ALAN WILLIAMS was born in 1935, the son of actor/playwright Emlyn Williams. He was educated at Stowe, Grenoble, Heidelberg and King's College, Cambridge.

As a reporter he has covered most of the world's worst trouble spots – Vietnam, Israel during the Six-Day War, Czechoslovakia, Ulster, Mozambique and Rhodesia. He has travelled widely and has achieved a controversial reputation both as a man and writer. In Algeria, the Foreign Office received complaints about him both from the French Army and from the Arabs. In Beirut, he encountered Kim Philby the day before the latter disappeared to Moscow. Before that, he was involved in the Hungarian Revolution, and masqueraded his way into East Germany when that country was virtually closed. He was a delegate from Cambridge to the World Youth Festival of Peace and Friendship in Warsaw where he and some friends smuggled a Polish student to the West.

This first-hand experience of adventure and intrigue has been put to superb use in his highly successful novels.

D1435043

Also by Alan Williams

Long Run South
Barbouze
Snake Water
The Purity League
The Tale of the Lazy Dog
The Beria Papers
Gentleman Traitor

Alan Williams

Shah-Mak

Panther

Granada Publishing Limited
Published in 1977 by Panther Books Ltd
Frogmore, St Albans, Herts AL2 2NF
Reprinted 1977

First published by Blond & Briggs Ltd 1976
Copyright © Alan Williams 1976
Made and printed in Great Britain by
Hazell Watson & Viney Ltd
Aylesbury, Bucks
Set in Linotype Granjon

For Claire Rawcliffe

The lower slopes of the Gotschnagrat were empty in the late January sun. Most of the sightseers were foreign tourists, still in their goggles and knitted caps, lips smeared white against snow burn, who had been cleared off the ski-slopes half an hour earlier. There were a few locals from the village of Wolfgang, midway between Klosters and Davos, together with a discreet showing of Swiss Police in their pale grey capes. In front of the crowd, at the foot of the ski-run, stood a row of dark men in square-shouldered overcoats and astrakhan hats, hands deep in their side pockets.

The man swept over the last crest of snow. His skis smacked down as he executed a neat Christie before cutting round, half squatting on his haunches, swooshed back in a spray of powdered snow, and came to a halt a few feet from the row of men in overcoats, who took their hands from their pockets and clapped.

A blue Cadillac with smoked windows slid up to the edge of the road with a soft thump of chains. It stopped long enough for the man to snap off his skis and jump inside, before being driven away in the direction of Klosters. A perceptive observer might have noticed that its wheels left unusually deep ruts in the snow. Three more cars appeared, gathered in the men in overcoats, and sped off in the wake of the Cadillac. All four cars carried diplomatic plates and Swiss Zollamt registration numbers.

From what the spectators had been able to glimpse of the man, he was slim, rather small, with a good head of dark silver hair and a beaky profile under wrap-around mirror glasses. He had been wearing a red, white and blue plastic anorak over a white polo-necked sweater and black skiing trousers.

The road was closed for five minutes until the convoy of cars had reached the steep track leading up to the large chalet, 'Le Soupir du Soleil', which stood concealed by trees 200 metres above Klosters. Here the ritual of arrival and departure was more pronounced. Men drifted out from behind conifers and banks of snow and surrounded the cars in a silent assembly, each facing in a different direction. More men whisked the doors open, bowing low as the silver-haired man stepped out of the Cadillac and walked across the snow-swept forecourt and up a flight of shallow granite steps.

The entrance hall, of plain, dark stained pine, was dominated by a bronze effigy above the stairs of a huge hybrid bird with the spread tail of a peacock, the talons of an eagle, and the head of a serpent spitting fire. Privileged guests to the chalet rarely noticed that the peacock fan was a spray of blue sapphires, the serpent's eye an emerald the size of a gull's egg, and the flames from its mouth rows of rubies.

A servant, in a white uniform buttoned to the throat, removed the man's skiing boots, while a second servant brought him a pair of embroidered slippers and a glass of apricot brandy. He swallowed the drink in a gulp; then walked, still in his wet plastic jacket, up the carpeted stair-case and along a corridor to a sauna, which was equipped with two telephones – internal and external lines – and a UHF radio.

Half an hour later, dressed in a loose-sleeved silk house-coat, he sat behind a wide desk reading through a stack of that day's international newspapers – the American, British and French in the originals, the Italian and German ones from translated résumés. He had replaced his wrap-around glasses with horn-rimmed spectacles, which magnified his cold, oily-black eyes; and he read intently, systematically, pausing to make notes in pencil. When he had finished the last page he touched a button under the table and a chunky man in a black suit appeared, bowed, and gathered up the heap of papers. The man behind the desk said, 'I am ready to see him.'

The retainer bowed again. 'Your Imperial Highness, I regret that the gentleman has not yet arrived.'

'He should have been here an hour ago. What explanation do you have?'

'A telegram, Your Imperial Highness' – the man bowed even lower this time – 'has informed us that there is fog at Zürich. The gentleman's plane has been obliged to land at Geneva.'

For a fraction of a second an expression of petulant anger crossed the face behind the desk. And in that instant it became an ugly, frightening face: the black unblinking eyes under their thick brows, as glossy as horses' hair; the fleshy nose deeply etched into the sides of his high cheek-bones; the thin, determined mouth – a hard face, a noble face, a face known through-out the world, admired, feared and reviled; now, in that moment, changed to the face of a spoilt, spiteful playboy with too much money and too much power – grown bored with both.

He recovered quickly. 'Bring me some coffee and tell Lutz to join me for chess.'

The retainer bowed three times and backed out of the room, opening the door behind him without turning. Two minutes later a blond man appeared carrying a chess set. His face was pale and impassive, without a smudge of eyebrow, giving him a naked albino appearance.

The man behind the desk nodded to a chair opposite. The retainer had returned with a silver coffee service. The Supreme and All-Powerful Ruler of the fourth richest nation in the world watched without speaking as the servant poured two cups of black coffee and the blond man called Lutz laid out the chess-men.

The Ruler won the first three games; halfway through the fourth the black-suited retainer bowed himself in. 'Your Imperial Majesty. The French gentleman has arrived.'

'I will see him tomorrow.' The Ruler's hand hovered over the chessboard. He looked up at his opponent. 'Lutz, you are not doing well. You are doing very badly.' He spoke in English, with a very slight accent. The retainer had withdrawn. *'Shah-Mak!'* the Ruler added, and allowed himself a small smile; 'Or, as the English say – "check"!'

Lutz put his head on one side and smiled. 'How could I win against you?'

'How could you, indeed?' said the Ruler. 'How could any-one?'

Two days later the Frenchman was finally summoned, by telephone, from his room in the Silvretta Hotel in Klosters, to the Serene Presence above the town. No one had been sent to fetch him and he had been obliged to take a taxi for the quarter of a mile from the hotel to the Imperial chalet.

Monsieur Charles Pol was very short and very fat: rolls of flesh squeezed into a shapeless oyster-white suit that had seen better days; a large egg-shaped head decorated with a goatee beard and a lick of hair pasted down across the brow in a kiss-curl. His general demeanour was that of a comic character who had wandered out of an eighteenth-century French farce. It would have required someone with special insight – or equipped with a file containing full details of the Frenchman's diverse career – to perceive that, behind his grotesque exterior, Charles Pol was a man to be taken seriously.

The Ruler had just such insight and just such a file. The latter lay open on the desk in front of him when Pol was shown in some time after noon, having waited for over two hours downstairs in a rest-room used by the bodyguards. The Ruler did not look up. He turned a page of the file, which was bound in plain grey covers and was as thick as a film script, and went on reading. Pol waddled down the length of the room and squeezed himself into the chair opposite his host.

'You seem to be a man with a great variety of interests, Monsieur Pol,' the Ruler said at last, in French, still without lifting his head. 'You have been an anarchist, a Marxist, a Resistance hero, a spy, a bandit, an organizer of terrorism, a financial adventurer with an unsavoury reputation.' He paused, then slowly raised his eyes. 'Do I do you justice?'

Pol beamed back at him, his cherry lips showing two pearly-white teeth. The Ruler observed with distaste that there were patches of sweat under the man's armpits and that the rim of his silk collar was also damp, and not quite clean.

'It is all surely a matter of interpretation, Your Highness. I have read descriptions of your own career which were certainly accurate, yet far from flattering.'

The Ruler's face remained quiet and closed. 'Monsieur, a man in my position quickly wearies of the repetitive lies and propaganda put about by enemies abroad. It is one of the ironies of the modern world that if I were the upstart head of a starving nation who went squealing to the United Nations begging for aid and arms, I should not only be helped – I should be universally respected and admired.

'But' – his eyelids drooped with an expression of contemptuous boredom – 'it is my evident misfortune not only to be the unchallenged ruler of a nation of some thirty million people, whose standard of living is rising faster than any other in the world, but also Supreme Commander of the largest and best equipped Army, Navy, and Air Force between the Mediterranean and India. My personal income last year was over 6000 million American dollars. I do not exaggerate when I claim to be the most powerful individual in the world. If I increase my oil revenues by one per cent – five per cent – fifty per cent – I can overnight, affect, distort, even destroy, the whole economic structure of Western civilization. I do not need the flattery of friends. As for the envy and hatred of my enemies' – he swept his hand dismissively – 'they do not disturb my sleep, I assure you.'

Monsieur Pol sighed. 'Are you telling me all this to impress me, Your Majesty? Or because you fear I might be ill informed?'

A faint shadow passed across the Ruler's face; he tapped the file in front of him. 'From your record you are a man who has indulged himself in many left-wing causes. I do not expect you to have any love for me, or even appreciate what I have done for my country. Although we have an ancient history, we are also – in the modern world – a very young country. We are no more than a child who is just beginning to walk and speak. And I am that child's father. In my country we have no parliamentary democracy. That is a luxury we cannot afford. It would be as foolish and as dangerous as allowing a child to play unguarded in a busy street. We also have no inflation, no strikes, no unemployment, one of the greatest social and industrial expansion programmes in the world, and a crime rate that is the lowest in the world.' He paused, his eyes hooded and unblinking. 'You are amused, Monsieur Pol?'

Pol gave a massive shrug which split a seam in his jacket. 'When Your Majesty talks of social and industrial progress, I presume you include the factory that was recently constructed outside your capital, Mamounia, and which I understand is devoted exclusively to the manufacture of artificial hands and feet?'

The Ruler gave a quick smile, showing small sharp teeth. 'You seem very well informed. And no doubt you will understand that in a rapidly advancing nation, old traditions die slowly. In France you still employ the guillotine. And yet, in the West, you are such masters of hypocrisy! When in my country a thief is caught and his hand is cut off, or when he tries to run away and his foot is cut off, you call it barbarism. Yet innocent citizens do not fear to walk the streets of our cities, Monsieur Pol, as they do in most Western countries. So why are you so anxious to criticize and condemn?'

'I do neither,' said Pol. 'On the contrary, I admire your progress. I am told that the amputations are no longer carried out in public, but under local anaesthetics in a special air-conditioned clinic.'

There was a pause. 'I trust you are not being impertinent, Monsieur Pol?'

'Your Majesty, I understood that you had summoned me here with the possible purpose of hiring my services. I certainly did not come to discuss the ethics of Your Majesty's rule. Since you have my file, you are probably aware that recently my circumstances have become somewhat straitened. You will also know that until a few months ago I myself, in a not too modest way, also enjoyed wealth and power. While I have never actually brought down a government, I have caused several to have bad indigestion. As for money, I too have enjoyed far more than was necessary to gratify those few appetites that are still left to me. But with respect to your own wealth and power, Your Majesty, let me say at once that I am more impressed by the genius of Yehudi Menuhin, or of the English novelist Graham Greene, or even by the culinary skills of the late Monsieur Point, proprietor of the "Pyramide".'

As the Frenchman finished speaking, the door opened on its well-oiled hinges and the black-suited retainer appeared. The Ruler said something in his own tongue and the man came across the room and stood behind Pol's chair.

The Ruler sat back and said to Pol, 'In my own country most of my subjects believe that I am endowed with powers of divine guidance. To a sophisticated person like yourself, this will seem like childish idealism – the simple totem worship of a primitive people in search of a tangible god. I admit that many of my people are still simple. But you must also remember that my throne has not been occupied for a few generations by one of your inbred European dynasties – a mongrel breed of Germans and Greeks, seedy Mediterranean princelings and Balkan impostors. The Emerald Throne of the *Hama'anah* – a legendary bird that draws its strength from the talons of the eagle, the beauty of the peacock, and the venom of the snake – has been occupied for more than 3000 years. It has withstood the assault and intrigue of almost every race and alliance, from the Greeks, the Huns, the Turks, the Tsars, the Arabs, and, in recent times, the infectious plague of international socialism. I carry on the ancient tradition of my throne without fear or favour. If I do not always expect love, at least I command respect.'

Pol turned his head enough to observe the rigid figure of the servant standing less than a foot from his shoulder. The man's hands hung straight at his sides, the fingers thick and square-tipped. His eyes did not move from his master's face.

Pol's lips parted in an impish grin. 'I think we already know enough of each other, Your Majesty, not to have to play the comedy between ourselves. I am a failed financier – a buccaneer – a bum – whatever it pleases you to call me. As for you, I know that your throne was seized in a coup d'état by a common Army sergeant who mutinied against his superiors, promoted himself Colonel, overthrew the old Imperial dynasty, and proclaimed himself King of Kings, Ruler of All Princes. You were merely his illegitimately begotten son.'

The Ruler said calmly, 'I think it was St Paul, in your Bible, who spoke of those who can suffer fools gladly, seeing they themselves are wise? Monsieur, you are a fool.'

'Perhaps,' said Pol. 'But it was Napoleon who said that the fool has one great advantage over the man of sense – he is always satisfied with himself.'

The Ruler murmured something and the retainer moved up against Pol's chair. A hand closed round the side of Pol's neck and the fingers hardened, squeezing and probing into the rolls of fat until they found the right spot. Pol's face turned blue; he tried to blink through the tears, and tasted bile choking his throat. It was several seconds before he could make out the Ruler's voice, slow and measured, with that tone of bored disdain.

'We are fortunately under Swiss territorial jurisdiction, Monsieur Pol. Otherwise I might be tempted to dispense with legal properties. It is not wise to call me a bastard and a fool.'

Pol dabbed a silk handkerchief to his eyes and cheeks, and smoothed its cool surface over the side of his neck. The carefully arranged kiss-curl was splayed out like a crushed spider on the shining dome of his forehead, and the sweat trickled down his cheeks, collecting in the folds of his chin. He wiped his eyes again and said, 'Your Majesty, I am surprised that a man in your position should want to descend to such clumsy and embarrassing dramatics. In my experience, one is always at a disadvantage talking business with somebody one has just reduced to tears.'

He sat back and blew his nose. The man at his elbow had not moved, his eyes again fixed on the Ruler's face. He is a poor bodyguard, thought Pol: he should be looking at me, not at this ageing emperor of his – this second-hand usurper of a desert kingdom grown suddenly rich on black gold – this prancing oriental peacock who's no better than some cheap tout who has just won a lottery and is now lecturing his friends and neighbours on how to manage their affairs. Not that Pol totally disapproved of the Ruler. For while he remained unimpressed by the man's vast wealth, Pol's Gallic sense of irony was aroused by the thought of this despotic arriviste now being free to bail out several insolvent Western nations, as well as controlling major industries in a number of others.

He peered across the desk and grinned. 'You are surely not fool enough to think me worth a little childish bullying before throwing me out into the snow? What do you want?'

The Ruler raised his eyes and nodded, and the bodyguard retreated soundlessly from the room. He turned to the dossier in front of him. 'During the Vietnam War you stole two billion dollars from the Americans and gave them to Hanoi. Did the Communists pay a commission on the deal?'

'They paid a commission,' said Pol. 'It was not large.'

'What were your motives?'

'I like to spit in the eye of Goliath. It is more satisfying than killing him – and a lot easier. Besides, if the operation had failed, I had nothing to lose. I was not there at the time.'

'You used mercenaries, of course?' The Ruler began to turn the pages of the file. 'On at least two other occasions in your career you have cheated the French, Soviet and British governments, and earned yourself approximately a million dollars playing one off against the other. You also appear to have successfully organized several African terrorist movements against the whites. These, I assume, were not so remunerative?'

'They paid my expenses.'

'Monsieur Pol, you have amassed great wealth through great

14

cunning and enterprise, and yet when my agents finally contacted you, you were living in a cheap hotel where it seems you were having trouble paying your bills. You are also banned from entering the United States and the Soviet Union, and a number of smaller countries where you have indulged your adventurous appetites. I understand that you are not very welcome here in Switzerland, after they rescinded your Resident's Permit last year and sequestered your villa on Lac Léman in order to settle your debts. Nor do I hear that your own compatriots are very happy about you, following certain double-dealings you did with the OAS after the Algerian War. It seems that only your reputation during the Resistance has kept you out of a French gaol.'

'I congratulate you on the thoroughness of your Intelligence Service,' said Pol. 'But as you will have seen from my dossier, I too have some experience of the spy trade and have usually found its practitioners disagreeable, incompetent, and prone to exaggerate. I have no wish to correct their mistakes for them, except to point out that I am still gainfully employed as the legal owner of a shop for ladies' undergarments behind the Gare St Lazare. As for my relations with the French authorities, I can assure you, Your Majesty, that while not official they are, in certain circles, more than merely cordial.'

The Ruler sat inspecting the knuckles of his manicured hands, on one of which he wore a single gold ring with a square emerald. 'Your views on Intelligence agents do not interest me, Monsieur Pol. I did not summon you here, in the middle of my short winter vacation, in order to discuss irrelevancies.'

'Why, then?'

The Ruler appeared to hesitate. He was not used to direct questions. 'How would you describe your present political leanings?' he said at last.

Pol began to pat down his kiss-curl. 'Where you are concerned, Your Majesty, my politics are what you pay for them. The more extreme, the higher the fee. What are you paying now?'

The Ruler closed Pol's dossier and pushed it away from him. Then he sat back and steepled his fingers together under that much photographed, deep-cleft chin. 'I am offering you two million English pounds sterling, Monsieur Pol. It will be paid in gold or any equivalent currency you choose to name. This sum will be sufficient to cover your personal fee, and all expenses.'

'To do what?' Pol's lips were parted, unsmiling, and the sweat had broken out again on his pink brow.

The Ruler was looking at him with his steady black stare. 'I want you to kill me, Monsieur Pol.'

Charles Pol gave a cooing giggle, almost a girl's giggle; and his right hand darted back under his jacket and beneath his waistband, groping into the deep recesses of his immense buttocks. Considering his extreme corpulence and the tightness of his clothing, this whole movement displayed an astonishing dexterity.

Before the Ruler fully realized what was happening, Pol's fat little hand had reappeared, clutching another folded white handkerchief. With a further giggle he thrust out his arm until his hand was less than twelve inches from the Ruler's face.

The Ruler flinched back, but quickly checked himself. Pol had unclenched his fingers and the handkerchief slowly opened like the petals of a flower, giving off a faint puff of pollen-like powder. The Ruler made another involuntary movement backwards, and remembering where the handkerchief had just come from, raised a hand to his nostrils; then he recognized the smell – it was the same talcum powder that he himself often used after bathing. For a moment he stared at Pol's hand with an expression of distaste and curiosity.

In the centre of the white petals lay what looked like a small grey cigarette lighter. Pol crooked his little finger and there was a tiny snap. A blade, less than two inches long and a centimetre wide, had transformed the object into a knife which was now pointing at the Ruler's throat. One edge was serrated with minute hook-like teeth, cut inwards so as to inflict the maximum damage on being withdrawn. It was also slightly hollowed, forming part of a metal tube protruding from the end of the handle. As the Ruler watched, Pol's thumb-nail snicked some hidden catch and a small leaden object rattled on to the desk and rolled across, almost into the Ruler's lap.

The Ruler's hand closed over it, and slowly lifted it as if he were inspecting a card at baccarat. 'Very neat,' he said. 'Neat and nasty. You were thoroughly searched when you came in, were you not?'

'Twice. But remember, we fat men possess certain advantages. The night before his execution, Hermann Goering secreted enough cyanide crystals in his body to have killed twenty men.'

'We also use metal detectors.'

Pol grinned. 'Yes. But you will observe that this little toy is made entirely of plastic, except for the soft-nosed bullet.'

The Ruler was looking at the .22 cartridge. A cross had been cut into the lead nose of the bullet. With a look of contempt, he dropped it into his pocket, then wiped his fingers on the desk top. 'A Mexican knife-gun,' he murmured, and reached out just as Pol pushed the blade back into the slim plastic handle. 'You will give me that, please. I do not like my employees carrying unauthorized weapons. The dum-dum bullet alone is proscribed by the Geneva Convention.'

Pol chuckled. 'I know. It is a toy that breaks all the rules – the only firearm that is banned throughout the United States, including Texas and Arizona. Very handy on a dance floor or in a crowded reception. You press it into the kidney or spleen, the blade shoots in, and *pop*! – no louder than a champagne cork. The dum-dum splits up inside and there is usually no exit wound.'

'Give it to me, please,' the Ruler repeated. Pol handed it to him, and the Ruler dropped it into his side pocket. 'Why did you show me this little toy? Possession of it would be enough to get you a prison sentence in most countries in the world – including my own.'

Pol gave a fat cherubic smile. 'Surely you do not begrudge me one small effort to impress you, Your Majesty? After all, you have asked me to kill you. I could have done it just now.'

This time the Ruler smiled back. 'Yes. But you would not have got away with it. Nor would you have been paid. That is what distinguishes the professional assassin from the random lunatic. I do not want a lunatic, Monsieur Pol. I want a genius. A man capable of committing the impossible crime. Of penetrating not only my National Security system, but also my personal Praetorian Guard.'

'And then escape?'

The Ruler sat back and gazed at a point above Pol's head. 'Whatever else I think of you, Monsieur Pol, I certainly do not underestimate your intelligence and sense of self-preservation. You do not imagine that an attempt on my life – whether it were successful or unsuccessful – would meet with clemency? Your death – and the death of any accomplices or hirelings you decided to use – would be a horrible one.'

'You must forgive a certain naïveté, Your Majesty, but even I am used to some degree of straight dealing. What you are suggesting sounds more like a fantasy – even a whim. But hardly a business proposition.'

'Monsieur Pol, I have already mentioned a straight fee of two million sterling. That is not a whimsical proposition. I am now going to give you brief and precise instructions on what you are to do. You will take no notes. When you leave here you will be searched again – thoroughly this time, I promise you – and if you are foolish enough to be carrying some clever little recording gadget, you would be wise to tell me now.'

'I have an excellent memory,' Pol replied. 'But before we begin, might I ask a favour? I would like a whisky. A large one, with no water or ice.'

'You shall have one.' As he spoke, the door opened and the retainer reappeared.

2

'It's going to rain,' the girl said, staring out across the canal at the steep narrow houses. 'If you'd got up earlier we could have done the whole round trip and been back by now.' It was an assured, arrogant voice, the voice of a girl who is used to getting her own way. 'And while we're about it,' she added, without turning her head, 'I think I'm being followed.'

'You're always being followed,' Owen Packer said, feeling the first drops of rain on his bare head. The motor-launch had come into sight under the bridge and the row of tourists pressed up to the edge of the landing stage. The girl glanced behind her, seemed about to say something, then thought better of it. Instead, she set her mouth in an exaggerated pout. 'You *knew* I wanted to look at the tulips. It's typical of you. You're so selfish.'

'We'd have been in perfectly good time for your bloody tulips,' Packer said sourly, 'if you'd just let me screw you this morning.'

'Please! Half the people here speak English!'

'To hell with the people here.' He avoided looking at her, aware that she was already attracting her fair share of looks from the tourists and passers-by. She was a small dark girl in tan culottes, with matching jacket and high-heeled boots. A scarlet beret had been arranged at a precarious angle on her fine black hair, and a pair of octagonal green-tinted sunglasses covered half her face. Her lipstick was blood-red and glistened even under the grey Dutch sky.

The motor-launch chugged round and bumped against the rubber tyres hanging under the landing stage. The girl took another glance behind her before stepping nimbly aboard, and without waiting for Owen Packer she made her way to the front of the glass-covered cabin. Packer allowed a few elderly women tourists to go ahead of him, before joining the girl. The seat beside her was already taken by a plump man with pebble-glasses and a pork-pie hat.

It was typical of her, Packer thought. Although his legs were much longer than hers, she somehow always managed to keep several paces ahead of him, whether they were entering hotels, restaurants, aeroplanes, or just walking in the street. Perhaps it was something to do with breeding, he decided gloomily.

His face was set to the window, already streaked with rain, and he looked out at the familiar postcard views of canals, houseboats, belfries, the replica of Van Gogh's swing-bridge. At least they had been spared a morning in the Rijksmuseum, filing through those rooms full of gloomy Dutch Masters. For although Sarah worked as what she called a 'personal secretary' to the director of a Bond Street art gallery, she showed no interest whatever in art. He often wondered what she was interested in – between the narrow giddy social life she led among her select friends in West End clubs during the week, and at country house-parties at weekends. What Packer called the Backgammon–Bollinger Brigade.

He was honest enough to realize that part of her attraction for him – perhaps the greater part – lay in her exclusiveness. In the early days after they had first met, when she had still shown some passion for him, she had taken him to a famous London shop and bought him a silver pen. Sarah Laval-Smith had paid by cheque, and when the assistant politely asked for her name and address on the back, she had pointed, with chilling arrogance, to the inscription at the top of the cheque. The name of the bank matched that of her signature.

He turned his head, enough to see her neighbour trying to talk to her. She was giving the man that wide alluring smile which she reserved for strangers. Owen Packer had long discovered that her sulks and wilful petulance were inflicted only on her intimates: a bitter privilege which he had learned to endure.

A girl had stood up in the front of the boat and was intoning a list of names and places, in Dutch, English, French, and German. It was raining hard by the time they reached the Grutsmolen. 'Here, ladies and gentlemen, you see one of the most famous windmills in Holland. As you will know, Holland has many hundreds of windmills. But the Grutsmolen is one of the largest and best preserved.'

Packer caught a glimpse of Sarah's neat profile beside the plump bespectacled face under the pork-pie hat. Very deliberately she lowered her large tinted glasses on to the end of her nose and gave Packer a wink. Like the spectacles, her eyes seemed a little too large for the rest of her face, which was of a startling prettiness, fine-boned and feline, with a fresh-skinned innocence that belied her natural self-confidence and aggression. Yet it was her eyes that remained her most striking feature: very dark, and sloping at an odd angle, as though a photograph of her had been cut exactly in half then put together again fractionally out of line. They gave her a sly, muckle-mouthed expression that was not conventionally beautiful, but extraordinarily attractive. For Owen Packer this attraction lost nothing in the knowledge, as her current consort, that much of her allure depended on arti-fact, including a set of false eyelashes and a broad colour scheme of skilfully applied eye-shadow.

When the boat stopped, Packer tried to take her arm, but she evaded him and reached the quayside well ahead of him. He caught up with her as she stood huddled, urchin-like in her rain-spattered beret, under the canvas awning. 'Still being followed?' he asked, with a forced grin.

She looked away. 'The man next to me said there are some wonderful tulip nurseries about two miles from here.'

'Bully for him. And you're ready to walk there in this pissing rain?'

'Why do you always have to sound so cross?' she pouted. 'You stay here and look at your windmill, and I'll take the bus. There's one every ten minutes. I'll see you back at the hotel this evening.'

'Thanks,' said Packer. He made an ineffectual attempt to kiss her, but she ducked artfully away.

'Please, my make-up!' she cried. 'The rain's done enough damage as it is.' She turned, smiling. 'Now go along and have a good look at your lovely windmill. It'll cheer you up.'

'I'm perfectly cheerful,' he said. 'I'm cheerful enough to take a running jump into the canal.'

She shrugged and adjusted the angle of her beret. 'You've been in a foul temper ever since you got up. I just hope you're nicer this evening.'

He watched her walk over to the bus. The man in the pork-pie hat was already aboard. Packer didn't wait to see if she sat next to him again, but turned and walked towards the mill.

Follow the rule book, he thought grimly: if I start a quarrel now, it'll just get worse. Though it couldn't be much worse than it was at the moment. This weekend expedition had gone badly from the start. The plane had been three hours late leaving, and Packer had mislaid his passport and traveller's cheques just before take-off. 'God, you're hopeless!' she'd cried. 'However did you become a Captain in the Army?' 'I wasn't in the Army,' he'd replied, 'I was on special duties.' 'Oh, how exciting and mysterious!' she'd taunted him, with her spiteful laugh. As with art and windmills, she appeared to have no interest in Packer's past career.

He entered the blue and white door of the Grutsmolen. The windmill stood on six storeys, of which the first three were living quarters – painstakingly preserved seventeenth-century Dutch interiors, like the inside of a giant dolls' house. Packer began to forget his frustrations as he climbed to the fourth floor; this would contain the machinery that never failed to fascinate him. But there was little machinery to be seen. Between the sloping walls were a couple of wooden bins and some rusted wheels. He climbed to the next floor and saw with disgust that the stones, 'horses', and grain chutes had been stripped out and replaced by a large circular table with a relief map of the Low Countries, showing a network of dykes and canals.

He started back down, scowling at the old Dutchman who had relieved him of two guilders for the entrance fee. Outside, both the launch and the bus had gone. He walked out into the rain and kicked viciously at the gravel path, and heard a shrill voice behind him – 'Engleesh?' – followed by a high-pitched laugh.

Packer turned and saw a short, immensely fat man, wet and flushed and grinning, swaying in front of a stationary taxi.

'Your wife, she leave you, hein?' – the man wiped some rain from the tip of his pointed beard – 'so we follow, hein?'

Packer took a step towards him; and even through the rain he could smell the gin on his breath. 'Who are you?' The man was obviously not English, which he had spoken with an absurdly distorted Cockney accent.

At this moment the fat man reverted to French. 'I thought I would catch you at the mill, but then the lady decides to disappear – *poof*! Comme toutes ces femmes emmerdantes!' He

22

stepped back and grappled unsteadily with the rear door of the taxi. 'Please, monsieur!' he cried, in his cooing voice.

Packer took another step forward and stopped. 'I didn't see you on the boat,' he said fiercely, 'so they must have told you at the hotel, and you came by taxi.' The man gave a giggle, which exploded into a belch. 'Who the hell are you?' Packer yelled.

'Oo the 'ell am I?' the fat man repeated, again in English; then with some difficulty he reached under his raincoat and pulled out a stout crocodile wallet from which he handed Packer a card.

Packer read, in embossed copperplate:

CHARLES AUGUSTE POL
(Légion d'Honneur)
Conseil d'Affaires
P.O. 248, Genève, La Suisse

Packer started to hand it back, but the Frenchman brushed him aside, at the same time managing to drag the taxi door open. 'Please, you are my guest!'

'I don't understand,' said Packer. 'Where do you want to take me?'

'To find the young lady, of course! Cherchez la femme!' He gave Packer a boss-eyed grin and rolled almost head first into the back of the taxi. The driver sat watching him with mild reproof; he had switched off the engine, but the meter was still running and showed over fifty guilders. Monsieur Charles Auguste Pol was being an unusually lucrative customer.

Packer still stood outside, holding the door open, while the Frenchman had already settled back into the corner, his thighs and buttocks filling more than half the space on the seat. Packer wondered, for one wild moment, whether the man were some eccentric private eye who had run amok on Dutch gin while employed by Sarah's family to obstruct Packer in this feeble spasm of foreign pleasure.

He said to the fat man in French, 'Will you please explain what this is all about? How you know about this girl and me, and why you're following us both?'

Charles Pol patted the seat beside him. 'All in good time, my friend! First we must find the lady.'

Reluctantly, and mostly because the rain had increased again,

Packer climbed into the taxi. Pol grunted something unintelligible and the driver started the engine. Packer quickly opened the window to relieve the fumes from his companion, which he now recognized as a mixture of Bols and sour sweat. He was wondering when the Frenchman had last had a bath, when the taxi turned out on to the autobahn south to Utrecht. The driver kept to the outside lane, going very fast.

'How far is this tulip nursery?' Packer asked, feeling the first twinge of unease.

Monsieur Pol flapped a hand which was like a freshly peeled shrimp. 'Do not disturb yourself, mon cher! You will soon be reunited with your loved one.'

'This is bloody ridiculous,' Packer muttered to himself; then, in French: 'Did you follow us from the hotel, or the airport, or out from London?'

Pol put a fat forefinger to his cherry lips. 'Shall we just say that I found the lady particularly *attractive*, as you say in English? That red beret is most coquettish. And so easy to follow!' He gave his giggle and wiped a string of spittle from his mouth.

Owen Packer was leaning against the open window, his head and shoulders wet with rain, and was trying to look round the driver to see if there was a registered number somewhere on the dashboard. He was unfamiliar with Dutch taxis. But before he had time, he was hurled back into the corner of his seat as the driver pulled across the centre lane, cutting dangerously in front of a little Daf that squealed at them with headlamps flashing; then swerved into the slip road which ran out along an embankment above the lowlands.

Packer's attention was momentarily distracted by a row of windmills on the horizon. He was relieved to see that the flat landscape was dotted with little houses and what looked like plots of vegetable garden.

'Relax, Monsieur Packer! We are soon there.'

Packer swung round in his seat. 'How do you know my name?'

Pol gave him a beady grin. 'Let us say that you are not entirely a stranger to me, Monsieur Packer. Or should I, perhaps, call you *Capitaine Packer*?' He sounded suddenly, disturbingly sober.

Packer was still trying to think of something to say when they

24

pulled into a muddy space and stopped. He had his hand on the door catch, and was out of the taxi before the driver had time to switch off. He backed away a couple of paces and stood with his body flexed, hands at his sides, fingers stiff. Even if Pol were armed, in his present state he should present little difficulty. It was the driver who worried Packer. From what he'd seen of him he looked young and fit.

But the driver did not move. Packer watched Pol clamber out, almost sitting down in the mud as he did so, his egg-shaped face streaming with sweat; then he came squelching round to the front of the taxi and clutched hold of Packer's arm, as though to steady himself from falling.

'We have arrived!' he gasped, and with his free hand he waved at a row of coaches parked next to a barn. Beyond, Packer could now see bright splashes of red and pink and yellow, and groups of people with umbrellas. Hardly the place for a quick showdown on the outskirts of Amsterdam, he thought. This was a civilized country, after all; which only made the intrusion of this drunk French 'business consultant', who had followed him here, and knew his name, even his former rank, all the more incongruous and mystifying.

'Come, mon cher, now we start the hunt for your little friend!' He was still holding Packer's arm, with a surprisingly firm grip; and began leading him past the row of coaches to the tulip fields. They made slow progress, with Pol's pear-shaped body wobbling and lurching on two tiny feet in what looked like ballet slippers, almost small enough for a child.

When they reached the edge of the field, Packer saw that it was not going to be easy to find Sarah. There were at least a hundred people moving among the tulip beds and her red beret would be lost in the blaze of colour. Even when he did find her, he wondered how the hell he was going to rid himself of this awful Frenchman. For Sarah possessed a particular aversion, which she did little to disguise, to all forms of both grossness and drunkenness. Even if Pol had been sober, Packer knew that she would hardly welcome him as a new-found holiday friend.

A moment later he realized that his anxieties would soon be settled, one way or the other. The rain had slackened to a drizzle, and Sarah's small familiar figure stood alone, near the barn, the scarlet beret pulled down aggressively over one eye. She was staring at a bed of unnaturally large yellow tulips. Unfortunately, Pol saw her at the same time, and evidently recognized her. He let out a whooping shriek, and with his free hand pulled a stone bottle of Bols gin from his pocket.

Packer shook himself free and began striding down the path towards Sarah. She noticed him when he was some yards away. 'Hallo. You were quick,' she said, without enthusiasm. 'What happened to the windmill?'

'Lousy.' He reached her and lowered his voice. 'You were right – somebody *was* following both of us.' He turned and nodded to where he had left Pol floundering on the edge of a tulip patch. 'The fat man over there, with the beard – is that the one?'

She looked back at Pol and shrugged. 'Never seen him before. He looks drunk.'

'He is – smashed out of his skull. What's more, he knows my name, and that I was a Captain, and he knows about you.'

As they both stood looking, Pol – with the grotesque abandon of a stage drunk – waved his bottle at them, unscrewed the top and began gulping from the neck. 'Who did you think was following you?' Packer persisted.

'No one important. That man I was sitting next to in the boat – he was French too, or at least he spoke French. He's gone now.'

She was interrupted by a yelp of laughter; and they both looked round in time to see Pol coming towards them at a lumbering, lurching trot, his open bottle held precariously aloft. He had covered half the distance when he came to grief. An unusually deep puddle tipped him off balance and sent him sprawling sideways into a bed of magnificent tulips. Many dozens of full-bodied blooms, each of which had been nursed from its earliest shoot to its present ripe maturity – to be bought and sold all over the world, to decorate great homes and palaces, to carry off prizes at international flower shows – now had their lush stems and fleshy petals crushed and flattened under the Frenchman's colossal weight.

A number of tourists were near enough to see; but all they did was gape. Pol himself was the first to recover. It would be incorrect to say that he got to his feet, but rather to his hands and knees; and it was in this position, like a monstrously inflated baby with a false beard, that he began to scramble forward on all fours – not back to the path, but even deeper into the tulip bed. He seemed to be taking a direct short cut to where Sarah and Packer were standing, about fifty feet away. He paused only once, to take a swig from the bottle which he had somehow managed to keep upright. On and on he came, leaving a wide, dishevelled path of decapitated flowers.

Then, from the direction of the barn, came a guttural roar, and a man with white hair and a brown stringy face began sprinting down the path towards Packer and Sarah, turning sharply left when he reached the original trough of chaos left by Pol. He was shouting all the way, and carrying a stick of thick knotted wood. Pol evidently neither saw nor heard him; for at the moment that the Dutchman brought the stick down across his elephantine haunches, Pol was at his Bols. There was a loud crack, followed by a snort, then a shrill yelping like an animal in pain.

Packer and Sarah watched the scene that followed with silent disbelief. Before the second blow could fall, Pol had rolled over on to his back and lashed out at the Dutchman's legs with his stone bottle; then, with astounding agility, he scrambled to his feet and flung himself at the man's throat. Although the Dutchman was a good foot taller, Pol quickly gained the advantage. The Dutchman tripped and fell over backwards, leaving Pol holding both the bottle and the stick. But instead of exploiting his advantage, the Frenchman turned away and began to run a berserk zig-zag trail through the tulips, thrashing wildly about him with the stick. Petals, leaves, shredded stems and clots of mud flew around him like floral shrapnel. He must have destroyed several hundred flowers before his energy was spent.

In the meantime, the old Dutchman had recovered and run back to the barn – presumably to call the Police.

Sarah began to laugh. Packer was all the more astonished, because not only was she a girl who rarely laughed, except when it was expected of her, but she had an almost fanatical love of flowers; and Pol was not merely gross, but had committed the two worst heresies in her book – he had massacred some of the finest blooms in the world, and was blind drunk to boot.

Pol reached them a moment later, his short fat arms flung out

27

in welcome. He had thrown away the stick and the empty bottle somewhere in the wreckage behind him.

'My friends! My dear, dear friends! *My little tulip!*' he shrieked, and to Packer's dismay flung both arms round Sarah's neck and gave her a smacking kiss on each cheek. Packer grabbed him by the shoulder and steadied him, fearful that he would topple over again and squash Sarah. She seemed too surprised to be angry; for several seconds she just stood staring at Pol, inhaling the fumes of Dutch gin and bad breath, not noticing that his open mackintosh and stained suit had left traces of mud and verdant slime on her impeccable culottes.

'Come on, let's get out of here,' Packer said to her. 'He's a bloody madman!' He pushed Pol back and pulled her free of him. 'Where's the bus?'

She gestured vaguely towards the barn. 'It's not due to leave for another twenty minutes.'

'The Police will be here at any moment,' Packer said, trying to lead her away from Pol.

'You're not afraid of the Police, are you?' she said. Her voice had a discreet veneer of insult that provoked in him a dull, powerless rage.

'Don't be bloody silly,' he muttered. 'But the Dutch'll half murder him when they get him. What he's done is like a foreigner crapping on a Union Jack outside Buckingham Palace.'

She drew in her breath with a hiss. 'I do wish,' she said, 'that you wouldn't be so fucking crude all the time.'

'You're one to talk,' he growled.

'I just can't stand talk about shit,' she said primly; then she glanced back again at Pol, and this time she smiled. He wiped his lips and smiled back, then hiccoughed. She said to Packer: 'We can't just leave him. After all, he brought you here – didn't he?'

'I don't know anything any more,' said Packer. 'I just know the fellow's a load of trouble. And I don't want him round our necks for the rest of the day.' He turned away, knowing at once that it was a mistake. If he had shown even the smallest sign of taking Pol's side, the girl would have turned on them both with the full venom of her disapproval. As it was, she turned and took Pol gently by the arm, and began to lead him back towards the taxi.

It was she, this time, who gave the driver the instructions, in English, to take them all back to the hotel. They had just reached the opposite carriage-way of the autobahn, in the direction of Amsterdam, when they saw the police van with its flashing blue beacon turn on to the slip road towards the tulip nursery.

From his seat in the back, crushed up against Sarah, Pol let out a luxurious fart. 'Ah, mes enfants! What an interesting afternoon – I haven't done anything like that in years. In fact, the last time, I think, was when I smashed Admiral Guerin's porcelain tea service aboard his flag-ship off Oran, in 1946.'

Sarah had turned her head away, and quickly rolled down the window.

The speed and strategy which Owen Packer displayed in removing Charles Pol beyond the limits of Dutch law impressed even Sarah – although she was careful not to show it.

Packer's eventual motives for deciding to befriend this gargantuan foreign intruder were twofold. Sarah was amused by the man – and even more amazing, she seemed to have taken a peculiar liking to him; and while Pol could not possibly prove a libidinous threat to Packer, he might yet prove to be a healing catalyst for him and Sarah. For Packer had come to realize that alone together their weekend in Amsterdam was doomed.

His second reason was curiosity. He wanted to find out why this grotesque, importuning Frenchman, who claimed to work from Geneva as a business consultant, should decide – while drunk in the middle of the morning – to follow him and Sarah on an expensive taxi ride into the country. Packer might have written the incident off as an alcoholic whim – inspired, perhaps, by Sarah's blood-red lipstick and scarlet beret – had it not been for those two vital details. Charles Pol knew both Packer's name and his former rank. And Packer was going to find out how and why.

The first stage of the rescue operation was to take Pol back to their hotel, where Packer paid off the taxi and bundled the Frenchman, dribbling and giggling, through the side entrance and up in the automatic lift, which was mercifully empty. They met no one in the corridor to their room. Inside, they lugged him unceremoniously into the bathroom; and while Sarah ordered black coffee from room service, Packer coaxed Pol into giving him the name of his own hotel.

They left him soaking in one of Sarah's bubble-baths, with instructions to answer the telephone, but not the door; hung a 'Do Not Disturb' sign outside, went downstairs and took a taxi to the Frenchman's hotel – the Amstel, one of the oldest and most select in Amsterdam. They entered the marble foyer – Sarah now dressed in casual Cardin and swinging a Gucci bag, Packer in suit and tie – and were told by Reception that Monsieur Pol had already settled his bill and was leaving that night.

Most of his luggage had been brought down; there remained only a few things in his suite, which he had intended to collect before two o'clock. The desk staff displayed an amiable deference, as soon as they found that the two of them were English; and while Sarah chatted to the ancient head porter, Packer explained to the desk clerk that Monsieur Pol had met with a slight but unfortunate accident. He would not be able to collect his luggage personally – but, of course, neither of them would be offended if one of the staff accompanied them upstairs, while they finished Pol's packing.

As Packer suspected, Pol existed in a state of opulent chaos. A half-full magnum of Krug stood uncorked on a side table, next to an unopened bottle of Johnnie Walker Black Label, which Packer eyed enviously. Sarah, who had been systematically going through the drawers, gave a shout of delight. In the bedside table she had found a fat roll of one-hundred-guilder notes, together with 7800 French francs in various denominations. Packer strode over and peeled off two of the Dutch notes, and put them in his wallet. 'That'll do for taxi fares, for a start.'

She stood, still holding the bundles of notes in each hand. For a moment the two of them looked at each other without expression. She spoke first: 'He'd never remember – he's far too drunk.'

Packer glanced at the door, where the hotel clerk was waiting discreetly out of sight in the passage; then shook his head. 'For a girl with your background, Sarah love, you seem pretty light fingered. Or maybe you're just greedy?'

'Why not? – if he gets drunk and leaves the stuff lying around everywhere?'

He took the notes from her hand and stuffed them into his inside pocket, next to his traveller's cheques. 'And he'd probably never counted them in the first place,' he said; then smiled. 'Don't worry, I'll let you have your cut, after we've deducted expenses – and a fee. Harbouring tulip butchers from justice isn't cheap, you know. He'll get what's left over – if there is any.'

'Anyone could tell you're a Welsh Jew,' she said, smiling, 'even if you don't look like one.'

Packer now began himself to examine the drawer by the bed. He picked out a vellum folder stamped with the image of a bird with a snake's head, talons and a blue and gold fanned tail. Inside was a first-class, open return ticket to Mamounia, capital of the second richest oil-producing nation in the Middle East. Pol was booked from Schiphol Airport, Amsterdam, but Packer observed that the ticket had been issued by the state's national airline in Zürich.

He put the folder into a monogrammed Louis Vuitton case, and rejoined Sarah in the bathroom where she was busily sweeping bottles of eau-de-cologne, deodorants, anti-perspirants, pills and patent medicines into a toilet case that was larger than Packer's hold-all.

He was smiling at the idea of Pol actually being vain, when he saw something lying half hidden under a very dirty ivory comb. It was an opened envelope, with an English stamp, addressed to M. Charles Pol, c/o American Express, Amsterdam. The postmark was London, but Packer could not make out the date stamp.

He turned it over. On the torn flap, above a familiar crest, were the initials SMRTS. Packer looked up and gazed at his gaunt image in the mirror, and saw his passionless blue eyes light up with the dawning of a great excitement. The envelope was empty.

Carefully, making sure that Sarah could not see, he folded it once and placed it in the zipped-up inner compartment of his wallet.

He made a final, swift check through the room, before they rejoined the hotel clerk outside. 'Thank God the Dutch are a trusting, English-loving people!' Packer muttered, as they rode down in the lift.

The only obstacle they encountered before leaving was the

polite insistence of the head porter on either a written or telephoned authorization from Pol himself. Packer had anticipated this. He had asked for a note from Pol, but the Frenchman had seemed to be in no state to write even his own name. Packer now took the precaution of putting the call through himself, from the public phone in the lobby, before summoning the head porter to answer it. Pol sounded drowsy, but was coherent enough to satisfy the old Dutchman.

A taxi had already been called, and while Pol's three elegant suitcases were being loaded into the boot, Packer ostentatiously gave the head porter their destination as Schiphol Airport, Lufthansa counter, in time for the 2.00 p.m. flight for Munich. Once inside, he instructed the driver to take them to their hotel.

The lobby reported no disturbances. Up in their room they found Pol still in the bathroom, dozing on the lavatory, with a half gnawed sandwich on his lap and an empty bottle of Vichy between his ankles. His cases were brought up a few minutes later. Packer forced the fat man's head brutally under the cold shower, where Pol squealed like a pig, then frog-marched him back into the bedroom where Sarah was going through the suitcases, selecting a fresh silk suit, silk shirt and tie, and a pair of miniature crocodile shoes.

'I'm leaving you to get him dressed,' Packer told her, 'while I go and fix up about a car. Come on, don't look so shocked! Just think of yourself as his nanny.' As he turned, he heard Pol urinating behind the open bathroom door.

The nearest hire-car bureau was only two blocks away. It took him less than ten minutes to complete the formalities and pay the deposit – out of Pol's roll of guilders. On reflection he decided that the more impressive the car, the less the risk of being stopped. In any case, Pol would be paying – all the way. Packer would make damn sure of that.

When he arrived back at the hotel, he began to feel uncomfortably like a chauffeur as he sat in the Mercedes 280 and watched the Vuitton cases, followed by Sarah and the freshly clad, pink and perfumed figure of Pol, emerge with a retinue of hotel staff to see them off.

A quarter of an hour later they joined the autobahn south to the Belgian border.

*   *   *

There was only one Dutch policeman at the border post beyond Breda – a man with shoulder-length blond hair in a net, who waved the Mercedes through without leaving the shelter of his guard-room. Packer drove for several more kilometres without seeing any more Police, and no Customs. It was when he turned on to the autoroute to Antwerp that he knew they were well into Belgian territory.

He felt more anticlimax than relief, the slowing of adrenalin, and a growing awareness of Sarah sitting slouched beside him, chain-smoking her Gitanes and complaining regularly of his hesitation at overtaking in the rain. More than anything, he felt in need of a drink. Meanwhile Pol snored in the back.

The landscape was closing in, the sky drawn across with electric cables, the horizon a line of dismal slag heaps and factories and the guttering glare of burning gas waste. The rain was now coming down so hard that even with the windshield wipers working at double speed, he could see little through the filth and spray flung up by an almost unbroken chain of juggernauts.

It was not quite four o'clock, on a late March afternoon – exactly three and a half hours since the slaughter of the tulips – when Packer manoeuvred the car across the heavy traffic, into the lane leading up to the minor ring-road round Antwerp.

It would be as good a place as any, he decided. The weather was foul, the light bad, and most drivers would be in a hurry. He slowed into the inside lane, almost under the bows of a TIR truck; then turned to Sarah. 'Wake him up!'

She hesitated, and turned in her seat. 'Much better to let him sleep,' she began.

'Do as I say,' he said. The road was curving over ragged marshland, cut diagonally by a canal. There were no houses, no paths, no signposts; and the only lights came from the traffic. Sarah leaned over the seat and shook Pol's knee. He grunted and snuffled, and Sarah ducked as the Frenchman rolled down his window and spat into the slipstream. 'Where are we?' he asked, in a clogged voice.

'In one of the great beauty spots of the Common Market,' said Packer. 'Anywhere in particular round here you want to be dropped off?' In the mirror he could see Pol's little wet eyes blinking. His foot touched the brake. 'You're getting out here,

Monsieur Pol. You and your beautiful luggage. The Belgians won't be too upset about a few Dutch tulips.'

'Les Belges?' Pol muttered.

Packer half turned and continued in French. 'Yes. But first I've got a few questions to ask. And I want the answers quickly. Otherwise we drop you here.' He had slowed the car down to less than twenty kilometres an hour. Sarah was busy lighting another cigarette, while Packer prolonged his moment of drama. Usually he was embarrassed by speaking French in front of Sarah, for her command of the language – with a beautifully refined accent – was one of the rarer attributes she had picked up from her finishing school near Lausanne. But the tension in the car released Packer's inhibitions.

'How did you get hold of my name and rank, Monsieur Pol?'

'Where are we, for God's sake?' Pol cried again.

'We're heading for the autoroute to Lille. But it's still a long way. And it's not a good day for hitch-hiking – even if it's legal.' He had pulled on to the emergency shoulder and stopped.

Pol's face loomed up in the mirror. 'You are trying to take advantage of my condition, Monsieur Packer. I am not accustomed to being treated in this manner.' He spoke with forced dignity, while Packer drummed his fingers on the wheel, in rhythm with the rain.

'As I see it, Monsieur Pol, we have three choices. We can either stay here all night until you talk. Or we can throw you out and drive on. Or I can turn round and drive you straight back to Amsterdam.' Pol was silent. Packer added: 'Why did you get so drunk this morning?'

Pol gave a gurgle of laughter. 'Oh, if you knew, if you knew! The troubles I have had – first a good card, then a bad card. A whole run of bad cards, now a run of good cards. I must be allowed to think.'

'Just tell me how you knew about us and why you followed us this morning.'

Sarah sat sideways, her tinted glasses pushed up on to her forehead, and looked first at one, then the other.

'It is a matter for serious discussion,' Pol said at last. 'Tête-à-tête, in the strictest confidence.'

'You followed us both, so you talk to us both. Are you some filthy private detective employed by her parents – ?'

Sarah gave a little gasp, but Pol cut her short. 'You underestimate me, mon cher Capitaine Packer.'

Packer switched off the engine. 'Now listen, Monsieur Pol. I got you out of a lot of trouble this morning. I'm not particularly interested in why you got drunk on the job. I just want to know what that job is, and why.'

Pol sat back with a miserable sigh. 'I am not feeling well. It is not just.'

'You'd find things a lot less just in a Dutch gaol,' Packer said reasonably. 'Unless they let you off with a stiff fine. Could you pay it?' He gave Sarah a quick wink which she did not return.

Pol groped inside his silk jacket and brought out his crocodile wallet. To Packer's surprise, and faint disappointment, he watched the Frenchman riffle through another stack of notes, whose value and nationality he could not see. 'I will pay you,' Pol croaked. 'Pay both of you. Pay you well. Just take me to a little spot where we can talk quietly.'

There was a silence, broken only by the rain muttering on the roof.

'Let's get on,' Sarah said in English. 'We can't just stay here on the side of the road. Anyway, it may all be a misunderstanding. Perhaps he saw us last night in the hotel and heard one of the porters call your name.'

'None of the porters called me "Captain",' said Packer savagely. 'No one's called me that in ten years.' He looked round to see if Pol had understood, but the Frenchman was busy spitting out of the window again. 'There's just one other thing,' said Packer. He took out his own wallet and extracted the folded envelope that he had found in Pol's hotel bathroom.

'Charles Pol!' he said loudly, and turned the envelope over, so that the Frenchman could see the back flap. 'SMRTS,' he read out. 'What are you doing running around with a crowd of madmen like that?'

'What?' Pol looked blearily back at him and a tear began to form in the corner of one eye.

'Listen. I found this in your room. It's addressed to you. The initials stand for SPECIAL MILITARY RESERVE TRAINING SCHOOL' – he spoke the words in English – 'Headquarters, Clifton, near Mead, Wiltshire. London office in High Holborn.' He paused.

Sarah gave a thin laugh. 'Off down Memory Lane again, are we?'

'You should be asking him that, not me,' said Packer, and thought, you stupid bitch! It was a long time now since he'd had anything exciting happen to him, and she'd be sure to try and take the cream off it.

Pol had reached out for the envelope and was looking at it with an expression of mild annoyance. 'Monsieur Packer,' he said at last, 'I think it would be best if we drove on. I know an excellent little spot in France – very quiet – where I can begin to explain things in full.'

As he spoke, a pair of headlamps flashed twice in the mirror, and a siren howled. A moment later a dark blue car screeched to a halt directly in front of them. Two policemen slowly got out and strolled towards them through the rain. Packer lowered his window, and a blunt red face with a moustache grunted, 'Nederlander?'

Packer opened the glove compartment and took out the car's papers. The man studied them for some time, while his companion had moved round to the back of the Mercedes. 'Passeports!' the red-faced man said.

Packer obliged, without a word. The man turned the pages and frowned, glanced at Sarah, then at Pol, and back at the passport. 'You know, please,' he said in English, with the ugly Flemish glottal, 'that you are forbidden absolutely to stop on this road?'

'I'm sorry,' said Packer, 'but my friend in the back is ill.'

The policeman stared at Pol, looked again at Sarah, then seemed to make up his mind. 'One thousand francs Belges.'

'Now just a minute – !' Packer began. He could feel Sarah watching him, testing him. 'My friend is ill!' he repeated, with a helpless gesture towards the back seat.

'One thousand francs Belges,' the red-faced man insisted, taking out a pink, carbon-backed pad. The second policeman had joined him from the back, his hand resting on his gun belt.

'Un instant s'il vous plaît.' Pol was leaning forward, smelling strongly of scent, reaching over Packer's shoulder and holding a card in a celluloid frame. The Frenchman said something rapidly, which Packer did not catch, and both policemen saluted.

As Pol's hand withdrew, all Packer could make out on the card was a diagonal red, white and blue stripe.

One of the policemen had moved out into the road, and now signalled them to go. For several seconds they rode in silence. 'These little theatricals, Monsieur Packer,' Pol said at last; 'they are unnecessary and undignified. This morning I was drunk and you were my friend. This afternoon I am sober and I hope I can be your friend.'

'Friendship requires trust,' said Packer.

Sarah interrupted, in English, 'Oh, don't be so bloody pompous, Owen!' – and she smiled at Pol. 'Where are we going, Monsieur?'

'A little place I know on the Somme Estuary, called Le Crotoy. The patron does an excellent soupe de poisson and fruits de mer. Drive to Lille, then on to Abbeville, and from there I will direct you.'

He's got himself into the driving seat, Packer thought bitterly; and I've lost the advantage. Cunning sod. If it hadn't been for Sarah, he'd have been inclined to press on with the interrogation; but Pol's performance with the Police had clearly drawn her well into his sphere of influence. From now on it would be two against one, with Packer up against the ropes.

'Naturally,' said Pol, 'you were treated abominably. The English are so quick to accuse our French justice, but even after the Algerian story we never treated our officers as you were treated.' He sipped his black coffee and sighed. 'To kill many men in war is called "duty". To kill one man, under special circumstances, so easily becomes a cause macabre, even a crime. You British are particularly vulnerable, of course. Your authorities hate nothing more than to be embarrassed; and the cause of that embarrassment is often sacrificed with a terrible fury.'

Owen Packer looked through the French windows across the mud flats of the estuary to the distant town of Saint Valery. The tide was out and the fishing boats were lolling under the jetty, showing their rusted bellies to the darkening sky. Outside the hotel there was a little square with a triangle of plane trees, their branches cropped like poodles, arranged around a statue of Joan of Arc. The fishermen, in their flat black caps and blue boiler-suits, were drinking downstairs in the bar, while Sarah was in Room 3, preening herself for the evening meal.

'You are absolutely forbidden to drink alcohol?' Pol asked abruptly.

'It is not advisable,' Packer said.

Pol did not pursue the matter. Together they watched the wild duck sweeping down over the mud flats. 'How did you feel when you killed this man?'

'Like putting a girlfriend off for dinner at the last moment.'

'You are very cynical for an Anglo-Saxon. I have never heard a man compare the act of killing to using a telephone.'

'You know what happened.'

'Yes,' said Pol. 'The British were playing nursemaid to one of those ridiculous old syphilitic sheikhs. The sheikh was senile and stupid enough to send his favourite son to Paris and Oxford, where the young man picked up a lot of dangerous ideas about progress and social reform, and other absurdities. He even went on a goodwill trip to Moscow, and when he got home to papa's kingdom, one of the first things he did was to attack the ancient custom of stoning women to death for adultery. Unfortunately the old man was a bit passé, and didn't seem too keen on either telling his boy to shut up, or on having his head chopped off. So the paternal British felt they had better take a hand in the affair.'

He grinned at Packer. 'You were a comparatively new boy at the game – a bright clean graduate. The commandant called you in and gave you a drink – eh?' He giggled. 'Maybe several?'

Packer said nothing.

'You were perhaps a little "cooked" as we say. And then he made you his proposition.'

'Oh God,' said Packer, 'get me something to drink. A brandy – or at least some beer.'

'You would not make such a suggestion, I think, if Mademoiselle Sarah were here?'

'What's that got to do with it?' Packer said angrily.

'You are an alcoholic.'

Packer stared at the floor. 'I don't know.'

Pol sat nodding slowly. 'You know. It is in your dossier. It was the main reason why they threw you out.'

Packer looked up quickly. 'They threw me out because I killed the wrong man.' He laughed nastily. 'Those Arabs are like the Chinese, they all look the same! But please, go on.'

'They found the poor fellow with a broken neck in his crashed sports car a few miles from the town. Apparently another bad habit he had picked up at Oxford – driving too fast while under the influence. Only, as I said, he wasn't the only one that night who had been enjoying himself. There was a certain Captain Packer who happened to be in Abud Zur, on some confidential mission for the British War Office. He had been drinking with his Commanding Officer just before the incident. Perhaps he had had one glass too many and had forgotten – or perhaps he did not know – that the old sheikh had more than one son. Two of them, to be precise, with almost identical names. So easy to confuse Arab names, don't you think, Capitaine Packer? And doubly unfortunate that they both drove English sports cars.'

'I was badly briefed.'

'Quite, quite. There is no need to upset yourself, my friend. The British authorities merely wanted to protect their own interests. They could hardly have you kill the original son after what had happened. Even the Arab conception of Fate has its limits! So they put you behind a desk in Aden, where you were in charge of leave schedules. That's when the little problem of drink began, I believe? It was soon so bad that they sent you back to England where you spent six weeks in a military hospital near Andover.' He paused. 'I do not remember the exact medical details, but it appears that your addiction to alcohol was accompanied by outbursts of extreme violence.'

Packer did not move. Pol stirred the dregs of his coffee and said gently, 'I have purposely begun at the end – at the tragic end. But it was not all tragedy. I know nothing of your family background, except that you went to one of those English private schools for the bourgeoisie, which you call "public" schools, I think?' He gave Packer a bright smirk. 'And afterwards you spent a year in Grenoble, where you learnt French. Then you were conscripted into the Army for two years, and after six months were sent to Malaya during the Emergency, where you underwent a training course at the Jungle Warfare School in Jahore Baru. From there you were sent on special anti-terrorist operations. The reports state that you did well.'

'What reports?'

Pol ignored him. 'Would you like me to go on?'

'Why not? Tell me the routine text-book stuff they taught me – the twenty-nine elementary ways of killing a man with one's hands and feet. Use of explosives, detonators, cyanide bullets, as well as all those sophisticated methods of interrogation which don't quite infringe the UN Charter of Human Rights.'

'You sound bitter, mon cher Capitaine?'

'Not at all. I'm nostalgic.' He leaned forward. 'Did your information tell you that I killed, personally, a total of forty-seven men in Malaya, eighteen in Cyprus, and two in Aden? Not counting the sheikh's son with the sports car. And all of them civilians. Students – professors – lawyers – ' he smiled ' – not necessarily terrorists, just left-wing intellectuals. Or do I shock you, perhaps?'

Pol's chins rippled with mirth. 'My dear friend, I know the whole routine from Indo-China and Algeria. The only difference is that you British, with your great reputation for fair play, gave up your glorious Empire like gentlemen. It didn't matter that a few gentlemen – like the good Capitaine Packer – were using their expertise to burst men's kidneys with their thumbs, or to half drown a suspect in a bucket of his own urine. Nothing mattered as long as the British public went on believing that their Army behaved like gentlemen, and no one told them otherwise.'

'At least we won in Malaya,' Packer scowled, 'and didn't leave a bloody mess like Indo-China.'

'This is not a political discussion, Monsieur Packer. I am interested in you as an individual. Let us go back to a small incident in Cyprus. There was a young secretary in the GOC's office in Nicosia, and there had been leaks to the Press about ill treatment of EOKA suspects. One night he had an unfortunate accident – fell out of a third-floor window, didn't he? – after a wild party at the Ledra Palace Hotel. Broke his spine – pauvre type. I understand he will never walk again. You were one of the guests at the party, of course.'

Packer sat stiffly forward on a mock Empire chair, listening with a mixture of bewilderment and rage to the accuracy of this cruel curriculum vitae from which the unknown Pol seemed to be selecting only atrocities and failures.

'I was discharged from the Army nearly ten years ago,' he said at last. 'Is that as far as your spies were able to dig?'

Pol spread his hands. 'The rest is a little mundane, mon cher Capitaine. You remained on the reserve, attached to this rather obscure organization – I cannot remember the name. Otherwise, you got a job for a short time as a bank security guard. What happened?'

'Nothing. Nobody tried to rob me or cosh me or take a shot at me. I got bored.'

'Then you enrolled as a student in an art school outside London.' Pol made a clucking noise. 'Rather out of character, surely? A killer with a love of art – that is hardly an English trait.'

'I'm Welsh. Anyay, how do you know? The War Office files aren't that thorough.'

'No, but the Police are. You seduced one of your fellow pupils and got her pregnant. When she asked for the money for an abortion, you said you didn't have any. Her brother entered the act and there was a fight. You were drunk. He was ten days in hospital and you spent three months in prison. The rest is eccentric, perhaps, but not entirely irrelevant. During your last dry-out in hospital you developed an odd skill, in the way of occupational therapy. You started building model windmills. Eventually you became so expert that you were able to sell them. You do it now as a full-time job.'

'You don't have to go on any more,' said Packer. 'That last bit isn't on any Army or Police file. Now just tell me how you got it all.'

'Does it matter?'

'Yes it does matter. When I wipe my arse, I like to do it in private. You wait until I'm having a quiet weekend in Amsterdam, then you pick me up with my girl in a tulip field and – rather cunningly, now I come to think of it – you contrive to have me run you across a couple of frontiers and sit me down in this hotel and expect me not to ask questions. Why France, anyway? Why not back in Amsterdam? Or, better still, London?'

'The answer to your last question,' said Pol, 'is that my presence in your country is not altogether welcome.'

'Then how the hell were you able to get the information in the first place?'

Pol sat with his fat little hands folded across his stomach, the kiss-curl and goatee looking stiff and artificial against the rest of his hairless face, like adornments on a huge Easter egg. 'I understand your point of view perfectly, Capitaine Packer. But please understand mine. Our relations with each other must, of necessity, be extremely delicate at this stage. I must win your complete confidence, while at the same time not betraying the confidence of my employer. And my employer, Capitaine Packer, is a man who plays the comedy with absolutely no one. That I promise you.'

'I'll take your word for it,' said Packer. 'What's the colour of his money? And what does he want done for it?'

Pol had turned his head without moving his vast body, and was watching the tide swirl in across the mud flats at the speed of trotting horses. 'For yourself, half a million English pounds,' he said at last; 'or the equivalent in gold, or any other currency you prefer, paid into the bank of your choice.'

Owen Packer sat very still and straight in his chair. He waited, watching Pol, saying nothing.

'Would you like some coffee?' Pol added, 'or perhaps a citron pressé?'

'I'd like a bloody big drink,' Packer muttered, in English.

'You know that is not permitted,' Pol replied gently, still in French. 'Your last medical report described your mental condition as emotional, but basically stable – providing you avoid alcohol.' He smiled. 'I sympathize deeply, mon cher.'

'The bastards. And they say England's a free country!' He looked at Pol. 'What's the job?'

Pol shifted his buttocks and belched. 'You are very direct, my friend. I hope – particularly after the unfortunate incident this morning – that you are taking me seriously?'

'Entirely seriously,' Packer replied, without irony; and repeated, 'What's the job?'

'Your old profession. Simply, to kill a man.'

Packer nodded. 'For half a million pounds?' He paused. 'The last I heard, the going rate in London was between two and three thousand. You must be getting into a pretty high-class league.'

Pol gave him a beady stare. 'I am certainly not hiring some cheap hoodlum with the brain of a dinosaur and the morals of a rattlesnake.'

'I'm flattered,' said Packer; 'but why me? The British Army turns out dozens of us every year. Some even have clean records.

They usually get jobs in public relations or industry – poor bastards. What makes me so special?'

'Your present occupation, mon cher. Your occupation of building model windmills and selling them extremely well to rich Americans. I have been shown an article in a New York magazine, containing photographs of your work. There was also a most interesting interview with yourself.'

'What the hell have model windmills got to do with killing a man for half a million pounds?' Packer growled.

'One detail which you revealed in the article struck me as particularly interesting. Although your models – certainly from the photographs in the magazine – are obviously most complex and detailed, you claim to build them without any plan or diagram. You start with a basic idea in your head and construct from there, building on each stage ad hoc. When a problem arises, you simply improvise. You also claim that you have never encountered a problem which has defeated you, and that you have never had to abandon a model before it was finished. It would also appear that these models are of a very high order.'

'They each take between six months and a year to build,' said Packer, 'and sell at an average of 12,000 dollars. It's a living – but it's about a hundredth of what you're offering me now. Why?'

Pol gazed out at the estuary where the tide was now full and the fishing boats were bobbing upright in the dusk. Lights winked at them from Saint Valery. It was nearly six o'clock. Packer wondered how long it would be before Sarah had finished painting her face and applying her fixtures and fittings; but Pol seemed in no hurry to come to the point.

'You construct a framework, then add the mechanism to fit the framework,' he was murmuring, half to himself, 'wheels that move other wheels – pulleys – ropes – ladders – trap-doors. Everything to fit exactly. Every detail made to measure, and to work. And all without a master plan.'

'You think a man can be killed like that?' Packer sneered. 'What we English call a "one-off job". A psychopath with a cheap rifle on the fifth floor of a school book depository – or a teenage student with a one-shot pistol standing in a crowded street in Sarajevo.'

Pol patted his belly. 'Not precisely. But already you have the principle. It is true that most successful assassinations in history have been what you might call "accidents", and that the really organized attempts – against Peter the Great, Napoleon, Queen Victoria, Hitler, de Gaulle – all failed. They failed because their planning was too careful, too grandiose, *too well organized*.' He gave a mischievous chuckle. 'I intend to construct a plan which is both organized *and* random.'

'You still haven't answered my question,' said Packer. 'Why me? Not because I killed a few men in Malaya and can stick some pieces of balsa wood together and flog them to a few dumb Texans as mobile art. That's not good enough, Monsieur Pol.'

'No,' said Pol, 'it isn't. Your great virtue, Capitaine Packer, is that you are a misfit – a flawed character – a failure.' He paused; Packer had gone rather pale and his long upper lip was sucked in against his teeth. He said nothing.

Pol went on: 'The man in question not only lives in the constant expectation of an assassination attempt, but several such attempts have already been made. Also, besides being one of the most closely guarded men in the world, he has an excellent Intelligence Service. We must assume at once that he will quickly get wind of any new plan. And the first thing he will do is to order his Security chiefs to draw up a full list of international suspects. A superficial list would not be difficult to compile. He would certainly receive the active assistance of almost every friendly Intelligence organization outside the Communist bloc. The first candidates would be his own nationals – refugees and self-exiles who oppose his régime. These would not, for obvious reasons, stand much chance on their own. But he will also be looking out for foreign mercenaries and "guns for hire". Here again, the most likely candidates will be those with clean records – in civilian life, at least. The professionals from Algeria, the Congo, the Yemen and Biafra, and perhaps a few disenchanted American veterans from Vietnam.'

'That would make one hell of a long list,' said Packer.

'Perhaps. But as I said, the gentleman in question has a very large Security force, consisting of many times more men than would ever join such a list.' He leaned forward with a creak of silk and pressed his thumbs together. 'But even supposing that one of these professionals escaped his surveillance, there would still be one flaw. The same flaw that blemishes all elaborate assassination attempts. The assassin, or assassins, will resort to the most subtle artifacts of the trade, as well as the most obvious. False passports, ingenious disguises, scientific weapons – the whole arsenal of what the Americans call "The Department of Dirty Tricks".' He flapped his hand dismissively.

'We, Capitaine Packer, will approach the matter rather differently. We will even indulge in a little double bluff. Our victim, if he is as thorough as I think he is, would probably include you in his original list of suspects. But not for long, I think. He will reason just as you did – that after a good start, you ruined your professional career, and ended with a history of alcoholism, criminal violence, and mental instability. Besides' – he chuckled – 'grown men who earn their living building model windmills, do not go around assassinating Heads of State.

'But there will be a second stage to our double bluff,' he went on. 'Besides you, I have also recruited a rather bizarre gentleman by the name of Samuel David Ryderbeit. He is already in the neighbourhood and – providing you are still willing – you will be meeting him soon. He is a very open character and does not require much explanation. It is enough to say that he was formerly a Rhodesian and has spent much of the last fifteen years hiring out his services – which are considerable – to various doubtful causes. He has these valuable qualities. He is a crack shot, with almost any weapon. He is one of the best pilots in the world – at least, on the free market. And he is totally without fear.'

Packer groaned. 'Oh God, not one of those! Another gun-happy White African killer! His sort they'll have on a list already, without even drawing up a new one.'

'The essence of a successful assassination,' Pol said calmly, 'is not merely precision of planning, or courage, or even luck. The vital element is that the victim should be *confused*. He may suspect a former counter-terrorist officer with an alcohol problem. He will certainly suspect Sammy Ryderbeit. But then there will be other, subtler elements that he will not suspect. While he is looking for the obvious, professional killer, his back will be turned to the real danger.'

There was a long pause. Packer watched Pol idly scratching his silk crotch. They could hear the burble of voices from the bar below. It was quite dark now.

45

'What real danger, Monsieur Pol?'

Pol tilted his chair perilously back and jerked his head at the wall. 'Next-door, my friend. In your room.'

Packer was not shocked or outraged. He was disappointed; for during the last half-hour he had begun to take Charles Pol almost seriously.

'Well, one thing's for certain,' he said at last : 'whoever you've got in your sights isn't going to have her on his list!'

'That is correct,' Pol said.

Packer paused and sat looking across at him. 'You've got an expensive sense of humour, haven't you?'

'I have been entrusted with enough money to afford one,' said Pol; and for a moment there was a hard gleam in his eyes which Packer had not seen before.

'You're serious, aren't you?' Packer said, suddenly beginning to doubt his judgement.

'Absolutely serious.'

Packer let out a long breath. 'All right, what does *her* dossier say? No, don't tell me. I can look it all up in the press-cuttings when I get back – gossip columns going back nearly eight years. She started young – on her seventeenth birthday, when Mama gave a ball for her at their family seat, and Papa gave her a car. She got broken in early. Most girls get hurt at least once, and some of them seem to get hurt the whole bloody time. But not this one. She's lived on and off with three different men, and each one of them she's sliced up like a razor. But that doesn't qualify her to help kill one of the world's leaders.'

'You love her?'

'Yes. It's been going on for just over a year now and every day's been like the Eastern Front.'

Pol spread his hands. 'You are being self-indulgent, my friend. What influence do you have over her?'

'None whatever. She does what she likes, when she likes, as she likes. The trouble is, she's a knockout. When she wants, she can be the most vivacious, amusing, exhilarating girl you can imagine.'

'I don't imagine these things,' said Pol. 'Your own sentiments for her are purely subjective. What concerns me is the effect she has on others. Of the three serious lovers whom you mentioned, I understand that at least two were considered to be among your country's most eligible young men. The third was connected with your aristocracy, and was married. Of course, she is very well connected socially herself. Not exactly la noblesse, I understand, but the true grande bourgeoisie. But what is her real secret?'

'Bedroom eyes,' said Packer, 'and style. The sort of girl who walks into a room and everyone, including the women, turns round to look at her. And most women, except her closest friends, loathe her.'

'She is acceptable in almost any society, however high,' Pol said softly, as though half to himself. 'Her family's fortunes are also in difficulties. The present economic situation in Great Britain, combined with certain Socialist measures to curb inheritance, threatens her father's wealth, while she herself has a humble job in an art gallery. It is hardly a satisfactory situation for a girl of class, n'est-ce pas?'

'She'll survive,' said Packer. 'If she'd been on the *Titanic*, you can bet your balls she'd have been in the first lifeboat – as a first-class passenger, of course. Her stated ambition is to live it up until she's thirty, then marry a rich man with at least one big house in the country, and perhaps a little place in Provence thrown in.'

'Is she greedy?'

'Selective. Spoiled. And broke. That's to say, she's always complaining about not having enough money, and I finish up paying the bills. And for her it's nothing but the best. Even her marmalade has to be twice as expensive as any other brand – not because of the taste, but because it comes in beautiful ceramic jars. She's always going on about how she loves beautiful things.'

'Does she love you?'

'No. She likes me, and she uses me. I also interest her, vaguely. She hasn't met anyone like me before. Not in her class, I'm afraid. The one thing she's really scared of is getting her name linked with mine in the gossip columns.'

Pol shook with laughter. 'You are lost, my friend! Have you ever tried beating her?'

Packer hesitated. 'No. I might end up killing her.'

'Ah, that would be a pity, mon cher' – he was still laughing – 'but I fear you are lost. No matter! It is all part of the human comedy. The immediate solution is to make you the rich man, then your problems are over.'

'Fine. And where does that leave her?'

'If you are careful, mon cher, it will leave her with a house in the country, and perhaps a farmhouse in Provence.'

Packer leaned forward; he spoke slowly, quietly. 'Monsieur Pol, do I understand that you intend to involve her in this little charade of yours?'

'My friend, in French we have a proverb: "There are never indiscreet questions, only indiscreet answers." I will reply as discreetly as I can. Mademoiselle Sarah is your affair. She appears to be a charming girl, and she might – with a little persuasion, and perhaps the offer of money – prove very useful to our enterprise. But that is entirely a matter for your own judgement. I am offering to employ you to draw up a plan – that is all. Whether I accept your plan, or insist that it be amended, is up to me. For the moment, I am merely your paymaster and *parrain*.'

They both looked up. Sarah had come in without knocking.

At dinner she was at her most sparkling. The restaurant had an entry in *Michelin*, and Pol had ordered generously and with imagination. He had chosen, for Sarah and himself, the best wines; and Packer found himself eating almost in silence while the two of them laughed and talked and drank together as freely as though this obscene old Frenchman had known her since she was a child.

She seemed to enjoy him enormously. Her eyes followed his with every word, flashing with mock flirtation; responding to all his jokes, not with her usual contrived gaiety but with genuine high spirits, her head thrown back, her shoulder rubbing up against him, like a cat caressing a vast silken sofa. Packer was all the more disconcerted for, whenever he was alone with her, he usually found her a rather humourless, even sullen character. Above all, he noticed that she appeared entirely to overlook Pol's habit of talking with his mouth full – a sin which Packer committed only at the risk of arousing her fury and revulsion – while their host continued to eat and talk his way through the meal with impunity, his goatee clotted thick and cherry lips smeared bright with grease.

For beneath his gross exterior, Charles Pol had charm. It was a comic but insidious charm; an alliance of the sybarite and the buffoon, overlaid with the seductive comfort of the magnanimous host; and towards the end of the evening Packer began to consider the outrageous possibility that the day's events might all be some obscure and elaborate ruse by which Pol intended to ensnare Sarah.

Such things had happened before. What could not be explained, however, was the vast compendium of information that Pol possessed about his and Sarah's backgrounds. This had been no ordinary pick-up. Its final execution in the tulip field might have been ludicrous, but its planning had been meticulous. The research itself must have taken weeks, even months, depending on Pol's sources of information – and this brought Packer back to perhaps the most puzzling aspect of the whole affair. Why had the Frenchman waited until the trip to Amsterdam to make contact? Pol had hinted that he was somehow persona non grata with the British authorities. Assuming that the man was genuinely trying to set up a major assassination, Packer was inclined to accept this explanation at its face value. But then how – without intimate access to certain of Packer's former colleagues in the Army, and perhaps a few indiscreet friends – could he know so much?

Sarah's case was relatively straightforward; half a day's research in the library of any of the big European newspaper offices would have revealed most of her background. Miss Sarah Pugh Laval-Smith was public property; Captain Owen Packer was not. For Pol to have obtained such information about *him* – both classified and obscure – would have demanded the resources of at least one major Intelligence organization, friendly or otherwise.

Packer decided that the Frenchman might, after all, be serious.

He sipped his Vichy water and watched the waiter put down the two balloon glasses of Armagnac in front of Pol and Sarah; and again detected, behind those epicene features across the table, a gleam in the Frenchman's little eyes which Sarah seemed to find entrancing, but which Packer had begun to mistrust.

They were now the last diners in the restaurant. Without consulting Sarah, Pol ordered two more Armagnacs. She often boasted to Packer about how she came from a hard-drinking family; and he had known her to get drunk many times, but always in an impeccably controlled way. Only her bad temper and those ritual 'bull shots' at lunch in the Ritz betrayed her. Her delicate features, painstakingly repaired with cosmetics, remained unblemished.

Pol drank a toast: 'To my two new, dear young friends!' – and Sarah lifted her glass to his and drank, without looking at Packer. It was one of her most tantalizing techniques – the way she assiduously ignored him in public, while bestowing on friends and strangers alike that brittle gaiety that was so alluring, and so venomous.

It was after midnight when they left the restaurant. Pol, his rosy face smeared and streaked with sweat, held them both tightly by the arm and wobbled between them on his slippered feet. He mounted the stairs with some difficulty, pausing every few steps, and once swayed perilously backwards as they neared the top. Packer felt gloomily sober.

They reached Pol's door first. He stopped and beamed. 'My children, I must offer you a last drink!' He winked at Packer. 'A glass of Vichy perhaps, Monsieur Packer?'

'Thank you,' said Packer, 'we're going to bed.' He released himself from Pol's grip and took Sarah's arm, which she instantly removed.

'Good night, Charles. Thank you for a marvellous evening!' She gave Pol her most devastating smile, and Pol smiled back, bright and benign, but without excitement.

'Bonne nuit!' he whispered loudly, and stumbled against his door as he opened it.

In their room Sarah began to undress at once, quickly and dispassionately, wearing only a pair of tight blue pants as she bent over the mirror, her back fully displayed to Packer. She began peeling off her eyelashes.

He tried to avoid looking at her, lay down on the bed and stared moodily at the ceiling. He knew the routine too well by now; it was less of an instinct than an animal scent, like a dog sniffing fear. Only with her it was resistance, truculence – worst of all, indifference. He caught a glimpse of her pale-nippled breasts in the mirror and saw them quiver slightly as she pulled two jade necklaces over her head, and heard her voice, limp and sulky, talking to her reflection: 'God, I'm tired.'

Packer looked away and fought the familiar temptation to coax her with soft lulling endearments, imagining it as it had been in the early months, with him standing behind her with one hand cupping her breast, slowly pinching the nipple, while the fingertips of his other gently prodded her pubic mound, feeling her thighs parting as he leaned down and began kissing the fluffy black hair at the nape of her neck. Now, with the passing of that year, the task of seduction had become inversely more difficult, more challenging, while his own approach had become clumsier and more artless, to the point when it was no more than a coarse and ineffectual grope.

He heard her rings clatter on to the table top, then felt the bed heave as she sank down on to it, curling up with her back towards him, pulling the sheet and blanket close up round her neck and shoulders. 'I'm so tired,' she said again; then, with a little sigh: 'Goodnight.'

He got up and began to undress, leaving on his boxer shorts, and wondered, in a flash of desperation, whether this might be the moment to offer her a share of half a million pounds. Every girl has her price, he thought. There had been times, increasingly during recent months, when he'd caught himself imagining luscious, fearful, unspeakable things he could do to her – or watch have done to her – wondering how much she would accept before submitting, each subtle and ghastly perversion calculated to within a few pounds.

He could feel her steady breathing, feigning sleep, as he climbed carefully in beside her, rigidly restraining himself from touching her, even with his knees or toes, until he felt that cold dead lump in his gut and a tiny pulse beating fast in his left temple. He reached up and turned out the light.

3

The peacock-blue diplomatic passport was cleared through a special gate, and the man walked out of Zürich's Kloten Airport eight minutes after his Boeing 727 had landed. It was 10.20 p.m. and snowing lightly. Outside, a black Peugeot stood with its engine idling. A plain-clothes chauffeur waited on the kerb, and whipped the rear door open as soon as the man emerged.

Even inside the car the man kept on his dark glasses and ankle-length vicuna coat, removing only his black astrakhan hat. An attaché case with four gold-plated locks was secured by a chain to his thin wrist, just below his Patek Philippe watch. The chauffeur drove fast but carefully, accelerating only when they joined the autoroute to Chur, where the Peugeot reached the 'advised' speed limit of 120 kmh. An hour later the chauffeur turned off at the intersection to Landquart.

At exactly two minutes to midnight they passed the sign marked Klosters, six miles below Davos. The Peugeot drove between the scattered chalets on the outskirts of the resort. The car then took a sharp left turn, passed a red and white No Entry sign, and began to climb a steep single track between pine trees, its surface freshly cleared of snow. A hundred yards further on, a couple of men stood on either side of the track, half hidden by the pines. As the Peugeot's headlights swept up between them, one of them flashed a pocket torch twice, and the chauffeur slowed down long enough for the man to read the Peugeot's numberplate. After another quarter of a mile they came in sight of the dark heavy-roofed shape of the chalet.

The Ruler received his visitor ten minutes later in the sauna lined with oozing pine logs. He was sitting on the centre step, naked except for a white towelling sarong. Despite the fierce heat, he sweated little. His body was well preserved, betraying its age only by a slightly hollow chest and small paunch.

As soon as the door closed, his visitor suppressed a gasp, bowed low three times, and began to breathe carefully. He was wearing a blue worsted suit and a neutral tie. Within seconds he felt the prickles of sweat on his sallow brow and along his upper lip, but he made no move to take off his jacket or loosen his collar. He remained standing, still holding the attaché case, which was no longer chained to his wrist.

The Ruler gave him a long stare, then reached out for a wooden ladle beside him, dipped it into the bucket on the step below, and poured the contents on to a pile of steaming stones against the wall. The water exploded with a sharp hiss, filling the room with a fog of steam. The visitor found himself gasping again, and blinking at the Ruler through tears of sweat.

The steam slowly subsided. The Ruler looked down at the little man in front of him. 'Welcome, Letif.'

Marmut bem Letif, newly appointed Minister of the Interior to the Imperial Court of the Emerald Throne in Mamounia, bowed again and produced a bunch of gilt keys with which he began to unlock, with his slippery fingers, each of the four locks on the case. He opened it, still standing, and balancing it awkwardly on his forearm, picked out three stapled sheets of pink paper closely covered with Arabic script. He began to hand them to the Ruler, but was waved back.

'The paperwork can wait until later. I have summoned you here, Letif, for a confidential audience. First, how do you find your new appointment?'

Letif licked the salt off his lips. 'It is indeed an honoured privilege, Your Imperial Highness. It carries with it great responsibilities.'

'Come, come, Letif. You talk like a diplomat. I have not summoned you more than 3000 miles to listen to bureaucratic platitudes. Here you are free to talk privately, in absolute confidence. I do not want the babblings of some fawning acolyte. I want the truth.'

Letif raised his head and looked at the Ruler with moist, yielding eyes. He felt the sweat running down his back. The Ruler seemed for a moment amused. 'You are shy, Letif. The experience of your new office has not yet taught you the harshness of authority. Let me help you. You have already made the acquaintance of your subordinate, Colonel Sham Tamat?'

Letif inclined his head in a nod, but said nothing.

'He is a hard man. A brutal man. But NAZAK is a hard and brutal organization. It guards the internal security of our nation,

Letif. We cannot afford – even for the benefit of our Western friends – to leave it in the hands of weak, sentimental liberals.'

Letif stood with his head resting on one of his narrow shoulders. There was a long pause.

'Something troubles you, Letif. I am your master, and you are directly responsible to me. You must tell me everything, however trivial it may seem.' The Ruler's tone was quiet and soothing.

A nerve began to twitch and tug at the damp skin around Letif's right eye. He spoke carefully, without looking at the Ruler. 'I am conscious of Your Imperial Highness's views about certain aspects concerning the work of Colonel Tamat and his organization. Last week, on the day after I received Your Imperial Highness's Seals of Office, the Colonel invited me privately to the headquarters of NAZAK. I witnessed one of his formal interrogations.'

He paused, and his dewy eyes seemed to be searching for something in the steamy gloom of the sauna. Again he smelled the brackish odour of the windowless cell, with its single strip of neon that fizzed and blinked from the ceiling; saw Colonel Tamat's large friendly figure beside him, in its well-tailored uniform the colour of dried dung, as the awful instrument was wheeled in, looking like a portable barbecue; then the girl being stripped from the waist down and strapped on to the grille, and then the screams and stench of scorched skin and urine, the flash as the lights fused, and Tamat's laugh bellowing through the darkness: 'The little bitch – pissed on to my beautiful barbecue à cheval – toasted her fat arse and she never told us a thing!'

'I am waiting,' said the Ruler; but before Letif could answer, his master had ladled more water on to the stones. When the noise had subsided, Letif replied.

'There was an accident. One of the prisoners – a girl, a student, – was electrocuted on Colonel Tamat's machine.'

The Ruler's eyes showed no expression. 'Sham Tamat is a good family man, but he has the instincts and appetites of a wild beast. He is also cunning, and will react quickly and cleverly when attacked. Minister Letif, I am going to entrust you with a delicate and difficult task. You must be wary of Colonel Tamat. I have many potential enemies in my kingdom – some of whom I know, some I do not – but Colonel Sham Tamat is a man who must be watched constantly. After myself, he is probably the only

54

person in the country who understands how to use real power. While he was still content to use that power in the interests of my nation, I was prepared to give him a free hand – even if it did mean allowing him to play with his revolting toys.

'However, I have taken a decision. I no longer trust Tamat, and I intend to take that power away from him. But it must be done without bloodshed. That is most important, Letif. I have no intention of advertising our country as just another snake pit of power feuds, like our cheap Arab neighbours. Over the next decade, Letif, my nation is destined to become one of the greatest powers in the world.'

A dull light shone in his black eyes as he sat forward, hands on his naked knees. 'But I intend that we should also become a civilized power. We will use civilized methods in everything from agriculture and industry to the treatment of our political enemies. Sham Tamat and his kind are not civilized. They will soon cease to have any place in our nation's destiny. Tamat will be destroyed, Letif, and you will be one of the instruments of his destruction.' He sat back and gave a short nod. 'Now to more general matters, Minister. What have you to report?'

Letif inclined his head again and rubbed his hands together as if he were washing them – the tell-tale gesture of the bazaar and the street pedlar. 'As always, Your Highness's divine guidance has been correct. On Tuesday evening Colonel Tamat paid a visit to the house of Doctor Zak, across the Gorge of Darak. After three hours they were joined by two junior members of the Pan-Islamic Socialist Brotherhood. They stayed until after two o'clock in the morning, when Tamat returned to Mamounia, while Doctor Zak and the two officers drove away to Saba where they boarded a light aircraft.' He glanced down at the papers in his hand, where his thumb had left a wet mark in the corner. 'I have the registration number here, but unfortunately we were unable to determine the plane's exact destination. However,' he added, his meek voice gathering confidence, 'the radar station at Bikar reported an unidentified plane flying into Iraq in the early morning.'

'There were no flights back into my country?' said the Ruler quietly.

'No, Your Highness.' Letif gave a limp smile. 'I am fully

confident that if there had been, your Imperial Air Defences would have intercepted them at once.'

'Not if they were small aircraft flying low. Our radar defences, Letif, are among the best in the world, but they are directed at high-flying bombers and missiles. But no matter. I do not want Doctor Zak and his friends apprehended – at least, not for the time being.'

Letif bowed. 'I understand, Your Imperial Highness.'

The Ruler picked up the wooden ladle and dipped it again in the bucket, but this time just stirred it around, as though testing a soup; then, to Letif's relief, he replaced it on the bench beside him.

'Minister, let us now turn to that difficult and delicate task I mentioned to you. In the last few days information has reached me, from secret sources outside our country, which indicates that an attempt is being planned against my life. I know that such attempts have become almost commonplace, but they have usually been the work of amateur fanatics and disaffected Army officers. My recent information, however, obliges me to treat this latest plot more seriously.

'The indications are that it is being planned abroad, and that the potential assassins are unknown to our Security services. I want you, Minister Letif, to identify these men – to isolate them, and eliminate them. In accomplishing this, you will have to manoeuvre most delicately — particularly where NAZAK and Colonel Tamat are concerned. Tamat has great enthusiasm and energy when it comes to torturing a few students with left-wing sympathies. But I fear that he lacks the subtlety to deal with a full-scale international plot against my person. What you confide in Colonel Tamat, I leave to your discretion. As Head of Internal Security, he will have to be told of the plot. But I advise that as your inquiries proceed, you keep him informed of only the most basic details.' He paused. 'You are blessed with my confidence, Letif. You will not fail me.'

Letif bowed again, his clothes clinging warm and wet to his skin, and his feet felt as though he were standing in mud. 'I understand, Your Imperial Highness.'

The Ruler smiled. 'What news do you bring of Her Majesty?'

'Her Imperial Highness is in excellent health, Your Imperial Highness. The Crown Prince, also.' Letif reached into his clammy pocket. 'I have here a list of purchases Her Imperial Highness asked me to make for her in Geneva and Paris.' He was speaking with a slow unctuous smile. 'Do I have your Imperial permission to carry out these requests?'

'You do not. You are not a valet, Marmut bem Letif. You are a public servant responsible to me and my thirty million subjects.' For a moment the Ruler's jaw muscles stiffened to suppress a yawn. 'That will be all, Minister. You will leave all the State documents with my adjutant.'

Marmut bem Letif gave another three bows, feeling the sweat trickle through his glossy hair, and murmured the ancient ritual words of farewell, before opening the door behind him and backing into the sudden delicious cool outside.

Up in his room, which had the spare pinewood décor of a skiing lodge, the Minister quickly peeled off his clothes and stood for several minutes under the cold shower. Then he lifted the telephone and summoned the Ruler's adjutant.

The café smelled of cooked lentils and stale cigarettes. The greasy zinc-topped tables were empty except for two workmen in blue overalls, slapping playing cards down between them without exchanging a word. The barman sat under a row of bottles reading *L'Equipe*. From the back room came a staccato rattle, as a very tall, thin, black-haired man in a charcoal suit played a ferocious game of table football with himself. His hands, which were long and slender, manipulated the row of knobs with agility and skill, knocking the little ball back and forth with a zig-zagging speed that was almost too quick to follow. The only times he paused were to take a drink from a glass of pastis on the table behind him.

He had been playing for more than half an hour when the two strangers came in. Although he was facing the door, he did not immediately look up, but went on spinning the wooden players, scoring two goals against one side, one against the other. The two men sat down opposite him and waited.

He straightened up, turned and took a deep drink, then stared at them both with a long yellow eye of astonishing brightness. His other eye was of the same cat-like colour, but with a curiously flat dead look, giving him the appearance of having a squint.

He put his glass down behind him and clapped his hands together. 'Garçon!' he yelled, in an accent which made it sound like 'gersin'. His good eye swivelled back and fixed on the younger of the two men, who was watching him warily.

'SAS?' the tall man said suddenly, in English.

'More or less,' said the other. 'Except they didn't give us a label.'

'Exclusive, eh?' The tall man nodded, then turned again and cried, 'Hey, garçon! Encore! Lazy dago bastard,' he muttered, and pulled up a chair. 'Captain Packer, isn't it?' – he pronounced it 'Pecker' – 'I'm Sammy. Good to meet you, soldier.' He held out a smooth hand. 'Full name's Samuel David Ryderbeit – but that's strictly off the record. Over the last fifteen years the name Ryderbeit's become a dirty word in just about every respectable country in the world.' He gave a sidelong leer at the second man. 'Eh, Charlie Boy?'

Charles Pol grinned, his thighs bulging over the sides of the chair. The barman sauntered in with a bottle of pastis and a jug of water. 'Tell him to bring two more glasses and leave the bottle,' said Ryderbeit, still in English. Pol translated the order, while Ryderbeit's good eye turned again on Packer. 'How far's the fat man here put you in the picture, soldier?'

Packer told him, in one sentence – a top assassination job, target as yet unknown, fee of half a million pounds.

Ryderbeit sneered into his empty glass: 'That's a bloody sight more than I'm getting! Five times more, to be exact. I'm just the hired heavy – so you must be bloody good!' His body leaned forward from the waist. 'Just how good?'

Packer said nothing. The waiter came back and poured their drinks. Packer put a hand over his glass and asked for a Perrier.

'TT, are we?' Ryderbeit cackled, his good eye shining out of his hooked face, which had a slightly greenish complexion and was totally hairless. His appearance suggested gypsy blood; though Packer deduced from his name that he might be Jewish; while his accent – clipped, almost prim, with the occasional un-certain drawl of the expatriate – was South African.

When Packer still said nothing, Ryderbeit downed his drink,

and aggressively poured himself another, adding very little water this time. 'I asked how good you were.'

'Good at what?'

Ryderbeit's eyelid drooped. 'Don't play funny with me, soldier. Killing, of course. What's your score?'

'Didn't Monsieur Pol tell you?'

Ryderbeit sighed. 'He said around sixty. Chinks and wogs mostly – but they hardly count. Not in my book, anyway. I've killed hundreds – mostly munts. But I've also killed a few whites. Ever killed a white man, soldier?'

'No,' said Packer. 'What's your form, Ryderbeit?'

'Fat Man didn't tell you?'

'I prefer to hear it from you.' Beside them, Pol sat sipping his pastis.

Ryderbeit said, 'I started the serious stuff in the Congo back in '62. Flew for Tshombe's Air Force in Katanga. And when that bust up I did a spell with Black Shramm's boys. That was rough, bloody rough – for the other side, I mean. For us it was a laugh all the way! Then there was Commando Four.'

'And then?'

'I knocked around – tried my hand at a bit of civilian life, in Europe, then in the Middle East. Usual game, getting hold of a few rich suckers and selling them things that didn't exist. Then I got a bit over-ambitious and tried to sell an obsolete US aircraft carrier to the Syrians. I got rumbled on that one and had to get out fast. I went East. Finished up flying out of Laos, dropping rice – and a few other things – for Air America, the CIA's private airline.'

Packer sipped his Perrier. 'I didn't think the Americans took on mercenaries out there?'

'Like hell they didn't! The Yanks are good boys – they all drink milk and pay their income tax and are in bed by ten every evening. 'He poured himself another drink. 'It was about that time I met up with this bastard' – he grinned and jabbed a thumb in the direction of Pol, without looking at him – 'and we pulled off a beautiful caper out of Saigon. Seized a planeload of green-backs worth about two billion dollars. We were all set up for the big time, only Fat Man here had other ideas. The whole fucking lot finished up in North Vietnam and I spent the next year in a stinking Hanoi gaol sewing Army tunics. I only got out when the final curtain came down on Indo-China, and they chucked me out into Burma, and the Burmese chucked me into India, then the Indians tried to chuck me back into South Africa, only Jo'burg Immigration took one look at my poor bloody passport and I was on the next plane out to Angola. Want me to go on?'

'You're Rhodesian, aren't you?'

'Originally. But I reckoned I had enough problems without being officially classified as a rebel against Her Majesty your bloody Queen. I've had a lot of nationalities in my time. At the moment I'm an Israeli – thanks to some nifty paperwork by Charlie Boy here.'

'And you've never been back to Rhodesia?'

Ryderbeit shrugged. 'Too many troubles. Wife troubles, mostly. Up there, and down in Jo'burg. You ever been married, soldier?'

Packer shook his head. There was a pause. The Rhodesian refilled his and Pol's glasses, then deliberately offered the bottle to Packer. 'Have some. It's good!' His eye glittered.

Packer shook his head.

'I never trust a man who won't drink,' Ryderbeit said slowly. 'Unless there's a bloody good reason.'

'There's a reason,' said Packer, trying to decide just how much Ryderbeit already knew about him from Pol. 'For that matter,' he added, to change the subject, 'how come you're so trusting with Charles here – after he dropped you in the shit in Hanoi? I don't suppose *he* spent much time sewing tunics for the Viet Cong.' He glanced at Pol, but the Frenchman did not seem to be listening.

'It's a long story,' said Ryderbeit. 'Let's just say "birds of a feather". He also owes me a lot of money – from that same sky-jacking caper. That's the reason I'm in on this deal.'

'And what are Pol's reasons for taking you?'

'Because I'm the best pilot I ever met. I can fly anything, drunk or sober, short of a B52 or a supersonic strike aircraft – and that's only because I never got the chance to try. I can also shoot straight.'

'How straight's that?'

'I can hit a man in the head at over a mile, given the right gun.'

'How much have you been told about this operation, Ryderbeit?'

'About as much as you. And just for the record, don't call me Ryderbeit. Sammy's okay, but my full legal name now is Daniel Spice-Handler, born Breslau, 1935, resident of Tel Aviv. Anyway, that's what my passport says, so it must be true.' He emptied the last of the pastis into his glass and swallowed it neat. Packer reckoned that he had drunk three-quarters of the bottle – not counting anything he had had before they'd arrived – yet he seemed unnaturally sober.

'Right,' said Packer. 'How's your French?'

'Ugly as sin, but it works.'

Packer turned to Pol. 'I understood we were working with clean slates. Yet this man's got a record that extends from Johannesburg to Ho Chi Minh City, and now he's hiding behind a phoney passport. What's the game?'

Pol reached out and patted Packer's knee. 'Do not disturb yourself, mon cher. Monsieur Sammy is an old friend. He is also what I call a "reserve force". In an emergency you could find his talents very useful. As for his history, we have already discussed the usefulness of the double bluff in our tactics. Sammy's record will prove an admirable distraction to our enemies.' He gave them both a reassuring smile. 'As former soldiers, you will both no doubt appreciate the value of diversionary tactics.' He suddenly heaved himself to his feet and clapped his hands together. 'Bien, mes amis! I am pleased you have made each other's acquaintance. I will arrange for you to meet again very soon.' He nodded at Ryderbeit, then gestured Packer towards the door.

Ryderbeit sat without moving, watching them with his one-eyed yellow glare. Only when they reached the door did he call out in English, 'Just remember, soldier. You blow me and I'll kill you.'

Packer followed Pol through the café without replying.

Outside, a sharp salt wind had come up, rattling the shutters down the street. From beyond the houses opposite they could smell the sea. They had left the hired Mercedes, with its Dutch numberplates, a couple of hundred yards up the street, and Pol was soon walking with an effort against the wind. Neither of them spoke until they were in the car.

'Eh alors?' the Frenchman gasped, letting his seat back while

Packer turned south on to the coast road from Berck-Plage to their hotel in Le Crotoy. 'So what were your impressions of Monsieur Sammy?'

'He's either a liar or he's mad. He may be both.'

Pol chuckled. 'He is a very serious man, I assure you. He is also a dangerous man. I tell you, sometimes he even frightens me.'

'What happened to his eye?'

'Ah, a woman did it to him – a Cambodian woman in Phnom Penh. She had discovered he was being unfaithful to her, and one night she stamped her high heel into his face while he was asleep.'

Packer felt a spasm of envy – the odious notion that if he could excite such passion in Sarah, it would be worth going one-eyed for the rest of his life.

'You can do me a favour, Charles. If I'm staying on, this is my last night with Sarah. I'd like to dine alone with her tonight.'

'Why? Do you suspect me of being a rival for your beautiful Sarah?'

Packer could feel the fat man shaking with silent laughter beside him. 'I want to be alone with her, that's all.'

There was a pause. 'Monsieur Packer' – Pol sounded in earnest this time – 'are you intending to discuss our little operation with her?'

'No. For a start, I don't even know what the operation is. And I'm certainly not going to discuss anything more – with you or anyone else – until the money's settled. As far as Sarah's concerned, I've got to be able to convince her of that country house – remember? And from the information you've given me so far, she probably wouldn't believe a word of it, anyway.'

'What would make her believe?'

'A Swiss numbered bank account.'

Pol nodded gravely. 'I like your Mademoiselle Sarah. She may have a conventional background, but I have also detected a nuance of rebellion in her. This is not unusual in girls of good family, but in her case she also has the advantage of a strong personality. She is a girl of determination, I think?'

'Unfortunately, yes.' Packer was staring ahead at the road. 'You seem to have taken a lot of interest in her.'

'But why not, mon cher? A strictly professional interest, of course!'

'She's a ruthless, calculating little bitch,' Packer said.

'Une fille méchante, hein? Good! That is just the girl we may need.'

Next morning Packer drove Sarah to Le Touquet Airport, where she caught the 9.15 British Caledonian flight to Gatwick.

Their farewell was polite and perfunctory. She had allowed him to make love to her the night before, and he had responded with resigned, bitter lust. Afterwards she had complained that he had made her sore and refused his advances again when they woke, preferring to concentrate on her breakfast and make-up.

He now saw her through the barrier, watching her scarlet beret bobbing among the drab line of weekend trippers returning from Paris; then walked away, passing the bar, where he hesitated for longer than usual, before hurrying to the car and driving very fast back to Le Crotoy.

That afternoon Packer and Pol returned to Berck-Plage. The beach was long and grey and empty; the bathing huts locked, the tricolours flapping in the wind. They chose the last bench on the esplanade, a hundred yards away from the nearest house.

Five minutes later Ryderbeit appeared silently from behind, wearing a floppy wide-brimmed hat. He sat down without a word, took out a cigar case and tapped out a fat Bolivar corona which he proceeded to light skilfully against the wind, shielding the flame under the brim of his hat. He inhaled deeply; then, with his good eye half closed against the smoke, peered slowly at Pol, who sat between them. 'All right, Fat Man,' he said, in his abominable French: 'The contract.'

Pol looked at him with mock surprise. 'You are not expecting to exchange signatures here? That must wait for the appropriate occasion – when we reach Switzerland.'

Ryderbeit gave a rasping cackle, then looked at Packer. This time he spoke in English: 'You're supposed to be my boss-man,

63

soldier. You explain what I mean by "the contract". I want to know who the "hit" is.'

Packer looked at the Frenchman. 'The name of the victim, Monsieur Pol.'

Pol grinned benignly. 'But of course. However, are you not being perhaps a little optimistic? He is not yet our victim.'

'Come on, you know what we're talking about,' Packer said irritably.

Pol was staring at the waves, which broke in angry white ridges a quarter of a mile away. A solitary figure in a blue rain-coat was strolling along the water's edge. Otherwise the whole horizon, as well as the houses behind them, seemed deserted. Pol began to speak, slowly and clearly. 'What I am about to tell you is, of course, in the most absolute confidence. I desire, I demand, that you never speak the man's name, or his title, or his country, even when talking among yourselves. You will refer to him simply as "The Ruler".' He sighed deeply, then spoke the man's full appellative, in six words.

Packer stared in front of him in silence. He was thinking, it's so fantastic, it just has to be true. Perhaps half a million wasn't so much after all.

Ryderbeit sucked at his cigar, and let out the smoke with a long hiss. 'That's going to be one sod of a job!' he muttered, in English. His eye looked round at Packer. 'As I said, you've been appointed boss-man. What's your brilliant view?'

'At a guess,' said Packer, in French, 'ninety-nine per cent impossible.'

Pol rummaged under his coat and took out a silver flask, un-screwed it, drank, and said, 'I have calculated it at more like sixty per cent. Our task – or rather your task, my dear Capitaine' – he broke off to smack his lips – 'is to concentrate on the forty per cent.'

Packer took his time before replying. He was watching the lone figure at the shore's edge, which had now stopped almost opposite them, and bent down to pick something out of the sand; paused, then flung the object casually into the waves. 'You're not just hiring me to help you kill the Ruler, Monsieur Pol. In these matters the actual killing – successful or otherwise – is only a part of the problem. The lesser part. Where we really start earn-ing our money is in the escape afterwards. And the man we're talking about is probably better guarded than anyone alive to-day.'

'Precisely,' said Pol; he sounded amused. 'You did not suppose I was paying you so handsomely just to give you some soft target like a European Prime Minister or the Queen of England, did you?'

'He has one of the largest, most efficient, and certainly most ruthless police forces in the world,' said Packer. 'It's called NAZAK, and its reputation is right up in the CIA–KGB league – and even nastier.'

Ryderbeit sniggered to himself. 'Electrodes on the balls and up girls' pussies, needles through the eardrums – I know the type. Not exactly polite, but they certainly bring the "smack of firm government"!' He drew again on his cigar. 'But there have been several attempts on the bastard's life already,' he added. 'I met a chap in Oman who told me what happened to one of the would-be assassins. Officially he was given the chop – literally – in public, just like the old days, plus one nice little refinement. If the sword doesn't cut through the neck first time, there's a statutory one-minute interval before the next stroke. With this poor sod it took seven minutes. But that wasn't all. This chap in Oman said it wasn't the execution that was so bad – it was what they did to him beforehand. I can't remember all the details, because it was a pretty long inventory. All I can say is, they didn't leave much out – or rather, much left.'

Packer felt a shock of dismay, accompanied by a cold hollow in his stomach. He was not thinking of himself, but of Sarah – relating Ryderbeit's words to her with appalling vividness. He was relieved only by Pol's reassuring voice beside him.

'You need not be too concerned about the Ruler's secret police. Like all absolute monarchs, his most dangerous enemies are to be found among his accomplices and henchmen.'

'Are you saying that NAZAK isn't reliable?' said Packer.

'Rumours are a poor substitute for the truth,' Pol replied ambiguously. 'However, as far as NAZAK is concerned, for the moment they are the Ruler's problem, not ours. Let us first consider the schedule. The Ruler is at the moment spending his annual two-month vacation in Switzerland, at his chalet outside Klosters. He is due to remain there for about another two weeks. The security arrangements, from what I have been able to gather, are shared between the Swiss Police and a retinue of a couple of hundred carefully chosen bodyguards. None of these – so I am reliably informed – belongs to NAZAK.'

Ryderbeit was looking sourly at the dead butt of his cigar, then flipped it over the concrete parapet on to the beach. 'What you're trying to say, Fat Man, is that even if the odds are still heavily against us in Switzerland, at least we won't get our balls cut off if we're caught?'

'It is a consideration, my dear Sammy. But not the first consideration.' Pol turned to Packer. 'The essence of this operation is to kill the Ruler, when and where the circumstances are most apposite. Fear of the consequences is neither noble nor helpful.' He gave Packer a mischievous wink, with a quick nod at Ryderbeit; then took another drink from his flask.

'Thank you, I'll have a spot of that too!' Ryderbeit said, and grabbed the flask out of Pol's hand before the Frenchman had time to screw it up. He took a long gulp from the flask, then handed it back to Pol, who was smiling cheerfully.

'The main point to remember about the Ruler's presence in Switzerland,' the Frenchman continued, 'is that officially he likes to make it known that this annual vacation is a purely informal affair. Klosters is a small skiing resort, less fashionable than Gstaad or Davos, and less snobbish than St Moritz. But it still attracts a large proportion of la grande bourgeoisie. During his stay in Klosters, the Ruler goes to some pains to behave – and to be seen to behave – like an ordinary tourist.'

'Some ordinary tourist!' Ryderbeit sneered.

Pol wagged a fat forefinger. 'You must understand, Sammy, that the Ruler is a very proud man. He is also a brave man; and, like most tyrants, he enjoys the illusion of being loved. He is fond of boasting about how he has his hand on the pulse of his people, and how he feels their love for him. He does not mention that the pulse is in their throat – ' he chuckled at his little joke, and went on.

'No matter! He is very sensitive to Western public opinion, and is at great pains – particularly in Klosters – to keep his bodyguards as inconspicuous as possible. That is not to say that he will be an easy target. But the problems and logistics of killing him and of escaping afterwards do not concern me. They are for you to deliberate and solve. That is what I am paying you for.'

'You're suggesting that Klosters provides our best opportunity?' said Packer.

'I am suggesting nothing. I am paying you not merely for action, but for ideas.' Pol shivered suddenly and hugged his short little arms together. 'I think it is time we returned, mes amis.'

Packer remained staring moodily along the esplanade to where the man in the blue raincoat was just climbing the steps off the beach, about 200 yards away. Pol and Ryderbeit had stood up. Packer followed a moment later. He waited until the other two had got into the Mercedes, then leaned in and said, 'I'm just going back to get some cigarettes.'

It took him three minutes to reach the nearest café. It was empty except for a waiter in a white apron wiping down the tables. Packer asked him for twenty Gitanes filtres and gave him a ten-franc note. The waiter fetched the blue packet, rang up the till, and handed him the change, which came to seven one-franc pieces and some centimes. Packer took the coins in his left hand and walked out.

The esplanade was still deserted except for a few parked cars. The Mercedes lay to his left. Without looking at it, Packer turned right and began walking briskly along the pavement. He passed a battered grey van, then, a few yards on, a Renault estate car. He was two paces beyond it when he swung round, jumped back, grabbed the handle on the driver's side with his right hand, and yanked the door wide open.

With his left hand still holding the roll of coins, Packer hit the man in the blue raincoat twice – two jabbing blows against his jaw and cheek-bone that sent his head bouncing sideways like a punch ball. He followed with a low thrust of his right hand, the stiffened fingers sinking low into the soft fat of the man's side and pulling upwards until he felt the lower ridge of the rib-cage, dragging the whole body towards him, at the same time lowering his forehead to meet the full impact of the man's left temple.

There was a grunt and the man made a flailing movement with his hands. Packer hit him again, full in the face this time, and heard the crunch of cartilage as a sharp pain bit into his knuckles. The man's head flopped back on to the plastic seat and lay still.

Packer checked the street in both directions, then climbed in over the driver, closed the door and went to work. His hands moved fast, running up the man's ankles, over his thighs and through his side pockets, under the armpits, before reaching inside his jacket. The man was carrying no weapon.

Packer took out a leather wallet stuffed with one-hundred French franc notes and a number of credit cards in the name of P-B. Chamaz. He transferred the money into his own wallet and tossed the one he had taken on to the floor; then he looked at the two passports. One was French, the other Lebanese. The photographs were different but bore a plausible resemblance to the thin aquiline face beside him, which was now bleeding thickly from the nose and mouth. The details in both passports corresponded, each made out in the name of Pierre-Baptiste Chamaz, born Beirut, 1936. His profession was described as 'Homme d'Affaires'.

Packer flicked through the pages of both. The French passport looked used on the outside, but its pages were suspiciously virginal except for a six-month Swiss Resident's Visa which had two months to run.

He now began to look, more carefully this time, through the Lebanese passport. It was older and well worn, with the gilt cedar tree and Arabic and Roman lettering almost rubbed off the frayed green cover. It had been issued in Beirut in 1972 and renewed three months ago by the Lebanese Consulate in Geneva. Its pages were crowded with a kaleidoscope of West European entry and exit stamps, with corresponding visas. The majority were for Switzerland and France. Packer noted that the most frequent point of entry and exit was Kloten Airport, Zürich. He counted five since January – the last one being an Eingang five days ago, with an Ausgang the day after.

But what interested him most was the last stamp of all, *Schiphol – IN*, dated three days ago – the day before he and Sarah had themselves arrived in Amsterdam. He searched hurriedly for the Exit stamp, and any entries from the Belgian and French frontiers, but could find none. Monsieur Chamaz had evidently used his French passport for this journey, knowing that it would not usually be stamped between EEC countries.

Packer would have liked to have checked the earlier entries, together with their dates – particularly Chamaz's visits to Switzerland – but time was running out. It was now twelve minutes since he had left the other two in the car.

He checked the street again, then replaced both passports in the same inside pocket, careful not to get blood on his sleeve; and now reached into the man's side pocket and removed a Minox camera and a tiny cartridge of film, the seals of which were broken. He leaned over the seat and made sure both rear doors were locked from the inside, took the keys from the ignition, got out and locked both front doors, checked the car's registration number, then started back towards the Mercedes.

Ryderbeit snarled beside him, 'Where the fuck have you been? Chasing tail in the local cat house?'

Packer ignored him. He turned to Pol and handed him the Minox and the cartridge. 'By courtesy of a Monsieur Pierre-Baptiste Chamaz, a businessman who enjoys both French and Lebanese nationality.' He started the engine, did a swift U-turn, and began to head back along the esplanade, away from the marooned Renault.

Ryderbeit had already noticed the blood-clotted teeth marks across the back of Packer's left hand. 'Been giving someone the old knuckle sandwich, eh, soldier?'

Packer waited until they were past the roundabout that marked the edge of the town, then began to tell them, calmly, in precise detail, what had happened and what he had found. 'I don't think he's bad enough for hospital,' he concluded; 'and I have an idea he won't be too keen to go to the Police. But unless he comes to before someone finds him, the Police may go to him, if only to get him out of the car.'

'You take risks, don't you?' Ryderbeit breathed.

Packer shrugged. 'Why? What can he tell them? Even if I made a mistake, all they've got is an innocent old-fashioned mugging.' He tapped the bulge of his wallet. 'Enough portraits of "Le Roi Soleil" to stand us all a nice weekend on the Riviera.'

Ryderbeit looked at him suspiciously. 'And supposing he's got the number of the bloody car?'

'If he's got the number of this car, Sammy, then it proves that he's just what I think he is.'

Pol now spoke for the first time. He had been sitting with a little notebook on his thigh, scribbling with a slim gold pencil. 'What is your own evaluation of this incident, my dear Packer?'

'He's a man who finds it convenient, or perhaps necessary, to travel to different countries on different passports. My guess is that the French one is forged. He travels as a Lebanese when he's on bona fide business, which seems to take him mostly to Switzerland. He probably uses the French one to slip over borders when he's in a hurry – like the day before yesterday, when he followed me and Sarah from Amsterdam.'

'When did you first spot him?' Ryderbeit asked.

'I didn't. It was Sarah who did, in a sense. That's to say she thought someone was following her on the boat in Amsterdam. Only – ironically – it was the wrong man.' He looked at Pol: 'Unless, of course, Chamaz somehow knew about your interest in me and Sarah *before* we got to the tulip fields?'

'That is absurd,' Pol said piously.

'Well, the only alternative explanation is that Chamaz followed you in the taxi. And you didn't spot him.'

'Mon cher, I was not myself that morning.'

'No, but you had enough wit to meet me at the windmill, without following on the boat.'

'I saw which boat you took, and I guessed that you would stop at the windmill.' Pol smiled. 'What you would call an inspired guess, yes?'

'Bloody well inspired – for someone in your condition.'

Pol frowned. 'You are not insinuating, mon cher, that I and Chamaz were working together?'

Packer looked at him steadily. 'I think I'll just have to take your word for that, Monsieur Pol. But the important thing is, Chamaz – according to his passport – arrived in Amsterdam the day before us. Is there any way that someone knew you were in Amsterdam to meet us?'

'Impossible,' Pol replied – rather too quickly, Packer thought.

Packer went on: 'The other point concerns Chamaz' trips to Switzerland. He always seems to come in through Zürich – travelling on his Lebanese passport – and Zürich is the nearest airport to Klosters.'

'You mentioned,' said Pol, looking at his notes, 'that he has a six-month visa for Switzerland.'

'Probably just convenience. The Ruler's largest European Embassy is in Paris. Chamaz may use it as a base, and perhaps he doesn't always want to be known to the French authorities as a Lebanese.'

'If he goes to the trouble of having two passports,' Ryderbeit said, 'and one of them is forged – or so you think – why wouldn't he have them in two different names? That's what I'd do.'

Packer nodded. 'Perhaps you would – until you got picked up on some stupid charge, like a drunk driving rap or getting raided in a club. Monsieur Chamaz may not be legal, but he likes to seem legal.'

'Yeah, and maybe he *is* legal. Have you thought of that, soldier boy? Nothing you've told us comes anywhere near proof.'

It was Pol who answered him. 'The film in this camera will decide the matter. A Minox is an unusual toy for a single man enjoying an afternoon by the seaside. There is also the number of his car. You say the last two figures were 69. That means the car is registered in Lyon.' He sighed. 'That is a long way to come to Berck-Plage, especially out of season. Mon cher Packer, you have acted with great agility and intelligence. I congratulate you.'

Ryderbeit was chewing at another cigar, staring sullenly at the road ahead.

Pol looked at his watch. 'I suggest, under these new circumstances, a small change of plan. We will drop Sammy at Abbeville railway station, as arranged. You, mon cher Packer, will drive to Paris with me – also as arranged – and return the car to the hire bureau at Orly. However, you will not join me on the plane to Geneva. Nor will you cancel your flight. Instead you will catch the night express from the Gare de l'Est. I would also prefer that you do not book a couchette, but travel second-class. It is disagreeable, I know, but it is best to leave no written record of your journey. As your training will have taught you, even the smallest precautions can sometimes be the most vital.'

'And what about you?' asked Packer.

'I,' Pol said smugly, 'will go Swissair, first-class as we agreed.'

4

The meeting was for three o'clock the next afternoon, at one of the open-air cafés on the Quai du Mont Blanc, overlooking Lake Geneva. Packer arrived a few minutes early to find Ryderbeit already there, sitting alone at a far table, his chair tipped perilously far back against the rail above the water.

He looked up from behind a copy of that day's *Herald Tribune*. 'Sit down, soldier.'

Packer was relieved to see that Ryderbeit had only a half glass of beer in front of him. The waiter arrived and Packer ordered a black coffee. Ryderbeit gave a crafty smile. 'So the Fat Man's actually paying you half a million?'

Packer made no reply. Ryderbeit leaned back against the rail and gave a low whistle. 'That's money, soldier! That's the sort of money that makes you worth knowing. But why sterling?' he added. 'Why not something nice and solid, like Swiss francs?'

Packer shrugged. 'Probably because whoever's behind this racket paid Pol originally in pounds, and it makes it easier for Pol to calculate our shares in pounds too.'

'Pol may be a lazy sod,' said Ryderbeit, 'but that explanation's a bit too simple – even for me.' He sipped his beer in silence. 'That somebody,' he said at last, 'or organization, or whatever, must deal in pounds. As their first trading currency, I mean.' He squinted slowly over his glass. 'Could they be British, d'you think?'

'Possible, but not probable. There aren't many people in Britain today with that sort of money to throw around. At least, not the sort of people who'd have the motive.'

'What about the hush-hush boys? MI6, or whatever they call themselves now?'

'Not a chance. The Ruler lent our Government 1000 million last year, and we've just landed a second order from him for Chieftain tanks, worth over 400 million.'

'Yeah, but what about your lefties? Those unions of yours, for instance?'

'Don't be bloody silly,' said Packer. 'Even if they had the

money – which they haven't – they're so thick they can't find their arses with both hands, let alone think up a scheme like this. Anyway, where's the motive?'

But Ryderbeit did not seem to be listening. 'Britain's buggered. Down the can, and just waiting for the international money boys to pull the plug on you.' He poked a lean finger at Packer's face. 'I tell you, soldier, I give you lot a couple of years and you'll be seeing those Ruskie T54s rolling down Piccadilly and Pall Mall!'

Packer smiled secretly at the vivid image of mobs pressing towards the City, sacking that noble banking house in St Mary Axe, before rampaging back into the West End and laying waste to the vilely exclusive club of which Sarah was a member and he was not. 'I think I'd prefer the tumbrils rumbling down Bond Street,' he said, 'with Madame Guillotine waiting in Berkeley Square.'

As he spoke, he was already wondering how Sarah would behave on the scaffold : with a certain patrician dignity, perhaps. Or would she be dragged screaming up the steps, wetting her pants as they strapped her face down and hauled up the knife? Except that with the Ruler's secret police, NAZAK, it would certainly not be so swift, and there would be no opportunity for heroics.

Ryderbeit's eye had narrowed suspiciously. 'And which side would you be on?'

'I just might take up knitting and enjoy the show.'

'You're not by any chance a fucking pinko, are you?'

'No. Just a class-conscious Celt.'

'Not Irish, I hope?'

'Welsh,' said Packer. 'My girl thinks we're the Lost Tribe, but that's just her way of showing off her blue blood.'

Ryderbeit nodded sympathetically. 'I'm a Heeb myself – third generation White African Jew. But don't think that makes me sentimental. When it comes to politics – particularly African politics – I'm strictly right of centre. They may have chucked me out of Rhodesia and South Africa, but the reasons were nothing to do with politics. I'm right behind the whites down there, don't worry.'

'Why should I worry?' said Packer. 'As long as you aren't too touchy about being Jewish,' he added.

'Just what's that supposed to mean?'

'It might make just that tiny bit of difference when the heat's turned on and one of their prime suspects is a right-wing Jew with an Israeli passport. At least, that's the sort of suspect they're going to be expecting. Otherwise, I was just narrowing down the odds on who might be behind this business. None of the Western powers, that's for sure. They love the Ruler. Besides his oil and petrodollars, he's our front-line defence East of Suez. In fact, most Western governments would pay hundreds of times what Pol's paying us just to keep him alive.'

'Am I reading you right, soldier' – Ryderbeit's voice was menacingly quiet – 'if I think you're suggesting that Fat Man's taking his graft from the Russkies?'

'Not necessarily. The Russians are interested in economic stability – at least, as far as it affects them. And if the Ruler gets knocked off, it's not only going to be the Middle East that would be in turmoil, but the whole capitalist world, including even the United States.'

'But the Russkies would just love that!' Ryderbeit cried.

'In theory, perhaps. But in practice, once the Ruler went, it might not be one of Moscow's boys who put on his socks. There are any number of eager little candidates waiting in the wings – half crazed would-be dictators, like they've got in Libya and Iraq and Syria, most of whose régimes make Moscow's look rather quaint and old fashioned.'

'Then who *would* kill him, for Christ's sake?'

'I don't know, Sammy. It's you who should be answering that question, not me.'

'Me?' Ryderbeit was suddenly alert. 'I know bugger all about politics.'

'Perhaps. But you know quite a lot about Charlie Pol. And Pol might be the clue.' He leaned closer across the table. 'What do you know about Pol, Sammy?'

Ryderbeit tilted back his chair again and peered at the sky. 'Just that he's a fat old crook who eats like a pig, drinks like a fish, and sweats like a sponge.'

'I'm talking about his politics,' said Packer. 'From what you told me about your Vietnam experience, he seems to have a pretty soft spot for Communists. Two billion dollars' worth, I think you said it was?'

'Yeah, well' – Ryderbeit paused, his manner evasive – 'Fat Man's something of an enigma. Getting to figure him out is like peeling an onion – there's always another skin underneath, and at the end of it, all you've got is tears in your eyes. I think he gets his kicks out of pretending to help the underdog, just as long as he stays top dog himself.'

'But do you trust him?'

'Trust him!' Ryderbeit brought the legs of his chair down with a loud clank. 'I'd trust him like I'd trust a blind guide dog to get me across the Place de la Concorde in the rush hour!'

'And do you think he'd try and cheat us?'

' 'Course he'll try and cheat us. And it's part of our job to see he fucking doesn't!' He paused to look at his watch. 'Where is the fat sod, anyway?' But even as he spoke his eye caught sight of Pol waddling between the tables towards them.

'Ah, mes chers amis!' He stood swaying forward, balancing on the balls of his feet, and smiling ecstatically. 'The moment has arrived. Before the sun has set, you will both be rich men. But we must hurry.'

Ryderbeit was left to settle the bill, while Packer followed Pol back to the street. It was still only just 3.30, and Swiss banks do not close until 4.00. Packer was expecting to find a taxi waiting, but instead Pol stopped beside a big Fiat sedan with Geneva plates. He handed a pair of keys to Packer. 'You drive, mon cher. I have more confidence in you than in Sammy.'

'Where to?' Packer asked, as Ryderbeit joined them.

'Take the autoroute to Lausanne,' Pol said, as he settled in beside Packer, with Ryderbeit in the back.

'Lausanne?' Packer cried. 'But I thought we were going to the bank?'

'We are,' Pol replied, with his roguish grin. 'A little place called Aalau between Berne and Basel, close to the German border. It's hardly marked on the map – so I don't expect you've ever heard of it.'

Packer pulled out into the traffic and was following the signs towards the autoroute. 'How long is it going to take?'

'It's 140 kilometres,' Pol said, leaning back luxuriously in his seat. 'But most of it's autoroute. We should make it by five.'

'It is a bank we're going to?' Packer said.

'Yes, mon cher. A very exclusive bank.'

Ryderbeit broke in, in English. ' "Bank" is the polite word they use round here. In the business they call them "Close Mouth Money Laundries".'

Packer turned again to Pol. 'And it stays open until five?'

Pol replied with supreme calm, 'It will stay open until we arrive.'

They had passed the derelict brick-red palace of the old League of Nations building and joined the autoroute. Packer said, 'You told me you didn't expect I'd ever heard of this place we're going to. Well I haven't. What's so special about it?'

'For a tourist, nothing. It is a very small, very dull Swiss town. But it has one peculiarity. It possesses more private banks than any city in Europe.'

'What's wrong with a bank in Geneva or Zürich?'

'Ah well, contrary to general belief, Geneva is not a large banking centre, and what business it does transact is entirely respectable.' He gave Packer an oblique grin. 'Whereas Zürich, and to a lesser extent Berne and Basel, nowadays deal mostly with big corporation money and international transactions. The little town of Aalau is more in our line.'

'You mean they're crooked?'

Pol sighed. 'You are being a trifle naïf, my friend. In Aalau they merely exact a slightly larger premium for secrecy, without fear or favour – that is how the town made its wealth. As I said, it is very close to the German border, which is along wooded hills and difficult to guard. The town first became rich when the Jews started smuggling their fortunes out of Germany after 1933. At the time, the Swiss weren't interested in German paper money – only in gold. And they gave the Jews thirty cents for every dollar's worth. Under the circumstances the Jews were grateful.

'Unfortunately, however, they were also still optimistic. Many of them returned to Germany, where they later disappeared up the chimneys of Dachau and Birkenau and Treblinka, while their family fortunes – estimated at several hundred million dollars – have continued ever since to ripen and multiply in the vaults of Aalau.'

'Do you mean to say,' Ryderbeit called from the back, 'that these lousy Swiss can just sit on that money, while good Jewish families go hungry?'

'There have been many attempts, particularly by the Jewish Agency, to persuade the Swiss authorities to have these accounts opened – if only to provide funds for victims of Nazi persecution. The Swiss have always refused.'

'It makes me like the Swiss more and more,' said Packer.

'Ah!' said Pol, 'but Aalau's big coup was to come at the end of the war, when the Nazis started trying to get *their* money out of Germany. And again the good burghers of Aalau insisted only on gold. They got it in all shapes and sizes. Bormann's believed to have made a personal deposit of bullion in March 1945, valued at between ten and twenty million dollars. Then there were the regular weekly visitors, known locally as the "dentists" – guards from nearby concentration camps who came down from Ulm carrying suitcases of gold rings and gold teeth – and the occasional gold spectacle frame.'

'Didn't anyone in Aalau baulk at that one?' said Packer.

Pol chuckled. 'Most of the professional people in Aalau are bankers, my friend. And as bankers they treat all customers alike, according to their financial standing.'

'Yeah, but what happened to those fucking Krauts?' Ryderbeit cried in English. 'Did they wait till the dust had settled, then draw out their loot and start chicken farms in Brazil, or just get fat running a nice modern factory in Düsseldorf to the glory of the European Economic Community? The bastards.' He spat towards the car ash-tray, then got out a cigar.

Packer turned again to Pol. 'Sammy wants to know if any of that Nazi money was ever claimed.'

'Very little. Most of the big Nazis were killed, or were too frightened to show up – even in Aalau – for fear of being charged with war crimes. If there's one thing the Swiss love, it's money; and one thing they hate is scandal.'

'But in Aalau they're a little less touchy than most?' said Packer. 'I mean, they don't mind having highly paid assassins on their books?'

'Not as long as our accounts remain in credit.'

Packer nodded. 'Sounds a nice place, this Aalau.'

'It is very quiet,' said Pol.

They reached the town an hour and ten minutes later, along a winding secondary road off the main Berne to Zürich highway. It was a narrow cheerless town, surrounded by hills that looked like storm clouds. The houses along the main street had the tidy, drab appearance of private business premises. Packer noticed that at least two out of three buildings were banks, their names usually proclaimed by a discreet bronze plaque beside the door.

Pol told him to stop at a house halfway down, and not to worry about the parking restriction. He bounced out of the car with great energy, pressed a bell in the polished door, and was shown in by a pale man in a grey tie and bifocals, who gave Packer – and particularly Ryderbeit – a fishy stare, before standing back and closing the door behind them.

He now led them down a marble passage into a deserted hall no larger than a private office, with two grilles, no partitions or counters; instead, half a dozen green leather-topped tables, each with its own pen set and pristine pad of blotting paper, and green leather swivel chairs placed on either side. Except for a digital clock with an electric calendar on the wall, the room was unadorned. It smelt neither fresh nor musty, but was filled with an antiseptic gloom.

The pale man in bifocals showed them through a door at the far end, into a quiet dark-panelled room with button-backed leather chairs arranged opposite an executive desk on which stood a white telephone, an intercom and a bronze bust of Voltaire.

A man rose from behind the desk and greeted them with a professional smile. Apart from his grey suit and gold cufflinks, he was not at all as Packer imagined a Swiss banker to be. He was a short, athletic man in his middle thirties, with a large head of wavy blond hair and that deep, slightly orange suntan that comes from the mountains.

His manner was cordial and relaxed. He obviously knew Pol well, but showed no trace of deference towards him – rather, a certain boisterous familiarity, as one who is privy to the secrets of another. He was a man to whom the fiscal rules of the outer world were irrelevant: Foreign Exchange controls mattered less to him than parking on a yellow line. After all, banking was just as respectable in the main street of Aalau as in St Mary Axe –

providing it remained within the limits of Swiss law; and in these matters Swiss law was almost limitless.

The formalities were swift and simple. An elderly man, with the grave servility of a wine waiter, appeared with two sheaves of documents which he placed on the desk, then withdrew. The young banker arranged the six copies in a neat row in front of him; then sat back and smiled.

'I think, for the benefit of our two new clients here, that I should explain something about our Swiss banking system. There are altogether more than 260 private banks in Switzerland. Most people – businessmen working for big companies, and even foreign governments – prefer to deal with the better known names like Le Crédit Suisse. But some people are happier to take advantage of the rather more specialized, personal services which we smaller banks are able to offer. The main service, of course, is secrecy. Complete and absolute secrecy. We ask no questions, and we give no answers.' He paused and ran his finger along the edge of the desk.

'However, we do impose conditions. These conditions vary from bank to bank – though only slightly.' He gave a quick glance at Pol. 'At this point I feel I should mention what is called "Swiss Negative Interest". I do so, because it is a practice often misunderstood by those unfamiliar with our methods. On an initial deposit of not less than $50,000, we levy an interest of seven and a half per cent.'

Ryderbeit let out a hiss. 'There's no misunderstanding so far as I'm concerned, mister. That's not banking – it's not even usury. It's bare-faced robbery!'

The banker held up his hand. 'Please. I have not finished. Here, at the Volkskantonale Bank, the minimum deposit accepted is $50,000. If it should fall below that sum – by even a few francs – the account is temporarily frozen, until further funds are received; and during that period an interest rate of nineteen per cent is levied.'

Ryderbeit was scowling fiercely at him, but said nothing. The banker went on.

'We have a further, more stringent condition. If the client's deposit drops below $25,000, his account is closed.'

'And if he pays in a couple of billion next day,' said Ryderbeit, 'is it opened again?'

'I regret, no.'

'Holy Moses!' Ryderbeit turned to Pol, his eye glaring dangerously. 'I'd rather keep my loot in a piggy bank!' His eye swivelled back on to the banker. 'What are we getting out of this crummy little place, anyway?'

'You are getting privacy,' the banker replied quietly. His face cleared, and he leaned forward with his arms on the desk. 'Now, for the details. It is usual for an individual account holder to be given a seven-figure number. Theoretically the client has only to produce this number, accompanied by his signature, which must correspond to that held by the bank, and he will be permitted to draw what funds he desires.

'However, in the recent climate of international crime – as well as with these meddlesome foreign government investigators – we have felt obliged to introduce a couple of simple extra precautions. We now require two Polaroid photographs in colour of each client – full face and profile – and' – he gave a small gesture of apology – 'a set of finger-prints.'

'And what guarantee do we have that these photos and prints aren't passed – unofficially, of course – to some foreign Intelligence agency?' Ryderbeit growled.

'You have no guarantee,' the banker said smoothly. 'But you have my word that it would be against the most basic ethics of our banking system.' He paused, and began to gather up the six documents from the desk; stood up and handed them across to Pol, together with a gold pen.

Pol glanced through them with an air of bored familiarity, scribbled his signature six times, then handed the pile to Packer. There were two copies on vellum, closely covered in copperplate typescript, in French, German, and English; and four duplicate sheets on onion-skin paper.

Packer studied them with a mixture of awe and suspicion. The English text was correct, and unusually lucid for such a document. The sum of £500,000 was typed both in figures and in words, next to its exact equivalent in more than two and a half million Swiss francs, down to the last centime, as calculated against the IMF index at noon the day before. At the foot of the page, above Pol's signature, were seven figures.

The document represented the formal opening of a joint numbered account, in his and Pol's names, which could be drawn

80

on only with the production of both their signatures. The pen-ultimate paragraph stipulated that in the event of the decease of Monsieur Pol, the account would be frozen in perpetuity. Packer noted that no such provision had been made in his case.

He turned to Pol and pointed out the omission. The French-man replied, with his mischievous chuckle: 'Mon cher Packer, you are surely not anticipating an accident, are you? Or a serious illness, perhaps?' His eyes glittered.

Packer glanced uneasily at the banker, who sat impressively behind the desk, his face a mask of indifference. Packer hesi-tated, unwilling to provoke an argument at such a delicate moment.

Pol was patting his belly, with a half nod towards the banker. 'I am sure we do not wish to take up any more of our friend's valuable time.' He reached out and handed Packer the gold pen. Packer declined it.

'Eh, alors?' Pol was frowning, but his eyes were still bright. 'Are you not satisfied with the arrangements, my friend?'

'Not satisfied at all.' Packer waited for Pol's response, but when none came, he went on: 'Charles, it's the old story – heads you win, tails I lose. I do all the thinking, take all the risks' – he was already ignoring the banker, as his voice grew with emo-tion – 'and just supposing we do succeed in carrying out the operation, and even escaping afterwards – then, *poof*! I get knocked down by a Rolls-Royce in Park Lane or fall out of the top-floor suite in the Georges V.' He broke off, all discretion gone now, with an expectant glance at Ryderbeit. 'Or perhaps just a bullet in the back of the neck.'

But Ryderbeit, like the banker, did not seem to be listening. He had taken out his cigar case, and without offering it to their host, or even asking his permission, was busy igniting one of his coronas.

Packer asked wearily, in English, 'What's your view, Sammy?'

'I got no views, soldier. It's none of my business.' He drew on his cigar, leaned back and breathed two blue tendrils of smoke through his nostrils. 'Remember, you're my boss-man,' he added, his eyes fixed on the ceiling. 'You take the decisions, not me.'

Packer had an angry suspicion that Ryderbeit was enjoying his discomfiture. He stood up and dropped the papers and pen on to the desk in front of the banker. 'I want an extra paragraph inserted on all six copies. Exactly the same wording as the last-but-one, but substituting my full name for that of Monsieur Pol here.'

He heard Ryderbeit's cackle from behind him. 'Good on you – you devious Welsh bastard! I once trusted the fat sod with a couple of *billion* US and finished up as a fucking seamstress for the Reds.'

The banker was looking at Pol. The Frenchman appeared quite unmoved. He gave a little nod. 'Do as Monsieur Packer instructs.'

The banker hesitated. 'It will necessitate a certain delay. In the meantime I will arrange for you to be photographed and finger-printed.' He had pressed a button with his foot, and the elderly man appeared without a sound, closing the door as though it might break in his hand. He stood slightly stooped over the desk, while the banker murmured rapid instructions, then handed him Packer's documents. The man left, without glancing once at the other three.

The banker now handed another set of documents to Ryderbeit, who began to study them with threatening concentration, his good eye squinting along each line of elegant typescript, while his dead one stared dully at the carpet and his cigar smouldered down between his fingers. He read them altogether three times, before accepting the gold pen; but although he seemed in a mood to haggle, he was evidently content. Pol knew Ryderbeit well enough not to chance his hand too far.

Ryderbeit finally signed, six times, in a slow careful hand, like a schoolboy's. From where Packer was sitting he could not read any of the details, but their lay-out looked similar to his own, except for one important difference. Pol's signature was missing. Ryderbeit tossed the gold pen in the air, caught it, threw it at the banker, who dropped it under the desk; then leaped up and gave a whooping cry. 'Now Samuel D. Ryderbeit is going to start living!'

Packer looked at him, with a trace of envy. 'You got the lot?'

'The lot.' Ryderbeit brought his hands together with a loud smack, while his cigar lay smoking unnoticed under his chair. 'A hundred thousand beautiful British pounds transferred into Swiss francs.' He reached the desk in a single stride and slapped the documents down in front of the banker.

'All nice and wrapped up, eh, Sammy?' Packer's voice was cold and steady. 'And no strings?'

Ryderbeit whirled round. 'Trouble, soldier?'

'Curiosity. A hundred thousand, just like that, without lifting a finger. Nobody's that generous – not even Uncle Charlie here.'

Ryderbeit's eye glinted nastily. 'I say, soldier, none of your fucking business.'

'It *is* my fucking business,' said Packer. 'From now on everything we do, right down to the smallest detail, is all my fucking business. What's more, I'm going to make it my further fucking business to find out.'

Ryderbeit hesitated, then returned to his chair and retrieved his cigar. He looked up at Packer with a crooked leer. 'All right, you bastard. I get twenty-five thousand on the nail. Another twenty-five when the deal's set up. And fifty thou' when we're home and dry. Okay?'

'No strings, no conditions?' said Packer.

Ryderbeit raised his hands, palms upwards. 'All clean as a nun's knickers. And rich and fancy-free to boot.' He looked round as the elderly retainer beckoned to them from the door.

The three of them followed him into a small white room with a plastic curtain, like a cubicle in a doctor's surgery. The Polaroid pictures were taken by remote control, from an eye in the wall; then they each filed ceremoniously past a desk, where they pressed their finger-tips on to a spongy black pad, then splayed them out on a set of headed documents, adding their signatures to each, before being given a towel and shown into a washroom, equipped with a patent destigmatizing lotion.

Back in the banker's inner sanctum, a fresh set of documents lay on the desk. The banker again handed them first to Pol. The Frenchman merely glanced at the added paragraph, before again scribbling his signature at the bottom of each sheet, and passing them across to Packer. Their eyes did not meet.

Packer satisfied himself that the wording was correct, then signed too: with a detached, passionless precision, surprised that his hand remained steady. His past dealings with bank managers had been mundane, awkward, sometimes unpleasant. This experience now left him with a sense of unreality: it reminded him of the bad old days when, after a heavy night, he used to wake early to find that he was still drunk; and, as then, when he now stood up, the floor did not feel entirely firm under his feet.

There was a final formality, when the banker unlocked a drawer and handed each of them a plain, thick, sealed envelope. These, he told them, contained their cheque books and the numbers of their separate accounts. He added that it was advisable to commit the figure to memory and destroy the paper afterwards.

'A useful hint in these matters,' he concluded, 'is to enter the figure in your address book as though it were a telephone number. Of course, as I said, the figure by itself would be useless to a third party without the signatures. But it could still cause embarrassment if it were to fall into the wrong hands.' He smiled innocently. 'We are always anxious to protect the interests of our clients in every possible way.' He gave each of them a muscular handshake and saw them through to the outer door.

They got into the Fiat, with Pol choosing the back seat this time, curling up his legs in the foetal position, with his hands cupped under his head for a pillow. Ryderbeit slid in beside Packer.

Before starting the car, Packer broke open his envelope, took out his cheque book and a slip of paper that was blank except for seven numbers, memorized them quickly, repeated them under his breath several times, then tore the paper into four pieces. Ryderbeit gave a low cackle close to his ear and snapped open a lighter, holding the flame under the torn scraps in Packer's hand. 'Taking it real seriously, aren't we, soldier?'

Packer held the four pieces until they scorched his fingers, then dropped the charred flakes into the ash-tray. Pol had begun to snore.

Packer turned on the headlamps, drove round a mean little square at the end of the street, and headed back towards the road to Lausanne.

'One thing puzzles me,' said Ryderbeit suddenly. 'You had the Fat Man sewn up back there. He tried that fast one on you, but that was probably just his sense of fun – or perhaps his way of testing you. What I don't understand is why you didn't go for the half million in a straight, simple account of your own, and no fucking about with joint signatures. Now, every time you want to draw even the petty cash, you've got to get Fat Man to agree.'

Packer nodded. 'You were the one who first said you didn't trust Pol. Maybe I don't trust him either. Maybe I don't trust him not to let me go ahead with this operation, then arrange for me to have a nasty accident at the end of it. Pol's original trick of fixing that joint account in the first place was a form of insurance. He didn't want *me* knocking him off. Now the tables are turned. Whatever happens – and however much Pol may want me out of the way – he's going to have to do some pretty agonizing thinking before he sacrifices that half million. United we stand, divided we're skint.'

'Fair enough, soldier.' Ryderbeit's voice was a hushed whisper in the dark of the car. ' 'Course, it doesn't stop *me* knocking *you* off. Or hadn't you thought of that?'

'No, I hadn't thought of it, Sammy. I hadn't thought of it because you're too sentimental and full of fun. You'd be lost without me and old Pol.'

Ryderbeit laughed, but said nothing.

They met for breakfast next morning at a café outside Geneva, on the Chamonix road. Pol was lapping up a bowl of hot chocolate with his omelette au jambon; Ryderbeit was drinking marc; and Packer had ordered black coffee and croissants.

They had arrived separately from their different hotels – Pol insisting that it was wiser not to be seen too often together. Again he had arrived late, and seemed for the moment more interested in his omelette; while Ryderbeit was unusually taciturn. Packer himself had slept badly and now felt a vague sense of trepidation.

It had taken him until the light of day to realize just how fully he was committed – irretrievably beholden to the Gallic clown across the table, Charles Pol, Swiller of Bols and Beheader of Tulips – this gross, deceptively comic buffoon who had intruded into his life by means of a drunken romp in the rain. For what had begun as an eccentric joke had flowered, with alarming rapidity, into a conspiracy of incalculable dimensions.

Pol wiped the chocolate from his mouth and beard, belched, and took a stiff buff envelope from inside his jacket. 'I have something here that will interest you both.'

While Ryderbeit called for another marc, Pol lifted the un-sealed flap of the envelope and shook out two glossy sheets of contact prints. There were several dozen on each, though the last half of the second sheet was blank. He shuffled the two sheets into the middle of the table, then flung an arm round Packer's shoulder and pulled him sideways in a huge hug, almost dragging him off his chair. 'I must congratulate you again, mon cher Capitaine. This is excellent work!'

Packer found himself once more breathing the rank odour of scent and sweat; he tried to struggle politely, but the Frenchman only squeezed him closer. And again Packer was amazed at how strong Pol was. He gave an energetic shrug, broke free, and picked up the sheets of contacts.

The pictures were so small that he had to hold them up to the light, peering at them from a few inches away. They looked at first like poor family snaps – fudged with sun spots, with the figures too small, bunched into a corner or blurred by movement. At first glance they would seem to have been taken either by a very inexperienced amateur, or by someone working under ex-ceptionally difficult circumstances.

With a few exceptions, which were mostly among the first rows on the completed sheet, the backgrounds were of a mono-tonous uniformity : bits of street, empty pavements, blank walls. The exceptions were several shots of Pol entering and leaving the Hotel Amstel. There were two more of him staggering through the tulips, but the detail was distorted by the rain and poor light. There were three of Packer's hired Mercedes – rear views on what looked like autoroutes. But in Le Crotoy, Chamaz had either lost his nerve or been biding his time. There were no pictures of Pol, Packer and Sarah together. The next half dozen shots had evidently been hurriedly snatched from inside a car : Pol and Packer walking along a street; Pol, Packer and Ryder-beit at a street corner; two of Ryderbeit and Packer walking together – although their faces were obscured. There were several that were either blotched shadows or had failed to come out at all.

Then suddenly, to Packer's dismay, there were three that were the clearest of all : they showed him and Sarah arriving at Le Touquet airport; waiting at the check-in counter – this one showed Sarah in clear profile; and him giving her a tentative embrace before she joined the queue through the gate.

The last two on the second sheet were long shots across the sand at Berck-Plage, showing the three of them on the beach.

Packer passed them to Ryderbeit, then turned back to Pol. 'It's not good. For starters, it's bloody bad.'

'I think it is excellent!' Pol cried. 'Thanks to your initiative we have plucked the evidence from under their noses. And since we have the negatives, there is no risk of Monsieur Chamaz having sent copies back to his masters.'

Packer nodded gravely, wondering if Pol were being un-usually optimistic, or again perhaps testing him. 'Yes, we've got two reels. But we've got no guarantee that there aren't others.'

Pol made a little pooh-poohing noise. 'You can see for yourself that the pictures cover our movements from Amsterdam to the moment you surprised him in his car. What do you fear?'

'First – before we've even sat down and made the most pro-visional plan of action – someone has sent an agent after us who's filmed us all – Sarah included – from the very beginning, before I even knew who you were. That's bad enough. But even with-out the films, this man Chamaz is going to be able to give a description of us, to whoever he works for – and we can guess who that is – and will probably be able to recognize us again.'

There was a pause. Ryderbeit slung the contacts back at Pol and swallowed the rest of his marc. His face was dark and mean. 'I tell you what I think,' he said at last. 'I think Packer Boy may be smart, but he's also soft.' He jabbed a slender finger at Packer's face. 'You shouldn't have just bloodied that bastard on the beach back there – you should have sent him straight up to the Great Reaper!'

Packer looked at him without expression. 'Sure. The moment Charles starts getting his team together, the Ruler sends a snooper after us. Not a very serious job – just a leg-man who can take a few snaps for the record. For all we know, the Ruler's got teams of men working the field all over Europe. But once one of those leg-men gets knocked off, the Ruler's got the odds narrowed down so finely he doesn't even have to go on looking. Beating Chamaz up was a risk, I grant you, but at least it could pass as a simple robbery – and anyway, I couldn't think of a better way of getting the films.'

He looked back at Pol. 'But there's an even more serious aspect

87

to all this. If Chamaz had got on to us here – or even in Le Crotoy – I'd have said it was pretty smart Intelligence work, and with a pretty efficient organization behind him. But he got on to us in Amsterdam. He even got on to me and Sarah – judging by these pics – before he got on to you, Charles. That doesn't sound like good Intelligence. It sounds like either a leak or collusion.'

Pol listened with his naughty smile; but in his eyes Packer detected that gleam of cunning. The fat man giggled. 'You are making a most impolite suggestion, mon cher. It is also an absurd suggestion. Why should I – who am paying you both so handsomely – wish to betray our operation?'

Packer said nothing, because he could think of no logical, even plausible, counter to Pol's reply. 'Right, let's forget about Chamaz for the moment. We came here to sign a few cheques. Sammy and I both want our ten per cent advance. I want £50,000 released from our joint account, which I propose to deposit in a bank in Geneva before lunch. I'm ready to sign, Charles.'

'One moment, please.' Pol's expression was suddenly solemn. 'Ten per cent is a great deal to pay for a few photographs. As I have already told you, I am employing you, Capitaine Packer, not only as a man of action, but of ideas. You acted, in a modest way, in Berck-Plage. But now I require something on a larger scale – your overall plan of action.'

'A provisional plan,' said Packer. He signalled for more coffee, then turned to Ryderbeit, who had just lit up a cigar. 'Can you ski, Sammy?'

'Sure I can.'

Packer frowned. 'I'm talking about snow skiing. You get much of that on the Rand or up in the rain forests of the Congo?'

Ryderbeit gave an evil grin. 'You ignorant Welsh provincial. Never heard of Kilimanjaro? The Atlas Mountains? The Lebanon?'

Packer nodded and turned back to Pol. 'We'll start with the shopping list. Sammy and I are going to buy our skis, boots and gear today in Geneva. *Buy* them mind – not hire them – because I want our names on as few records as possible. We'll also hold on to that Fiat of yours, Charles. We're going to need a car, and again I don't want to leave my signature and particulars with any rental people, like a bloody paper-chase for the police to follow.

'Now for the more important things. We're going to need two large-scale maps – 1/100th, or even bigger, if possible – of the Davos–Klosters area. And not one of those glossy brochure jobs they do for the tourists. Preferably an Army or aerial survey map that marks exact contours and distances, as well as ski runs. Particularly the ski runs.'

Pol had taken out his notebook and was scribbling in it with his gold pencil.

'I also want two pairs of miniature 12 × 20 Zeiss binoculars, with glare shields, and two Polaroid cameras with telescopic lenses. Nothing too big or showy – the sort of thing a camera-crazy tourist might have without attracting undue attention. And it must be able to take a reasonably clear picture up to 1000 yards.' He waited while Pol finished writing.

'And lastly, three pocket-sized R/T sets with a UHF range of at least three miles.'

Ryderbeit's voice growled from the end of the table: 'You said "lastly", soldier. But you're forgetting the most important things of all. The hardware.'

'We'll choose that when we know exactly what we're up against.'

'Look, soldier' – Ryderbeit leaned forward, blowing cigar smoke into Packer's eyes – 'that's still our priority Number One item. The other stuff's a cinch, but guns aren't things you can pick up in a supermarket, especially not in Switzerland, for Christ's sake! And I don't want a clapped-out antique from the Boer War. I have a respect for guns. Like women with jewellery, I only go for the best.'

'You'll get the best,' Pol put in gently. 'Providing the gun is still being manufactured, or is in circulation, and does not re-quire very special modifications, I think I can satisfy you within a matter of hours.' He looked at Packer. 'Anything else, mon cher?'

'Yes. I want as detailed a schedule as possible of the Ruler's movements in Klosters. And the exact day on which he plans to leave.'

5

The Ruler lay stretched out on a long chair, his eyes closed behind the mirror lenses, feeling the Alpine glare burning through the film of scented oil which had been massaged into his cheeks and jowls and across his broad forehead. His nose was protected by a shield of black plastic.

Through the thin mountain air the chatter of far-off voices drifted up from the crowds of tourists queueing for the cable car up the Gotschnagrat; occasionally a spray of girls' laughter reached him, like a peal of tiny bells. He felt relaxed, isolated, almost free. Here, in the sanctuary of his chalet, 'Le Soupir du Soleil', he could enjoy his power in privacy, mercifully spared the company of frivolous women, nagging diplomats, obsequious courtiers and foreign emissaries with their begging bowls.

Yet even on this terrace above Klosters, separated from his people by more than 3000 miles, the channels of Absolute Power – from his Ministries in the capital, Mamounia, to the smallest Police posts in the desert villages – still flowed directly to and from him, maintained by a complex radio system which occupied the whole top floor of the chalet, its wavelengths kept alive twenty-four hours a day, receiving and transmitting in codes that changed every hour, on UHF frequencies that changed every fifteen minutes. It was said that not even a white line could be painted on a road without the Ruler's personal sanction.

This morning, as he lay under the cloudless sky, digesting his regular breakfast of fruit juice, one slice of toast and two cups of black coffee, one thought troubled his self-confidence. It concerned his nation's health, which was as one with his own. In a growing child, mild bouts of neurosis were bound to occur, but in recent months a certain organ in the national body had begun to show more serious symptoms. For while his brain despatched messages to which his country's muscles responded perfectly, the central nervous system – which was encapsulated in his Security and Intelligence organization, NAZAK – was coming dangerously close to schizophrenia. The Ruler suspected, but still without absolute proof, that the leaders of NAZAK – 'the Supreme Committee for Counter-Terrorism and Public Safety' – were no longer loyal.

His worries were lulled by the faint throb of a helicopter across the valley. He pushed up his mirror glasses and peered through the diamond-sharp sunlight, just as the tiny dragonfly shape dipped below the dark wall of the Wang, on the south-west face of the Gotschnagrat. For several seconds the sound was lost, carried away by a changing current of air; then returned, this time with a loud beat that pulsated down the valley, as the slender silver-grey machine throbbed across the town, in the vague direction of 'Le Soupir du Soleil'.

The Ruler watched casually as it approached. The sight was not unusual and was unlikely to arouse much interest among the tourists and townsfolk below. Whenever the weather was clear there was always a Swiss Army helicopter somewhere in the area, drifting over the mountain peaks and tacking up and down the valley. Few people would notice that the machines always hovered for several seconds when they were over the forest of pines that hid the large chalet on the eastern slopes above the town.

It was the avalanche season, and many passes and ski-runs were closed. This winter had seen heavy snow, and with the coming of spring the Swiss authorities had doubled their precautions. Several times in the past two weeks the silence of the valley had been shattered by the echoes of mortar fire, followed by the roar of avalanches brought down prematurely.

The Ruler watched the helicopter come within a few hundred metres of the chalet, then stop, suspended above the sharp points of the pines for perhaps five seconds before the skeleton tail swung sideways-on, and there was a flash of reflected sunlight from the glass bubble cabin.

The Ruler felt a stab of panic, dispelled at once by a sense of outrage at his own weakness. He prided himself on his personal courage; and the fact that each morning when the sky was clear he exposed himself, alone, for half an hour, below the ring of naked mountains, was surely proof of this.

Yet there was always a moment – a fleeting second when his eye caught a gleam of refracted light from the mountains: from a pair of goggles, or a ski-stick perhaps: or some sudden, unexplained noise from the town, amplified and distorted by the echo-chamber of the valleys – when he instinctively flinched, his hand starting automatically to the alarm button set into the tiles beneath his chair. And it was in such moments that he became frighteningly aware of the fragile mortality of his slight, ageing body.

He waited until the helicopter began to move again, its nose dipping as it rose and chugged off in the direction of St Moritz. The Ruler pulled down his glasses and closed his eyes.

He was woken from a dreamless doze by a voice beside him. 'I am sorry to disturb you, but we have received a message from the Ministry of the Interior.' It spoke English, with a quiet familiarity, and just a trace of German accent. 'It is from the Minister himself, so I thought you would like to see it at once.'

The Ruler turned his mirror gaze up to the young blond man beside him and took the typed sheet of decoded message that was held out to him. He read it quickly and handed it back. 'Destroy it, Lutz. I do not want even a copy kept for the Black File.'

He felt the man's shadow move across his face, shutting off the warm sun; and a chill crept through his tight-fitting black sweater and skiing trousers. 'All right, Lutz, that is all.' But the shadow remained across him.

'Please, you will be sending no reply?' the German asked.

'No.' The Ruler was relieved to feel the sun flow back over him again. He looked at his watch, which was of pale gold with a platinum twenty-four-hour dial that showed the time in all the major capitals of Europe and the Middle East.

In Mamounia, the sun would be at its zenith, and for the next four hours all activity in the capital would be stilled, as the timeless tradition of the siesta was enjoyed from the very highest in the land, down to the stall keepers and bazaar pedlars and fly-encrusted beggars. Only Marmut bem Letif would be awake and abroad. For of one thing the Ruler was certain: his new young Minister of the Interior did not pass the idle hours sleeping, begetting babies, or committing other harmless sins. Letif used this dead quarter of the day to pursue the special nature of his new office: skulking to some secret rendezvous; wallowing in the shaded marble pool and eating iced melon at the feet of Colonel Tamat and his fat noisy wife; or drinking mint tea with Doctor Zak and his circle of precocious Western-educated

Marxist disciples. Letif would only return to his modest villa outside the capital late at night, when the Ruler's work was done.

The Ruler knew that he was running a serious risk in entrusting so much to one individual. But with the present delicate balance of power, he preferred to trust himself to one man rather than to a dubious hegemony of a State Committee – or worse, to the hosts of acolytes who gathered round his throne like moths round a flame.

For the Ruler had chosen Letif with cunning. To the man's colleagues – and especially to those unsubtle minds inside NAZAK – Marmut bem Letif was just such an acolyte. A nobody whose loyalty could be bent to the strongest will at hand. His unexpected elevation from a desk in the Ministry of Trade to his new office was seen by all as merely another puppet appointment. Only now there were others, besides the Ruler, who aspired to play the puppet master; and to these men Letif appeared, in his ultra-sensitive position as Minister of the Interior, to be the perfect, pliable creature of their power dreams.

But there was another, more sentimental reason why the Ruler had chosen Letif. For the young man was the only legitimate son of Hamid the Fox – later named Hamid the Martyr – one of the heroes of the long War of Liberation, which had ended in 1927 with the Glorious Reawakening, when the palsied carcass of the old feudal order had been finally dismembered, and the Ruler's father had mounted the Emerald Throne of the *Hama'anah*. But not before his trusted lieutenant, Hamid the Fox, had fallen into the defenders' hands and suffered a death whose details the Ruler had first heard as a child on his father's knee, and which even now he shrank from contemplating.

Marmut bem Letif had only been an infant at the time – born from the loins of a Maronnite Christian who had died in childbirth – and Marmut had been suckled by goats and nursed by camp followers of the rebel army. From such harsh beginnings, he was soon to be included in the élite of the new régime; and after studying abroad, he returned as one of the best educated men of his generation.

The Ruler had quickly detected in Letif certain characteristics which had made Hamid the Fox the scourge of the old régime. Letif was quiet and cautious and dedicated; but he was also devious, cynical and ambitious, with a predisposition to intrigue.

He was not an arrogant or flamboyant figure, but this the Ruler found reassuring; and while he realized that Letif's ultimate disloyalty could cost him dearly, he was impelled by the perverse streak of the gambler. Rather than destroy Letif, the Ruler had decided to use him.

He shook himself awake. Such thoughts, enjoyed in the comfortable isolation of the Swiss Alps, were mere self-indulgence, of which he felt himself unworthy. He sat up and pressed a second bell under his chair, next to the alarm. A servant moved out from the shadows of the wall. 'Summon Herr Metzner,' the Ruler commanded. The servant bowed three times and vanished.

The young German appeared on the terrace a moment later. The Ruler nodded. 'Lutz, I regret that I do not have time for chess today. I have other problems to solve. Have them call my Embassy in Paris. I want Second Secretary Ashak. And the call will be put through the K-scrambler.' He paused. 'Is that understood?'

The German stared at his twin reflections in the Ruler's glasses. 'The K-scrambler – ?' he began.

'Yes, Lutz? Please go on.'

The German scraped a shoe on the tiles. 'I was curious,' he began again, his pale eyes fixed on the mirror lenses below him.

'Curious about what, Lutz?' The Ruler's voice was like dry ice.

'I thought we no longer used the K-scrambler,' the German murmured.

'You are misinformed. The line is still operational. It is merely that of late I have grown tired of sharing all my conversations with Colonel Tamat and his colleagues.' The Ruler stretched himself like a cat and stood up, resting his hand on the German's shoulder. 'Colonel Tamat is a most vigilant public servant, Lutz. But even I must allow myself some privacy.' His finger-tips stroked the German's slim shoulder, feeling for the collar-bone. 'Something still worries you?' he added caressingly.

Lutz blinked and lowered his pink eyelids, trying to avoid those two shining mirrors only a few inches from his face. The Ruler gave off a metallic, bitter-sweet smell, like a well-oiled weapon.

'I was only thinking' – the German hesitated again, shifting his other foot – 'I was thinking that perhaps the Colonel will be surprised to hear you use this line after so many days.'

'Surprised? My dear Lutz, why should he be? As I said, the line is still operational. In any case, it is not I who will be using it. *You* will talk to Second Secretary Ashak.' His forefinger and thumb dug gently into the muscle under the German's neck. 'You will tell the Second Secretary that the Lebanese gentleman, Monsieur Chamaz, is to be issued with diplomatic papers, and is to leave the Embassy at once. He will proceed by car to Basel with the utmost secrecy. If the Second Secretary should ask why the gentleman is not to go by air, you will explain that I do not wish there to be a record of his journey, even with the civil airlines. Whereas the frontier formalities on roads between France and Switzerland have almost ceased to exist.'

There was silence. In the town below, the queues for the cable car behind the railway station had dispersed; a car hooted from the road up to Davos; a jingle of bells reached them from a horse sleigh down by the ice rink. The Ruler had fractionally lowered his voice, as though afraid that they themselves would be overheard.

'That is all understood, Lutz?'

'Yes. But the address – the destination in Basel?'

'You will give the address as the usual "safe house".' His finger and thumb squeezed the muscle and felt it stiffen. The German winced. 'Something still troubles you, my dear Lutz? Tell me – we have no secrets.'

The German opened his mouth, then shut it again, like a fish. 'I do not know everything,' he said quietly, 'but I know there are some things that must stay secret. Because it is better for me, yes?'

'Yes.' The Ruler's hand relaxed and patted the German's shoulder. 'Far better. But as my personal adjutant here in Switzerland, you are entitled to know all that you feel necessary to know.'

The German took a step back, leaving the Ruler's hand hovering awkwardly. 'I will call the Embassy,' he said in his stiff English, and turned.

'And Lutz!' the Ruler called after him. 'When you have finished, have some champagne sent to my office. And two glasses. You look as though you need some refreshment.'

Left alone, the Ruler stood gazing out at the dazzling

panorama of jagged white against the back-drop of frozen blue. He loved Switzerland: not only for its climate and scenic beauty – luxurious retreat from his arid kingdom – but also because it reminded him of the very best hotel: the management, discreetly invisible, provided all that was demanded, as long as the price was right.

In his study he removed the plastic shield from his nose and exchanged the mirror glasses for his black-rimmed spectacles, which gave him the appearance of an austere banker, and began to consult a map of Europe. Basel straddled the Rhine, at a junction with the French and German frontiers; and he pondered upon which of the four most likely routes from Paris the driver would choose. Colonel Tamat's men were not going to find it easy; thus the exercise would be instructive in two ways. It would test the effectiveness of NAZAK's organizational abilities in France and Switzerland, and it would settle the question of Colonel Tamat's loyalty, one way or the other. For as the faithful Lutz had pointed out, the fact that the instructions to Paris had been given on the K-scrambler meant that NAZAK would automatically intercept them. It remained to be seen whether the NAZAK agent in Paris already appreciated the importance of Pierre-Baptiste Chamaz – enough to request instructions from Colonel Tamat himself – and whether the Colonel realized the trap and did nothing, or responded with his characteristic efficiency and ruthlessness.

He looked up as Lutz came in carrying a tray with an opened bottle of champagne in an ice bucket and two chilled glasses. He watched him, secretly amused. Poor Lutz, he thought; the boy looked so earnest, and still worried. The Ruler wondered how much he suspected.

He was relieved to notice that the German's hand was quite steady as he poured the champagne.

Marmut bem Letif could not sleep that afternoon. Alone in his villa outside Mamounia, he lay naked in the half dark of his curtained room, waiting. Even with the air-conditioning turned up full, the sheet beneath him bore the wet imprint of his frail body.

At 3.42 the telephone purred by the bed. He sprang up, as though convulsed, lifted the receiver and listened to the few seconds of absolute silence; then the harsh familiar voice, very clear over the top secret line:

'Minister? The man Chamaz has just left the Boulevard des Capucines. He is being driven to Switzerland – to Basel. That will mean Dr Hubel's place, will it not?'

Letif felt his hand growing moist round the receiver. Hubel, he thought to himself; and could imagine the Colonel's scowling face the other end. For Colonel Tamat hated the very idea of Dr Hubel – that clever little Swiss brain surgeon who was busy tutoring the Ruler in the most sophisticated techniques of interrogation. To Sham Tamat the man represented more than a threat – he was a personal insult. Only too soon the Colonel would see his mediaeval instruments of agony – crudely updated with electronic accessories – made redundant by the clinical use of drugs, auto-suggestion, and other mind-bending mumbo-jumbo of medical science.

Letif whispered back into the mouthpiece, 'You are to keep away from Dr Hubel. That is an order. You understand?'

There was a short silence. Colonel Tamat was not used to taking orders.

'The car is being followed,' he said at last. 'I just hope – for the Doctor's sake – that my men do not lose it. If they do, I regard it as my duty to proceed with the ultimate plan.' He paused. 'You will be returning to the Ministry?' he added.

'Yes, I shall be returning.' Letif heard a click and the line went dead.

In the stillness of the darkened room he heard a ringing in his ears. Sweat seeped down his smooth chest and collected in driblets on his thin hairless legs. His nose twitched, like that of an animal scenting danger. For the first time in his life, he felt pangs of real fear.

Several times he wondered if he should lift the phone again and call Switzerland direct. He had had the villa debugged only ten days ago, but there was no guarantee against the insidious workings of NAZAK: his villa was no more immune to them than it was to woodlice and dry rot.

If only I had more time, he thought: time to amass a nice little nest-egg in one of those Swiss banks, as all his colleagues did. But he still had time to cut his losses and run. His diplomatic passport required no exit visa; and there would surely be no lack of interested parties abroad who would pay well for information on the inside workings of the Ruler's empire.

He sat on the bed and stared at the telephone, and wondered if there would be another summons to Europe. He decided that if there were, before this evening, he would sever all ties with Tamat and confide totally in the Ruler.

At precisely 12.30 p.m. – three hours behind Mamounia time – a silver-grey Citroën CX drove out of the side gate of the Ruler's Embassy in Paris with its peacock-blue, gold-crested shield above the main entrance.

The car moved through the lunch-time traffic, turning east towards the Péripherique, where it joined the south-bound carriage-way, pulling out into the fast lane and ignoring the 60 kmh speed limit. A black Peugeot radio-taxi kept a comfortable hundred metres behind.

The Citroën carried three men, two in the front and one in the back. The car's one distinctive feature was a tall aerial which bent back in the slipstream like a fishing-rod. As the driver approached the Porte Vincennes exit leading to the RN4, the taxi closed in fast. The Citroën passed the third and final sign marking the intersection, and the taxi flashed its headlights twice.

Drawn up on the shoulder of the emergency lane, twenty yards in front of the intersection, was a white BMW 30 SI, its engine idling. There were two men inside. As the taxi passed them, the driver of the BMW drew smoothly out into the traffic, also heading south-west along the Péripherique. The man beside him was talking into a radio microphone.

The driver had moved into the outside lane, using the horn and flashing the cars ahead; but it was not until they were past the junction to the Porte d'Italie that he caught sight of the Citroën. It had slowed down to join the heavy traffic that was heading for the autoroute, south to Lyon and Marseilles.

The driver of the BMW placed himself several cars behind the Citroën. They passed the Orly exit and the junction west to Orléans; then the autoroute spread into six lanes, stretching flat and straight into a dim, rain-soaked horizon. Here the driver of the BMW felt able to draw back until the Citroën was almost out of sight.

There were no turnings for the next twenty kilometres, before the toll gates. When the BMW reached them, the Citroën was already second in the queue for the fast gate, and drove through a full minute before the BMW – enough to put nearly a kilometre between them.

The two men in the BMW snapped on safety belts and were pressed back in their seats as the engine hummed powerfully through the automatic gears, the tyres drumming on the concrete surface. The rain clouds were drawing closer, the sky ahead darkening over the pale ribbon of road that stretched unbroken for 300 miles to Lyon.

The passenger had unfolded a map of France on which a number of exits from the autoroute were ringed in red. There were altogether eighteen on this stretch; though the most likely ones for the Citroën to take were in the wine-rich Côte d'Or, between Auxerre and Beaune.

Neither he nor the driver had spoken since leaving the Péripherique. Their manner was calm, methodical, bored: they reacted as though this were a routine run that they made every day of the week.

Fifteen kilometres beyond the toll gate, the BMW closed in on the Citroën, but for several seconds the car ahead held obstinately to the outside lane. The BMW flashed its lights again and its horn howled above the slipstream as it drew dangerously close. The sloping rear window of the Citroën was shaded green, but the two men in the car behind it could just make out the shape of a man's head.

The Citroën finally pulled over, and the BMW slid effortlessly past, neither its passenger nor driver glancing at the other car.

From now on the two men in the BMW followed the rule book. The next exit, to Nemours, was twenty-nine kilometres ahead. When they were five kilometres from it, the BMW slowed until the low silhouette of the Citroën showed in its mirror. If the men in the Citroën were expecting to be followed, they would normally be looking for a car behind, not in front; but even if the Citroën's driver were anticipating this technique, it was virtually impossible – on a long stretch of road where most cars would be travelling several hundred kilometres – for him to be ever certain of his pursuer. The real problems for the men in the BMW would arise when their quarry left the autoroute.

As they approached the Nemours exit, the Citroën was again in the outside lane, overtaking everything except the BMW, which had now pulled out of sight. A few minutes later they hit the rain.

The BMW driver switched on his side lights. Four seconds later a pair of yellow fish-eyed headlamps flared in his mirror. He pulled over, momentarily blinded by a fog of spray. A glowing red bar of light swept past and shrank into the blurred twilight of the storm.

The BMW had slowed to under 100 kmh and was now keeping to the centre lane. The Citroën passed them a few minutes later, ten kilometres before the exit to Courtenay. The radio under the BMW dashboard crackled to life. The passenger pressed the switch of the hand microphone and spoke back slowly and deliberately : the target was past Courtenay – next exit, Auxerre.

The autoroute was beginning to curve and climb through an ugly rock-strewn landscape where convoys of juggernauts were bunched together, wheezing at walking pace along the inside lane. The BMW passed a sign marked *Diversion*; then a diagonal row of orange beacons, and a bulldozer parked on the soft shoulder which had been churned up into a yellow swamp blistered by rain.

The traffic was now crowded into single file, crawling uphill with the belching juggernauts. The Citroën was only three cars in front of the BMW; and directly in front of the Citroën was the car that had raced past them several minutes ago, with its glowing bar of red rear lights. The men in the BMW recognized the long, low sledge shape of the Maserati.

At the same moment the radio crackled again, its instructions brief and precise. The passenger acknowledged them, then flicked a switch under the dashboard that sent out a deep, steady whine. He sat back and lit two cigarettes, passing one to the driver. 'They might have warned us,' he said.

'They never warn us,' the driver said, with a slight shrug of his big square shoulders.

*　　　*　　　*

There were about a dozen elderly men in the café, hunched over pine tables, drinking thimbles of framboise, poire, and other white spirits popular in the Jura. They scarcely seemed to notice as the three strangers entered, bringing with them a blast of cold air.

The proprietor took them for foreign businessmen on their way to Switzerland. For although the café was in a desolate spot on a minor road through the mountains east of Besançon, strangers were not unusual. Tourists often used the narrow cross-country road as a short-cut from Dijon down to Berne or up to Basel.

The three men sat at a corner table and ordered coffee. They talked quietly, urgently, emphasizing every word with quick didactic gestures; then one of them got up and asked the proprietor, in thickly accented French, if he could use the telephone for a long-distance call. He was shown into a corner under the stairs where he stayed a full five minutes. As the proprietor went through to the kitchen, he heard the man talking in a language which he had never heard before.

When the stranger returned to his table, he had a pinched, tight-mouthed expression. He said something without sitting down and the other two got up, leaving their coffees half drunk. The man left a 100-franc note, without waiting for the bill or the telephone charge, and the three of them marched out.

On the sloping gravel parking lot were two cars that stood out instantly from the other, local vehicles. One was the silver-grey Citroën CX; the other, the long, low, elegant shape of a maroon Maserati with wire wheels and four exhaust pipes as wide as trumpets. There was just one person inside, the driver – a dark man in a sports jacket who was leaning back in the bucket seat, smoking a cigarette and reading a map.

The man who had made the telephone call hesitated. He already had the Citroën keys in his hand, and now clenched his fist so that the sharp metal edges jutted out between his knuckles. One of his companions murmured to him, and the man frowned and stood staring at the reclining figure in the Maserati, who did not even look round. The man grunted and opened the Citroën door, and the other two followed. As they drove away, they saw that the man in the Maserati had still not moved.

During the climb to the Col, the driver's hands had begun to sweat on the wheel as he wrenched the Citroën round the steep blind bends between dense pines, with a shriek of tyres and an almost continuous blast on the horn, his eyes flitting every few seconds from the road to the mirror; but this time there was no car behind. He found himself growing angry, slamming his fist against the gear lever, causing the smooth cushioned car to shudder at each turn. He was not frightened of danger, but he hated disorder – and above all, he hated and feared things that made no sense. And that Maserati made no sense – no sense at all! His two companions, sensing his anger, did not disturb him.

They reached the Col, and began the corkscrew descent, still in silence. Again, as they rounded each bend, the driver glanced in his mirror, but there was still no sign of the Maserati. They now came to a particularly treacherous corner, where the outside shoulder of the road had partially subsided, the surface cracked and buckled like charred wood, sloping down to the edge of a gully. The remains of a triangular 'Danger' sign, symbolically bent and dented, with the black painted exclamation mark half erased by rust, leaned crookedly backwards out of a pile of grit.

The driver swung the Citroën into the centre of the road, keeping his thumb down on the horn, while his right hand changed violently down into second gear. The car bucked and the engine gave a shrill whine that carried above the sound of the horn. It slewed sideways, the rear wheels stopping less than a foot from the edge, while the front driving wheels shrieked in a dry skid, scrabbling for a grip on the steep camber.

The driver uttered a long imaginative obscenity, as the wheels caught and the car swerved back into the centre of the road. He had slowed to 30 kmh, but completed the turn and was confronted by another bend, less than twenty yards ahead, where the road doubled back almost beneath them.

Here there was a second danger signal: this time a portable reflector triangle that had been set up a few feet from the edge. But it was not this that had warned the driver. A man was standing on the bank opposite, half hidden in the shadow of the trees; and a few yards beyond and below him, in a shallow lay-by scooped out of the bend, stood a white BMW 30 SI, with Paris plates.

The Citroën had jerked to a halt, and for the first time the driver took his thumb off the horn. He opened his mouth to shout, but the words were shattered by a sound like a paper bag bursting, and the windshield turned a frosty white. A shower of crystals hit his face, and something harder struck his jaw and chest. The force smacked his head back against the seat, and the air was sealed in his lungs. When he tried to breathe, the lower part of his face felt loose and odd, like a bagful of pebbles. In those last seconds he heard the staccato *bop! bop! bop!* – and this time the whole windshield crumbled into the car, like a sheet of crushed ice. The driver experienced a blinding light, then nothing.

The man beside him was wedged under the dashboard, shot between the eyes. His shoulders and hair were spattered with glass and splinters of bone from the pulpy grey hole which the soft-nosed bullet had torn out of the back of his head. He had managed to lift the mat off the floor, and his hands had locked round the plastic stock of an automatic carbine, when the bullet struck.

In the back seat the third man had reacted first by lunging at the offside door, away from the gunman, then had apparently thought better of it and flung himself on the floor. He was unarmed, and knew that he had no chance of reaching the carbine under the front seat. His only hope was to feign death, waiting until the gunman arrived to study his results, then to attack him hand-to-hand, and to try and disarm him.

The man under the trees now slithered down the stony bank and reached the road. He was holding another, stubbier carbine with a curved magazine that jogged against his thigh as he came forward. He paused, listening. Silence. He made a brief signal to the BMW below, and drew from his raincoat what looked like a pale green beer can. He walked forward until he was a dozen paces from the Citroën.

There was no movement from the car. Using the thumb of his left hand, which still held the carbine, he raised the can, ripped a length of wire out of it, and lobbed it uphill where it bounced neatly between the Citroën's front wheels.

It exploded a second later, lifting the car a couple of inches off the road where it seemed to hang suspended above a glaring bubble of light, as though a gigantic flash bulb had gone off, throwing the surrounding pines into unnatural relief.

The man had turned and begun running as soon as he had

thrown the bomb. He was halfway to the BMW, when there was a second explosion, as the Citroën's fuel tank ignited. For several seconds the glowing white light all around turned a warmer orange. He reached the car below, where the driver already had the engine running. The BMW began to move before the man had time to close the door.

Above them a cauliflower of smoke was rising to the top of the trees; and under it, the ball of fire was now turning a livid green in which the black skeleton of the Citroën shimmered and shrank, its chassis now sunk on to the road where it was beginning to melt and spread out over the liquid tarmac in pools of white-hot metal.

The Police arrived twenty minutes later, when the fire was still burning with a dense white smoke that gave off impenetrable fumes. Two convoys of traffic had gathered along the road in both directions; and the Police radioed for reinforcements with fire-fighting and breathing equipment.

It was not until the next day that forensic experts confirmed that the burning explosive had been white phosphorus – a rare and lethal substance, restricted almost entirely to military use. The Police Routière had no record of such a load being transported anywhere in France on the previous day; and no military establishment in the country had reported the loss or theft of white phosphorus.

The forensic report could only state that at least two people had died in the car; for apart from a small amount of body fat adhering to the melted metal and congealed tarmac, which had been scraped up with the chassis, only the remains of several teeth had been found; and these had belonged to more than one person.

The Inspector who had been called in from the Police Criminelle in Dijon, ordered a further, more intensive examination of the wreckage, together with a thorough search of the area surrounding the fire. By the following evening the make of car had been identified as the Citroën CX, though the number-plates, chassis and engine markings had been obliterated.

The Police also made three important discoveries. The first

was a fragment of metal, deformed at one end but almost intact at the other. For some time the experts were perplexed. They tried fitting it to every known part of the Citroën mechanism, and checked it against all known car accessories. It was one of the ballistics experts who finally recognized it as part of an American MI6 carbine.

The second discovery was of eighteen empty 7.62mm shells, scattered over a small area on the bank of the road opposite where the wreck had been found. At first the Police were again puzzled by the markings round the firing cap; until the same ballistics expert confirmed that they were Russian, and that the shells fitted the Kalashnikov AK 47, the standard Soviet sub-machine gun.

The third, perhaps most important find, was a curved disc, blackened but unmelted by the heat, with two holes in each end. In the laboratory it was cleaned, and found to bear the engraved name 'Pierre-Baptiste Chamaz' and what appeared to be an inscription in Arabic. The metal was identified as a rare heat-resistant alloy used in the aerospace industry, and not available on the open market.

The Inspector was satisfied that it was part of an identity bracelet, belonging perhaps to a pilot or fireman – someone who faced the regular hazard of being burnt to death. He was also satisfied that he had a case of murder on his hands. The fact that at least two weapons had been used – one American, the other of Communist origin – also suggested a political motive. Reluctantly – for he was an ambitious man – he now referred the case to Paris, but not before he had given an extended Press conference during which he was photographed from many angles, holding up Chamaz's identity bracelet, the fragment of the American carbine, and a number of Russian machine-gun shells.

The case received wide publicity in both the local and national Press. A squad of detectives from the capital had meanwhile set up their headquarters in Besançon, with open lines to the DST* – The French Security Service – and to Interpol headquarters, both in Paris. No record could be found on the files of either organization relating to a Monsieur Pierre-Baptiste Chamaz. But

---

* *Direction de la Surveillance du Territoire*

a Professor of Arabic, from Grenoble University, translated the inscription on the bracelet as 'Silence Speaks the Truth'.

It was the third day before the Police obtained their first tentative lead: the proprietor of the Café du Col, on the road eight kilometres away from the scene of the incident, remembered the three strangers who had entered the café about half an hour before the Police were first alerted – which meant around ten minutes before the explosion. His description of the three was not inspired, but he did remember that they had arrived in a Citroën; and one of them had made a long-distance telephone call in a language which the proprietor insisted was not European.

Here the Police had their first and only piece of luck. The café telephone was not yet on automatic, and all long-distance calls had to go through the operator in Besançon. Enquiries at the town's Central Post Office, giving the time of the call to the nearest quarter of an hour, produced an operator who remembered it at once. The man had been abrupt and impatient, she said; he had asked, in a foreign accent, for a Paris number. When she had told him there would be a slight delay, he had shouted at her that it was 'a matter of the most supreme priority', adding the phrase, 'un appel diplomatique d'urgence!'

She looked up her file for that afternoon and found the number, which Paris reported as unlisted and belonging to an address in the Seventeenth Arondissement under the subscriber's name of Bloch.

That evening three armed plain-clothes officers from the DST called at the address – a top-floor flat in a dingy house behind the Place Clichy. The old concierge told them that during the ten months that Monsieur Bloch had rented the flat, he had never even set eyes on him. The officers went upstairs and found a door with a complicated triple lock which could not be picked by the usual methods. A Police locksmith was called, and was only able to release two of the locks; the third had to be cut by oxyacetylene.

Inside they found a two-roomed flat. The air was stale, the utility furniture thick with dust. There was a single bed with a bare mattress; a tiny bathroom with no towel, soap, or lavatory paper; the kitchenette had no crockery or utensils; the main room was bare of books, magazines, old newspapers, even ash-trays. The only individual features were a reproduction of Van Gogh's *Sunflowers* and a black telephone of unusual design, with four coloured buttons instead of a dial. The officers made an intensive search of the flat, even removing planks of uncarpeted floor and sounding every inch of the walls, but found nothing.

The DST now concentrated on the telephone. They had discovered that it was not a direct line, but connected to a scrambler – a device that is illegal in France, except where permission is granted under special circumstances, usually at the behest of the Embassy of a friendly power. In this case, no such permission had been given.

When the officers tried the number from an outside phone, it rang for a full two minutes; then a man's voice, with a slight accent, answered, 'Michel ici.' The officer asked to whom he was speaking. The voice replied, 'What number do you want?' Careful not to alert suspicion, the officer quoted back the number with the last two digits reversed. 'You have the wrong number,' the voice said, and the line went dead.

Later that night a man strolled past the house, noticed the plain-clothes agent just inside the front door, and went on to a café at the corner, where he asked for a jeton and shut himself into the phone booth. Next morning, when the engineers arrived at the house to disintegrate the scrambler, they found the line had already been disconnected.

The DST, as well as the authorities in the Rue du Palais, provoked by the wide Press coverage, which was now degenerating into reckless speculation – including reports of a clandestine Police operation against Arab terrorists in France – were working desperately to break the case.

But after five days the only further information they had obtained was the method by which Monsieur Bloch – who was again unknown to either the DST or Interpol – paid his rent. This was settled by a regular banker's draft drawn on a small independent bank in Basel. The DST contacted the Swiss Police Financière, who replied that the money came from a numbered account, and that the payments had been stopped two days previously – on the same day that the scrambler had been disconnected.

The only consolation left to the authorities was the fact that

107

the Press, also starved of further facts, was becoming bored with the story; and finally dropped it altogether.

The file marked 'Chamaz/Bloch/Michel', however, remained open but unsolved.

Marmut bem Letif sat small and listless behind an enormous desk, which was bare except for a platinum pen set, a dictating machine, and three telephones – black, green, and red. From the wall opposite, the Ruler gazed impersonally down at him out of a heavy gilt frame.

He glanced at his watch yet again, and looked nervously at the red telephone. It was past seven o'clock: there must be news soon. He licked his lips and swallowed hard. He was still un-acclimatized to the air-conditioning, which dried his nose and mouth and gave him a sore throat.

Behind him, beyond the huge picture window, the city lay nine floors below in the red haze of evening. Through the bullet-proof glass the roar of rush-hour traffic reached him only as a muted hum. He turned in his swivel chair and looked out across the flat baked brown roofs to the sweep of high sugar-white buildings rising along the old Front de Mer – now renamed the Avenue of the Glorious Reawakening – and could see the great emptiness of the tideless Gulf, its surface broken for a moment by a tiny white trail in the wake of a water-skier.

He spun back to the desk as the red telephone gave a single peal, and a green light began winking on the dial. He grabbed the receiver, listened, muttered something and hung up; then reaching into the desk drawer, brought out a bottle of Chivas Regal and poured himself half a tumbler, which he swallowed neat. It was a dangerous luxury, but one which seemed to fit the occasion. While alcohol was not officially outlawed in the country, it was severely disapproved of – particularly among the Ruler's servants – and could only be obtained, at extravagant prices, in the more exclusive hotels and restaurants that catered for foreign tourists.

He sat sucking a peppermint to clear his breath, and waited for Colonel Sham Tamat, Chief of NAZAK and the Incorrup-tible Guardian of the Nation's Public Safety.

Either from deference to Letif's rank, or to emphasize his

civilian as well as military status, the Colonel was not in uniform. He wore an English suit of grey worsted, silk tie by Pucci and shoes by Gucci, while his big fleshy face bore an expression of smug contentment. He strode across the deep white carpet and clasped both hands round Letif's limp wrist. Only the width of the desk seemed to prevent him embracing the little man.

'Fortune smiles upon us today, Minister!' He sank into a chair under the portrait of the Ruler. 'The dirty Levantine – the one they call Chamaz – is departed this day to his maker. It was not easy – particularly at such short notice – but I had my best men on the job, and they cooked the cur good and proper! Roasted him, to be exact – with half a litre of white phosphorus. Chamaz and the two Embassy guards – *shnouf!* ' – he pinched his finger and thumb together as though snuffing out a candle – 'cremated on the spot, with no funeral expenses for the French taxpayers.' He swung a leg over the arm of the chair and gave Letif a sly white grin.

'My chief man in Paris has also reported some interesting background information. It appears that Monsieur Chamaz – who also carried a French passport, incidentally – had not been very clever. He had apparently been assigned to follow someone in the north of France. But that someone seems to have spotted him, beaten him up, and robbed him of some very important photographs he had been taking. He then travelled to Paris and took asylum at our Embassy where his case was handled by that crafty lizard, Second Secretary Ashak – who, as we well know, has no love for my Organization. I might add, my dear Minister, that it is an outstanding tribute to my men in Paris that they were able to find out so much so quickly.'

'Most of this I know already,' Letif replied, with quiet authority. 'What else did they find out?'

The Colonel's face darkened. 'You must appreciate, Minister, that my men were operating under extremely adverse conditions. As you know, the Diplomatic Corps is notoriously uncooperative with my Organization, and Second Secretary Ashak has lips as tight as a snake's arsehole. When Chamaz turned up, Ashak was careful not to talk to him at the Embassy. But one of my men works on the desk, and has sharp eyes and a long memory. He recognized the Levantine as an errand boy for the Almighty's Inner Circle, and was able to alert his Chief.

'Meanwhile, Ashak questioned Chamaz in a nearby café, where it was not easy to follow all of the conversation. However, my man did gather that the films would have helped to identify certain foreign individuals who are plotting against the State.'

Letif sat forward, sucking his soft finger-tips. 'Did Chamaz say how many individuals – and what nationality they are?'

'There are at least three men involved, and one of them is French. He is said to be very fat and to have a beard. My man reports that several times he heard Chamaz use the phrase "le gros barbu".'

'And the other two? Are they foreigners too?'

Colonel Tamat shook his head impatiently. 'I do not know the nationality of the others. As I said, the conversation took place in a café – and you know what those cafés in Paris are like. It was surprising that my man was able to overhear anything at all.'

Letif appeared unimpressed. He had lowered his head, as though to avoid those two sets of eyes staring at him across the room. He wondered whom he could trust: which meant, who was the more likely to win – Tamat or His Imperial Highness? They could not both win, that was for certain. When he spoke, his voice had that shy, slightly apologetic tone which his colleagues misinterpreted as a sign of weakness.

'You mentioned, Colonel, that these individuals might be plotting against His Serene Imperial Highness' life. Are you implying that in a matter of such grave importance, Second Secretary Ashak has been deliberately withholding information from NAZAK?'

The Colonel replied, with a polite layer of insult, 'Minister, you are new to your office, but even so, the niceties of the present political situation cannot have entirely escaped you. Relations between myself and His Imperial Highness have recently become – shall we say, chilly? I am a loyal public servant, as you know, and where duty is concerned, I acquit myself not only with ability but with passion. No one in the State can doubt this – least of all, my enemies.'

'Do I detect, Colonel, that you make a subtle distinction between your loyalty and duty to the State on the one hand – and to His Imperial Highness on the other?'

'That is an impertinent suggestion, Minister. His Highness

and the State are one. It is a lesson that our children learn from the moment they are born; it is shouted from the radio, from the television, from every loudspeaker in the streets. It is engraved in marble above the entrance to my office. I am surprised you do not have it inscribed on the wall of this room.' His voice was like that of a man delivering a sermon.

There was silence. The red sky was darkening outside the window, and Letif's head appeared as a narrow silhouette, its expression invisible. 'The Ruler no longer trusts NAZAK, Colonel. And, as you well know, he does not trust you.'

Tamat removed his leg from the arm of the chair and took out a big polished Dunhill pipe, which he began to fill from a leather pouch. His movements were slow, methodical, giving him time to think.

'You are accusing me of treason, Minister? That is a grave affair' – he tamped down the tobacco in the rosewood bowl, then struck a match and held it between his fingers – 'but it is your affair, Letif. Your own personal affair.' He blew the match out, stood up and dropped it in the base of the pen set on the desk; for Letif, outwardly loyal to the Ruler's every whim and prejudice, kept no ash-trays in his office.

The Colonel stood looking down at Letif's sleek black head and sloping shoulders, and noticed that the white suit which had been hastily ordered from Rome, to embellish his new appointment, already looked worn and baggy. Marmut bem Letif, the Colonel reflected, filled his high office about as well as he filled his clothes.

'We are both aware that every word of this conversation is on tape,' Letif said in a dry whisper. 'I also know that those tapes will be handled only by you, or by those closest to you, in whom you have complete trust. I am therefore not fearful of what I am now going to say, Colonel.'

Tamat had returned to his chair, where his big powerful body sat relaxed, his eyes showing mild amusement. 'Yes, Minister?'

'His Imperial Highness' life is in danger, Colonel Tamat. As I have already informed you, a plot is being organized abroad, recruiting foreign mercenaries to assassinate our Head of State and overthrow the régime.'

'Well? There have been attempts before on his life. It is a national hazard we have to put up with, like sandstorms and cholera. The Ruler is well enough protected, I assure you.'

'I am not so sure,' said Letif. 'No man is inviolate. And how well is he protected against his protectors?'

There was a pause. Colonel Tamat lit another match, this time putting it to his pipe and sucking until a flame jumped out of the bowl. He breathed smoke in a slow haze in front of his face. 'You will please explain that last remark, Minister.'

'There are many people in our country who wish His Highness dead. They are not all revolutionary riff-raff and Baathist scum. Some of them are respectable and highly favoured.'

Tamat put another match to his pipe, and this time dropped the burnt end on the carpet. 'What is your point, Minister?'

'You have contacts – very close contacts, sometimes – with some of these favoured people.'

'Give me one name, Letif.'

'Dr Zak, for example.'

Colonel Tamat choked on his pipe, and hastily spat into a silk handkerchief which he folded back into his breast pocket. 'You have no proof,' he said, with forced arrogance.

'I do not require proof,' Letif replied, 'any more than you require proof before you submit one of your prisoners to the bastinado, or the electrodes, or your favourite barbecue à cheval. But if I did need proof, I would question why the good Doctor is still alive and well.'

He gave a faint smile, which Tamat could not see. 'When I took tea with him two days ago,' Letif added, 'the old man seemed in excellent spirits.'

'I can assure you, Minister,' Tamat said in a low voice, 'that Dr Zak's file is clean.'

'No doubt – since you are responsible for the file,' Letif murmured; and his doe eyes looked steadily back at the Colonel. 'But we are straying from the point. We were discussing a matter of national urgency – a plot to assassinate our beloved monarch. There is one factor, Colonel, which you seem to have overlooked – or perhaps you have forgotten? In the matter of the agent, Chamaz, you admit that your men were operating under highly difficult circumstances. Not only did they receive no cooperation from the Inner Circle – as you call it – but they appear to have been actively excluded from the whole affair. Yet this man Chamaz claimed to have photographs that might identify the would-be assassins. So what do you do? Do you attempt to kidnap Chamaz and interrogate him yourself? Or, better still, hold him until the moment is ripe for him to recognize the assassins? For that is what Ashak and his friends were surely trying to do – tuck Chamaz away in Dr Hubel's house in Basel and wait for an opportune moment. Are you still with me, Colonel?'

Tamat did not reply. His pipe had gone out, and he stared out at the dark blue, maroon-streaked sky. Letif's soft cloying voice went on:

'I ask again, Colonel – what did you do? And I will give you the answer. You did the one thing that, for any Security Chief, is the ultimate and unpardonable sin – you destroyed the evidence. You eliminated the star witness – the only witness – who could have identified these would-be assassins of His Imperial Highness.'

The Colonel flushed darkly and his eyes showed flecks of orange. He was renowned for his dangerous temper, and Letif watched him warily. For several seconds Colonel Tamat did nothing; then he deliberately unscrewed the stem of his pipe and poured several gobs of brown dottle on to the white carpet. Letif looked on impassively, knowing that this room, with its expensive fittings, might well be a passing luxury.

'You are suggesting – ?' Tamat's voice broke, and he spat again into his handkerchief, which this time he folded and used to wipe his forehead. 'What are you suggesting?' he added hoarsely.

Letif spoke with gentle persuasion. 'I am not interested in your motives, Colonel. It is your tactics which concern me. While your strategy is bold and effective, it lacks subtlety. You have attacked, Colonel – but not on your own initiative. You were drawn into that attack. It is my opinion that you have been drawn into a trap.'

He waited, but the Colonel was silent. 'It is my opinion that the Ruler and his friends intended you to kill Chamaz. They despatched him across France like a fat worm on a long line and a big hook. You swallowed that worm this afternoon. You also swallowed the hook. You must now, my dear Colonel, expect His Highness to start pulling in the line.'

Colonel Tamat's expression had become choleric; but when

he spoke, the sneer in his voice was warped by suspicion. 'Why would the ruler want Chamaz dead?'

'You are sure Chamaz is dead?'

'Don't play the monkey with me, Letif!' Tamat roared. 'I have a good sense of humour, but I do not appreciate jokes at my expense.'

Letif ignored the outburst. 'You say the men were carbonized?'

'That's what my confidential source reported.'

'Did your source state that Chamaz had been positively identified?'

Tamat drew in his breath, and this time his voice was barely in control. 'The man who organized the operation did an excellent job. He had just two hours in which to make his plans. He assures me there was no mistake. And I trust his word. He is a good man – one of my best.'

'I do not doubt it,' said Letif. 'They certainly did not make it easy for him – or for you, otherwise you would have been suspicious. You see, Colonel, they were *relying* on your man's expertise. And they have been rewarded.'

'Who?' Tamat barked.

'Ashak, for instance. And His Imperial Highness, of course.'

Tamat sat in uneasy silence. At the back of his arrogant mind, a doubt was beginning to stir.

'Why did you have Chamaz killed?' Letif said at last. 'Or rather, why did you *want* him killed?'

'You still doubt that he is dead?' Tamat growled.

'I don't know that he is dead any more than the French Police know. I suggest you contact your man in Paris and confirm that he made a positive identification of Chamaz before he bombed the car.'

Colonel Tamat stood up. His eyes had grown tired with trying to read Letif's expression across the darkening room. 'I think your inferences are dangerous and without foundation, Minister.' He spoke with none of his natural authority. 'It is your privilege to have your own opinions and suspicions. But I must warn you, if you are unwise enough to try and act on them I shall be obliged to report this whole conversation to the full Council of Ministers, and to His Highness himself.'

'No,' said Letif. 'It is *you* who will not dare to act. You will not dare to, because today you have placed yourself under heavy suspicion. There is an international plot to kill His Highness, and yet this afternoon you attempted to liquidate a vital witness.'

Tamat stood in the middle of the room, jaw muscles working as though trying to dislodge something from between his teeth. 'You are being naïf, Minister. You should know that when an agent bungles his job he does not get rewarded with a reprimand – or a cosy bed in Dr Hubel's house in Basel. What my men did this afternoon was standard procedure.'

Letif lifted his hands in a small gesture of resignation. 'I am not convinced that His Highness will see it that way.'

Tamat, who had turned towards the door, wheeled round and peered angrily at the slight hunched silhouette behind the desk. 'You dare accuse NAZAK of treason!'

Letif cut him short. 'Do not waste your breath, Colonel. You have already said enough this evening to merit a slow official death. Just take a little advice. From now on, do not act too hastily. You and I may soon need each other.'

Colonel Tamat swung round and collided with the door, muttering ferociously, and marched out into the neon-white glare of the corridor, slamming the door behind him. Ten yards away a guard came to attention, smacking the butt of his rifle in salute. The Colonel's two plain-clothes bodyguards joined him at the lift. He rode between them and walked through the double security check, out into the dry heat of night, where a black armour-plated car with bullet-proof windows and self-sealing tyres awaited him between two motor-cycle outriders.

Colonel Tamat sank into the back and listened to the rising howl of the motor-cycle sirens as they sliced through the traffic, in the direction of his marble residence in the foothills outside the city.

He rode in sullen silence, irritated by the proximity of the two bodyguards on either side of him. Such routine precautions seemed suddenly irrelevant. It was not those staring crowds outside in the streets that he now had to fear.

6

The motorcade had disappeared down the road to Klosters; the Police had dispersed to their own cars; and the tourists at the foot of the slopes were making their way up to the Kulm Hotel. One of them was a tall figure with lank black hair sprouting from under a powder-blue pixie hat, orange sun goggles, a faded khaki-green jacket and white doeskin boots over his skiing trousers. Round his neck was slung a Polaroid camera, with a telescopic lens.

He climbed to the hotel terrace and sat down at a table where Owen Packer was drinking lemon tea. A small pair of binoculars lay half hidden under his leather mittens. He looked up and nodded. 'Same time, same place. I made it just two minutes up on his time yesterday. We don't need a computer to work out a schedule like that.'

Ryderbeit ripped the last exposure out of his Polaroid and pushed it across to Packer. It was still tacky, and showed a blurred silver-haired skier in a red, white and blue anorak coming to a halt among a crowd of men. 'Family snap,' he said, smiling. 'I could pick him off with a peashooter.'

'Sure. But you wouldn't get fifty yards.'

Ryderbeit pushed up his goggles and squinted for a moment at the still-deserted slopes above. 'I grant you, the sod doesn't stint himself on hired help. It's just a question of how good they are.'

'They're lousy,' said Packer. 'They miss the first and most important trick of the game – the art of standing around doing bugger all and looking convincing about it. Those boys look like stand-ins out of Central Casting for some thirties B-movies. They're not only lousy, they're laughable!'

Ryderbeit had turned and snapped his fingers for a waitress. 'Could try a Magnum .38 with a silencer, plus a diversion. Bit of plastique explosive under one of the tables – then perhaps toss a couple of grenades. Ten, twenty people killed – lots more wounded. It might work.'

Packer brought both hands down on the table and slopped tea into his saucer. 'Listen, Sammy, we're not organizing a cheap hit-and-run massacre. You're a big boy now – you're not playing nigger hunters in the bush any more. This time it's serious. Which reminds me' – he looked more closely at Ryderbeit's khaki jacket, which was of a distinctly military cut, and of a thin material more suited to jungle than to snow. On the left arm was a ragged shoulder flash bearing the remnants of an embroidered yellow lion's head. 'Do you have to stick out like the Bad Fairy at the Princess's christening? I mean, I know you're not conventional, but that outfit rather demands attention, don't you think?'

Ryderbeit looked up as a plump blonde waitress appeared. He ordered a bottle of white wine, gave her a lewd wink with his good eye, and she walked swiftly away.

He looked back at Packer and grinned. 'Look, soldier, I don't mind listening to your advice, just as long as you don't expect me to take it. You were taught by the rule book – the British Army rule book. That means you're a professional. And the professionals teach you that top-grade assassins, like master spies, are supposed to be grey, faceless men – they merge with the crowd and disappear in the mist. You think I look like a top international assassin?'

Packer stared irritably at the slopes, where the first skiers were appearing above the woods, now that the Gotschnagrat had been reopened following the Ruler's afternoon run. He had to concede that Ryderbeit's reasoning contained a degree of specious logic.

'Out of the four days we've been here,' he said, 'on three of them the Ruler's come down the same run, at exactly the same time. The cable car's closed to tourists at 3.30. At 3.40 he and his entourage go aboard, and at four o'clock he gets out at the top of the Gotschnagrat. We know from yesterday that he doesn't hang around at the restaurant, except to put on his skis.'

The waitress arrived with a bottle of wine, showed it to Ryderbeit, then drew the cork and poured a glass, keeping her face averted from his Cyclopean leer. He lifted the glass and squinted over the rim, watching her broad hips swaying away between the tables. 'I could sure slip her a length,' he murmured. 'You don't suppose the Fat Man could fix me up with something, do you? I mean, do you think one of the big hotels here might run a service?' He saw Packer's grin and stopped. 'Ah, forget it. I guess a Swiss brothel's what you'd call the ultimate contradiction in terms, like a driving licence in Braille?'

They both laughed. 'Why a brothel?' said Packer. 'Surely there's enough stuff running around on the slopes?'

'Yeah.' Ryderbeit emptied his glass and poured himself another. 'It's okay for you, soldier. You've got that nice bit of fluff tucked away waiting for you down in the Chesa Hotel – while all Samuel D. Ryderbeit's got is a B-grade pension with a narrow little bed and a few dirty handkerchiefs. Incidentally, just when am I to have the gracious honour of meeting your famous Miss Duval-Smithington-Jones, or whatever she's called? Even Fat Man says she's quite an eyeful – and that's some compliment, considering the krauts chopped off his nuts more than a quarter of a century ago.' He leaned closer to Packer. 'He says she's a pretty classy number. You worried I might frighten her?'

'She can look after herself,' Packer said dully.

'Yeah, I bet she can. Your English upper classes aren't licked yet, that's for sure. They stick together like the bloody Masons.'

Packer said nothing: he was thinking of Sarah, preening herself in the tea-room of the Chesa Grishuna – she was too lazy to ski – and no doubt succeeding, with that subtle, effortless allure, in insinuating herself into some smart corner of Klosters' international set.

The day after they had arrived here from Geneva, Packer had phoned her in London, catching her on the third call at 2.20 a.m., and had invited her out, paying for her air ticket, first-class return, from his £50,000 – a symbolically extravagant first nibble at his numbered nest-egg.

She had accepted at once, telling him that the owner of the Bond Street gallery had gone to New York and she had a free week. Packer, who had not consulted Pol beforehand, had anticipated some resistance from the Frenchman – perhaps for fear that Sarah would attract the attention of the Ruler's ubiquitous retainers, who were to be found at all times of day, and most of the night, sitting alone or in pairs in every big café and restaurant in the town. But Pol, who had taken up residence in the Silvretta Hotel – where he was rarely to be found – had been quite delighted by the prospect of her arrival.

Ryderbeit had finished his third glass of wine and was lighting a cigar. 'Let me tell you something, soldier – you get yourself snarled up in the ruling classes, and you've got to be either a masochist or a sadist. In my case, I preferred the role of sadist.'

'You've had experience, then?'

'Three times. My first two wives were Brits out of the top drawer – South African Brits, which is even worse. The third was heiress to a Bolivian tin mine, and Big Daddy didn't approve of her marrying a Red Sea Pedestrian.' Packer looked puzzled. 'Jew to you, soldier. Anyway, they were three real rich bitches, no worries. And they all loved me madly, and I treated them like dog shit. The second one didn't just divorce me, she got me thrown out of the bloody White Republic.'

'For what?'

'We had a bit of a fight.'

'Just a fight?'

'Well –' Ryderbeit peered over his glass at a pair of slim tanned girls in matching white fur hats – 'well, I did a bit of handiwork with some scissors. Snipped off a nipple. Jo'burg Police weren't too pleased about that. I did a year in the can, then they stamped something rude in my passport and bade me farewell.'

Packer sat and watched the skiers winding gracefully down the slopes. He tapped the Polaroid snap on the table. 'You don't need guts or brains to maim a wife, Sammy. But this fellow's different. I want your views.'

'He's not a good skier. Not bad for his age, but nothing like as good as he wants people to think. You noticed those fancy Christies he did just before he stopped? All crap. He's like a diver making a lot of splash. That boy's strictly in the après ski playboy class.'

'I agree. And that's why he always chooses the Mähder run – the easiest. There are several down the Gotschnagrat, some of them very difficult, including the Wang, but none of the spectators down here in Wolfgang are going to know which one he's taken.'

Ryderbeit frowned. 'According to the map, there are half a dozen other runs that are just as easy – here and in Davos. And why does he always choose exactly the same time? It's too simple, soldier. If I wasn't a trusting bastard, I'd start suspecting it might be a set-up.'

'All the other runs,' said Packer, 'the Parsenn, the Weissfluh-joch, the one down to Küblis – are either too difficult or too long. And length's important, because every extra metre means an added security risk. But there's another reason – and it also explains his regular timing. As we know, whenever he goes skiing, he gives an hour's warning so they can empty the cable car up the Gotschnagrat and have the runs clear by the time he gets to the top. If he decided to make a different run every day, at a different time, he'd have half the ski-lifts, cable cars and runs round Klosters and Davos more or less permanently suspended or closed. And that wouldn't fit in with his image as the happy monarch on holiday.'

Ryderbeit had squashed out his half-smoked cigar and sat for some time with his lips moving silently; then his good eye swivelled round to Packer. 'So it looks like being the Mähder run? High-velocity rifle with telescopic sights, at a range of up to 1000 metres. We'd have to do it from one of the higher runs. Pick him off at a downward angle, taking into account rising air currents, distorted distances, as well as snow glare, which in these altitudes can make it seem like you're shooting underwater. Also, the target's going to be moving downhill – weaving, changing position every second.' He paused. 'I still prefer the idea of the cable car – especially with this schedule he keeps. Fat Man agreed to get me the plastique, and thought it a very smart idea smuggling it into the hut at the bottom, hidden in a big pâté sandwich.'

'It sounds smart,' said Packer, 'but it's not. Because even if you got into the hut and put the plastique under one of the cable drums – with, say, a two-hour fuse stuck into it – and *if* the Ruler decided to ride up that afternoon, they not only use that one hour's notice he gives them to clear the car, but to check every inch of cable as it passes through all the huts – up at the Gotschnagrat station, *and* the Gotschnaboden, the halfway stop. You might not get caught, but you wouldn't kill the Ruler either.'

'Just a lousy old pâté sandwich that someone chucked away behind the winding machinery? Do you think they'd actually taste the pâté – let alone look for the detonator?'

'You forget you're in Switzerland, Sammy. They'd hate that

sandwich dirtying up their clean little Gotschnabahn hut, whether it contained pâté or plastique.'

Ryderbeit sat back and sighed. 'You're not the first person to shoot me down in flames, soldier. But I'm always up there, flying again. Now, try this one for size. I get up in the woods, just under where the cable car passes up to the Gotschnaboden. I've got perfect cover, and I've also got a .417 Magnum – commonly known as an "elephant gun". Just as the car gets over the halfway mark, I let fly at the traction cable and *twang!* – the whole caboosh and its Imperial load goes zinging down the wires, *splatter!* into that tidy little hut at the bottom. Okay?'

'Not okay at all. You're supposed to know about ballistics, aren't you? Or are guns to you just things with triggers and barrels which are used to blast off at black men and wild animals when they're not looking?'

'Easy, soldier.' Ryderbeit's eye had become a bright yellow slit, and his knuckles had whitened round his empty wine glass. 'You tell me what I ought to know about ballistics.'

'I'll tell you what you ought to know about those Gotschnabahn cables. The traction cable is over an inch thick, and made up of several hundred spliced steel wires that would take half an hour of oxyacetylene to cut through. It's also greased twice a day. Any bullet would just bounce off. You could get a hundred bullets hitting the same spot, and they'd hardly make a scratch.'

'What about the tension cables?'

'Same story. Except there are two of them.'

Ryderbeit emptied the wine bottle into his glass, and gave his wild cackle. 'You're all right, soldier. I was only feeling you out. That idea was just a lead-up. But on the right principle, mind. We both agree that trying to pick him off in the cable car itself would be something like thirty to one against – bearing in mind that he goes up with the thing packed with bodyguards, all about the same height and build as him, and after the first shot – unless one of us got him first time round – they'd all be lying on the floor and we'd need an armour-piercing weapon to get any closer.'

He grinned cunningly. 'Which is what I propose we do. People walking around on mountains carry a lot of heavy equipment, and there's no reason why a couple of innocents like us shouldn't wander up into those woods one sunny morning lugging a couple of 122mm rockets with sticky bomb shells. That way we could roast the whole car-load alive – in memory of your old pal, Chamaz, if the papers yesterday were anything to go by.'

Packer was shaking his head. 'I have to disappoint you again, Sammy. At eight o'clock this morning I was stopped by four Swiss Police with guard dogs only 200 yards beyond the Got-schnabahn hut. By 3.30 this afternoon you can bet they had those woods sealed off like the Gulag Archipelago.'

'There's the second stage, above the Gotschnaboden,' said Ryderbeit. He showed no sign of being disheartened; he was already signalling for another bottle of wine.

'The second stage,' said Packer, 'is the Wang. I'm not for one moment questioning your ability as a skier, Sammy, but you'd have to be pretty good to come down holding a Kalashnikov 122 in your hands, firing it as you went – because there's nowhere to stop on the Wang, where you'd be doing speeds of up to seventy mph.'

Ryderbeit said nothing until his wine arrived, and then drank two glasses straight off. 'You're a gloomy sort of sod, aren't you?' he said at last, 'even for a Brit. Supposing *you* come up with some ideas. That's what you're being paid for, isn't it?'

'My idea's been the same all along. If we're going to get him, it has to be somewhere on that run' – Packer nodded across the road – 'between here and the Gotschnagrat restaurant. Or rather, just below the restaurant. In fact, somewhere on the T-bar.'

Ryderbeit frowned. 'Sorry, soldier, but where I learned to ski we didn't have any fancy time-saving gadgets. We walked, or rather climbed. What exactly is the difference between a T-bar and a chair lift?'

'A chair lift carries the skiers in mid-air, suspended from a cable, and would make a much smoother target – while the T-bar is just an inverted T which scoops you up under the arse and pulls you up the mountain with your skis on the ground, follow-ing every contour of the track.'

Ryderbeit nodded gravely. 'So it's not only going to be a moving target – probably receding – but jerking and bumping all the way. Right?'

'That's what we'll have to find out. Tomorrow morning we're going up the Gotschnagrat to try those runs. We'll take as many pictures as we can and compare them with the maps. There'll be men spotting the slopes with binoculars, and maybe even a few choppers around. So anything under 500 metres is out. I suggest as near 1000 metres as possible.'

Ryderbeit let out a low whistle. 'Holy Moses! You know what a man looks like through telescopic sights at 1000 metres? Like a tiny bloody tadpole – which means a head shot, or nothing. And that's not all. If you're right, and he only goes skiing at four o'clock, wherever we're stuck overlooking the T-bar, we're going to have the sun coming in low at around ninety degrees. So we'll have shadows as well as snow glare.'

'The more difficult it is,' Packer said, 'the more chance we have of getting away. If we can find a spot on any of the parallel runs that gives us a clear range of that T-bar – and we only need a few seconds – we can kill him and get down here to Wolfgang, pick up the car, and be through Klosters even before the alarm's given.'

He had paused, leaning across the table until he could smell the wine on Ryderbeit's breath. 'Now the matter of the guns. I'm talking to Pol at seven this evening. He promises to get what we need by tomorrow night. I suggest a couple of Armalites – 5.56mm assault rifles – with self-adjusting anti-glare telescopic sights.'

The skin round Ryderbeit's good eye crinkled into a sneer. 'Those are gimmick guns, soldier – cheap and flashy – typical Yankee toys. Give me the old Lee Enfield .303, or the World War II Browning any day. Those were real guns, even if they don't make them any more.'

'The Armalite isn't cheap for a start. It's also small – no longer than a racing ski – and it's light.'

'Yeah. It's made of plastic.' Ryderbeit spat deliberately between his doeskin boots. 'No serious gun's made of plastic,' he added, and poured himself more wine.

'The bullet is also plastic,' said Packer. 'And as you probably know, instead of the usual spinning motion, the Armalite round has a lobbing trajectory, so that its impact is even more lethal than a soft-nosed bullet or a dum-dum. And that, for us, is the vital factor – that, and the fact that it has a stopping power of up to nearly two miles, and is accurate up to around one mile. You pointed out yourself that the target's going to be very small, very difficult – moving, shimmering and distorted. With any ordinary rifle, in order to hit him in a fatal spot – the spine, heart, or head – we have to be ninety per cent lucky. And we're not going to have time for more than three shots each at the most. But with an Armalite, that little plastic bullet has only got to hit him, in the elbow or the ankle, or just wing him, and the lobbing movement sends the bullet tearing round inside his body, ripping his limbs off.'

'Ah, it's dirty,' Ryderbeit growled; then looked up with a bright leer; 'but I grant you, it's beautifully dirty! To be truthful, I am being a bit jealous just now. You see, we never got anything fancy like that in the Congo or Biafra – just the usual lousy old hardware. Perhaps it's made me a little conservative.'

He poured the last of the second bottle of wine. 'But you think the Fat Man can get hold of a couple of Armalites – in Switzerland?'

Packer smiled. 'If somebody's prepared to pay enough to give me a cut of half a million, I guess an Armalite's going to be about as difficult to buy out here as a tin of Nescafé.' He called for the bill and waited while Ryderbeit drank his wine.

'Where is Pol, by the way?' Ryderbeit said at last.

'I don't know. He's phoning me at the Chesa. He hasn't been in Klosters since yesterday morning.'

Ryderbeit made no comment; nor did he make any move to help settle the bill. Only when they were halfway to the Fiat did he say, 'Just to be on the safe side, soldier, ask the Fat Man for six rounds each. It's a quick-firing weapon, you know.'

Packer nodded. They drove most of the way back down to Klosters in silence. Over the last stretch, Ryderbeit was leaning forward, straining his one eye for a glimpse of the cables up to the Gotschnagrat, which was already in heavy shadow.

'You know, soldier – and I don't want you laughing until I've finished – I've got half an idea to hire a twin-engined Executive jet and fix a nice sharp piece of metal between the undercarriage, then fly down that valley and nick those cables like pieces of string. Remember that accident on Mont Blanc a few years ago? – when a Mystère fighter cut the traction cable halfway up the mountain, and the pilot didn't even know what had happened until after he'd landed?'

'And what speed do you think he was doing?'

Ryderbeit shrugged. 'A few hundred knots.'

'And how fast do you think you could fly down that valley, keeping right up against the trees or the Wang in order to cut the cables near the top?'

Ryderbeit snarled something in Afrikaans; then got out a cigar, snicked the end with his teeth, and lit it from the dashboard lighter. 'Okay, soldier, you win again. I guess those Executive jobs are best left to giving the fat cats a smooth ride without upsetting their secretaries' champagne. A pity, though.'

Packer turned off the main road, just before the stony river, and drove down between two rows of dank grey houses which led to Ryderbeit's pension. 'Till tomorrow at eight o'clock sharp, at the Gotschnabahn Hut,' Packer said, stopping the car.

Ryderbeit got out and gave a gallant wave. 'My regards to the Fat Man – the sod! And give your girl a big something from me.'

He waved again, this time with a hint of loneliness as he mounted his dingy doorstep and fumbled for his key, following Pol's instructions to keep a strictly low profile during their stay in Klosters.

7

When Charles Pol was shown into the Ruler's presence, shortly after noon next day, he had been kept waiting only forty minutes. He was received in the same room, where the Ruler sat behind his desk, wearing a lounge suit and his horn-rimmed spectacles.

'Welcome, Monsieur. Be seated.' He sat back and gave Pol his long oily stare. 'Are you a chess player, Monsieur Pol?'

'I have played. But I am not good.'

'You surprise me. I am an excellent player. I have taken on some of the Grand Masters, and often it is I who have called *shah-mak*. Perhaps you are unfamiliar with the term? It is an ancient word in my language meaning, literally, "Death to the King". You call it, I believe, "checkmate"?'

There was a pause. Pol sensed something disquietingly casual about the Ruler's manner. 'You have surely not invited me here to play chess?' Pol asked, with his mischievous grin.

'No. I mentioned the game because it has a certain irony – one which you, as a Frenchman, may appreciate. When I first summoned you here, I had selected you from a long list of international scoundrels. I preferred you because your record proved you to be not only a professional – ruthless and ingenious – but also an eccentric. You enjoy intrigue. You enjoy it like a game, and the higher the stakes, the greater the pleasure. You do not contradict me, I see?'

Pol waited, saying nothing.

'I summoned you here, on that first occasion, to ask you to play a very special game with me. I even paid you a fortune to do so. I invited you to *shah-mak* me.'

He smiled like a razor. 'In such a context, do you not find the word magnificently ironic? Perhaps we should have invented a new word – "Death to the King of Kings, Prince of Princes"? But I fear I must disappoint you, Monsieur Pol. Our little game is over. I have put away the chessboard, and the pieces. Including you.' He raised his hand, as though he expected Pol to interrupt. 'I am not asking for the money back. I am asking simply that the operation be cancelled and all evidence destroyed.'

'Evidence?'

'You are being dull, Monsieur Pol. You have recruited accomplices – professional assassins whose only loyalty is to the money you pay them. I do not want them to become an embarrassment to me.'

'Your Majesty, let me explain something. You have referred to this operation as a game. I prefer to compare it to a clock – a highly complex clock which, on your instructions, I have wound up, and which is now beginning to tick. It is not easy to stop a clock once it has started.'

'It can be broken.'

'That was not part of the contract.'

'Do not be ridiculous. You have received from me a very large sum of money. So far you have done little to deserve it. You have, however, remained discreet about your plans. I know, at least, how many accomplices you have, although I still do not know their identity.'

'No. You lost a useful pawn there. According to the papers, it was burnt to a cinder on a lonely road in south-east France. The French Police are treating the case as one of political murder.'

The Ruler's stare was black and unblinking. 'I have no knowledge of the case, beyond what I too have read in the Press.'

'The man's name was Pierre-Baptiste Chamaz. Before his accident, he had been following me for several days, and had taken photographs of myself and my accomplices. Those photographs were fortunately intercepted.'

The Ruler gave a bored shrug. 'You should report such information to the Police, not me. I am not interested.'

'It is perhaps as well that I have not reported it to the Police, Your Majesty. By the way, why was Chamaz wearing an identity bracelet?'

'I do not know. Many people wear St Christophers. You are beginning to waste my time, Monsieur Pol.'

'St Christophers, Your Majesty, are not usually made of heat-resistant alloy. However, it certainly ensured that poor Monsieur Chamaz got his name in the papers.' Pol's face softened into a grin. 'Your Majesty, may I ask you a question?'

The Ruler waited, expressionless. Pol went on: 'Why, precisely, did you hire me to kill you?'

There was a pause before the Ruler replied. 'Monsieur Pol, it seems I must give you some advice. You are like a man who puts his hand into the fire to see if it will get burned. You enquire into matters which do not concern you. However, I suspect that you are also a man who could prove more troublesome if your curiosity is not satisfied. Let it be sufficient for me to say that I have recently had cause to question the loyalty of certain of my subjects. By allowing them to know that my life might be in danger from foreign assassins, I was able – by a relatively simple ruse – to test their loyalty, and find it wanting.'

'An expensive ruse,' Pol murmured, without enthusiasm. He was too old a hand to be impressed, let alone daunted, by the fantastic machinations of this inflated modern satrap. But Pol was also too careful to let any such disbelief show. He waited for the Ruler to continue.

'But a small price to pay for the security of my State.' He paused again, his eyes not moving from the Frenchman's face. 'Monsieur Pol, I must remind you once more that it is unwise to become too concerned in the affairs of a country like mine. I have been reluctantly obliged to implicate you, and certain other outsiders, in what has strictly been a matter of internal politics. Unfortunately, once outsiders become involved, they find themselves in a quicksand – the more they struggle, the deeper they are sucked in, until they are buried. Let your accomplices struggle, Monsieur Pol. You relax and listen to what I now have to say.'

From the moment that he walked out of 'Le Soupir du Soleil' and entered the chauffeur-driven car which was to take him back into Klosters, Pol knew that he was frightened.

It was not a rational fear; for Pol had learned to distinguish degrees of fear as the police distinguish types of crime. As the Ruler's dossier had said, the Frenchman had tangled with some of the roughest outfits in the game. Not just hoodlums, but the real professionals. Yet all these organizations – the Falange, the Gestapo, the OAS and CIA and KGB – all had one common characteristic. They employed craftsmen. They had a job to do: a job to extract and evaluate information; sometimes they paid for that information with cash, asylum, immunity from arrest, sometimes by sparing their clients the maximum pain, mutilation, death.

But his Serene Imperial Highness, the Ruler of the Emerald Throne of the *Hama'anah*, belonged to another breed altogether. And as the car drew up outside the Silvretta Hotel, and Pol stepped out into the dry cold air, he realized that the Ruler was probably the one man of whom he had ever been really frightened in his life.

The Ruler was not merely a tyrant; nor even a simple megalomaniac. He was a mortal living in the centre of a fantastic dream, which had been turned to reality by billions of barrels of oil, and by his capacity to hold, single-handed, the intricate economies of the Western world perpetually hostage to his slightest whim. His domestic politics, in which he had temporarily involved Pol, he treated as no more than a casual game; and Pol – who, as the Ruler had accurately observed, loved to play games himself – was all too aware of the frivolous menace of such a man.

The fact that Pol had already deposited detailed accounts of his dealings with the Ruler at two banks – one in Switzerland and one in France – and a separate copy with a highly placed friend in the Palais de Justice in Paris, would not, he realized dismally, cause the Ruler much discomfort. Pol's reputation, both in France and abroad, was not, unhappily, without blemish.

He felt tired and cold as he entered the lobby, and thought he might have a chill coming on. At the desk he left some lengthy instructions, including an order for a double club sandwich to be sent up to his room, where he did not wish to be disturbed until 6.30.

Upstairs he poured a stiff brandy which he drank in the bath; but afterwards, as he sat naked on the bed, he felt no better. The first bite of the sandwich had made him feel queasy and he had put the tray outside the door. He sat and watched the sweat trickling over the rolls of flesh, gathering in a salty pool in his massive navel and spilling over into his pubic beard, above the withered suture between his legs where a series of surgeons had spent months repairing what was left of his manhood.

Besides his own safety, what worried him most was how to protect Packer long enough for them to come to some arrangement about the money in Aalau. Pol had already cleared well over a million pounds on the operation, after paying both Ryderbeit's and Packer's shares. But even in such a crisis, it seemed to him immoral that he should risk losing his half of the further £500,000 in that joint account with Packer.

The one thought that finally lulled him into a fitful sleep was the memory of the 21,000 Swiss francs he had spent yesterday in Geneva, after his pleasant little détour to Talloires. For if events worked out as he now anticipated, Mademoiselle Sarah Laval-Smith was probably the best investment he owned.

When the telephone by the bed woke him at exactly 6.30, his malaise had returned; the sheets were rumpled, and his whole body ached as though it had been expertly beaten all over.

Ryderbeit was already in the hut when Packer arrived. He sat sprawled back against the wall, one hand holding a tumbler of mahogany liquid, the other, one of his eight-inch coronas.

Packer had already discovered, during the run that morning, that although the Rhodesian had only one eye and had spent most of his life in the tropics, he was a recklessly adroit skier; while Packer was tired and out of practice. This second run of the day, down one of the fastest pistes on the Gotschnagrat, had left him bruised and bad tempered, as he unclipped his skis and clumped into the hut, which smelled of sauerkraut and wet wool. The only other customers were a group of noisy Germans ranged along a table, drinking gluhwein.

Ryderbeit had a pile of Polaroid exposures spread out like playing cards, next to a large cloth-backed military map. As Packer stood in front of him, shaking the snow off his clothes like a dog after a swim, he noticed several rings in red felt-tip down the spine of brown-shaded mountain. From the last of these a straight line – in the same red – stretched diagonally across the map and ended in a spray of arrows, each touching a black line broken with little strokes, like a centipede.

'Okay, soldier?'

Packer nodded, pulled off his mittens, unhoisted his rucksack, and took out a similar map; sat down and drew another stack of photographs from his anorak pocket.

A large muddy-faced girl appeared in front of them. Ryderbeit eyed her with disapproval. 'What are you having, soldier?' Mine's a teeny triple Scotch.'

'Apfelsaft, bitte,' Packer told the girl, and Ryderbeit cackled. 'Still being a good boy, eh?'

Packer ignored him. He looked again at Ryderbeit's map, then unfolded his own, on which he had made similar markings, but in green. He compared the two, nodded, and ran his finger down the red rings on Ryderbeit's. 'These are all possibles?' he asked.

Ryderbeit said, 'Uh-huh,' and drew on his cigar. Packer tapped the black centipede on his own map.

'This is the T-bar up to the Mähder run, okay? According to this, it covers almost exactly 600 metres. Taking into account the undulations, we'll call it 700 yards. When I went on it this morning it took twelve minutes and nineteen seconds. That puts its speed at between four and five mph – a brisk walking pace.'

Ryderbeit took a deep drink and said, 'Fine. But it gets worse.'

'Yes, it's a rear sighting. But it's also at a thirty-two-degree angle, remember, so the target will seem slower.'

Ryderbeit shook his head. 'Not through a telescopic lens, it won't. You're getting forgetful, Packer Boy. At 860-odd metres, his speed's going to look twice as fast!' He ran his finger along the red line he had drawn across the two white grooves of valley; then tapped the brown-shaded ridges between them. 'But this is what's going to give us the real shit. Even as late as four o'clock there's still going to be a lot of shimmer, like panes of distorting glass.'

'Which point have you chosen?'

Ryderbeit tapped the red ring from which he had drawn the line across the centre of the T-bar. 'Barring accidents, it should take me ten minutes to get down to Wolfgang.'

'And how long have you got up there?'

'Seven seconds.'

'And you'll have him in your sights all the time?'

'No.' Ryderbeit shuffled through the pile of photographs and selected three, which he arranged in order. The first showed a small blurred figure in a half-sitting position, against a white background. In the second shot the figure's head was disappearing over a ridge of snow; then reappearing in the third. 'I got three to four seconds from when he first shows, and less than

131

three when he's over the hump,' he added. 'But for a hundred thou' I can't really complain.'

Packer smiled. 'If you're as good as you say you are, Sammy, he'll be a sitting duck.'

'Yeah. Trouble is, so will I.' Ryderbeit swallowed the rest of his whisky and waved his tumbler at the girl behind the bar; then again tapped the red ring on his map. 'This gives me the best sighting, but it's also a fucking horrible place to stop. I got to do a bloody smart turn, on forty-five degrees of ice, or I go smack over the edge, thirty feet down on to bare rocks. Then there's always the danger of some bastard running into the back of me. This afternoon I was lucky – got three clear minutes to make the sightings and take a few snaps before anyone came past. That run gets pretty busy this time of day. So if I'm going to keep this thing nice and quiet – just between me and the Ruler – I'm going to have to be bloody quick and bloody lucky.'

'It should be a lot clearer when he comes up,' said Packer. 'They empty the cable car for him, remember?' He paused. 'What about cover?'

'Sod all. The back of the bend is a wall of soft snow going right up over the shoulder of the mountain. The map marks it as a green avalanche hazard – which is medium.'

'What about trees?'

'No chance. The nearest are well below the bend, and a good five minutes' climb.'

'These other sites' – Packer brushed his fingers down the row of red rings – 'what's wrong with them?'

'They're all about the same, except the range gets longer and none of them give a sighting of more than five seconds. And even with an Armalite, that's cutting the odds pretty fine.'

Packer nodded slowly. The waitress brought Ryderbeit another sturdy drink which he half emptied; then he sat eyeing Packer along the length of his cigar. 'What about these Armalites, soldier? You think the Fat Man's going to come through?'

'You know him better than I do,' said Packer.

'Yeah.' Ryderbeit sighed and drank some more whisky. 'Did he say how the guns are going to be made up?'

'No need. An Armalite's about the length of a short ski, and we'll take them up in genuine ski bags.'

Ryderbeit leered nastily. 'A pair of Armalites with the latest self-adjusting telescopic sights – standard skiing equipment these days, eh? I just wonder that nobody's thought of it before.' Packer said nothing. Ryderbeit leaned back and breathed smoke at the ceiling. 'You know anything about these new sights? Do they need shooting in?'

'They shouldn't, if they and the gun are new. But if you're worried, we can find somewhere quiet – up near Davos, on the Weissfluhjoch, round about the time they're popping off mortars to bring down avalanches.'

'It's not that that's worrying me, soldier.' He smiled, sly and cat-like. 'I'm worried about you and Fat Man. I'm thinking you may be setting me up on this mountain as a patsy.'

'You've drunk too much, Sammy. Remember, I'm going to be up on this mountain too.'

'Yeah' – Ryderbeit's eye gleamed – 'but you haven't told me where.'

Packer turned to his own map and pointed to one of the green crosses. 'About 300 yards above you. And the range from the T-bar is nearly 100 metres further than yours. But it also gives a more parallel target, so our odds are about even.'

'Except you've got tree cover,' Ryderbeit scowled. 'And your run'll get you down to Wolfgang a good few minutes before me.'

He swallowed the rest of his Scotch, then leaned down as though to adjust one of his boots, and brought his head up, smiling this time. In his left hand was a small short-nosed automatic with a grip that was hidden in his slender palm. It looked to Packer like the sort of weapon that used to be called a 'lady's gun'. But still lethal within six feet – providing you knew how to use it. And Ryderbeit no doubt did, however much whisky he'd drunk.

Packer felt a familiar chill spreading through his gut. He laid both hands carefully on the table. 'All right, Sammy, just tell me what's on your mind.'

'I already told you, Packer Boy. I been thinking that you and Fat Man want me up on this mountain to make a dummy run, so you can both collect the chips.'

'I don't understand.'

'You don't?' Ryderbeit snickered. 'Well, I'll tell you. I've just had a funny thought. And that thought tells me that the mysterious Mister Big behind all this – the one who's paid Fat Man to set up this caper – is maybe the same joker we're supposed to be knocking off on that T-bar.'

'That's bloody daft.' Packer felt his palms growing moist on the cold table top. Ryderbeit was crouching forward, his fingers folded round the little gun which was pointing loosely down at Packer's groin. He was not touching the trigger. Packer glanced at the table of Germans, then at the waitress; but no one was looking at them.

'Why daft? Never heard of a man trying to buy a bit of popularity by hiring a hit-man to make a botched attempt on his life?'

Packer smiled swiftly, trying to humour him. 'You mean like Idi Amin – once a week – just to prove he's divine?'

Ryderbeit snapped his fingers. 'Right on the nail, soldier! Though Idi's a trifle crude, even for a munt. I was thinking of something a bit smarter – the kind of trick that might appeal to a crafty A-One shit like the Ruler.'

'Such as?' Packer said, in a quiet tight voice; he was trying not to look at the black eye of the gun, which was now near enough for him to grab without his even having to move his body.

'Soldier, the way I see it is this. The Ruler pays Fat Man a nice big sum to arrange a botched assassination attempt – something fancy that catches the imagination but doesn't quite succeed. Something like getting shot at while enjoying his innocent annual vacation in Switzerland. Shooting skiers must be even worse than shooting grouse out of season?'

'I'm sure it is. Put away the gun, Sammy. What's it for, anyway?'

'What's a gun for?' Ryderbeit repeated sleepily; he looked at his empty tumbler, then at the waitress, hesitated, then leaned down and replaced the little gun in his boot. He grinned. 'No offence, I hope, soldier? I need a gun sometimes – like I need a drink. Sometimes I need both. Like just now.'

'What was so special about just now?' Packer said; his hands were still sweating.

'Just that I was thinking how convenient it would be for Fat Man to put me up here on the mountain to take a shot at the Ruler – who, for all we know, can be a stand-in with a lovely silver wig – while you, Packer Boy, are perched up there in the trees, and the second I pull the trigger and blow the dummy's head off, you pull your trigger – at a nice easy range – and chop me up like horse meat.'

Packer looked wearily into Ryderbeit's unblinking yellow eye. 'Why would Pol want me to do that, Sammy?'

'Because Fat Man is as crooked as a mountain road and as shifty as a shit-house rat, with morals lower than the basic wage. He's already swindled me out of millions, and although he hasn't got me on his conscience – because the bastard doesn't have a conscience – he sure has me on his mind. He's so far only paid me £25,000, remember – and to get me off his back, that would be cheap at the price.'

'Well, if it's any comfort to you, I'm not going to shoot you. For a start, I hardly think you're worth £500,000. And anyway, we've been seen around too much together. But that's not all. You're not the only one who's got things on your mind, Sammy.'

Ryderbeit's eye narrowed. 'Meaning what?'

Packer took a deep breath. 'I'm just thinking of something else old Pol said when he first briefed me in that hotel in France. Before he had even mentioned the Ruler, he talked of the great advantages of what he called "diversionary tactics". Then he mentioned you – painting you as a typical mercenary killer – adding, for good measure, that you were an excellent pilot.'

Ryderbeit inclined his head. 'Thanks. What else did the bastard say?'

'I can't remember his exact words. But he did also mention that the vital element in an assassination of this scale is that the victim should be confused.'

'You've sure got me confused, soldier. Just what the hell are you driving at?'

'Pol took the trouble to track me down to Amsterdam, Sammy, because I have a fairly tough military record, plus a few black marks, which he claims will rule me out from most police suspect lists. He also threw in a sop about my talents for improvisation – apparently on the evidence that for the last few years I've earned my daily bread building model windmills for American millionaires.'

Ryderbeit was shaking his head. 'Either you're cracked, soldier, or Fat Man is. What have bloody windmills got to do with all this?'

'Probably nothing. I think that Pol may intend using you and me as the fall-guys – what he calls his "diversionary tactics" – to make the Ruler think he's being threatened by the most conventional method possible. And what could be more conventional than trying to knock him off on these ski slopes?'

'It's not going to be that easy,' Ryderbeit growled.

'No, but it's not going to be so difficult that it's worth a total of £600,000 between us to Charles Pol – or anyone else, for that matter. And I'm getting £500,000, remember? And for what? For ideas – those were Pol's words, weren't they? What ideas? Studying a map and marking a few ski runs and taking a couple of shots with a high-velocity rifle? He'd have half the Army veterans in the world queueing up for a job like that – and for a hundredth of the price.'

Ryderbeit's good eye had rolled up towards the high sun-streaked peak of the Gotschnagrat. 'Stop playing around, soldier,' he said softly. 'You've been paid for ideas, so let's hear them.'

'I'll lay it on the line, Sammy. Pol said something else in that hotel room in France. He said that while the Ruler will be expecting obvious, professional killers, his back will be turned to the real danger.'

'Go on.'

'He was referring to Sarah. What he called "another, subtler element".'

Ryderbeit's face was quite calm. 'And you think that's why he chose you?' he said at last.

'It seems more than probable.'

Ryderbeit stroked his chin. 'As I said, I don't know the girl – but she must have something bloody special to pull you in half a million quid. What is it?'

'I don't know. And Pol isn't the sort of person who'd tell me, unless he wants to.'

There was a long silence. Ryderbeit did not even touch his Scotch. He said, finally, 'All right, soldier, so it looks as though we may be in the hot seat. But we're being paid bloody well for it, so we can't argue. I'll accept that Fat Man may be setting us up on this mountain for a dummy run – or a diversion, as he calls it. He may even think we can knock the Ruler off first time round. If not, maybe he will use your little Sarah. Well, that's going to be her problem. As for us, we've been paid to do a job, so I guess we'd better do it.' He paused. 'Now there's one last item on the agenda. What about the signals? I suppose we'll have to risk an open radio link?'

'Well, even if the Police are monitoring all UHF transmissions within a good five-mile radius of the Gotschnagrat, the mountains play strange tricks with wavelengths, and they can't be sure all the time what they're picking up. For our purposes we need just one phrase – one word, even. And to anyone listening in, that could mean anything.'

Ryderbeit sat nodding his head with a peculiarly regular movement, like a chicken, his dead eye lurching up and down and his good one still fixing Packer with its yellow stare. 'That little word, soldier, has got to be spoken at the Gotschnagrat restaurant, the moment the Ruler sets off down to the bottom of the T-bar. And who's going to speak the word? Pol?'

Packer laughed. 'I rather get the impression that Pol prefers to be somewhere else when the action's taking place.'

Ryderbeit laughed too. 'Yeah, the cunning sod So who speaks?'

'Sarah.'

'You bastard! You mean you're going to put her up in the eagle's nest, surrounded by the whole gang of goons, while we're all snug on our mountain perches nearly a mile away?'

'Can you think of anyone better? In fact, if you do think about it, she's the ideal person. Any of us hanging around the Gotschnagrat restaurant when the Ruler appears would automatically arouse suspicion. But not a girl – not this girl.'

'You said she doesn't even ski.'

'She's good enough to fool around.'

'But what's she supposed to be doing up there?'

'Taking pics of the royal party. Why not? He might even invite her for a drink.'

'Yeah, why not? And when does she get to send the message – when she goes for a pee?' Ryderbeit shook his head. 'Those pocket R/Ts don't work too well indoors.'

'She'll find a way. She's not stupid, believe me.'

Ryderbeit nodded. 'Yeah, I believe you. Okay, you bastard. When are you going to tell her? Or does she know already?'

'Not yet.'

'Are you going to tell her everything?'

'If I have to.'

'Yeah, that's what I'm afraid of. I don't know the lady, mind, but if she's anything like the rest of her type, I'd lay evens on her either getting all shirty and threatening to run to the law, or more likely just yapping her mouth off back in some flashy night spot in London Town. Those upper-crust bitches never could keep their fucking mouths shut! I suppose you'll have to pay her?' he added savagely.

'That's my business.' Packer looked at his watch. 'Time we got going.' He turned and signalled for the bill. Again Ryderbeit made no effort to pay, but walked out in front of him through the door. Packer found him outside with his skis already strapped on, adjusting his goggles, gloves and sticks.

Ryderbeit pushed off first down the well-packed piste into the gathering gloom. Packer was not able to catch up with him.

Packer looked for Sarah in the Chesa tea-room, and in the downstairs bar; then collected their key from the desk, where he was told there were no messages.

The maid had been to their room since he left: the sheets changed, Sarah's clothes folded out of sight, her lotions and paints and accessories tidied into rows on the dressing-table. No whiff of scent, no fresh imprint on her bed. It was as though someone were trying to expunge all trace of her.

He went through and ran a bath, squirting in a few drops of Badedas, which Sarah never travelled without; then straightened up and looked in the mirror. Under the yellow light his eyes had that odd, wild look that Sarah said she so hated.

The hell with her, he thought, and leaned on the basin. God, I need a drink. Damn that Rhodesian Jew and his silly little 'lady's gun'. But then, what was a gun for if it wasn't meant to make you feel nervous?

He turned off the bath, went into the bedroom, considered taking one of Sarah's ten-milligram Valiums – another essential she never left behind – but decided against it; and with a sense of righteous self-denial stretched out on his bed. He had forgotten about the bath.

He dozed, eyes half open, and come to with a start. The light was still on, the room empty. He looked at his watch. 7.40. He was ten minutes late. He stood up and pulled on his anorak, with the map still folded inside; went downstairs, took another look round the tea-room, then handed in his key and went out into the chill dusk.

A sharp breeze had come up and the slush was already freezing on the short slope down to the Silvretta Hotel. To his right, behind the railway station, the cables of the Gotschnabahn whined against the black wall of mountain. The last car had come down at 6.00 p.m.

Inside the hotel he collided with a woman going out, and swore before apologizing. He blinked round the bright lobby and for a moment had trouble getting his bearings. The desk clerk surveyed him with discreet disapproval. 'I have come to see Monsieur Cassis,' said Packer.

'Your name, please?'

'Burton. B-u-r-t-o-n.'

The clerk consulted a list, lifted a house telephone, glanced down and murmured into the mouthpiece, then hung up. He nodded at Packer. 'Monsieur Cassis will see you. Room 104.'

Packer walked away to the lift.

'Ah, come in – my friend! Please, be comfortable!' Pol held the door open, shuffling sideways in a pair of flip-flops that were several sizes too large for his tiny feet. He waved Packer towards a wing-chair covered in shiny brown rayon.

It was a big room, full of ornamental drapes and reproduction furniture, now strewn with the same disorder that Packer had found in Pol's room in Amsterdam. One Louis Vuitton suitcase stood open and only half unpacked in the middle of the floor. Packer found a chair and sat down, after removing a brand-new shirt, still in its wrapper.

'You look tired, Charles.'

'Yes.' Pol had waddled back to a sofa and slumped down next to a large open box balanced on the arm. He gave an exhausted flap of his hands. 'Yes, I am a little tired. I have passed an energetic day.' He plucked a chocolate the size of an egg out of the box and squeezed it between his red lips. The rest of his face had a waxen pallor, with mushroom pouches under the eyes; his silk shirt was crumpled, tieless, with the buttons done up wrong; the zip of his oyster-white trousers was open. Packer had the impression that he had disturbed him, probably from sleep.

'You would like tea or coffee?' Pol mumbled through chocolate; 'or perhaps some Passeuger water?'

'Nothing, thank you.'

Pol licked his fingers, then wiped them fastidiously on a tissue he had pulled from a carton beside him, and which he now dropped at his feet. The carpet round him was littered with them, like white carnations. He smiled – a rather forced smile, Packer thought. 'You also look tired, my dear Packer. Was your expedition up the mountain a success?'

'Moderately.'

There was an uncomfortable pause. It was very warm in the room, with a sweet clinging odour – stale after-shave, or deodorant perhaps. 'But *you* had a satisfactory day?' Packer asked finally. Pol nodded. 'Did you get the' – Packer glanced round the room, hesitated – 'did you get everything we need?'

'Yes, yes.' Pol ate another chocolate, and another crumpled tissue joined the rest on the carpet.

Packer was disconcerted. He was used to a boisterous Pol: a great rubbery rogue with a twinkling self-confidence wrapped in refined self-indulgence. But this was a shell of the man: sagging, listless, almost as though he'd grown too small for his voluminous clothes.

'Charles, are you sure you're all right? You look ill.'

'I told you – I am a little tired.' His eyes moved dully over Packer's face, then away again. He heaved himself up and trotted heavily over to a side table where he poured himself a brandy. Packer waited until he had sunk back again on to the sofa.

'Charles, I want to talk about Sammy.'

'Ah? He has been misbehaving again?'

'Well, he pulled a gun on me in the hut. Admittedly, it wasn't much of a gun, and nobody saw it. But it was a little irregular, don't you think?'

'Irregular?' A small grin started across Pol's enormous features, then seemed to give up. 'It is in character. But you did not attempt to take it away from him?'

'I did not. In my experience, the only time people get hit by toy guns is by accident.'

Pol wagged his head. 'Ah, Sammy is very wicked! But you must not trouble yourself too much about his little idiosyncrasies.

For him guns are merely the tools of his trade – like a hammer to a carpenter or a typewriter to a journalist.'

'Thank you. I'm reassured.' Packer felt himself getting angry.

Pol spread his hands in innocent despair. 'One must accept Sammy for what he is.'

'He's a madman. He also drinks too much.'

Pol sighed; he looked bored. 'He is a very competent drinker. I have known him land a four-engined plane on a curving dam after he had drunk most of a bottle of bourbon. He is also no fool.'

'No,' said Packer. 'He thinks he's being set up on that mountain as a diversion. Come to that, I'm beginning to have the same idea myself.'

'Oh?' Pol looked only mildly interested.

'When we first talked over this plan, Charles, you made great play of how we wouldn't be going in for the conventional gadgets of the killing business – rifles with telescopic sights, and that sort of thing. You talked about a more subtle approach. There's nothing very subtle about sitting up the Gotschnagrat with an Armalite.'

Pol ate another chocolate and said nothing. Packer went on: 'Sammy's also got some wild idea that you and the Ruler may be in cahoots, and that this whole business had been planned by the Ruler himself – to get himself some dramatic publicity. Is there anything in that?'

'It is ridiculous,' Pol replied, rather quickly. 'It is nonsense – a pure fantasy of Sammy's.' He sipped his brandy. 'But let us turn now to a more substantial subject – the incident concerning Monsieur Chamaz. You have read the papers, of course? What is your opinion?'

'About the burning of Chamaz and his car?'

'About the man himself – and his whole behaviour before you detected him.'

'Lousy. Lousy enough to be spotted, that is.'

'By you, yes. But then, you are an expert.'

'Well, it's rather a matter of degree, isn't it? It would depend, for instance, on whether Chamaz's bosses *knew* I was an expert.'

'Yes, of course.' Pol paused. 'I forget – when was the first time you suspected he was following us? In Amsterdam?'

'No. As I told you, Sarah thought she was being followed then

– but that's almost a reflex action with her. And usually she's right – only not for the reason we're thinking of.'

'Quite. But when did *you* become aware of it?'

'I noticed a car – a Renault – parked down the side of the hotel in Le Crotoy.'

'Why that particular car?'

'An old girlfriend had one. Then, when I dropped Sarah at Le Touquet, I saw it again outside the airport restaurant.'

'Exactly the same car? A Renault is not uncommon, you know.'

'It was exactly the same car,' Packer said firmly. 'The first four numbers of the registration were 1956 – the year of Suez. I'm sentimental.'

Pol did not smile. 'A nice coincidence, perhaps?'

Packer shrugged. 'In this game we were taught that there's no such thing as coincidence – just luck, sometimes. You learn to watch out for a man's shoes, watch strap, way of walking – a car with a scratch down the side, extra wing mirror, looped aerial. You don't bother so much about the numberplate – that can be easily changed. The man may change his clothes, too. But it's a funny thing, they very often forget to change their shoes, and always their watches.'

Pol popped another chocolate into his mouth and munched thoughtfully. 'You are saying that our friend Chamaz was careless?'

'I'd say at the beginning – in Amsterdam – he did all right. But then, I wasn't suspecting anything. It wasn't until we got into France, and you explained the plan to me, that I started getting sensitive. I had an idea we might be followed. I also had a lucky break – the car and the number. From then it was just a matter of waiting until he exposed himself – which he did, on the front at Berck-Plage.'

There was a pause. 'Capitaine Packer, would you say there was anything at all unusual – at all bizarre – about the way Chamaz operated?'

'That rather depends on who organized him. I'd say it was small-time, a one-man outfit – which is too little when it comes to tailing three people.'

'What would you have expected?' asked Pol.

'If we are dealing with the Ruler – which I assume we are –

142

I'd say it was very odd that he didn't use a team, working twenty-four hours. And at least two cars.'

'How are you certain there was only one man?' Pol asked.

'I'm not.'

'So there could have been others?'

Packer thought for a moment. 'There could have been. But if Chamaz had been working in a team, he'd have probably faded out after getting into France – certainly after Sammy came on the scene. As it was, he was left out on a limb. He'd have done as well to have walked right into the hotel and shown us his two passports by way of introduction.'

'You do not think, perhaps, that he was acting as a decoy?' said Pol. 'That he actually *intended* you to catch him?'

'With the films on him? That wouldn't make sense – under normal circumstances, that is.'

'You are suggesting that this was not normal?'

'I don't know how normally competent the Ruler is. But after I first talked to you, I did some homework back in London, and I learned, among other things, that his Secret Police, NAZAK, was wet-nursed by the French, and more recently tutored by British advisors. You know more about French techniques than I do, but I can assure you, even the British – and our authorities are as mean as they come – only allow a man to operate on his own if it's a short-term surveillance. Which means that the Ruler – or whoever gave Chamaz his orders – was either being damned clumsy or damned forgetful.'

'In other words,' Pol said slowly, 'you are saying that Chamaz *was* inviting capture?'

'I wouldn't say definitely. He may just have been incompetent. Like you get incompetent plumbers and brain-surgeons and Prime Ministers.'

Pol gave a strained chuckle. 'You are being perhaps a little presumptuous, are you not, mon cher? The Ruler – if it was the Ruler – was not necessarily to know that you did have expert training in this game.'

'Maybe not. But you were asking for my opinion, based on experience. And in my experience, in Malaya and Cyprus and the Trucial States, this sort of job would have been given what we called a "grand slam". I mean, if NAZAK is anything like as good as they say it is, and they'd got a smell of an assassination attempt against their Ruler, they'd have called in the big battalions. When I used to work this kind of job, even on a small scale – trailing a suspect group of terrorists – we always used at least two men to cover every one, doubling up if they decided to move around. And *we* worked on a shoestring. But it's my guess that NAZAK take themselves pretty seriously, and on a job like this they should have used at least a dozen men, and a relay of cars.'

'Twelve men?' Pol was sweating, and very pale.

'Maybe twenty.'

Pol slapped his thigh. 'Thank you, mon cher. If it interests you your opinion is not different from my own.' He inspected his empty brandy glass and placed it delicately on the arm of the sofa. 'Now let us discuss the arrangements for tomorrow.'

'Tomorrow?'

'Yes. His Imperial Majesty will be riding up on the Gotschnabahn tomorrow at 3.40 as usual. He should arrive at the top at 3.50. That means' – he raised his naked eyebrows – 'that he will reach the T-bar at almost exactly four o'clock, I think? The weather report for tomorrow says that it will be fair.'

'Wait a minute. You say he's going up tomorrow. At 3.40? Arriving at the Gotschnagrat at four o'clock?'

Pol nodded. Packer was looking at him carefully. 'How do you know?'

'Me?' Pol grinned and reached for a chocolate, but did not eat it. 'Mon cher Packer, the Ruler's movements are known to half the population of Klosters! Half the locals talk about nothing else.'

Packer went on watching him, waiting until he had masticated his chocolate and wiped his lips clean. 'Sammy said something else this afternoon, Charles. He said he thought that maybe you had your nose stuck into the Ruler's camp.'

Pol gave a look of false surprise. 'And what could he have meant by that?'

'Just what he said. He thinks you and the Ruler are pretty close.'

Poll attempted a mischievous grin, but it failed him. 'I told you not to concern yourself with Sammy's fantasies.'

'I'd have said he was perhaps being more shrewd than fantastic,' said Packer. 'The Ruler keeps himself to a pretty tight schedule out here, and he also keeps it pretty secret. He may always use the same ski run, at the same time – but not necessarily every day. When he does decide to go skiing, he gives just an hour's notice. Yet you happen to know – twenty hours ahead of schedule – that he's going up tomorrow.'

Pol's shoulders slumped wearily. 'Please, mon cher, you have an important job before you. And part of that job is not to ask questions. It is a bad military principle. Now, you have the map?'

Packer took it out of the pocket of his anorak and walked over with it, unfolding it across Pol's thighs. The Frenchman ate a couple more chocolates while he examined the green markings. Packer explained the two firing positions, the various trajectories, distances and attendant problems.

Pol seemed to be only half listening; and towards the end of Packer's speech his manner even grew impatient. His fat finger jabbed at the green cross which marked Packer's position on the run; and Packer noticed with some dismay, that his finger-nail – usually as shiny as mother-of-pearl – was this evening not quite clean.

'You are here – yes?' Pol looked up at him, his face beaded with sweat. Packer just nodded; he had already explained this detail a few moments earlier.

'Your position is above Sammy's,' Pol murmured; 'but you have further to ski down.'

'I know.' Packer was becoming puzzled: this, too, he had already explained to Pol; and he said again, patiently, 'The range is about a hundred metres longer, but the position of the target is slightly easier than Sammy's.'

Pol gave him a slow dull stare, then giggled: and Packer realized, with a physical shock, that what he had mistaken for exhaustion was really fear. And when Charles Pol became afraid, it was time for Packer to start worrying.

Pol said, 'Tomorrow, Sammy will not kill the Ruler. He will not kill anyone.'

'Oh?'

Pol giggled again. 'And you, my dear friend, will not kill the Ruler either. You will kill Sammy.'

*   *   *

Packer was standing very close to him. He could see the sweat glistening on his kiss-curl and on the shiny dome of his head, and he could smell the man's sweet fleshy aroma like an over-ripe hothouse plant.

'You are joking, Charles.'

'I am afraid that I am serious.'

Packer nodded. His voice was quiet, without emotion. 'This isn't in the contract, Charles.'

'Please do not be absurd. You know there is no contract. You have merely agreed to carry out my instructions in respect of a certain operation. And I must remind you that you are technically my employee. You may be a joint signatory to our bank account, but that does not preclude you from carrying out your obligations. That means, my dear Packer, that you must earn your money.'

'Half a million pounds to kill a one-eyed expatriate mercenary at a range of 300 metres?'

'You mean *can*, or *will*?'

'I mean, from your position here on the map you will be able to see Sammy, as well as the T-bar?'

'Of course. Otherwise, how do we synchronize the shots?'

Pol nodded. 'Bien. You will proceed with the plan exactly as you have just explained it to me, until the moment that Sammy takes aim. Your timing here will have to be impeccable. You will shoot him dead in the same second that he tries to shoot the Ruler. If you miss, the situation could become extremely disagreeable.'

Packer picked up the map and returned to his chair. Pol fetched himself a fresh brandy and swallowed most of it on his way back to the sofa.

'You do not look happy, mon cher. You should be relieved. It is surely easier to kill a stateless nomad than the Ruler of one of the richest countries in the world? Or perhaps you are entertaining some absurd British scruples about killing a friend and colleague?'

'Shit to that. Sammy's hardly a friend, and colleagues don't usually pull guns on you over a quiet chat.'

'So you are satisfied?'

'As satisfied as you are, Charles. And you're about as satisfied as a Chief Eunuch in the Playboy Club.'

The Frenchman winced, but said nothing. He was watching Packer with his beady stare.

'Listen, Charles. Part of what you're paying me is for ideas, not for scruples. The hell with scruples. What puzzles me is how an old pro like you came to get yourself into this mess. Here we are, less than a week out of port, and you've got us both – and Sammy – all nicely lined up to be killed.'

'I do not understand you.' Pol's face had turned the colour of greaseproof paper.

'You understand. You went up to see the Ruler today. Or somebody pretty close to him. And you were told that the plot's been discovered, and you've got to remove all the evidence. Or perhaps Sammy's theory was right after all, and the Ruler – for some devious political motive – hired you to try and kill him. Then something goes wrong, which makes him change his mind, and he suddenly calls the whole plan off. Am I right?'

Pol looked unhappy, but still said nothing. Packer nodded. 'Of course, he knows all about you, and he may know something about me and Sammy – from Chamaz, for one. Unless you were kind enough to tell him yourself? Then he summons you to the chalet and orders you to get your second-in-command to kill the fall-guy – Samuel D. Ryderbeit. Okay?'

Pol ducked his mouth to his glass and saw it was empty. He hesitated, and when he looked up his little eyes had grown crafty. 'You forget that I have been paid a considerable fortune. I have no intention of giving it back.'

'You realize, Charles, that you're as good as confessing that the Ruler did hire you for this job?'

Pol spread his hands and was again silent.

'Anyway, the Ruler's not going to worry about money. But he is going to worry about you and me and Sammy. And supposing I do kill that mad Rhodesian tomorrow, and even manage to get off the mountain and out of the country – who kills me? You?'

Pol began to laugh, but it was a hang-dog laugh, like a bad comedian laughing at his own joke. 'You are not being very intelligent, mon cher Capitaine. Must I remind you again that you are a co-signatory of our account? Do you really believe that I would kill you and forfeit half a million pounds?'

'The Ruler could always make it up to you. Half a million to

147

him is like a new pair of shoes to a shop-girl. He might even throw in a pair of tights. You'd look good in those, Charles.'

'Do not be facetious,' Pol said, with dignity.

Packer smiled. 'I'll respect your sensibilities. But I'm not so sure about your good sense. I don't give a damn what happens to Sammy – except that what happens to him is going to happen to all of us. The Ruler may, or may not, have hired you to kill me. What is absolutely certain is that he's not going to allow any of us to run around on the loose. I can kill Sammy tomorrow. I might even be able to kill the Ruler tomorrow – if your information is correct. And you could no doubt get me killed pretty soon afterwards. But after that you're wide open. You're dead, Charles.' He grinned, and crossed himself.

Poll was breathing hard, and the sweat had begun to drip from the end of his goatee. 'So what do you suggest?'

Packer put his hands on his knees and gave Pol a solemn, patronizing frown. 'Everybody else seems to be behaving so badly in this affair, I think it's perhaps about time we set an example and started being moral. The Ruler – or someone – has paid us all good money to do a difficult and dangerous job. I think it's only right that we should carry out our original instructions, and do just what we've been paid to do. We kill the Ruler – before he kills us.'

Pol was still laughing as he slopped more brandy into his glass. His belly seemed to have swollen to its normal proportions, and now wobbled and shook inside its folds of silk, while his eyes were soaked pink. Packer's words had even restored colour to his cheeks.

'Before you drink any more,' Packer said, 'where's the equipment?'

Poll had to pause and dab a tissue to his eyes before he could reply. 'It has all been sent to your hotel – don't worry.'

'To the Chesa? You must be mad!'

Pol raised his free hand soothingly as he tottered back to the sofa. 'You must not be so nervous, mon cher. The material has all been prepared in genuine sporting wrappings. They are even ready to be taken up the mountain, as we discussed.' He sank with a great grunt into the sofa and smiled. The shadow had passed : Charles Auguste Pol was himself again.

Packer said, 'A pair of Armalites – mint condition – self-adjusting telescopic sights; two packets with six rounds each. Right?'

'Tout en règle,' Pol said cheerfully. 'I have also acquired the very latest Japanese radios, no larger than a cigarette packet.' He winked. 'And I've even made some discreet enquiries among certain Swiss friends of mine, and have determined the two wavelengths used out here by the Army and the Police. You will find that all three sets have been adjusted accordingly. Which brings me to another little matter – our charming accomplice, Mademoiselle Sarah.' He gave a playful nod and lifted his glass in a mock toast. 'You have not told her yet?'

'Not yet.'

'And when do you intend to?'

'When the time is right.'

'Mon cher, you make it sound like a proposal of marriage !' He winked again. 'She will not refuse you, I promise you.'

Packer sat and scowled across the room at him. 'You and Sarah make a bloody marvellous couple,' he muttered. 'Big-hearted Uncle Charles and his naughty little wayward niece, playing games at killing people on the skiing slopes of Klosters.'

He stood up and pulled on his anorak, folding the map again carefully in the inside pocket. 'When are you leaving here. Monsieur Cassis?'

'Soon, Mister Burton,' Pol replied with a short bow. 'When the times comes for us to meet again, I shall know how to find you. Now' – he looked ostentatiously at his watch – 'I think it is time you went in search of your Sarah before she falls prey to the advances of these abominable après-ski scavengers.'

Packer crossed to the door, then stopped. 'By the way, what happened today that upset you so much?'

'Ah, no – just a moment of depression. Le cafard, mon cher. Only fools are permanently happy.'

'Goodnight, Charles.' As Packer opened the door he knew that Pol had not been telling the truth. He wondered what this sly French bastard now had in mind for poor Ryderbeit. But the matter was still in Packer's hands : and Packer had already decided what he was going to do.

8

It was 8.30 p.m. when he got back to the Chesa; but few people in Klosters dined much before 9.00, so he ran no more than the usual risk of missing Sarah.

The desk clerk informed him that Miss Laval-Smith had returned an hour ago, but had since come down again and left her key. A quantity of skiing equipment had also been delivered to their room in the past hour, Packer was told. He took his key and thanked the clerk, just hoping Sarah hadn't had the chance to open the parcels already.

She had left her mark on the room with as much unruly panache as Pol: the dressing-table was littered with bottles and jars and greasy cotton balls; while both beds were draped with dresses which she had discarded for the evening. He reflected, with mournful irony, that while in her mews flat in Knightsbridge she maintained a régime of tyrannical tidiness – even ordering Packer never to leave the lavatory seat up, because that was 'ugly' – the moment she was abroad, liberated by foreign servants in strange hotels, she lapsed into slovenly détente.

The only contradictory note was a message scrawled in blood-red lipstick across the bathroom mirror: 'DO YOU ALWAYS LEAVE YOUR DIRTY WATER IN AFTER HAVINGABATH???' – the final three words elided for lack of space. She had added no indication of where she had gone, or when she would be returning.

Then he saw the parcels. There were three of them, piled on the luggage stand inside the door, and they had obviously not been disturbed. There were two zipped-up plastic packs, like golf bags, each bearing the distinctive red and white markings of Hartmann Products – manufacturers of the latest make of short, high-speed, fibreglass ski, with patent safety bindings.

The third parcel was about the size of a cigar box, wrapped in plain brown paper, sealed with Sellotape, and with no inscription.

Packer made sure the door was locked; then pulled down the top pack and ripped open the zip. What he saw caused him to blink in amazement. He let go of the bag and part of its contents caught him a sharp blow on the shins. It was a short, fibreglass ski, painted the same brilliant red and white as the bag.

For several seconds he stared, bewildered; then he unzipped the second pack, and found another, identical pair of skis. In each bag was also a pair of aluminium sticks with red and white plastic hand-straps. For a moment he tested the sticks, to see if the handles unscrewed or came to pieces, in case Pol had concealed in them some ingenious conversion of the Armalite. But they seemed innocent enough. He tossed them back on the stand, and now turned to the brown-paper parcel.

It had clearly been wrapped by a professional, and in order to open it Packer would have to use Sarah's nail scissors to cut the tightly sealed corners. But first he took the precaution of sliding his fingers over the smooth sides of the box, feeling for the tell-tale strip of metal spring that would release the detonator. There was none.

He cut the paper edges, still taking no chances, and peeled off the wrapping. Inside was a dark blue leather case with the small gilt signature of GRIMA engraved on the top left-hand corner. He snapped open the catch and looked down at a cushion of tissue paper. Lying on it was a card covered in a messy Biro scrawl, in French: *'Cher Monsieur Packer! Forgive an old man who is still young enough to enjoy playing games. Give this to your beloved Sarah!'* – he had misspelt it 'Sara' – *'and remember the words of Charles Pol: Women are even more treacherous than policemen and politicians – if you cannot seduce them, buy them!'*

Packer lifted the tissue paper. On the black velvet lining was spread a necklace made up of cubes of pale gold, sprouting fibrous stars that were cleverly asymmetrical. In the centre was an emerald the size of a little finger-nail. His first reaction was to wonder, idiotically, how Pol knew that emeralds were Sarah's favourite jewel.

He put the card in his pocket, replaced the tissue paper, closed the box, and put it away in a drawer of the dressing-table; then walked over between the beds and lifted the telephone. 'Hotel Silvretta, please.' While he waited he was surprised at how calm he felt. The phone crackled in his ear: 'Hotel Silvretta, bitte.'

'Monsieur Cassis, please.'

'One minute, please.' The voice was a bored purr, and the silence that followed seemed very long. 'Hello, please. I regret, Monsieur Cassis has vacated the hotel.'

'*What!*' Packer controlled himself. 'He was there only twenty minutes ago – there has been some mistake.'

'One minute, please.'

Packer sat down on the bed; his knees had begun to shake.

'Hello, please. Yes, Monsieur Cassis has just left the hotel.'

'With his luggage? It's impossible! He must have just gone out. Did he say when he'd be back?' He found he was shouting, and steadied himself. 'I wish to leave an urgent message for Monsieur Cassis. From a Mister' – he hesitated, wondering if the fraudulent Burton was any longer relevant.

The Swiss voice, in its excruciatingly accurate English, cut him short : 'I regret, sir. Monsieur Cassis has checked out. He is no longer in the hotel.'

'For Christ's sake! Did he pay his bill?' Packer almost heard the outraged intake of breath the other end.

'Certainly. His bill is in order.'

'What about his luggage? Did he leave with any luggage?'

The voice grew prim and officious. 'I am not permitted to discuss our clients' affairs. If you wish to make further enquiries you must address yourself to the manager.'

'Wait a minute!' Packer shouted, before the man had time to hang up. 'This is a matter of desperate urgency. Did Monsieur Cassis leave a forwarding address?'

'One minute, please.' Again it seemed a very long time before the voice came back. 'Hello, please. Monsieur Cassis has left no forwarding address.'

Packer stared at his feet and said, 'Thank you,' and laid the receiver back in its cradle. Then he went into the bathroom, filled the basin with icy water and plunged his whole head in, still wearing his sweater and anorak. In the glass, behind Sarah's graffiti, his face was white. He took the hand towel and slowly dried the back of his neck.

The craziest thing of all, he thought, was that he should be so shocked and upset at being let off the hook. Half an hour ago he had been given the assignment to kill a man – unquestionably the most dramatic assignment he had ever received. And now he was free: free, with two brand-new sets of Hartmann racing skis, and a present for Sarah that must have cost several thousand pounds. The trouble was, it didn't make sense. It made no bloody sense at all.

He tried, as in the heat of battle, to rationalize, calculate the odds, evaluate the enemy's tactics. But who was the enemy? Pol? The Ruler?

He had thought of going straight back to the Silvretta and demanding to see Pol's room; but he remembered those watery official eyes behind the desk and knew it would be useless. It was possible that Pol had instructed the clerk to lie to all callers; but far more probable that Pol had indeed left – had already planned to leave before Packer had arrived – and that the open suitcase he had seen had merely been the last of Pol's packing.

No, one thing was certain: Charles Pol was scared, and was running for his life. The skis, and the expensive trinket from Grima, had perhaps been more of a reflex action – a devious grand geste, rather than a calculated deception. Otherwise Pol's motives – his supposed contract to kill the Ruler, the scrupulous ritual at Aalau, and his joint signature with Packer for half a million pounds – all now seemed as confused and improbable as that first grotesque image of him running amok in the tulip field.

Packer took off his anorak and sweater, finished drying his face and hair, put on a clean shirt and the linen jacket which Sarah had bought for him a year ago, and went down again to look for her.

The tea-room, restaurant, and downstairs bar were even noisier and more crowded than before: the girls lean and tanned, with small hips and strong good legs, well exhibited in their uniforms of skin-tight stretch-pants; the men confident and well nourished, of no determinate age or nationality, but sharing an easy camaraderie – the hall-mark of that society circuit that embraces the playboy pens of the Western world. Packer eyed them with weary contempt, relieved that he was not one of them, yet resentful that they did not seek him out for membership.

In the bar he bumped into a handsome man who splashed whisky over his sleeve. The man laughed and Packer clenched his fist. Easy, he thought: this is neither the time nor place to start picking at that social chip on your shoulder. He found the bar, and after using his elbows with some agility, managed to get a glass of mineral water. It was several more minutes before he saw Sarah.

She was squeezed up against the wall in a corner, her scarlet lips parted in their practised smile; her dark hair arranged with raffish abandon; wearing a wide-sleeved Peruvian peasant shirt, loosely knotted emerald-green cravat, and white bell-bottomed trousers that skilfully made the best of her hips while concealing her ankles, which were her least lovely feature. She had an almost empty glass of white wine in her hand.

The man she was talking to had his back to Packer. He was very tall, and his face, which was bent down almost at right angles as he talked to her, was hidden under an immense sealskin hat with the wide brim turned down over his ears. The rest of his long body was sheathed in a suit of brownish-grey sharkskin, over a pleated white shirt, unbuttoned to the navel and revealing, on his hairless olive chest, a chain with a gold Star of David. Despite the concealed night-club lighting, he was wearing dark glasses. It was a few seconds before Packer realized that it was Ryderbeit.

The Rhodesian had been talking eagerly to Sarah. When he saw Packer his expression behind the dark glasses was mute; he did not smile, just nodded. 'Evening, soldier-boy. You don't have to make the introductions – we already done it ourselves.'

Sarah had turned, and it seemed to Packer that her smile became slightly insecure, like a window coming loose at the hinges. 'Hallo. You know each other then?' She sounded uncertain of her ground.

Ryderbeit was drinking a white spirit, but he showed no trace of drunkenness. He bent his face back over Sarah and said, 'I was just telling Miss Laval-Smith about the most beautiful and dangerous creature in the world' – the fingers of his left hand traced a quick slithering movement through the air, and Sarah gave an exaggerated shudder – 'our old friend, the green mamba. I knew a bastard once who ran over one on a motor-bike, and the thing came after him and caught up with him, and they both presented themselves to the Great Reaper a few minutes later.'

'Horrible!' Sarah said brightly. 'At home we get lots of adders

154

in the summer, but I can't even stand grass snakes. They give me the creeps.'

Ryderbeit lifted his head and cackled. 'Penis envy, my darling!' He stood leering down at her, while she smiled back, with artificial amusement. Then she turned to Packer. 'Your friend here has been telling me some really dreadful things. All about people having their livers eaten while they were still alive.'

Ryderbeit swallowed his drink and handed Packer the empty glass. 'Be a friend and get me another, soldier. Kirschwasser. A nice big one with a lot of nothing.'

'Get your own,' Packer growled.

Sarah gave him a quick frown, then smiled and handed him her own glass too. 'I'd like some more wine, Owen. Chablis, please.'

Ryderbeit rocked back on his heels and showed his small canine teeth. 'Good on you, soldier. See you in about a month's time.'

Packer paused dramatically; then took both their glasses and began to shoulder his way back towards the bar. When he returned five minutes later, Ryderbeit was alone, leaning against the wall and staring at the floor.

'Don't tell me,' Packer said, with morose triumph. 'That old Red Sea Pedestrian charm failed you at the last minute, and she's gone off with a skiing instructor?'

Ryderbeit reached for his fresh glass, emptied it in a gulp, then stood shaking his head. 'Holy Moses, boy! I don't say she's my type, but I could sure sink the sausage there! I bet she performs like a can of worms with an outboard motor.'

'Where's she gone?'

Ryderbeit shook his head again. 'Big bald sod with a couple of plums in his mouth came over and called her "darling", and she called him "DJ", which appears to be short for D'Arcy-James. *D'Arcy-bloody-James!*' he repeated in a shrill moan; then looked at Packer with a pitying smile. 'As I said, soldier, I've been round the track with three lovelies like your Sarah, and I'll tell you something for nothing. They're all hard, fully paid-up professional bitches. Leave them to the D'Arcy-Jameses of this world, and all the other Hooray-Henrys!'

Packer bowed. 'I'm deeply indebted to you for your sentiments, Samuel. Let's get on to a lighter subject like, for instance, our friend Charles Pol.'

'So? What's he done?'

'He's buggered off, that's all.'

'And the guns?' Ryderbeit said, in a hushed whisper, even against the music.

'I think you'd better come upstairs, Sammy, to my room. Sarah'll be busy for hours. I've got something rather amusing to show you.'

He put Sarah's full glass of Chablis on the floor in the corner, and led the way back to the door.

'Frankly, boy, I don't see what our problem is.' Ryderbeit had come over and was sitting on the bed opposite Packer, where he refreshed his glass from what was left of the bottle of vodka that Sarah had bought in the Duty Free at Heathrow. He was still wearing his hat, but had taken off his dark glasses. His good eye now had a raw glitter, though he seemed otherwise in full control.

'Just look at it realistically,' he went on: 'What have we got and what have we lost? Well, we both got ourselves a nice few smackers in our respective banks for doing fuck all. We've had a week's skiing on the firm. We've each picked up a bloody good camera and pair of kraut binoculars. And now it seems we've had a last-minute bonus – two sets of Hartmann skis. And those things aren't cheap, I tell you.' He leaned back on the pillow and drank contentedly.

'And another thing,' he went on: 'I also got myself a lovely new identity – Daniel Spice-Handler, remember? Company Director, Tel Aviv.' He drained the glass, then held it up and twirled it lovingly between his long supple fingers. 'I just don't see what you're getting so windy about, soldier. Fat Man's scarpered. So what? He's not our bloody nanny.'

Packer looked at the lean hooked profile under the brim of the sealskin hat, and wondered if Ryderbeit were just a fool who managed to survive, or a cunning scoundrel who played at being a fool. Since coming up to the room, Packer had told him every-thing – with the exception of Pol's little gift from Grima; and he had only omitted it because he felt that, in some ambiguous way, it humiliated him in his relations with Sarah. Besides, Ryderbeit would probably insist on reselling it and splitting the profit.

Packer said at last, 'So you really think we can walk out of this as though nothing has happened?'

'Why not? We ain't done anything illegal. Who's gonna stop us?'

'His Serene Imperial Highness in the chalet up the hill – for one. And he's enough, as far as I'm concerned.'

'Sod His Serene Highness,' Ryderbeit said cheerfully. 'This is Switzerland, remember – not the bloody Sands of Araby.'

'It doesn't matter if it's Switzerland or Swaziland. A man like the Ruler doesn't do his own laundry, you know.'

Ryderbeit turned his head and gave Packer a sleepy stare. 'All right, soldier, piss off back to London with that rich little bitch of yours and start living.'

'Sammy,' Packer said, with grim patience, 'you say you know Charles Pol pretty well. You ever known him scared?'

Ryderbeit got up and poured himself the last of Sarah's vodka. 'Like you said he looked this evening, you mean?' He shrugged. 'Well, you said yourself you thought he just looked tired and ill. I'd say just that – too much booze. I've seen it plenty of times.'

'He was scared, Sammy. Shit scared. You and I know what it's like. Fear's something you don't see – you feel it, like sex appeal. And Pol had it tonight – badly. Fear, I mean,' he added; and Ryderbeit laughed, without humour.

'Okay, soldier – you were hired to do the thinking. So think up something good and let's hear it.'

'You thought it up, Sammy – that idea of yours up in the hut this afternoon when you poked your gun at me. You may have been right after all. For some reason the Ruler wanted to fake his own assassination, and he picked Pol, because the old Frenchman has a pretty wide experience in these matters and Pol somehow got on to me. You, of course, were half on his pay roll already.'

'So why's Pol skipped?' Ryderbeit broke in.

'I can only guess. But I think he went up to "Le Soupir du Soleil" today to get his final orders, and when he got there he found that the Ruler had changed his mind. The operation was off. Now, Pol's no man's fool – nor has he exactly led a sheltered life. Yet something today convinced him that he was in mortal peril. So he did the only thing he could do – he played for time. He agreed to help the Ruler clear up the evidence for him. And that was shrewd, because the Ruler's the sort of man who likes things to be done properly, and it would obviously be tidier all round if he got his hirelings to start killing themselves off, instead of having to use his own people to do it. And as I told you, he's planning to start with you, using me as the trigger-man.'

Ryderbeit leaned back and squinted at the ceiling, the cords of muscle in his throat stretched taut under the gold chain and Star of David. 'Am I supposed to assume that I've been spared, soldier?' he said finally. 'That thou hast weighed me in the balance and found me not wanting?'

'You can assume what you like,' said Packer. 'I'm not going to kill you tomorrow, because I wasn't hired to kill you.'

Ryderbeit's eye rolled slowly round until it held Packer's with its dry glitter. 'That sounds a trifle too moral to me, soldier. And I've never trusted people with morals. They have a nasty habit of putting those first, and selling you up shit-creek if they don't agree with you.'

'Even if I had the morals of a Miami estate agent,' said Packer, 'I still don't have a gun.'

'Yeah.' Ryderbeit's fingers caressed the hard angle of his jaw. His eye was staring across at the red and white bags by the door. 'What happened to those guns, by the way? And why the funny swap for the skis?'

Packer shrugged. 'You know Pol better than I do. He likes to play games. There are some people, one hears, who get their kicks out of sending their friends beautifully wrapped parcels containing dogs' turds. Maybe it was the same with old Charles – it tickled his sense of humour to have me come back here to unwrap the guns in their ski bags, only to find they were skis all the time!'

'Pretty funny sense of humour.'

'Hilarious,' said Packer. Expensive, too, he thought; but it still didn't prove anything except, perhaps, that Pol was not really interested in money, only in its effect on others. A few thousand pounds frivolously expended on a spoilt little foreign girl he hardly knew, probably stimulated some hidden vanity in the man; in any case, it would hardly make much of a dent in his fee from the Ruler – however much that was.

Ryderbeit was looking at him with a seriousness that Packer had not seen before. 'Okay, soldier. I'll buy it so far – on approval. Only one thing doesn't figure. How the hell does Fat Man think you can shoot me on the Gotschnagrat tomorrow afternoon without a gun?'

Packer nodded. 'Yes, it's bothered me a bit, too. It could be an initiative test, of course – to see if I've got the wit and contacts to find myself a high-velocity rifle in a fashionable Swiss skiing resort, at about eighteen hours' notice. What do you think, Sammy?'

Ryderbeit peered into his empty glass. 'I'm thinking I'm still thirsty. You don't have anything more to drink up here, do you?'

'Only Sarah's perfume – if you like Guerlain's "Chamade".'

'Skip it. I'll get something down at the bar.'

'I'll get it,' said Packer. 'You've shown yourself enough round here.' He stood up. Ryderbeit tilted back the brim of his hat and leered at him.

'Sort of anxious, aren't you, boy – in case your Miss Sarah takes a shine to me, maybe?'

'Petrified.'

Ryderbeit raised his hand. 'Thanks, soldier. I'll switch back to Scotch – Johnnie Walker Black Label – if they've got it. And if you need any help with Sarah's boyfriend, just let me know.'

Packer went out and closed the door, checking that he had the key. Something moved at the end of the corridor, but when he looked there was no one there. It was a hotel, after all, and he didn't have exclusive rights. He was just being careful, like a man walking through snake country.

He went to the stairs.

Sarah was somewhere in the middle of the dance floor, looking as though she were performing a gymnastic exercise. It was impossible to see who was her partner.

Packer was in no hurry to signal his presence to her. He returned to the bar, where he was finally relieved of the equivalent of £8 in exchange for a bottle of Scotch of dubious pedigree.

As he came away, the music stopped and he found himself walking against the crush of dancers. He almost tripped over Sarah in the dark, striking her with the end of the whisky bottle which he was holding, unwrapped, like an Indian club. She gave a yelp, then saw him and sucked in her mouth in a theatrical pout. At the same moment a bald, youngish man with a soft-hard face and a pearl pin in his white neckerchief, stepped between them and said, 'Can't you damn well look where you're going?'

'It's all right, DJ, he's a friend of mine.' She smiled obliquely at each of them. 'Owen Packer – D'Arcy-James,' and she added a multi-barrelled name which Packer missed as the music started again. He glared at the man, then blinked. People were pushing into them from all sides; two men in dark suits were watching them from a table in an alcove. One of them was wearing dark glasses. Packer was vaguely aware that D'Arcy-James was waiting to have his hand shaken. His fingers were big and clammy. 'I'm sorry, I didn't realize' – he gave a hearty smile – 'such a damn awful crowd in here.'

'Terrible,' Packer murmured. Sarah was guiding them towards a table. He followed her as though he were walking in deep snow.

There were two other men at the table, and a girl in a head-scarf with the scraped features of a model. One of the men wore a dinner-jacket and they were all smiling. Packer felt very cold and stood with his back to the room, with that familiar prickly sensation along the nape of his neck.

D'Arcy-James began making the introductions, but Packer had difficulty concentrating. He found himself standing, still holding the whisky bottle, and muttering something about having to go. Sarah hissed below him: 'What's the matter with you? You're not drunk, are you?'

'I wish to God I were,' he said, and made a formal apology to D'Arcy-James, who interrupted, shouting above the music, 'We've asked Sarah over to a party tomorrow night in St Moritz. Hope you'll be able to come too!'

'Maybe,' said Packer coldly; and as he turned, saw Sarah sitting tightly on her chair, her face rigid with embarrassment. He leaned over her. 'I must see you, up in the room. It's urgent. In a quarter of an hour – no longer.'

'I'll see,' she said, in a small blank voice.

He nodded and repeated, 'A quarter of an hour!' in a harsh whisper, and left.

As he pushed his way across the floor he kept his eyes on the entrance, away from the tables along the wall; reached the narrow winding staircase, which he climbed two steps at a time; came to the lobby and began to run. By the time he reached the room his body was damp with sweat, yet he still felt cold. His hands shook as he rammed the key into the lock.

Ryderbeit was still stretched out on Sarah's bed, his eyes hidden under the brim of his huge hat. One of his eight-inch cigars now pointed at the ceiling, sending up a thin spiral of smoke. He seemed peaceful.

'You've been taking your time, haven't you, soldier?' He spoke without moving his head.

'Not any more! We're on our way, Sammy. Out of here – out of Klosters – out of Switzerland.'

The Rhodesian lazily pushed up his hat and took a long draw on the cigar. 'Little Sarah been giving you trouble, soldier?' As he spoke, he reached out and removed the bottle of whisky from Packer's hand, then lay contemplating the label with distaste. 'What sort of Swiss piss is this?'

Packer said, 'Ever seen a dead man come back to life? Not just an ordinary dead man, but one who's been melted down with white phosphorus, so that they've had to scrape him off the tarmac?'

Ryderbeit's good eye opened wider. 'You ain't by any chance been having a quick drink down there, have you? I mean, the tension hasn't been getting a bit too much for your tender nerves?'

Packer went on looking at him. 'He's downstairs in the bar, Sammy. He and another fellow – just sitting quietly watching the dancing.'

'*Who*'s sitting downstairs?' Ryderbeit roared, and unscrewed the cap of the bottle.

'Pierre-Baptiste Chamaz, last seen unconscious in a car in Berck-Plage. He'd been taking seaside snaps, remember?'

'You talked to him?'

'What for – to apologize?'

Ryderbeit tasted his whisky and scowled. 'How can you be so bloody sure? The lighting's pretty bad down there – and anyway, all wogs look the same.'

'All right, I admit he was also wearing dark glasses – probably to cover a black eye – but the side of his face was swollen, and he still has a badly cut lip. Besides, you always recognize a man you've beaten up – it's a form of intimacy, like sex.'

'Okay. So just supposing it is the same man – don't you think it pretty bloody funny of them to use him again on the same tail, once he's been rumbled?'

'No, it's logical – providing Chamaz is still the only person who can identify us together, or separately.'

Ryderbeit sat up slowly and took a long drink from the bottle. 'So you think they may be getting ready to put the finger on us? And in lovely neutral Switzerland too' – he shook his head – 'that's naughty of somebody, that is!'

'Sarah should be up in a few minutes,' said Packer, 'then we're getting out.' He was already throwing clothes into suitcases, taking a reckless pleasure in clearing the dressing-table with one sweep of his arm and loading Sarah's toilet equipment with a soggy crash into her Gucci grip-bag.

Ryderbeit did not move. 'Just one small thing, soldier. A little development while you were downstairs. It appears that the management made a slight boo-boo this afternoon – forgot to deliver another set of goodies.' He pointed his cigar towards the door. 'Somebody's spoiling you, soldier. Another couple of sets of beautiful brand-new skis – only this lot was delivered earlier, about five this afternoon. The day porter has had them downstairs in the back room until just now. Take a look.'

Another two bags were piled by the door, next to the Hartmann equipment. They were blue and white this time and marked 'Top-Ski'. Packer unzipped the first one and drew out a slim object, about three feet long, wrapped in olive-green oilcloth, buttoned up at both ends.

He tore them open and pulled out a length of smoky-brown plastic tubing with a narrow breech, box clip and skeleton stock. There was also a smaller, bulkier parcel inside the bag, in similar wrappings. It contained a stubby telescopic sight, studded with knobs like a musical instrument.

Packer rapidly snapped off the box clip and looked at the venomous, tapering grey plastic bullet in its gunmetal cartridge. He shook out all six, weighed them in his palm, then slipped them expertly back in. He now turned to the third package, which was about a foot square, covered in shiny black plastic, with two straps at the top and a zip underneath. Again – more from instinct than caution – he ran his fingers over every inch of its surface, even sniffed it, before undoing the straps and opening it.

The three Hitachi R/T sets, still in their styrofoam casings, looked pleasingly like small transistor radios.

'Beautiful, eh?' Ryderbeit was lying back, watching him with a placid smile.

Packer replaced the Armalite in its ski bag and turned, breathing slowly. 'Did the porter say who brought these over?'

'A very large gentleman,' Ryderbeit mimicked. 'A French gentleman with a beard. Satisfied?'

'No.' Packer reached the door, then turned. 'And throw in the rest of my packing, will you? You might even start on Sarah's wardrobe. Pretend they're for a jumble-sale.'

The corridor and the stairs again seemed empty. The night porter was alone. Packer asked him about the parcels which had been sent up to his room, and the man began hastily apologizing for the muddle, but Packer cut him short. 'The *first* parcels – the ones that were sent up earlier, while I was out – can you find out who brought them here?'

The man nodded. 'I will have to ask my colleague.' He went behind a desk and began to telephone, while Packer watched the tea-room and the stairs down to the bar. He looked at his watch. It was 9.50: just over ten minutes since he'd left Sarah.

The porter returned. 'Sir, I regret, I cannot be of great assistance. My colleague thinks the parcels were brought by a chauffeur. A man in uniform.'

'Was he Swiss?'

'I cannot be certain, sir, but my colleague thinks that he was a foreigner.' His eyes dropped and he looked embarrassed. 'Perhaps I should not mention it, sir, but my colleague says that he left a large tip.'

'In Swiss francs?'

'No, sir. American dollars. But my colleague does not think that he was American.' He gave a deprecating bow and began to turn away.

'Wait a minute,' Packer called. 'My friend upstairs was told that the second lot of parcels was brought this afternoon by a big Frenchman with a beard.' The porter nodded. 'Did he bring anything else, later on? A small box in brown paper? It was also sent up to my room this afternoon when I was out.'

The porter frowned, then looked up with a smile. 'Ah yes! There was another parcel – a small one, as you say – delivered this evening just after you had gone out. At about seven o'clock, I think.'

Packer moved closer. 'Can you remember who brought it?'

'Yes. It was a messenger from the Hotel Silvretta.'

'You have been very kind.' Packer turned back towards the stairs. The riddle of Pol's opulent farewell gift to Sarah was still not solved; but at least he now knew that the necklace and the unsolicited Hartmann skis were not connected. He took another look at the stairs down to the bar, then bounded back up to his room.

Ryderbeit had evidently been applying himself to his task with some zest. He had already emptied two drawers of Sarah's blouses and scarves and underclothes and stuffed them, like dirty laundry, into her smart, well-travelled suitcases; and was now ransacking the cupboard full of her dresses.

'Right!' Packer said, closing the door. 'Pol delivered the goods on time all right. And someone else, who sounds suspiciously like one of the Ruler's boys, delivered the first little present – the Hartmann skis – before I got back.'

For the moment Ryderbeit's unfamiliar assignment seemed to fill him with more enthusiasm than Packer's news; and Packer had an ugly thought. He went quickly to the dressing-table and checked the left-hand drawer. The case from Grima was still there and looked untouched. He took it out and slipped it down the side of his own suitcase. 'I'm just going to have another look at those skis, Sammy.'

This time he unzipped the Hartmann bags with the same caution that he had used when he had first opened the Grima case. He checked both pairs of skis, paying special attention to the patent safety bindings, but could find nothing abnormal. He then drew out the two pairs of sticks.

They were of the standard length, and about half an inch thick. The material was a shiny alloy whose main advantages were strength and lightness. Packer balanced one of them midway on the palm of his hand. He guessed it weighed at least five ounces, perhaps a little more. In any case, it was certainly not lighter than any other ski-sticks he had used. He also noticed that it was slightly heavier at the pointed end, even taking into account the circular snow guards.

Very steadily, carefully, he carried the stick on his outstretched hand across to his bed, opposite where Ryderbeit was gleefully screwing up an Yves St Laurent cocktail dress to the size of a grapefruit and punching it into the top of Packer's leather hold-all.

Packer sat down and fingered the tip of the stick. It was about two inches long, and did not seem to be welded into the alloy frame. He took the point between his finger and thumb and applied a very slight pressure upwards, into the stick. The point did not move, but he could sense that it was not firm. Once again he balanced the weight of the whole stick on his hand. Hartmann's hadn't won their world reputation like this. The thing was at least two ounces too heavy.

He now examined the handle. Above the red and white straps, the top of the stick was a concave knob. He felt it for weight and seemed satisfied. 'Sammy, I'm going downstairs for a moment. If Sarah comes up before I get back, watch out for her right foot – she has a nasty habit of kicking one on the shin if she's not happy.'

He went downstairs again, out into the freezing night, to the taxi rank near the darkened railway station. It took him five minutes' haggling, and a deposit of a 100-franc note, before he got what he wanted. He folded them under his jacket and returned to the hotel, where Ryderbeit had finished packing and had their luggage marshalled in an impressive row inside the door. The room looked surprisingly spartan and tidy. There was still no sign of Sarah.

Packer took out an oil-clogged monkey-wrench from inside his jacket, together with a length of wire and a pair of pliers; then sat down on the bed, with one of the ski-sticks across his knees, and took hold of the monkey-wrench. He looked at Ryderbeit and paused. 'Sammy, this may be a bit tricky. If you feel like going for a little walk, I won't hold it against you.'

'I'll stay.' Ryderbeit had stopped in the middle of the floor and was watching him, holding the open whisky bottle which was already a third empty. 'I trust you're not going to fuck up a perfectly decent ski-stick?'

Packer said nothing. Although the alloy was thin, it was very strong. His arm was aching by the time he saw the first crack in the metal. He screwed the jaws of the wrench tighter, until the top of the stick was almost flattened. His mouth was dry. The alloy was now beginning to split on both sides. He gave a final twist, and the handle cracked off just above the straps.

'You got a knife?' he asked Ryderbeit. 'Preferably with a short strong blade?'

Ryderbeit brought over a thick bone-handled scouting knife with half a dozen blades. 'I just hope the hell you know what you're doing, soldier.'

He watched as Packer selected a short wedge-shaped blade, prised it between the pinched, jagged ends of the stick, and slowly forced them open again. Packer looked inside but could see nothing, then, moving closer to the bedside light, he took the piece of wire and very gently inserted it into the alloy stem. After about three inches, it touched something: not hard, but not yielding either.

He took a deep breath and wished to God he could have some of Ryderbeit's whisky. This was the worst part, he knew; he began to press the wire in at a slight angle, levering it round with a gentle prodding motion. Then he tipped the whole stick up and poured a few crumbs of greyish substance into his hand. They looked like a mixture of putty and pâté de campagne.

Ryderbeit was now standing directly over him, drinking and watching. He saw the crumbled particles in Packer's hand and nodded solemnly. 'So they're being really serious, eh? Nothing crude like jelly or old dynamite – but our old friend, "la plastique". Must be a couple of years since I last saw that stuff. How have they set it, d'you think?'

'Well, it's certainly not a trembler, or we wouldn't be here now. And I doubt it's on a time fuse, because they'd hardly want the scandal of blowing us up in the hotel. In any case, they'd have no guarantee they'd get us together. No, my guess is that it's a simple percussion fuse' – Packer tapped the point of the stick – 'with this thing sliding in on a spring and setting off the detonator. But it's pretty firm, and it would take pressure to set it off. Like pushing oneself through heavy snow.'

'So the bastards were calculating that we couldn't resist using a pair of Hartmanns, and would blow ourselves up on the slopes? Nice and tidy, and not too many innocent casualties.'

'Well, at least we know the score.' Packer was carefully pouring the particles of explosive back into the stick, then picked up the pliers and squeezed the ends together again. He had just finished when the telephone rang. He grabbed it, but did not have time to answer. Sarah's voice came over clear and fast, with that familiar tone of apology masking wilful determination.

'. . . it's the most lovely chalet in Klosters, and this man Steiner has some beautiful early Italian furniture. And there should be lots of interesting people there . . .' Packer started to interrupt, but she cut through him like an actress. 'One thing – are you still with that frightful colonial – Sammy something? – because if you are you'll have to get rid of him.'

Packer yelled into the phone: 'We're not going to any lovely chalet, Sarah! We're checking out! – tonight – *now*! And don't argue. Your packing's all done. I'll meet you at the desk in three minutes.'

'Why? What's happened?'

'I can't explain on the phone. Just believe me – it's serious. Okay?'

'I suppose so,' she said doubtfully; then added, 'What on earth am I going to tell the others?'

'As little as possible,' Packer said, and hung up.

He finished parcelling up the two booby-trapped ski-sticks and piled them up with the rest of the luggage. 'You wait here,' he told Ryderbeit; 'I'm going down to settle the bill and get someone to bring our things down. Don't answer the telephone, or the door, except to the porter.'

Downstairs, while the cashier was making out the bill, Packer went outside and returned the monkey-wrench, wire and pliers, and retrieved his 100-franc deposit. He then fetched the Fiat and brought it up to the hotel entrance. He went inside in time to see the porter struggling down the stairs, laden with Sarah's cases and Packer's hold-all; while Ryderbeit followed with all four ski-bags, and the box of walkie-talkies under his arm. While he and the porter went outside to load the car, Packer stood at the top of the stairs down to the bar and looked furiously at his watch. If Sarah had decided to go with her friends to this chalet after all, he wondered how he could stop her. To try and force her away, in front of D'Arcy-James and the others, would not only be embarrassing, but would harden her will conclusively. The one card he still had to play was the Grima necklace; but he wanted to save that for a more propitious occasion.

She appeared quite suddenly beside him, unsmiling but serene. He was carrying her coat and scarlet beret, and helped her on with them.

'Now perhaps you'll tell me what this is all about,' she said, as they reached the door.

'Later,' he said, and hurried her into the back of the Fiat. Something about his manner must have convinced her that he was in earnest.

From the front passenger seat Ryderbeit grinned at her under the brim of his hat, but her expression remained neutral. Packer headed the car down towards the river, into the drab street where Ryderbeit was lodging. He let him out at the door of his pension and turned the car round. While they waited, Sarah sat well back in the corner, arrogant and aloof.

Ryderbeit was evidently as adept at his own packing as at other people's, and was inside less than ten minutes. For most of these, Sarah sat in silence smoking a Gitane. Finally she said, 'Owen, I don't understand what's going on, except that you're behaving very oddly. I just hope you haven't been drinking.'

'I have not been drinking. I'll tell you the whole story when we're out of here.'

Ryderbeit's tall shape appeared a few moments later, lugging an immense misshapen grip-bag of bandolier-like complexity, its brown leather stained and scarred, the whole thing bound up and bulging with straps and buckles and zipped-up pockets. He had some difficulty forcing it into the boot; and when he got back into the car he had the whisky bottle out again, now nearly empty, and offered it to Sarah. She refused it. Ryderbeit smiled and touched his fingertips to her cheek. 'Holy Moses! It's real!' he muttered, and she flinched away.

Ryderbeit cackled and drank from the bottle, while Packer drove back up into the town, heading for the road down to Landquart.

'We're not going to Davos?' Ryderbeit asked.

Packer shook his head. 'Too obvious.'

'Where, then?'

'Chur.'

'Chur! Nobody ever goes to Chur – it's the arsehole of the Alps.'

'That's just why we're going there,' said Packer.

Charles Pol had missed the last train to Landquart, with its connection to Zürich, and instead had had to hire a taxi. For one of the disadvantages of Swiss life, he had discovered, was that it is the only country in Europe where trains do not run at night.

It was after twelve when he arrived at Geneva's Cointrin Airport. In various pockets of his voluminous clothes he was carrying the total equivalent of US $800,000, in high denomination Swiss, French and German notes. He went to the MEA desk and found that the next flight to Beirut left at eight in the morning. He booked himself a first-class single ticket in the name of Monsieur Cassis, which corresponded to that in one of his passports.

His choice of destination was deliberate; for Pol recognized that the Ruler would not think at once of hunting down his quarry in his own back-yard. Besides, Pol had friends in Beirut – powerful friends among the old Franco-Arab fraternity who had no love for this arrogant despot, this self-deified Croesus who had suddenly flourished all-powerful close to their more humble borders. Let the Ruler make his own plans. Pol would make his.

He checked in at the Airport Hotel, and put in for a 6.00 a.m. call with a substantial breakfast.

9

The hotel in Chur was a cheerless establishment where a stout unsmiling woman took charge of their passports and made them pay in advance. Sarah complained that she had not yet eaten, but the kitchen was closed, and there was nothing but salami and cheese. Packer arranged to have some sent to their room.

They carried up their own luggage. While Ryderbeit had taken charge of the Armalites and the radios, Packer preferred to keep the 'plastique' Hartmann equipment in his own room. It was not that he exactly distrusted Ryderbeit; but he had a nasty image of the Rhodesian finishing the bottle of Scotch, then attempting to test Packer's theory about the percussion fuses.

Ryderbeit had been given a room next to theirs. Packer was anxious to be rid of him, and be alone with Sarah. To his relief Ryderbeit made no effort to inflict his presence.

'Goodnight, children! If you run out of ideas, or need any help, just wake me.' He waved a free hand, cast a lewd grin at Sarah, then disappeared into his room.

Sarah sat down on the double bed and waited until Packer had closed the door. 'All right,' she said at last. 'What's going on?'

'We're in trouble, angel.'

'Trouble?' She sounded half amused. 'You mean you're frightened of something, here – in Switzerland?'

'I didn't say I was frightened. I just don't want to get killed. And someone's trying to kill us – Sammy and me, that is.'

'You're mad.'

He shook his head. 'I wish I were.' He waited for her to light a cigarette, then went on: 'It began in Amsterdam – when we first met Charles Pol.' He kept his voice level, matter of fact, as at a military briefing; for this was one of those rare occasions when he had complete mastery over her.

He told the story in careful chronological order, leaving nothing out; and she listened with that maddening inertia that could so easily be mistaken for boredom. She listened without interrupting, chain-smoking. When he had finished she just nodded and said, 'What did you do with the sticks?'

'Over there' – he nodded at the pile of luggage in the corner.

'But aren't they dangerous?'

'Very. But not unless they're used.'

She was silent for a moment; then looked suddenly worried. 'But isn't it dangerous just having them here?'

He smiled. 'I could put a match to the stuff,' he said easily, 'and it wouldn't burn. I could throw it in a fire – bash it with a hammer – even eat it – and it'd still be quite harmless.'

'So how do you get it to go off?'

'It needs a detonator. As I said, that only goes off if you push in the points at the end – when you go skiing.'

'And that's what they hoped you'd do?' There was a faint note of panic in her voice now, which pleased him.

'Don't worry. We're in no danger here.'

'And if you don't go skiing, and don't get blown up, what then?'

'Then they'll no doubt try something else.'

She sat sucking the tip of her thumb. 'But do you really believe the Ruler's behind all this?' she asked finally. 'It sounds so fantastic, I mean, these people I was with tonight – those friends of DJ's – they've got friends who *know* him. He's a very civilized man.'

'I'm sure he is. He's even been to Buckingham Palace a few times.' There was another pause. He decided the time had come to frighten her.

'I told you there was that secret agent of the Ruler's down in the bar tonight,' he said slowly. 'The one who saw me and Sammy in France, and who was supposed to have been murdered. Well, he saw us together at Le Touquet – which might have been a casual weekend – but he saw us together again tonight. That's why he was sent to Klosters – to find out if Sammy and I had any accomplices.'

'What are we going to do, then?'

'We're going to kill the Ruler.'

'We?' Her mouth, usually so mobile, had gone slack.

'I want you to listen to me very carefully, Sarah.' And he explained to her how she was to ride up to the Gotschnagrat restaurant tomorrow afternoon, and be there at four o'clock when the Ruler arrived; and how she was to send a simple message over the R/T radio. 'That's all you have to do – just wait for him to leave the restaurant, and say a couple of words.'

'Very nice' – her voice had become quiet and sulky – 'for you and Sammy and Charles Pol. You've all been paid a lot of money.'

He went over and took her gently by the shoulders. Her body felt strangely frail. 'Sarah, love, if you do what I'm asking, I'll buy you that latest Porsche convertible, silver-grey with a black hood.'

She looked up at him with a funny crooked smile. 'You're bloody sure of yourself, aren't you, Owen?' Her voice gave him the uncomfortable feeling that she was holding something back. He decided now was the moment to produce his ace.

He went over to his hold-all and took out the Grima case, concealing it from her view as he walked back to the bed; then, with a little bow, he laid it on her lap. She opened it, lifted the tissue wrappings, and looked at the necklace as though it were some household utensil. She made no move to try it on. 'When did you get this?' she said at last.

'Does it matter?'

'The only branches Grima have outside London are in New York, Paris and Geneva. I suppose you sneaked off to Geneva while you were pretending to be skiing?' She replaced the tissue paper and snapped the box shut. 'And no message? No billet doux? You don't believe in treating a girl with much delicacy, do you, Mister Packer?' There was a chill in her voice now. 'Do you?' she repeated.

He stood in front of her, not moving, not speaking.

'You shit!' she yelled. 'You mean little shit!' She looked up at him with ferocious triumph. 'You never went to Geneva. But I did! I went the day before yesterday, with Charles Pol. We went into France and had lunch at Père Bise. And on the way back, through Geneva, he stopped at the Grima shop, and he made me wait in the taxi.' She threw her head back and laughed. 'And how are you going to worm your way out of this one? You should have stuck to the Porsche.'

Packer nodded and sat down on the corner of the bed, not looking at her. 'What were you doing with Charles Pol?'

She gave him a bright taunting smile. 'Enjoying myself. He brings out the little girl in me. And he's wonderful company.'

'And you spent the whole day with him just enjoying his wonderful company?'

She shrugged irritably. 'I was bored and glad of something to do.'

'And what did you do – talk? And what did you talk about, Sarah?'

'What do you mean?'

'Just what I said. You didn't just spend the whole day looking into each other's eyes and singing duets.'

She gave him a look of flagrant dislike. 'We talked about lots of things. I can't remember.'

'Try and remember.'

Suddenly she shook her head so that her hair dropped across her face, half hiding her eyes. 'Oh this is bloody silly! I go out for the day with a mutual friend and I have to remember every damned thing we talked about.'

'One of the things you talked about,' Packer said slowly, 'was the little matter of the radio message from the Gotschnagrat restaurant tomorrow afternoon.'

There was a long pause, broken by a rumble and cough from the plumbing. A truck changed gear outside in the street. Sarah sat with her shoulders hunched forward, again sucking the tip of her thumb.

'All right!' she cried at last. 'If you know, why do you bloody well ask?'

'What was the message he told you to send?'

She hesitated. 'Something in French. We thought it would sound better. Something like: "It's getting cold. I'm going home".' Her tone was again sulky and evasive.

'And how much is he paying you?'

'I don't think that's any of your business.' She had pulled her shoulders back and addressed him as though he were some insolent servant.

'Everything to do with this operation is my business,' he told her patiently. 'For a start, I want to make sure that Pol's not under-paying you.'

'Like buying me a Porsche, I suppose? Well, Owen Packer, I can tell you that Charles Pol is a lot more generous than that.'

'And has he paid you yet?'

'He's made the arrangements, thank you. And don't worry, they're quite satisfactory.'

Packer did not try to argue. As a banker's daughter she probably knew more about such affairs than he did; and whether she could trust Pol or not was her business, not his.

She yawned and started to take off her bracelets. 'I'm going to bed. We've got a lot to do tomorrow.'

'You're sure you still want to go through with it?'

'Why not? Don't you?'

'The situation's changed since the day before yesterday, Sarah. Pol's buggered off, for a start.'

'Well, there was nothing for him to do hanging around Klosters. I thought he was leaving all the planning to you?'

For a moment Packer wondered whether, deliberately or otherwise, she had misunderstood everything he had told her. The alternative was that Pol had already begun to draw her into his own secret plans for the future: what he called the 'other, subtler element'. But at this stage Packer decided that it would be too dangerous to question her further. He said, 'I mean, the situation with the Ruler has changed. He has cancelled the operation.'

'You're not taking orders from the Ruler. You're arranging things for Charles Pol.' She stood up and fetched her grip-bag. 'And as Pol agrees, if the Ruler wants us all killed, I suggest we get on with the job as quickly as possible. Oh bloody hell!' – she had opened her case, and now rounded on him, her face taut with fury – 'did you pack this?'

He shook his head. 'Sammy did. He's a mercenary, not a valet.'

She paused, then began quickly undressing. 'Goodnight, Captain Packer. I always knew you were an officer and a gentleman.'

It was 3.32 by her watch, which was two minutes ahead of the clock in the Gotschnagrat restaurant. They had stopped serving lunch half an hour earlier than usual, and the waiters were discreetly making out bills before they had been demanded. On the terrace the tables were empty, except for a few lizard-skinned sun-addicts sitting with their oiled faces tilted west, sopping up the last of the ultra-violet before the sun slid behind the peak of the Weissfluh.

Sarah was sitting on a bench about 200 yards above the restaurant building. The sky was clear and it was very cold. She wore a smart white windcheater above her black stretch-pants, a fur hat with ear-flaps turned down, and a pair of the largest dark glasses she had been able to find in town that morning. She realized, with some irony, that it was probably the first time in her life that she had ever wished to conceal her attractions.

She was also carrying her own Instamatic camera, which she occasionally pretended to use; and beside her on the bench was her Gucci handbag, containing her make-up, pill case, purse, a packet of Gitanes, a headscarf, and the Hitachi R/T set.

There had been only one awkward moment since she had arrived on the mountain half an hour ago. She had sat out on the terrace and ordered a salad and a vodka martini, when a stout young man with yellow hair, whom she had taken to be a German, had tried to talk to her. He had been unusually persistent, while her practised technique of defence and counter-attack had not been wholly successful, and she had had to change tables.

At 3.40 the cable car rumbled into the shed just below the restaurant. But no skiers appeared: instead, a column of bulkily dressed men dispersed among the terrace tables and were ignored by the waiters.

Two minutes later the cable car started down again. Sarah glanced around her. The slopes were very bright and bare, with hollows of dark shadow. She noticed that one of the men on the terrace was looking up at her, lifting a pair of binoculars as though inspecting the view.

She stretched back on the bench and pretended to doze.

Packer had a light lunch in Davos, bought yesterday's English newspapers, and a dozen postcards with stamps for abroad, then took the funicular railway, the Parsennbahn, up to the Weissfluhjoch, the last station below the Weissfluhgipel, the highest peak in the area.

The morning rush of skiers had cleared, and the sloping car

was half empty. He was able to lay the 'Top-Ski' bag on the seat beside him without attracting attention. He kept a constant but unobtrusive look-out for Chamaz, or his companion from the Chesa bar the night before, but he noticed neither of them.

By the time he reached the Weissfluhjoch he was fairly certain he was 'clean'. If his reckoning had so far been reasonably correct, the Ruler had set two traps for today and would be content to wait and see which sprang first: either Packer acted on Pol's instructions and shot Ryderbeit, or Packer and the Rhodesian blew themselves to pieces with the Hartmann sticks. (But both sets of skis, with the deadly sticks, were now safely deposited in the left-luggage office at the railway station, and the ticket had been burned.)

Packer's nerves were calm; and it was more in a mood of resigned anticipation, rather than anxiety, that he stepped into the diamond-white glare outside the Weissfluhjoch station.

There was a hut with a bar and cafeteria, and a few benches out in the sun. It was perfect skiing weather, and the slopes were sprinkled with streaking zigzagging figures. Packer was leaving himself plenty of time. He was already more than thirty minutes ahead of schedule. He drank a couple of cups of black coffee, then went out and began to write postcards on one of the benches.

The day had so far been uneventful, except for an orchestrated tantrum by Sarah on discovering the condition of the rest of her clothes – an offence which she prepared to attribute to him rather than to Ryderbeit. Her fury had lasted the whole journey back to Klosters, where they had dropped her at the Hotel Vereina, a safe distance from the Chesa.

It was only after they had left her that Packer remembered to check that the radios, still in their pristine packings, had batteries. But however scared Pol might have been the night before, he was not a man to neglect details.

With fifteen minutes still to spare, Packer had a last coffee, fitted the 'Top-Ski' bag to the straps under his rucksack, which contained his binoculars, chocolate, and an extra sweater; clipped on his real skis and set off at a careful pace down the two miles of fairly gentle run to the Parsenn Hut.

Here he had eight minutes in hand. As usual, the hut was crowded with boisterous groups of skiers taking a late lunch and drinking on the terrace. Without unstrapping the 'Top-Skis', he sauntered between the tables, giving himself plenty of time to pick out any of the Ruler's henchmen. Again he saw no one suspicious. By the time he was outside again, he had four minutes in hand. Eighteen minutes to go.

He fitted his skis back on and started off down the last lap towards the Mähderlift.

Ryderbeit had ridden up on the Parsennbahn an hour before Packer, while the funicular was still busy, on the loose assumption that his appearance would be less conspicuous in a crowd. He was again wearing his blue pixie cap, but on Packer's orders he had discarded his combat tunic for a quilted blue anorak, and he was to wear his goggles at all times. Packer knew that it would be useless to forbid him to drink.

When they had parted, in the main street of Davos, Ryderbeit had been oddly silent. Packer was not surprised : Pol had ordered him to kill Ryderbeit, so that while Packer had assured the Rhodesian once again that this was not part of his contract, Ryderbeit's experience of life had not left him with a trusting disposition.

At the Weissfluhjoch station he had fortified himself with a couple of large Steinhaegers, chased down with a mug of beer; then joined the queue for the short steep Gipfelbahn to the summit of the Weissfluh. Like Packer he was leaving himself plenty of time, ostensibly in case of hold-ups, but in fact to allow himself decent pauses in which to refresh himself. For unlike Packer, Ryderbeit drew a natural satisfaction from taking risks, both calculated and fortuitous – a satisfaction which increased in proportion to the perils involved.

Another of Packer's strictures upon him that morning was that he must, under all circumstances, avoid creating a scene. At the Gipfel Hut the first thing Ryderbeit did was to come close to a fight with two beefy young men, one of whom he accused of taking his chair while he was having a pee. They spoke French, but Ryderbeit recognized their accent as Belgian, and said something to them in a patois he had picked up in the Congo, which made them flinch, then slink away. But they would remember him.

In the hut he consumed three more Steinhaegers and three more beers, until he had left himself less than eight minutes to cover the five miles to his position on that treacherous bend overlooking the T-bar.

The first leg was an easy run. The snow was excellent and Ryderbeit used his skills to the full. He was the kind of skier who is hated both by professionals and amateurs. He broke every rule of the slopes: racing up behind slower skiers and swerving past them without warning, cutting across them on bends and using his sticks as menacing weapons when someone either failed to notice him or move out of his way in time.

Just above the Parsenn Hut he rounded a bend and came up behind a girl who was wobbling precariously. He made no attempt to slow down, merely swerved a fraction to the side and passed so close to her that his stick caught her a neat cut across her hips and his nearside ski came within an inch of slicing into her ankle. He heard her yelp, and with a glance back, saw her tumble into a crooked sprawl. He grinned and raced on down towards the hut. The thought that she would remember him, too, did not worry him.

At the hut he had to waste two valuable minutes taking off his skis and walking across the flat snow to the head of the Gruobenalp run, where he could calculate on reaching speeds of up to sixty miles an hour. But here again, like a gambler on a winning streak, he could not resist the compulsion to take unnecessary risks.

The run was relatively clear, and his speed soon brought an exhilaration that blinded him to thought. He was 200 yards past the bend before he realized. He pulled up with a Christie that almost threw him on his back; then looked at his watch. He had less than a minute to go. Without panic, he took off his skis and started back up the icy glistening piste, keeping to the soft shoulder where the snow gave him more grip, and where he was less likely to meet skiers coming down.

He reached the bend overlooking the T-bar exactly thirty-two seconds behind schedule.

At exactly 3.49 by her watch, Sarah heard the rumble of the

cable car, then a pause as it bumped along the ramp inside the shed below the Gotschnagrat restaurant. At the same moment, from behind her, came a loud clattering noise that reminded her of a London taxi. She looked up and saw the long shadow of a helicopter rippling across the snow above her. The side door of the cockpit was open and a man was leaning forward, scanning the ground through binoculars.

When she looked away she saw one of the men from the terrace tables below walking up towards her. She had prepared herself for this, and picked up her camera. Her movements were unhurried, although her hands had begun to shake inside their fur mittens, as she went through the motions of winding the film. She peered through the viewfinder just as the man reached her.

He was thin and high-shouldered, with deep eyes in a dry, grainy, ageless face. He stopped a few feet in front of her and smiled with a mouthful of metal teeth. 'Excuse me, mademoiselle, I regret to intrude' – he spoke French with a strong accent – 'but I am obliged to supervise all strangers during the presence of His Imperial Highness.' He gave a short bow.

The effect of her smile was muted by her dark glasses, but it was enough to make the man lower his eyes. Behind and below him, Sarah saw a group of about half a dozen men walking up from the cable car hut to the restaurant.

'I hope I am permitted to take a photograph of His Majesty?' she replied, in her immaculate finishing-school French.

The man gave another bow. 'Of course it is permitted. His Imperial Highness has absolutely no desire to interfere with visitors here. But unfortunately' – his eyes flickered sideways to the Gucci bag on the bench beside her – 'His Imperial Highness is a very important man, and mademoiselle will appreciate that certain precautions must be taken to ensure his safety.' He held out his hand. 'May I look inside your bag, mademoiselle?'

'Certainly.' She opened it and held it out to him. He stepped forward and took it, and with the discreet efficiency of an experienced Customs official, he ran his hands swiftly through the contents and lifted out the Hitachi R/T set.

'This is your radio, yes?' He stood looking down at her with a professional stare. She gave a sharp laugh which sounded very loud in the Alpine stillness. The helicopter had moved away, and she could hear the clink of glasses on the terrace.

'You do not think I stole it, do you?'

The man's face stiffened at the sarcasm; he looked down at the tiny radio in her hand. 'It is very small for a radio,' he said. 'I have never seen one so small before.'

'No – my fiancé bought it for me in Hong Kong. They are the very latest models. I have never seen one like it before either.' As she spoke, she reached out for the bag.

The man hesitated for perhaps three seconds; then, with a delicate, almost feminine movement, he replaced the radio in the bag and handed it back to her, again with his little bow. 'Merci, mademoiselle. Bonne journée.'

He turned, and Sarah noticed a movement among the terrace tables. The Imperial party had disappeared inside the restaurant, and she guessed that the few remaining guests were also being supervised. The man was crunching down the slope, when she called after him, 'How do I recognize His Majesty?'

The man turned and looked back at her. 'You have never seen photographs of him?'

She smiled innocently. 'Oh, I know what he looks like. But how do I recognize him when he goes skiing?'

He paused, then took a step back towards her. She realized her mistake even before he had begun speaking. 'With your permission, mademoiselle, I will indicate His Imperial Highness as soon as he appears.'

She watched helplessly as he came back towards her.

'You will permit me to sit down, mademoiselle?'

It took Packer one minute and forty seconds, from the moment he unstrapped the 'Top-Ski' bag until he had the sights screwed into the stock of the Armalite and the sling adjusted to a snug comfortable fit. The last thing he did was clip the glare shield on to the sight and test it against the slanting sun; then he propped the gun against a pine tree, hidden from the piste.

He leaned against the tree, with the radio tucked into the side pocket of his anorak, its short aerial pulled out, the receiver button pushed down. His watch – synchronized with Ryderbeit's and Sarah's before they parted – showed a few seconds after 3.59.

He waited for a couple of skiers to pass, then swept his binoculars across the horizon. The T-bar was empty, the wooden hoists swinging slightly in the wind as they climbed over the slope.

He turned the binoculars down, to the bend which Ryderbeit had chosen for himself, beyond a ridge of snow and a deep gully. Ryderbeit was not there. Packer knew that the man was no coward, but in the tangle of mistrust, treachery and expedience which had ensnared them since Packer's meeting with Pol the night before, Ryderbeit might well have decided to take his £25,000 and run for it.

Packer did not recognize him at first. He had been watching the ski run above the bend, when he happened to move the binoculars down slightly and saw the lean loping figure carrying his skis on his shoulder, moving up through the soft snow below the bend. Every now and again he broke into a run, his arms spread for balance, scrabbling his way up the last slope, as the second hand on Packer's watch crept round to 4.00.

'You are here alone?' the man said. He had dropped the 'mademoiselle', and his voice had a nudging intimacy which repelled her. It also frightened her. Her eyes, hidden behind the dark glasses, kept glancing down for some movement from the restaurant. She was surprised that the Ruler preferred to delay indoors, rather than out on the terrace. Was he afraid of being so exposed? Or maybe he was just bored with the sun?

She said, with cold politeness, 'I prefer to be alone. That is why I came up here.'

'You told me you came up to photograph His Imperial Highness,' the men replied, and she felt his sleeve touch hers. She shivered.

'Yes, if I have the chance. It's not important.'

In the silence that followed, she shifted slightly away from him, but still felt the subtle pressure of his arm against hers. 'When I asked if you were alone,' he said, 'I intended to enquire whether you were alone in Klosters. But that is a foolish question, n'est-ce pas? For such a pretty girl to be alone in a place like this would be impossible! Ah, but I forgot – you have a fiancé, of course. He gave you that radio.' He looked pointedly down at the Gucci bag which she had gathered on to her knee.

This time she shifted a deliberate six inches away from him. 'Monsieur, my fiancé does not like me talking to strangers.'

The man's face cracked into a metallic grin. 'I think your fiancé is very strict,' he said, his voice rising as the helicopter returned. At the same time Sarah saw a group of six men emerging from the door of the restaurant. Two more followed, carrying bundles of skis.

She said briskly, 'Which one is His Majesty?'

The man beside her looked down and saw the Royal party for the first time. They were already fitting on their skis. 'He is the one in the middle, wearing the red and blue jacket.'

She saw a slim erect figure with grey hair and black goggles. Beside him was a blond man in a bright yellow anorak. They dug in their sticks and pushed off together across the flat snow, slightly ahead of the others.

Sarah had already snapped her camera several times, at random, her mind working frenetically, fighting down the panic. She was only half aware of the man talking to her against the ear-shattering roar of the helicopter, which was now making a low sweep over the restaurant. She saw the Ruler and his party reach the end of the flat stretch, and, with a thrust of their sticks, begin to move down the shallow 400-metre run towards the foot of the T-bar.

She turned to the man beside her and shouted above the noise, 'Please, I told you, I want to be alone!'

He replied with a smile and did not move. In desperation she opened the bag on her lap and, pretending to fumble for some make-up, she pushed the transmitting button on the R/T set. Then she remembered the aerial. She pulled it out to its full eighteen inches, and at the same moment, with her index finger, snapped on to 'Receive'. There was a crackle of static, just audible above the helicopter, which was tacking away down the valley. The Royal party disappeared over the ridge of snow.

She turned to the man and said irritably, 'It's no good – it's the mountains. I can't get anything' – and with a deft two-finger movement she switched the set back on to 'Transmit'. *It's getting cold,* she added, *'I'm going home.'* She switched the radio off, pushed down the aerial, closed the bag and stood up. 'Thank you, monsieur. Au revoir.' She began walking at a brisk but unhurried pace down towards the cable car hut; and she knew by his shadow that he was following her. He caught up with her when they were a few yards from the restaurant.

'Mademoiselle, perhaps you would allow me the honour of offering you a little refreshment before you leave?'

'Thank you, I must go,' she replied, quickening her pace round the foot of the terrace, where two men in long overcoats stood watching her with a weary indifference.

It was only when she was inside the hut that she found she was at last alone. The little platform was deserted, vibrating with the high-pitched hum of the cable running over the enormous traction wheel.

Then she realized how cold she was. She looked up anxiously for the red light to come on above the door into the attendant's office. Below, the cables hung empty as far as the first stanchion, then dropped out of sight. At any moment she expected her solicitous companion to reappear, and perhaps ask to take a closer look at the radio. She considered for a moment trying to hide it somewhere – burying it out in the snow – but reasoned that if he did come, and she no longer had it, his suspicions would be confirmed.

A bell had begun ringing. The red light came on. The uniformed attendant appeared and asked to see her ticket. Below, the car had just appeared over the ridge. It seemed to come on very slowly, crept up into the hut, finally stopped. The attendant slid the door open for her. Inside she was still alone. She stumbled to the front of the car and sat down on one of the flap-seats and began to shake. She opened her bag, swallowed a couple of Valium, and exchanged her fur hat for the headscarf.

The car began to move. As it lurched over the stanchion and dropped down above the sheer wall of the Wang, she leaned her forehead against the icy window and thought she was going to be sick.

Ryderbeit scrambled backwards up the icy slope, using his sticks and heels for leverage. The position he finally selected left him standing almost vertically, his weight balanced precariously against the ice. It was not a good position for any activity, let alone shooting a high-velocity rifle accurately at 800 metres' range.

He had unstrapped his 'Top-Ski' bag, and tested the telescopic sights. The T-bar came clearly into focus, through a faint bluish light behind the hair-line cross. There was surprisingly little haze or shimmer, and no glare through the shield.

He glanced back up the mountain, to the tree line, and tried to calculate where Packer was waiting. Holy Moses! he thought, if that bastard tries anything! He didn't think Packer was likely to shoot a colleague in the back; but then he was reckoning without that fat ogre, Pol, and his insidious influence.

4.02 p.m., and the radio in his pocket was still silent. Had that smart little bitch up on the Gotschnagrat 'snafued'? Pushed the wrong button, or maybe just changed her mind? Packer had said she was a great one for that.

Ryderbeit lifted the telescopic lens again and focused the cross of the hair-line on one of the empty bars. As it swung out of sight, the radio crackled in his pocket and a faint metallic voice, almost sexless, said, 'Il devient froid – je rentre chez moi.' Then silence.

Three skiers passed in close formation. Hell, he thought, if one of them happens to come by at the crucial moment. Well, he'd made provision for that: he'd shoot the sod and leave the Swiss Police to sort that one out too.

He looked at his watch. They had reckoned on three clear minutes from the moment the call signal went out. When the second hand registered two minutes and thirty seconds, Ryderbeit lifted the Armalite and took aim.

He had removed his gloves and his hands were beginning to feel the cold. He stood braced back against the ice, the cross of the hair-line sights trained on the exact point where the T-bar came into view.

At 4.05 a helicopter approached from the direction of the Gotschnagrat. It didn't worry him at first, except that its noise threatened to drown the sound of any approaching skiers. He brought his eye up from the sights and watched it hovering above the T-bar; he guessed that the Royal party must have arrived.

Another two long minutes passed. His fingers were numb and his arms ached. Get on with it, Your Imperial Fucking Highness. Perhaps the bastard had broken a binding, or twisted his ankle coming down from the restaurant.

Come on! Get your Serene bum under that bar and *move!*
Ryderbeit was not a man given to panic, but he hated waiting.

There was a bad moment when a sudden gust of wind swept
against the mountain, sending up a flurry of powdered snow. As
it cleared, two men bobbed into the sights, riding abreast on the
T-bar. Then another two. All identical, in dark skiing clothes
and matching caps, like uniforms. A third pair slid into the
circular frame. The one on the right was a blond man in a yellow
jacket. On his left, a man with grey hair, in a red, white and blue
anorak and black goggles.

Holy Moses, they're making it easy, he thought.

He kept them in the sights for just under two seconds, following the man on the left until the hair-line cross held steadily to a
point in the centre of his grey hair, exactly level with the goggles.
Then he squeezed the trigger.

The recoil jerked the sights up, and in the ice-cold stillness the
explosion was as sharp as a whip crack, followed by a series of
rapid shattering echoes which seemed to grow louder and louder.

Even through the noise, he heard the second shot, above and
behind him, followed by more echoes. He was still following the
two bare-headed men on the T-bar, who were now gliding, or
rather slithering, like a couple of drunks, with only the impetus
of the bar under their buttocks keeping them upright. The blond
man seemed oddly misshapen, shrunk and lopsided, and Ryderbeit saw something yellow lying in the snow behind him.

The man on the left was lolling forward, and his grey head
had become dark and jagged – not a head at all, but two cliffs of
cheek-bone sagging backwards from the neck – while his
anorak, through the bluish lens, was turning the same dark
colour as his head. Then both figures toppled sideways, crump-
ling up in the snow with their skis sprawled out behind them. At
the same moment the two men riding on the bar behind leaped
forward, unclipped their skis, and began to run up the track.
Neither of the men on the ground moved.

The helicopter had reappeared, dipping its tail and dropping
down over the T-bar, the noise of its engine muffled by the
double echoes of the shots that were still bouncing down the

valley. Ryderbeit had unslung the Armalite, snapped off the telescopic sights, and was reaching for the empty 'Top-Ski' bag when he became aware of another sound. A deeper, heavier sound, like the first thunder of a storm.

The mountains distorted its direction, but as it grew louder he guessed that it came from high above, rising and spreading with a rumbling growl, until the echoes of the shots and the sound of the helicopter were shut out altogether. He had just zipped up the ski bag when he felt, even through his thick boots with their plastic mouldings, a faint tremor. A couple of skiers flashed round the bend and one of them saw him and yelled something, waving upwards with his stick.

Ryderbeit had no time to follow Packer's instructions and bury the ski bag and the radio in the soft snow. Instead, he dropped them where he stood, grabbed his own sticks and skis, and scrambled down the slope. The snow at the bottom was trembling; and the noise from above was now a steady roar like the sound of a heavy sea. As he rammed his boots into the ski bindings, he glanced upwards. Beyond the steep ridge above him, the deep blue of the sky was turning pale, smudged with white clouds that were growing thicker as he watched, swelling out into great cauliflower formations whose edges caught the sun with brilliant colours.

His excitement smothered all fear. He knew he was now going to have to ski as he had never skied before, or perhaps ever again. With a powerful thrust of his sticks he started down the run. The first few hundred yards allowed him only moderate speeds but they also gave him time to think. The whole run was now vibrating, as though he were skiing over corrugated iron, and the roar from above was growing louder, and seemed to be spreading.

He came to a ridge over a long steep slope where there were two pistes – one that zigzagged down, and a second one, with fewer tracks, which descended vertically. Ryderbeit braced his knees and his skis leapt over the edge, and he felt the freezing blast of air scooping back his cheeks as he leaned forward, knees flexed, his sticks pressed back against his thighs to cut down the wind resistance.

Ahead lay a line of trees; and through the yellow light of his goggles, his one eye glimpsed, as though looking at a film in slow motion, the stems of the huge pines snapping off at the roots and tumbling down under the bubbling channel of snow which carried behind it a long white cloud.

The piste turned left before the trees, and he was now skiing parallel, and only about fifty feet away from the avalanche. He reckoned his speed at between fifty and sixty miles an hour; but the snow was moving faster, and also beginning to spread. Behind him the whole mountain was smothered in white cloud.

A second stream of snow had reached the top of the ridge that he had just crossed, and now came pouring over the side like milk boiling over in a saucepan. Ryderbeit saw that if he followed the piste he would be cut off and buried within a few seconds.

He turned left and decided to risk the soft snow. With his skis pressed together and his body balanced forward as far as the bindings would permit, he was still able to maintain a high speed. The danger now lay in hidden rocks. After the heavy snow earlier in the season, these would be well hidden; and apart from the occasional mound and undulation he would have to rely on instinct and luck – two elements in which he had an enduring faith.

Below, beyond another ridge, he could see the dark pool of more woods – thicker this time, just above Wolfgang. The run from here down to the village became gentler, but whether it would slow the avalanche depended on how much impetus it was drawing from the snow above. His only hope was that the trees would help to break it up. He risked a glance behind him and saw the snow crawling down the slope like a great white hand, the fingers outstretched and reaching down towards him, the nearest one less than 200 feet behind him, and coming closer. He guessed that the snow must be travelling at nearly eighty miles an hour.

He thought of throwing away his sticks, not only to break resistance, but to make him more free to manoeuvre; but he remembered having heard that if one got caught and buried in an avalanche, there were only two things to do : get your skis off and roll into a ball, before you were torn limb from limb, then try to push your sticks up through the surface so that the search parties could find you.

But Ryderbeit already saw his chances narrowing. Another

glance behind showed him the approaching hand was beginning to bunch into a fist, with huge boulders for knuckles. This part of the avalanche seemed to be slowing, but the outer fingers were still racing ahead, until the one on the right, which was taking a direct course down the mountain towards Wolfgang, had overtaken him.

A few seconds later he was cut off from the last stretch of the normal run down to the village. He saw a solitary skier below him make a desperate effort to escape into the deep snow. The tip of the finger reached him, and the figure with its skis and sticks whirled like a catherine wheel and was gone.

And now Ryderbeit noticed something else – something that seemed contrary to the laws of nature. So far the avalanche had been flowing like cascading water, its path following that of least resistance, in search of its own level. Suddenly, a few hundred feet from the trees above Wolfgang, one of the outlying fingers which had already overtaken him took a sharp turn and exploded in a burst of powdered snow, then continued at a much slower pace towards the woods. The first trees had already been crushed, and the ones behind were bent backwards like the bristles of a brush; but they did not break. The snow spread out with the consistency of clotted cream, rising in places to the tops of the pines. But the main impetus of the avalanche had been halted.

Ryderbeit now changed direction and headed for the woods, through a trough of deep snow where the tips of his skis sank several inches below the crusty surface. The noise above was beginning to subside and the air was now full of the clatter of helicopters.

He hit the piste about fifty feet beyond the wall of tumbled snow and rocks where the avalanche had finally spent itself against the trees. Two minutes later he was in Wolfgang.

The road in front of the Kulm Hotel was blocked by cars and crowds, with more cars crawling up the road from Klosters, followed by the ugly panting of sirens. As Ryderbeit kicked off his skis, he was surrounded by people asking what had happened. He forced his way through, without answering, and made for the tiny railway station. It seemed to be the only spot that was deserted. At the same time he noticed that there were no cars coming down from Davos.

He turned and headed for the hotel, where he struggled through the crowded lobby and was told what he had already suspected : both the road and railway from Davos to Klosters were blocked.

He left his skis and sticks in the rack outside the hotel, where they would probably remain for days without being noticed; lit a cigar, and began to run, at a clumsy jog-trot in his heavy boots, down the road towards Klosters. With luck he could be in the Vereina Hotel in twenty minutes; but he had no chance of making the 4.30 train to Landquart, for the connecting express to Zürich.

Packer had heard the avalanche as he was about to bury his gun and radio behind the tree. It took him several seconds to realize what was happening. His first reaction was irritation at seeing that his own shot – the second one – had missed the Ruler and hit his partner on the T-bar.

Then he heard the noise : and for a moment just stood and watched the progress of the avalanche with a peculiar detachment. It was only later that he came to appreciate the special advantages of the disaster.

The mainstream of the snow passed well below him; and he knew, with the same detachment, that Sammy Ryderbeit would be dead within a few seconds. The thought neither shocked nor saddened him, any more than he had liked or disliked Ryderbeit. The Rhodesian had served his purpose, and now they were rid of him. Packer even felt a dishonourable sense of relief; for once the deed was done, Ryderbeit would always have been a liability. Even if he had disappeared, sooner or later he would have managed to commit some indiscretion or outrage, and so keep the trail alight.

Packer waited until the full force of the avalanche had passed and saw, far above, the great slabs of naked mountainside – a patchwork of black rock and dead brown grass – like a cake with the icing scraped off. Then he put on his skis and began the four-mile run down the Schwartzalp to Klosters. He had just time to see, across the three ridges of snow, the helicopter settle beside the T-bar where a group of men had crowded round the bodies like ants round two scraps of meat.

A quarter of an hour later he reached the edge of the town;

it was jammed with traffic which had been pushed on to the side of the road to make way for the ambulances, police cars and rescue teams. It took him another ten minutes on foot, carrying his skis, to reach the station where he had left the Fiat; and another five to edge the car up through the crowded streets to the Vereina Hotel.

The lobby, lounge and bar were packed and full of static tension – people standing, waiting, shouting questions without getting answers. Packer left his skis at the door, and on his way through to the bar heard voices claiming that ten people had been killed – thirty – fifty – Wolfgang was cut off – half the village had been buried – had been wiped out altogether. A large German with an orange moustache was announcing, with grave relish, that a Swiss police officer had just informed him that at least 200 were dead.

Packer found Sarah sitting by herself on the far stool of the bar. She was still wearing her dark glasses and headscarf, and was staring at the bottles behind the counter, both hands round a glass of thick brown liquid that looked like soup.

She saw him in the mirror, and did not even turn as he slipped on to the stool beside hers. He leaned forward to kiss her, but she jerked her head sideways so that his lips brushed her ear.

'What happened?' she asked. 'Apart from bringing the whole mountain down?'

'He's dead.'

'You're sure?'

'Well, even through telescopic sights I could see that his head ended at his lower teeth –'

Her hand flew to her mouth. 'Please! Do you have to go into such horrible detail? You know that sort of thing makes me sick.'

'You had something to do with it,' he reminded her. She said nothing, but gulped her drink.

Packer paused. 'Ryderbeit's dead too,' he said slowly.

'What?'

'The avalanche. He was right underneath it.'

'Did you see him die?'

'It was too far away. But nobody could have got out of that. He was a good skier – wonderful balance and plenty of guts – but to outrun an avalanche you have to be in the Olympic class.

And bloody lucky.' He shook his head. 'I'm afraid skiing on Kilimanjaro and in the Lebanon just isn't the same thing. And his luck gave out too.' He shrugged. 'Poor Sammy.'

Sarah made no comment. Packer leaned on the bar, his forehead on his hands. He felt sick with exhaustion. Out of the din of voices he heard the big German yelling, in ugly English, 'There was shootings on the mountain! Some bloody Swiss Army fool bringing down an avalanche on the Weissfluh – then *wham* ! – both sides of the mountain come down!' 'It was probably those damn choppers,' an American voice called. 'They've been flying far too low – protecting that goddamn emperor up in the big chalet. Something like this was bound to happen.' 'I tell you, this whole bloody business is the fault of that damned emperor fellow,' the German declared loudly.

Sarah finished her drink and asked for another. Packer lifted his head and peered at her. Her expression behind the dark glasses was stiff and pale.

'And you?' he said. 'It went all right?'

'Easy as pie,' she answered; but there was a nervous edge to her voice.

'No hitches?' he said gently.

'Oh, just some creep who came up and searched my bag, then tried to pick me up.'

'Did he find the radio?'

She gave a brittle laugh. 'The fool thought it was a transistor. I sent the message while he was watching.'

'Christ,' Packer breathed; then smiled. 'You're a brave girl, Sarah.'

'Thank you.' The barman put down another glass of brown liquid in front of her. Packer nodded at it. 'What's that?'

'A "bull shot". Vodka and consommé. Don't you remember, I used to drink it in the Ritz at lunchtime? When we first met, while I was going through my wild phase.'

He looked at her wearily. 'It seems a long time ago. Come to think of it, I suppose it was. You used to say you were in love with me.'

She laughed. 'Only after I'd had a few drinks.' She lifted the glass and took a swallow worthy of Sammy Ryderbeit. Then she sat very still, staring straight ahead.

Packer said at last, 'We ought to go. The road down to Landquart will be full of ambulances and relief teams, and it's going to be a slow drive. We must try to make it before they start setting up road-blocks.'

'Owen – I'm not going.'

'You're what?'

'I'm not going with you.'

He blinked and licked his lips. 'What the hell are you saying?'

'I'm staying here.'

'To do what?' he asked, gaping at her.

'I'm going to that party in St Moritz tonight. Don't you remember – the one we were invited to last night in the Chesa when you walked out on me?'

He sat up and rounded on her. 'Don't be a bloody little fool! The Ruler's been assassinated and you were in on it. You were seen with me last night by that agent, Chamaz. And that's just for starters.'

'Yes, I've been thinking about that,' she replied, with exasperating coolness. 'He also saw me with DJ and Jocelyn and Serena Knox-Partington – and Jo's head of one of the biggest electrical firms in Britain. You think they'll try and bump him off too?'

Packer had closed his eyes. 'One of the Ruler's men also saw you up at the Gotschnagrat,' he said feebly.

'He'll never recognize me – not the way I was dressed.'

'What did you do with the radio?'

'Don't worry, nobody'll find it until the snow melts.'

'Did you leave any finger-prints?' he asked desperately, playing for time now.

'Don't be silly. You don't think I'd go up the mountain without gloves, do you?' She signalled for the bill. Packer made a belated attempt to intervene, but she had already got her purse out. It seemed a depressingly final gesture.

'When are you coming back to London?'

'I don't know.' She slid off her stool and stood facing him, their eyes level. 'I'm sorry, Owen, but it's all over. I can't explain properly – and anyway, you've got to go. It's too dangerous for us to stay together. And that business with the necklace last night, well' – her voice filled with sudden righteousness – 'that's just something I can't forget. I'm sorry. But there it is. Now, can you give me a lift – just down to the town? I can't walk,' she added, 'because you've got all my cases in the car, remember?'

She stood beside him, waiting. Packer could think of nothing to say: nothing sensible nor dramatic, not even outraged pleading came to his lips. He sat staring at the pool of melted snow that had spread out under his boots on the floor.

'Come on,' she said.

He followed her dumbly, through the crowds, into the street outside which lay in the shadow of the mountain, filled with a macabre carnival air, its music a cacophony of sirens and motorhorns. He unlocked the car and they got in. 'Well, where to?'

'The Chesa. I've got to meet DJ there in half an hour.' She paused as he started the engine. 'Don't try to come in. It won't do any good.'

He did an angry three-point turn, oblivious of the crowds. 'You're going to have one hell of a time getting to St Moritz,' he said at last; 'if you get there at all.'

'That's all right. Jo Knox-Partington's got a private helicopter laid on.'

'You think you'll get air clearance with all this going on? They've got half the Swiss Air Force up there at the moment.' He was driving on his brakes, his hand on the horn, weaving and jolting through the crowds.

'Oh well, if we don't,' Sarah said lightly, 'we'll just have to go by car. It won't matter getting there late – it's an all-night party.' They had reached the main street where there was an almost unbroken convoy of traffic moving in the direction of the Wolfgang–Davos road. 'I'm sorry about Sammy,' she added. 'But he wasn't really much of a friend of yours, was he? Still, it was a horrible thing to happen.'

Packer said nothing. He shot forward into a gap between two cars, and pulled up outside the Chesa Grishuna Hotel; got out, unlocked the boot, and after pushing Ryderbeit's gigantic bag to one side, lifted out Sarah's cases and laid them in the snow. When he looked up, she was standing in front of him, her little mittened hand held out.

'Goodbye, Owen.'

He breathed in, and nodded. 'You'll be getting in touch with Charles Pol, of course?'

'I expect so.'

Then he lost his temper; grabbed her arm and jerked her round. 'Did Pol pay you ten per cent down, and the rest when the Ruler was dead? Just to get up there on the mountain and say half a dozen words into a radio? While Sammy and I take all the risks and do the job – and Sammy gets killed doing it – and you choose this moment to run out on us, just to enjoy some bloody upper-crust jamboree where you can pick up a millionaire or two!'

She managed to wriggle free and stepped back, white-faced, the lipstick smeared like blood at the corner of her mouth. 'Well, that's it! That's the end! Absolutely the end. Now go away – go away and don't ever try to see me again.'

She turned and began to give instructions to a porter who had appeared from the hotel. Packer slammed the Fiat boot shut and stood for a moment watching Sarah's trim little figure walking into the porch of the Chesa, her head high and her Gucci bag swinging at her side. Then he got back into the car.

He drove almost without seeing, without swerving, relying on his horn and his headlamps. The crowds scattered, leaping out of his way and howling abuse after him. He parked outside the Vereina and stumbled back towards the bar.

There was a man on the stool where Sarah had been sitting. Packer stood at the bar without looking at him. The voices all round him were thumping at his head, so that he had to lean forward and put his hands over his ears to prevent himself from screaming.

A hand closed round his wrist and pulled his arm down. 'Hello, soldier. You look all in.'

'She'd got her claws well into you, hadn't she? You poor bastard.'

'I loved her,' Packer said, in a cold dead voice.

'You're well out of it, soldier. Over the wall, I call it.'

'I still love her.'

Ryderbeit cackled. 'Don't be bloody soft! What do you plan on doing? Running down to the Chesa and duffing up that Arcy-James bastard, then carrying the maiden off on your white steed to faraway parts?' He slapped Packer on the shoulder.

'What you need is a bloody good drink.'

'Maybe I do.' For the first time Packer realized how thirsty he was. Ryderbeit was back on a triple Scotch and had lit up one of his coronas. His ordeal, which he had briefly described to Packer, had left him uncannily calm.

'What upsets me is the way she used us,' Packer said bleakly.

'Shit! She didn't use us – we used her. And Charlie Pol used all of us. But enough of your Miss Sarah bloody Laval-Smith. She's history. We've got to think of ourselves now. My route's blocked – no trains while they bring up the rescue teams. It'll have to be the car. What's your reckoning on how long they'll take to put up road blocks?'

'Well, there was a chopper on the spot right away – but my guess is they'll be looking for a party of the Ruler's compatriots, or for some of his Arab neighbours. They can't detain every tourist in Klosters and Davos.' He called to the barman for Ryderbeit's bill, and bought a couple of bottles of Apfelsaft for the journey.

'Come on, let's go.'

The road down to Landquart was an almost continuous queue of traffic both ways. At intervals police cars stood with flashing blue beacons, but no one was as yet inspecting any vehicles going down except for the odd casual glance.

Ryderbeit chuckled. 'If any of those Arabian fat cats are holidaying up here, I guess they're likely to spend a nice few hours with the boys in grey!'

'We haven't considered the Ruler's own boys,' said Packer.

'They'll probably be running around chasing their tails. With the big boss-man dead, they'll be like a swarm of bees when the queen's been knocked off.'

Packer nodded dubiously, as a policeman waved them on. 'I suppose you're right. The chain of command goes back to Mamounia, and I doubt there's anyone big enough here to take any immediate decisions. They'll be too busy worrying about him being dead.'

'Holy Moses, he's dead all right!' Ryderbeit said, and settled back in his seat to light another cigar.

It took them nearly four hours to cover the forty kilometres to Landquart; but here the traffic suddenly dispersed as they joined the stretch of autoroute past Sargans, on the main road to Zürich.

'Are we clean?' said Ryderbeit at last.

Packer glanced again in the mirror. 'For the moment.'

Ryderbeit sat stroking his hairless chin. 'When it comes to a diversion, soldier, an avalanche takes a lot of beating.' He paused, then gave a shout. 'Holy Moses, we've been forgetting something!' And he switched on the radio above his knees, pressing several buttons until he found a channel in French.

The voice was speaking with the hurried, improvised tone of an announcer whose scheduled programmes have been cancelled, to make way for up-to-the-minute news flashes. Full details of the avalanche were still uncertain, although it was officially confirmed that at least thirty people were dead and many more missing.

After a number of contradictory interviews with eye witnesses, the announcer broke in with an official bulletin:

'The authorities are also investigating the report of two shots, which witnesses heard fired a few seconds before the avalanche commenced. It has not been established where these shots came from, or who was responsible, but rumours that they were fired by soldiers of the Swiss Army on local manoeuvres have been rigorously denied by the military authorities. The police, meanwhile, are conducting intensive investigations. We will be bringing you further instant coverage of the Davos–Klosters catastrophe as soon as we receive news.'

The voice gave way to rather unseemly light music. Ryderbeit said, 'That's bloody weird. You know what? Somebody's put the muzzle on. Now I can understand the Ruler being able to swing the lead out here, but how the hell do those underlings up in the chalet get the cops to clam up on his murder?'

'Could be they're worried about the publicity. Remember, these Swiss'll go to any lengths to protect their tourist trade. Just look how they covered up on that cholera epidemic in Zermatt a few years ago.'

'Sounds just a trifle too pat for me, soldier.'

They drove for some time in silence, reaching the end of the strip of autoroute, where they rejoined the main road along the edge of Lake Walensee.

There was no other traffic in sight, and Packer was cruising at ninety kmh when he rounded a bend on the dark lakeside and saw in his headlamps, directly in front of him, the back of an unlit panel-truck. He twitched the wheel to the left and slammed on the brakes, throwing Ryderbeit out of his seat and crushing his cigar in a shower of flaming ash against the windscreen.

The Fiat's wing clipped the rear corner of the truck, and Ryderbeit yelled, 'Bastard! Don't stop – it's his own bloody fault!'

But Packer had to stop. He felt the whole car rumble and the power-steering began to swerve wildly under his hands. The car was slewing across the road in a bumpy skid, away from the lakeside, and stopped with a violent jolt against the left-hand bank. Ryderbeit yelled, 'Lights – *out*!' – and as Packer groped for the switch, Ryderbeit slid down on his knees and grabbed Packer round the waist. 'Down!'

Packer squeezed himself beneath the wheel, kneeling under the dashboard. 'Easy,' Ryderbeit whispered. 'We'll get out my door – then lie flat as a corpse.'

As he spoke, there was a crack and a splintering of glass. The rear window smashed and something thumped into the back of Packer's seat. Ryderbeit had his door wedged half-open against the bank and slithered out. Packer followed, his hands touching frozen mud. Too late he remembered his gloves in the back of the car.

The darkness was almost total, as he slid down into an icy ditch. Ryderbeit had moved off silently into the night, and the only sound now was the distant hum from the autoroute. Then, almost simultaneously, there were two cracks from ahead, followed by the clink of the Fiat's shatter-proof windshield. Packer had seen no muzzle-fire, but guessed that the shots had come from their side of the road, opposite the dark blur of the panel-truck which he could just make out, about fifty feet away.

Ryderbeit's whisper reached him out of the darkness ahead. 'You stay put. The car'll give you cover for the moment.' As he spoke a pair of headlamps swept round the bend, throwing the panel-truck into hard relief, and dazzling them both as they pressed themselves flat into the icy mud of the ditch.

It was a TIR lorry with a trailer, and going slow enough to just manage to swerve out from behind the unlit panel-truck. Its air-horn bellowed with fury, but it roared on, its eight double tyres covering Packer with a freezing spray. Its headlamps had given Packer a glimpse of Ryderbeit, now halfway between the Fiat and a point level with the panel-truck, moving, belly flat in the mud, with the rhythm of a snake. At the same time, Packer had made out the silhouette of a shelving buttress ahead, probably a duct leading down into the ditch.

For a moment a deep black quiet closed round them; then the darkness was sliced by two more glares of light – stationary this time – and, without looking up over the edge of the ditch, Packer knew that they came from the panel-truck. Both beams were centred on the Fiat.

There was a short pause. Packer pulled himself along on his elbows, until he was a safe distance from the double beam, then took another quick look over the edge. A big squat man was moving forward along the lakeside, shoulders hunched, holding something against his stomach. He made no sound.

He passed level with where Packer was lying and came within a few yards of the Fiat; paused, then ducked across the road. Packer lowered his head and heard a couple of loud popping noises and a tinkle of glass as the truck's headlamps went out. Packer had forgotten all about Ryderbeit's little 'lady's gun'.

He was already out of the ditch, still with a clear impression in his mind of where the man had been standing. He lifted one foot and took a step forward, resting his heavy ski boot down as gently as though he were walking on glass. He still could not see the man, but he could sense him. He could feel that tense bulk of bone and flesh standing a few feet away, gripping his gun with both hands and wondering what to do. In a second he would decide: deprived of the light, he'd either take cover behind the Fiat, or more likely make a dash back to the truck.

In that second, Packer moved. He lunged forward with his arms flung out, fingers rigid, and heard a shuffle in the dark as his elbow collided with something solid and padded. He turned, measuring the distance by instinct, then kicked out his right boot with all his force, feeling the man's shins collapse under him.

There was a howl and the leather-clad body crashed against

him. The next moment Packer was holding the man up, and could smell the garlic on his gasping breath, together with a thick honey-scented hair oil. His left hand reached down for the gun; but the man had remembered it too, and brought it up with a painful smack against Packer's wrist.

Packer chopped his right hand down on the man's forearm and jabbed his knee up into his groin. Both blows connected, though the man's heavy coat protected him from the worst injury. Packer kicked him again, quickly, on both shins, then, applying all the strength in his frozen hands, he wrenched down the man's wrist. But the man did not let go. He was immensely strong. The gun was pointing harmlessly at the road, when there was the sound of another car behind them. A moment later the shape of his opponent began to form out of the darkness.

Packer calculated that he had perhaps three clear seconds in which to disengage himself from this indecent embrace in the middle of the road, as well as to neutralize the gun. The headlamps were growing brighter and the noise of the approaching car drowned the man's short heavy breathing. Packer tightened his left hand round the gun wrist, kicked again, savagely at the knee-cap, and squeezed off the man's scream by locking his right hand round the side of his neck and pressing his thumb down.

The car was 100 yards away and the man was beginning to squirm, giving out a high-pitched rasping sound, like a rusty ratchet. In the glow from behind, Packer could see the saliva bubbling at the edges of his clenched lips.

He squeezed harder, feeling the stiff rubbery artery flattening under the pressure; then something heavy hit the side of his boot and clattered on to the road. Still without letting go of the man's wrist or neck, Packer kicked the gun into the ditch. As he did so, the man collapsed.

Packer was hauling his dead weight to the side of the road when the car reached them. It had slowed down and the driver had opened his window. 'Il y a un accident?' he called.

'Rien de sérieux,' Packer replied. He smiled and imitated the motion of drinking.

The man in the car smiled back, rolled up his window, and drove on.

Packer bundled the gunman's inert body face-down into the ditch, groped about in the mud, and finally retrieved the man's weapon – a heavy long-barrelled .38. The safety catch was off and he marvelled that it had not fired during their struggle.

Now he was ready. He turned and began to run, with long crouching steps, again in pitch darkness, down the bed of the ditch towards the invisible buttress ahead. The question now was how many were there? The only way to find out was to draw their fire, and pinpoint the muzzle flashes.

There was no sign of Ryderbeit. When Packer calculated he was halfway to the duct, he threw himself flat and called quietly, 'Sammy!'

From the darkness ahead came a faint slithering. 'Soldier?' Ryderbeit appeared, serpent-like, beside him. 'You get him?'

'Yes. And his gun.'

Ryderbeit reached out and ran his fingers over the weapon. 'Nice. Nice, soldier! Where is he?'

'In the ditch by the car, sleeping. What about your boy?'

'Nowhere. Vanished. Bloody ghost man.'

They ducked down as another car swept round the bend and passed, this time without slowing down.

'There must be more than one,' Packer said, his lips almost touching Ryderbeit's ear. 'They'd never pull a stunt like this single-handed.'

'Yeah, but where is the bastard? The only cover he's got is here and the truck – and I've checked both.'

'Maybe we've scared him off. Anyway, no point in hanging around. Let's have a look at the Fiat.'

'We won't be using that Fiat again,' Ryderbeit said, and Packer felt something sharp prod into his chest. He took hold of what felt like a length of heavy chain, but instead of links, it was made up of barbed spikes welded into double crosses. At the end of it was a length of cord.

'I found it under the truck,' said Ryderbeit. 'An old trick. You must have seen it dozens of times. Throw it across the road just as the car's coming – all four tyres *kaput* – then haul it back in before anything else comes past. Still, at least we're breathing. Let's get our luggage out before the sightseers start getting here.' He had already pushed past Packer and was moving back down the ditch.

Packer stuffed the gun under his belt and followed. He found Ryderbeit bending over the gunman, his hands feeling under his coat. 'First blood, soldier. You killed him.' He glanced both ways to make sure the road was clear. 'Quick – get his legs.' He was already lifting the body under the arms, and Packer grabbed the ankles, and they began to stagger with quick sideways steps back towards the truck.

They carried the body round to the rear where Ryderbeit let his load drop; there was a dull clonk as the gunman's head hit the tarmac; then Ryderbeit had both panel doors open, slid the body in feet first, and slammed the doors.

Packer was already in the driving seat; and only then did he remember that the Rhodesian had shot out both headlamps. He climbed down and rejoined Ryderbeit, at the Fiat. 'No lights, Sammy.'

'No sweat,' the Rhodesian answered cheerfully. 'We'll drive on sidelights.'

'Like hell we will. Any idea what the Swiss police are like on traffic offences? And that's all we need – picked up for driving without lights, with a corpse in the back.'

'You law-abiding sod! But maybe you're right. We'll stash our gear in the truck, then back up round the bend and find a quiet spot where we can lie low till first light.'

He unlocked the boot and they began groping for their luggage. Ryderbeit hauled out his great case and started to lug it across to the truck, while Packer checked the inside of the Fiat and removed the plastic folder containing the hire-car documents and insurance, made out to M. Cassis, resident of Liechtenstein. Then he locked all the doors and carried his grip-bag over to the lakeside, where he paused to throw the car keys into the black water. But instead of a splash, there came a muffled bang from inside the truck.

He dropped his case, grabbed the gun out of his belt, and, crouching down, began to zigzag forward towards the nearside of the truck. He was close enough to distinguish the shape of the bonnet with its two blind headlamps, when he heard a quick step ahead, then Ryderbeit's voice. 'Packer, you bastard! What are you doing – having a crap?'

Packer ran round to the rear of the truck, still holding the gun in both hands. The panel doors were open, and above the red glow of the rear lights he could see Ryderbeit's case resting on the body of the gunman.

'There was a shot,' Packer said breathlessly.

'Yeah, there was a shot. Now get your case – we're moving.'

'But the shot – ?'

Ryderbeit looked at him with a crooked sneer. 'Get your stuff. I'll explain when we're aboard.'

Packer fetched his case from beside the lake and slung it in beside the dead gunman, then slammed the doors. 'Any idea where we can hide up?' he asked.

'Yeah, there's a lay-by just back behind the bend.' Ryderbeit grinned and pointed at his good eye. 'Awake or asleep, drunk or sober, an old hunter never misses anything.'

Packer nodded. 'You lead the way, behind the truck, to warn any traffic.' He got up into the driving seat, his frozen fingers fumbling along the dashboard, and found there were no keys. He switched on the inside light, climbed over the seat, and dragged Ryderbeit's bag off the body. If the keys weren't in the ignition, they must be in someone's pocket – it was just a question of whose pocket.

The man lay on his belly, his head turned towards the side of the truck, his arms stretched stiffly beside him. In the cramped space Packer had some difficulty rolling the corpse on to its side. He found the keys in the man's overcoat pocket. Feeling the tension subside, he had just rolled the body back on to its stomach, when he noticed a smear of blood along the rim of the man's collar. He looked closer, and saw that the short black hairs at the back of the neck were matted and wet.

He leaned over and began prodding carefully, like a doctor. The wound was just behind the man's ear. It was only a small hole – a hole made by a .22, at the most. A lady's gun.

He climbed thoughtfully back into the driving seat, switched off the interior light, and started the engine. There were no reversing lights, so he had to move slowly, guided by Ryderbeit's tall figure waving him impatiently on. Beyond the bend was a short path leading up to a clearing surrounded by trees: evidently a lay-by for picnickers wanting to enjoy a view of the lake. The ideal spot. While darkness lasted they would be invisible from the road – unless someone were looking for them.

Ryderbeit joined him in the passenger seat and tapped out a cigar. Packer nodded towards the back of the truck. 'What made you think he was still alive?' he said casually.

Ryderbeit bit the end of his cigar and spat out the leaf. 'It's like with certain animals, soldier – snakes in particular. You think you've killed the little bastards, then half an hour later they come twitching back to life.'

'So you shot him?'

'I shot him.' Ryderbeit leaned back and grinned over the flame of a match. 'Something troubling you, soldier? Your conscience, maybe?'

'Yes, something is troubling me. But it's not my conscience – though it does have something to do with our friend back there. I don't like his having been alone.'

'Shit, if he'd had anyone with him, he'd have shown up by now.'

'Now just think for a minute, Sammy. We've run into a carefully staged ambush, timed to the second' – he pointed to a large metal box under the dashboard, beside Ryderbeit's knee – 'using a powerful UHF R/T, certainly strong enough to pick up Klosters. Even in the mayhem of the avalanche, someone must have seen us leaving, while they probably had a "lamp-lighter" – "watch-dog" to you – back up the road to signal our approach. And our friend in the back knows how long it takes for a car to get here, and he has the Fiat's full description, waits till we come round the bend, then chucks out his spiked chain.'

'What the hell are you getting at?' Ryderbeit drawled. 'I'm not a babe in arms – I can figure how an ambush is set up. I've set up dozens myself.'

'Alone?'

Ryderbeit was silent for some time, sucking steadily at his cigar, which gave off a dull glow, like the cockpit lighting of an aircraft at night. 'So what do you figure?' he said at last. 'You'd think that if the Ruler's boys had rumbled us back there in Klosters, they'd have done better going to the Swiss Police? Or maybe the Ruler's fussy about other people clearing up his own shit?'

'The Ruler's dead,' Packer said.

Ryderbeit's eye flashed at him. 'Yeah. And he's not got a long arm, but it reaches out from under the winding-sheet!'

There was another pause. 'All I know,' said Packer at last, 'is that you don't set up an ambush with an elaborate radio link-up, on a busy international road, with just one man against two.'

'What do you expect from a bunch of wogs? The Ruler's

people may be getting fat on oil, but they're still a load of desert rats with crabs up their arses. They don't have the same refined techniques as you and me, soldier.'

'Hell they don't. Their Intelligence boys were trained by the West, only without Western scruples. They certainly know enough not to set up an ambush with odds like this one.'

Again Ryderbeit was silent. During the drive up to the lay-by, Packer had had the heater turned on full; but now the engine was off, it was growing bitterly cold. He climbed over into the back again and got his anorak, gloves, and an extra sweater out of his case and put them on. Then he paused, looking down at the half-hidden body of the gunman; took off his gloves and began going through the dead man's pockets.

There was very little: a crumpled packet of Swiss cigarettes and a 'cricket' lighter, a cheap plastic wallet containing a few hundred Swiss francs, and a cracked, dog-eared photograph of a stout woman standing beside a small boy. He searched the wallet again, but it was unnaturally empty, like that of a man preparing for suicide. Packer removed the money, stuffed it into his trouser pocket; then returned to his seat.

'Who was he?' said Ryderbeit.

'Nobody. No passport, credit cards, driving licence – nothing.'

Ryderbeit yawned. 'He's dark enough to be a wog, but you can't always tell. That's the trouble with the world. Too many wogs and munts swarming all over us and getting us white men by the balls. Well, at least we've knocked off one of the biggest bastards of them all. That's a nice thought to sleep on.'

He stamped out his cigar, then curled up like a cat with his head on one side and his good eye closed, while his glass one stared at the dashboard.

Packer could not sleep. His body was stiff with cold, and the gruesome events of the last half-hour became a blur, giving way to a parade of provocative images: dinner by candle-light, fondue bourguignon, plump shiny men in dinner-jackets, fragile women with sharp eyes and brittle voices. He looked at his watch. It was going to be a long night.

He tried again to unravel the puzzle of the ambush: the speed and ease with which he and Ryderbeit had been picked up in

Klosters, despite the confusion following the avalanche. Then this solitary gunman, operating in the dark against two targets, without knowing whether they were armed or not.

The problem did not resolve itself, but at least it concentrated his mind, and dulled the clear cruel workings of his imagination as it followed Sarah from table to table, candle-light to chandelier, drawing her admirers and pinning them down like butterflies. After her ordeal on the mountain today, she'd probably drink too much, and if there was someone in St Moritz with a little extra specious appeal, she might even go back and sleep with him. But not until she'd enjoyed the party. She wouldn't be naked and writhing in some strange hotel bed until the party was over. She hated to miss parties. She'd wait until first light. Like us, Packer thought.

She was like a cat. She hated being touched, even in bed, unless she was in just the right mood, with just the right person. A cat, he thought: slow, soft-footed, stalking movements, coming closer. He whipped round in his seat, then ducked forward, cracking his head against the metal door. He started to yell something, when the air exploded round him like an enormous paper bag and he felt the tiny stings of broken glass against his neck and ears.

He snapped down the handle and flung the door open with all his weight behind it, knocking the man outside clean off balance; then sprang out head-first arms extended as though he were diving. One set of fingers collided with cloth, the other scraped a rough jaw. He had his feet on the ground now and his thumb in the man's mouth, crooked back to avoid the teeth and tearing the flesh sideways, while the index finger of his other hand jabbed with a sickening squelch into an eye. The man folded up with a grunt that was little more than an apologetic cough.

At that moment Packer's mind lost control, and his body – trained during months of discipline back at the camp in Wiltshire – flew into action. He lunged forward and seized a tuft of short hair; pulled it down and brought his knee up into the man's still invisible face, then chopped his left hand down with all its might on to the man's neck. His adversary, who was now kneeling, made no sound. Packer lifted the man's head and felt something hard ram into his ribs.

He gave a yell of rage, for allowing his skills in unarmed combat to master his reason. The gun. He should have gone for that right from the start. But now the man had the gun in his ribs, and Packer knew – with a kind of timeless rationality – that he had a fraction of a second left to live. Instinctively, one hand reached under his anorak for the dead man's gun, while the other slammed down towards the barrel pressing into him just below his heart. The shot came before he could reach either.

Packer was knocked backwards against the open door : though the impact came from no bullet, but from the weight of the man in front of him, whose whole body had collapsed to the ground. Packer felt dizzy and weak at the knees, and there was a warm sticky feeling round his nose and mouth. He licked his lips and they tasted sweet and salty. He was licking blood, but it wasn't his own.

The light came on inside the truck and Ryderbeit slid down, the tiny gun folded inside his long fingers. He kicked at the body on the ground, then bent over it. The face was smeared with blood, but not enough to hide the little hole between the eyes.

Ryderbeit smiled. 'You're a brutal bastard, Packer-Boy, but that sort of fighting's strictly back-alley stuff. These boys may be tough, but they also use hardware. Or maybe you think that's against the rules?'

'Come on, get him into the truck.'

10

Sarah had not entirely enjoyed herself.

She had drunk too many vodkas to start with, and too much champagne later on. Jocelyn Knox-Partington's helicopter trip had been cancelled, and the drive to St Moritz had been perfectly hellish. She had ridden with DJ in his Jensen, behind the Knox-Partingtons' Bentley; and after the snail's pace down to Landquart, DJ had tried to make up time by taking the narrow icy road through Tiefencastel at reckless speeds, with at least two nasty skids; and the foremost terror in Sarah's life was to be maimed or disfigured in a car accident.

She had arrived at St Moritz in an evil temper. They were late for dinner, and her humour was not improved by finding that she had less than half an hour in which to bath, change, and prepare her face, in a large suite in the Palace Hotel which, she learned, had been taken by their host – DJ's friend, Mr Steiner.

Dinner in the local restaurant – which had been taken over by their party – was too crowded, too noisy, with too much drinking, too many people shouting and laughing; and at the end some of the men had even started throwing rolls and butter pats at each other. Several of them had made clumsy passes at her, including DJ and Knox-Partington. She had resisted them all, not always with good grace, and later, while she was repairing her lipstick in the Ladies' Room, she was joined by Mrs Knox-Partington, who remarked into the mirror, with acid humour, 'I'd be grateful if you'd take Jocelyn off my hands this evening – in fact, for the rest of the holiday. He certainly seems keen enough!'

Then the King Club under the Palace Hotel, with its tables jammed together like furniture in a warehouse; a swirling kaleidoscope of coloured light cutting through a haze of cigarette and cigar smoke; the pounding, ear-numbing bombardment of half a dozen hi-fi speakers. Sarah had accepted a few dances, which had fortunately demanded no physical contact with her partners, and for the rest of the evening she drank. And the more she drank, the more she found her mind wandering back to Owen Packer.

Poor Owen. He'd looked so tired when she'd left him. Not shocked or furious or desperate – just exhausted. It had been a moment she had been dreading for months now; for she knew – as he had known – that the relationship could not last. Yet when it had come, in that crowded bar at the Vereina, he had accepted it so mildly; all she could think of now was his poor tired face as he helped her out with her bags at the door of the Chesa.

She realized, with dismay, that she missed him.

She was bored – bored with this babbling gaggle round her; and for all his faults – his moodiness and social ill grace and sexual demands, Owen Packer had never exactly bored her. And as her mind became more fuzzy with champagne, she remembered a remark he had once made about her set of friends: 'I don't think much of their small talk, but I don't think much of their big talk either.'

Tonight the small talk had been pathetic, terrible. There had been a lot of chatter about the avalanche, but mostly about the inconvenience it had caused; then the ski talk – endless, boasting, competitive ski talk, broken occasionally by the mention of an engagement back in England, the suspected break-up of a marriage, an impending bankruptcy, parties given or about to be given in Dorset and Scotland and Knightsbridge and Mayfair and Marbella and Cannes. Then back to the avalanche.

But not one mention of His Serene Imperial Highness, the Ruler of the Emerald Throne of the *Hama'anah*, and what had happened to him.

She was now sitting upstairs in the Gothic gloom of the main hall of the Grand Hotel. The walls, with their pitch-pine panelling and dark drapes, kept starting to revolve round her. She held herself very straight at the end of a leather sofa, with a glass of Cointreau perched on her knee. At a comfortable distance sat her host, Mr Shiva Steiner.

He was a broad, well-proportioned man with dove-grey hair, small shrewd eyes, and pronounced Semitic features – although DJ had made a point of claiming that he was not Jewish. He had apparently built his fortune in South Africa, before moving to London where he had cashed in on the Australian nickel boom in the sixties, and was today a powerful figure in the oil world. Above all, Mr Shiva Steiner was eminently relaxed. He had been talking in a cosmopolitan voice which Sarah found pleasant and reassuring, while not actually listening to what he was saying.

It was after three o'clock; apart from a tired-looking huissier, they were the only people left in the hall. From under the floor came the boom of the King Club, like an underground train.

Mr Shiva Steiner was saying, 'In point of fact, I still have a couple of seats to fill on the plane. And, if you permit me to say so, you would be more than a mere passenger – you would be a positive adornment to our party.'

She smiled back at him, still only half taking in what he had said, and sipped her Cointreau.

Steiner went on, 'And if you will forgive a slight immodesty, I assure you that my house is most comfortable. On one side lie the mountains, on the other the blue waters of the Gulf.'

She said sleepily, 'But won't things have changed? I mean, after today?'

'Today?' His eyebrows tilted. 'What is so important about today?'

'But the Ruler – ?' Sarah's lips parted and she stared dumbly at him.

'Yes – what about the Ruler?'

'He's dead – isn't he?' she replied, in a small flat voice.

'Dead? My dear mademoiselle' – he gave a light laugh – 'I sincerely hope not! It is a most inconvenient hour for me to have to start telephoning my financial colleagues. But wherever did you get such an idea?'

She sat very still. The walls were no longer revolving, and the vulpine features at the end of the sofa came into sharp focus. 'I heard –' she began, but Shiva Steiner lifted a jewelled finger and motioned unobtrusively to the huissier at the end of the hall.

'You heard?' he said gently.

'I heard it in Klosters this afternoon. In the hotel. There were a lot of people talking and there was a German – I think he was a German – and he was telling everyone that there had been shooting on the mountain just before the avalanche' – the words had begun to flow even faster than she could think – 'he said someone had shot the Ruler, and that it was the shot that had set off the avalanche.'

Steiner glanced up at the huissier, then pointed at Sarah's glass. 'And did he say the Ruler had been killed?'

'I think – maybe' – she blinked at the pair of bright little eyes watching her along the sofa – 'maybe he said it, or someone else did.' She tried to smile. 'So it isn't true?' she added.

'Well, it certainly wasn't true at six o'clock this evening.'

'You mean, there was nothing on the news?'

'I did not hear the news,' said Steiner; 'but I did speak to His Imperial Highness.'

She found herself repeating his words : 'You spoke to His Imperial Highness.' Her eyes were open wide, her mouth felt dry.

Steiner gave her a lubricious smile. 'I speak to His Highness almost every evening at six – if not on the telephone, I visit him at his chalet.'

His hands spread out in a deprecating gesture. 'My dear young lady, my business interests do not only involve money – for what is money but scraps of printed paper? I deal in something more substantial – oil. That is why I can afford to be generous – to fly my friends in a private jet to Mamounia so that they may relax and be happy at my expense. You will not, I hope, think me impertinent if I include you as one of my friends?'

She looked up. The huissier stood beside her with a fresh glass of Cointreau on a silver tray.

11

They had started off as soon as they could make out the silhouette of the trees around them, with the mists rising from the lake below. It was 5.40 – just about safe, and legal, to drive on side lights only – with the road to Zürich still almost deserted.

Packer again took the wheel. His eyes stung from lack of sleep and his limbs ached; for unlike Ryderbeit he had slept only in snatches, his body refusing to relax, his senses alert to the smallest sound, the faintest hint of movement in the darkness outside.

Their departure was surprisingly, even suspiciously, uneventful. They passed the Fiat still at the edge of the road, resting on its flattened tyres, with its smashed rear window catching the rising sun.

As Pol had emphasized, to assassinate a public figure, however securely guarded, did not call for any special talent; the real skill lay in escaping afterwards.

Their original plan, which had been finalized in the hotel in Chur the morning before, had been for Packer and Sarah to take the Fiat to Zürich Airport, where they would leave it in the parking lot and book themselves one-way tickets to Singapore – the remotest spot they could think of where British subjects do not require a visa. It was a thin ruse, but it might cost the police – and anyone else who was interested – a few critical hours. Meanwhile, the two of them had intended to take the airport bus – more anonymous than a taxi – into the city centre, where they would make their way to the railway station and board the first train leaving. It wouldn't matter where.

Ryderbeit had agreed to a similar schedule, but travelling separately, on the 4.30 train down to Landquart, and on to Zürich, where he too would disappear, armed with the identity of Daniel Spice-Handler. There had been no mention of their ever meeting again.

Subsequent events had changed all this: first the avalanche, then Sarah's wilful disloyalty, and now this mysterious ambush, which had been carried out despite the confusion following the

Ruler's murder. However, Packer was determined to stick to the original plan as closely as possible. Even if his phoney flight to the Far East was not picked up, he calculated that the airports and roads would be checked first. The era of the railway was over – which might give them an hour or two's grace.

Meanwhile, they had already lost more than six hours, he remembered; and it was still a good ninety minutes' drive to Zürich, where they would arrive in the middle of the early rush hour. With their cargo of corpses, it was a risk they could not take; and he had already decided to make for the nearest town, Näfels, thirty kilometres away, at the beginning of the main stretch of autoroute to Zürich. Here they would leave the truck in a quiet street, and take a train or bus.

He was driving fast. The traffic was still light, but he was becoming increasingly puzzled, with a conflict of relief and anxiety, by the total absence of any police on the road. Fourteen hours ago one of the most powerful men in the world had been assassinated less than fifty miles away; yet the Swiss authorities – proud hosts on whose territory the Ruler had been slaughtered – had so far not even thrown up a single road-block.

Packer had not communicated his misgivings to Ryderbeit, who showed contempt for all potential danger, reacting only when that danger became imperatively real. In any case, the Rhodesian was now fully occupied, searching the body of the second gunman, which they had been unable to do during darkness for fear of turning on the interior light.

When Ryderbeit climbed back into his seat, he looked disgruntled. He had pocketed a fat sum of Swiss francs from the man's wallet, which again had been otherwise empty. The only mark of identity was a season ticket in a celluloid holder, valid for the Gotschnabahn for one month, with six days to run. It was made out in the name of *A. G. ESMET*, nationality Turkish. The photograph showed a heavy face with a dark jaw and a low forehead. Certainly not Chamaz; nor did Packer think it was Chamaz's companion whom he had seen two nights ago in the Chesa bar.

Ryderbeit wiped the wallet and season-ticket holder clean before tossing them into the back of the truck. 'First a Lebanese – now a stinking Turk,' he muttered. 'Seems they recruit their cowboys and gorillas from neighbouring countries, so it doesn't embarrass the Imperial Household when one of them gets nobbled, eh?'

'I don't suppose it fools the Swiss for long,' Packer said, thinking again: Where *are* those cool efficient Swiss? At the same time he remembered something else – that damn window next to him, with its neat bullet-hole surrounded by a web of cracked glass. The side windows did not roll down, but slid open, and it would only need one inquisitive eye to spot the damage; for even if the average Swiss wasn't used to gun-fights in real life, he still watched them on television. Packer cursed himself for not having smashed out the whole window while they were in the lay-by; for now it was too late. The traffic was beginning to build up towards the entrance to the autoroute.

'You know something, soldier?' Ryderbeit said casually. 'We should have dumped our two passengers in the lake. They wouldn't have swum.'

Packer did not laugh with him. He was becoming irritated by Ryderbeit's easy manner; the man didn't even need a shave, while Packer kept catching his own grizzled, red-eyed image in the driving mirror.

Näfels was a spruce dreary town off the tourist belt, its streets already crowded with industrious early risers. Packer headed for what looked like the centre. He saw an arrow marked 'Bahnhof' on a lamp-post, swung the wheel and cut left across the oncoming traffic. A whistle blew and he heard a shout from behind. He hesitated, then pulled up.

The man came round the front of the truck, noting the registration, then stopped by Packer's half-open window. 'Vous parlez français?' he asked, in his odious Swiss-German accent.

Packer nodded, not moving his eyes from the man's face. Under the grey képi it was an absurdly young face. There was a ripe yellow pustule at the edge of his nostril and his mouth had the churlish officiousness that is a substitute for authority.

'You saw the red light back there?' the policeman said.

'It was green when we crossed. I am sure it was green,' Packer smiled into the boyish eyes, desperate to keep the young man's attention from straying to the bullet-hole which was less than six inches between them.

'Where are you going to?'

'Geneva,' Packer said quickly, remembering that the truck carried Geneva plates.

'This is not the way to Geneva.' And the policeman's eyes strayed past Packer's shoulder to the back of the truck. 'You need the autoroute to Zürich.' There followed one of those timeless pauses that is the trademark of all policemen. The man was still looking into the back of the truck. 'What are you carrying?' he said at last.

Packer detected a slight sound beside him, as Ryderbeit slid his hand under his anorak. Packer decided to take the offensive. 'We're stopping at the station to collect the luggage of some friends in St Moritz. As you know, the railway has been cut off by the avalanche. These friends are important people' – he leaned forward and gave a slow nod – 'and it would be most unfortunate if they missed their belongings owing to a small misunderstanding.'

As he spoke, he heard a sizzle as Ryderbeit drew down the zip of his anorak. Christ, he thought, all we need now is to shoot a cop.

The policeman stepped back and said, 'In future you must drive with more attention. You could have caused an accident.' He pointed up the street. 'If you want the station, it is the second turning on the left. And next time be careful of the lights.' He saluted and walked away round the back of the truck.

Packer's hands were shaking as he double checked in the mirror before pulling out into the traffic. Beside him Ryderbeit let out a low cackle. 'I'd like to have seen that kid's face if he'd looked in the back! He'd have probably fainted.'

Packer nodded. 'He's also going to make an excellent witness when they find this truck.'

They didn't speak again until they were in the square opposite the station. Packer cruised round and saw what looked like a warehouse with an alley leading round the back. He drove up to it, turned the corner, and found himself facing a dead end. There was no one in sight, and the only other vehicle was a cart loaded with freshly sawn logs.

It took them less than two minutes to unload their luggage, toss the two dead men's guns into the back of the truck, lock all the doors, and run back into the square, where Packer dropped the keys into a litter bin. The station had only two platforms and the train for Zürich was already in.

From now on, it was decided, they did not keep too closely together. Packer bought the tickets, while Ryderbeit made for the bar. The train was leaving in four minutes, but at this point Packer did not care whether Ryderbeit caught it or not.

The carriage was only half-full, mostly with coarsely dressed Mediterranean types who looked like immigrant workers. Packer settled himself into a window seat, stretched his head back, and felt the full impact of exhaustion. The train jolted into motion and the rhythm of the wheels carried him into a deep sleep.

He was woken by someone shaking his shoulder. He blinked into the dark glasses and hooked face of Ryderbeit, who had slid into the seat beside him. He had a couple of newspapers in his hand. 'Can you read Kraut?' he demanded, and thrust the papers on to Packer's lap.

One was obviously a local paper; the other was the *Neue Züricher Zeitung*. Packer stared blearily at the local paper, which had a banner headline in red, over a huge photograph depicting a wall of snow and a column of men with long poles. He reflected that the aftermath of an avalanche was rather like the end of a battle – except there are rarely any bodies to be seen. Neither make good photographs.

The headline proclaimed: KILLER AVALANCHE IN KLOSTERS AND DAVOS: AT LEAST 31 DEAD, MANY MISSING, GOVERNMENT DECLARES STATE OF EMERGENCY. The story filled the front page, and overflowed inside, with more photographs.

He turned to the *Neue Züricher Zeitung*. The lead story concerned Cyprus; a second story was about Kissinger; and the avalanche claimed four columns at the bottom of the page. Packer hunted quickly through the rest of the paper, wondering if his sketchy German had missed something.

Ryderbeit was watching him with a sly grin. 'I always heard journalists were a load of lazy bums, but they can't be this bad. It's the gag, soldier. The iron muzzle, padlock and all.'

He paused, then sucked in his breath in a hiss. 'He was dressed in his usual black sweater and red, white and blue anorak. Wraparound glasses, gorgeous silver hair – the Serene Imperial Pin-Up Boy himself. And I sent that lovely little plastic pellet smack into the Imperial cranium so they'll have to melt the snow all around and put it through a sieve to find the pieces. Yet – yet!' – his fingers stabbed viciously at the newspapers on Packer's knee – 'it's the assassination of the decade and it doesn't get one fucking mention!'

Packer was very awake now. 'Even our old friend, Chamaz, got quite decent coverage. And he wasn't even dead!'

'You telling me the Ruler's not dead?' Ryderbeit said quietly.

'It's the only thing I can think of for the moment. Maybe I'll come up with something more brilliant later on. But two days ago the Ruler tells Pol that the operation's off. He also tells Pol to carry on with the original plan – with the difference that I've got to knock you off, instead of the Ruler. And the Ruler's not the kind of man to have scruples about sending up an understudy, just to find out what our reaction would be.'

'Maybe – if he *is* alive – he thinks we were killed in the avalanche?'

'So why did he set up the ambush?'

Ryderbeit pulled a sour face. 'How the hell could he be so sure? Unless he set up the ambush to find out?'

'That presupposes that his boys had the Fiat under observation.' Packer sighed. 'It's possible, even probable, with Chamaz still on our tail. Klosters is a small place. Come to think of it, so is St Moritz.'

Ryderbeit's eye squinted round at him. 'What's that supposed to mean?'

'I was just thinking of a girl I used to know.' Packer leaned against the window and closed his eyes. 'Wake me when we get to Zürich.'

'Well, this is it. As the sentimentalists say, I hate goodbyes at railway stations.' Ryderbeit clapped both hands on to Packer's shoulders. 'Do we keep in touch, soldier?' He grinned. 'All right, I stopped being sensitive a long time ago. I'm a pariah. People hire me – use me – sometimes even pay me. Then they get shot of me like I'm carrying bubonic plague.'

Packer cut him short. 'Is there anywhere I can get hold of you?'

'Ah, there's a touch of humanity!' Ryderbeit shook his head. 'You might try the American Express in Rome – the eyeties are one of the few people I haven't crossed so far, and they've got a lousy secret police. You might also try the Tel Aviv Hilton. And the name's Spice-Handler, remember – once again the Wandering White African Jew.'

The Zürich station loud-speaker was announcing the imminent departure of the 9.10 express to Geneva. 'For Christ's sake lie low and don't splash your money around,' Packer said, picking up his case. 'And be careful with that toy gun of yours – especially when you go through airport checks.'

'Always keeping to the right side of the road, eh, soldier? You know, you're still a miserable bastard – but I guess I'd be the same if I had to foreswear the Demon Drink. Fact is' – and for a moment Packer had a disconcerting glimpse of Ryderbeit embarrassed – 'with all we've been through, I've quite got to like you, soldier. Some day we might work together again.'

'Yes. And if my theory about the Ruler is correct, that day may be sooner than you think.'

A whistle blew; Packer turned and ran down the platform, just managing to leap aboard the last carriage as the train began to move. When he looked back, Ryderbeit had gone.

The open carriage offered him no cover. It was crowded, mostly with sober-faced men in business suits with despatch cases resting on their laps. Packer noted each one – first those facing him, then, after a visit to the toilet, observing the rest on the way back to his seat.

At each of the three stops – Berne, Fribourg, Lausanne – he changed carriages, leaving the train with his luggage, and only reboarding when the whistle blew. Again, it was more his senses than his eyes that were alert: he was no longer looking out for the square-shouldered, dull-eyed gorilla with his cheap ill-fitting suit bulging in the wrong places and taking half an hour to read one paragraph in the newspaper.

He was looking for someone quiet, typical – a face in the commuter crowd – a face that would reappear just once too often.

Eighty minutes later, when they drew into Geneva Central Station, Packer still felt 'clean' – or as clean as he could hope to feel over the coming months. He had spotted only one mild suspect on the train, but he had disappeared at Lausanne while Packer was changing carriages. After the abortive ambush, he was not under-rating the Ruler's capacity for following through with a 'grand slam', even here in Switzerland, and even with him and Ryderbeit now split up. Packer was taking no chances.

In the terminal's wash-and-brush-up emporium, he changed into a light suit, and at last rid himself of his ski boots, which had begun to weigh him down like a convict's ball and chain. He also bought all the French papers and the *Herald Tribune*.

The avalanche was again given wide coverage, but with few fresh facts. One French paper, however, carried a report alleging that the disaster had been started by gunfire. There followed another denial by the Swiss Army that any soldiers were responsible, but the report also reminded its readers that the Ruler maintained a staff of 200 highly trained and heavily armed bodyguards at his chalet in Klosters, ending with an implication that an attempt might have been made yesterday on the Ruler's life.

Le Journal de Genève, like its staid sister, the *Neue Züricher Zeitung*, gave the avalanche unsensational coverage, but added a brief paragraph quoting the Chief of the Graubunden Canton Police, who had spoken to a member of the Ruler's household, who in turn had denied that any of His Majesty's servants were responsible for any alleged shots. Packer wondered how many petrodollars those words had cost His Serene Highness – or whether it was just part of the contract for his resident's permit.

Alone, Packer felt a dull sense of inertia – of isolation, even anti-climax. He knew he could not return to London. The Ruler maintained a large Embassy in London and his relations with the Foreign Office were cordial – ingratiatingly so, on the British side, since Her Britannic Majesty's Exchequer was already in hock for over £1000 million to the Ruler, with another £500 million rumoured to be on the negotiating table. Besides, London meant an empty flat and a telephone that wouldn't ring, and nothing to do but work on his model windmills as occupational therapy.

The pain of losing Sarah had returned as the train pulled out of the station, bound for Lyon. Customs and Immigration were perfunctory; but again – perhaps now as much to keep his mind occupied as to protect himself – he kept a close but discreet watch on his fellow passengers.

There were no stops before Lyon. Here he caught the Rapide to Marseilles, arriving an hour and twenty minutes later. He checked the time-table, went out to the nearest tabac and bought writing paper and envelopes; then sat in a café, ordered a citron pressé and a large black coffee, and wrote, under the date, but with no headed address:

Dear Uncle Charles,
You will by now no doubt have heard the unfortunate news, and I can only say that I regret it as much as you. Clearly we must meet, as soon as possible, to decide what to do next, as well as settle our outstanding financial arrangements. My address, until further notice, will be the Poste Restante in Béziers.
With my best sentiments, Your trusting nephew,

O.W.

He sealed the envelope and addressed it to:

Monsieur Cassis,
c/o Volkskantonaler Bank,
Aalau,
Suisse.

He mailed it from the Post Office in the station. With forty minutes to wait for his train to Béziers, he occupied himself irritably leafing through the midday editions of the local papers. They had all taken up the rumour of an assassination attempt on the Ruler – two of them with banner head-lines – but the impact of the stories was dulled by cautious speculation. None of the papers carried any substance for the rumour.

Meanwhile, the Ruler and Pierre-Baptiste Chamaz seemed to have one thing in common. They were both alive. Chamaz had also identified Packer and Ryderbeit, and probably Sarah; and the Ruler had laid the bait – several baits – to see which way they would jump. He had been able to scare Pol enough to make him disappear; while Packer and Ryderbeit had been brave enough, or stupid enough, to stay around and carry the operation through.

The Ruler had made one clumsy attempt to kill them both last night – but a little failure like that would either needle his pride or whet his appetite, or both. It certainly would not deter him.

Packer realized that for the first time in his life he was not only utterly alone – he was on the run. And – like Pol – running for his life. For Pol and Ryderbeit, however, this was no doubt a mere professional chore: they changed identities, loyalties, allegiances, as other men change their socks. Even Sarah, with her cool and ignorant sense of social immunity, had had the nerve to stay put – indeed, to risk attending some swank 'do' in St Moritz where there was a good chance that some of the Ruler's associates might even be guests. But Sarah wouldn't think of that, of course. Sarah would be purring over that fat cheque Pol had given her, and deciding about what dress to wear.

Packer began to wonder how much Pol had paid her. He had paid her something, certainly. But for all his exuberance Charles Pol was a hard and careful man. He had paid Packer ten per cent against the rest when the deed was done. Would he have imposed the same conditions on Sarah? She had seemed confident enough in the hotel in Chur two nights ago, when she had spurned his offer of the Porsche – which suggested that any down payment she had received, or been promised, must be in the region of Packer's. But what for? To press a button and mutter one sentence into a portable radio? Or did that fat, sly, giggling villain have other plans for her? Plans as bold, but far more subtle than the ones at which Packer and Ryderbeit had so mysteriously failed?

If Sarah was to have got her other ninety per cent when the Ruler was dead, she would not only be feeling somewhat cast down by the news, or rather, lack of it – as well as furious at Packer and Ryderbeit, whom she would automatically blame – but she would also be just as keen as Packer to get in touch with Charles Pol.

Packer found a bureau de change in the station and exchanged half his Swiss francs for French money – enough to last him comfortably for at least a month – and the other into traveller's cheques. By the time he had retrieved his luggage, the train was about to leave. The second class was packed to standing room, mostly with noisy blue-chinned men from the Midi, laden with wine and parcels of food.

This time he chose the single first-class carriage, where he found an empty compartment. As soon as the train started he pulled down the blinds on both sides and tried to sleep. The door slid open and a man in a white suit and two-tone shoes came in, carrying an expensive leather grip-bag. He muttered a greeting, and Packer noticed that he had a lot of gold fillings. He also wore dark glasses, and an obvious toupée, like a little mat on the front of his head.

He sat down in the corner opposite Packer, and took out a copy of *Le Figaro* which he opened at the financial pages. Packer observed him with half-closed eyes. He had a long thin face, deeply creased like a sheet of paper that has been folded and unfolded many times. He certainly did not conform to the pattern of the Ruler's regular retinue, or to their race; besides, for a 'leg man' he was far too obvious. Unless, of course, he was operating as a sophisticated 'lamplighter' – one of the higher echelon who would risk playing it close as a double bluff. It was possible he had a couple of gorillas riding second-class, chewing garlic and spitting melon pips; with perhaps a radio in an inside pocket, which could be operated from the toilet.

Outside, under a misty sun, the grey-blue wastes of the Camargue swept past. The man in the toupée was still studying the fluctuations on the Bourse, without removing his dark glasses.

Packer went into the first-class toilet and began to shave. Despite his tan, his face had a drawn, yellow look and his eyes were dull with puffed red linings.

Shortly after he returned to his compartment the train began to slow into Arles, where there was a five-minute stop. He decided to give any 'lamplighters' the benefit of the doubt. No one joined them in the compartment, Toupée was happy with his financial sums, and Packer slept.

He slept so heavily that the conductor had to shake him several times. Packer asked how long it was to Nîmes. The conductor told him five minutes. Packer began to pull down his case. Toupée had now turned to the sports page. Chess or canasta looked more like his kind of game; but then you could never tell.

The train drew up at the platform and Packer slid open the door. Toupée did not even look up.

He waited on the platform for three minutes, then reboarded the first-class carriage at the other end, and this time found a compartment occupied by two nuns. He slumped down and slept for the next hour and a quarter – through the stop at Montpellier – until he was woken by the rasping voice, like a klaxon, announcing '*Béziers . . . Béziers . . .*'

He took down his case again, bowed to the nuns, and climbed out. Then, on an impulse, he jumped back aboard and ran down the corridor to his old compartment. Toupée's seat was empty. He turned abruptly, and the tall thin figure in his dark glasses and two-tone shoes was standing in front of him.

Packer grinned. 'It is forbidden to use the toilet during stops,' he said in French, reciting from the universal litany of the SNCF.

'I was merely washing my hands, monsieur,' he replied, with no trace of annoyance. A very tolerant, civilized man, thought Packer, who merely nodded and returned to where he had left his case on the platform. He picked it up and began to carry it across to the barrier. He looked back once, but the windows of the first-class carriage were empty.

He walked through and signalled to a taxi in the square outside.

12

Sarah had a hangover. It was very cold on the terrace of the Palace Hotel and the sun-light hurt her eyes, even behind dark glasses. D'Arcy-James had suggested a light omelette, and Jocelyn Knox-Partington had countered with an offer of eggs and bacon.

It was Mr Shiva Steiner who solved her problem; and without even consulting her, he had effortlessly summoned a waiter and ordered her a 'Harvey Wallbanger', before explaining the ingredients to her as though they were part of a game : one-third vodka, one-third Galliano, and the rest pure orange juice. 'The best cocktails are like the best lovers,' he said, patting her fur mitten across the table, 'severe but gentle, and the results delectable.'

DJ had stood up to greet a party of boisterous men in skiing gear, and Knox-Partington had stopped a snappily dressed American with whom he was trying to arrange a backgammon game.

'You have not changed your mind, I hope, mademoiselle?' Shiva Steiner's voice transmitted the reassurance of a very good doctor. Sarah guessed that his hands, too, would have the cool dry touch of a doctor's.

She gave a quick laugh. 'Why should I? Provided there are no strings.'

'Ah, my dear young lady' – Steiner's gaze moved out across the white roofs of St Moritz – 'one makes a down payment – one takes a small percentage.'

Sarah winced behind her dark glasses. Her café au lait had grown cold in front of her and was covered with a wrinkled grey skin. 'That sounds rather mercenary, Mr Steiner.'

'You are a romantic, I think?'

Sarah shrugged, pulling her silk cashmere poncho closer around her shoulders. 'I don't know. You'd better ask one of my friends.'

'Or your lovers, perhaps?' Shiva Steiner laughed – a pleasant laugh without the least innuendo. But she did not laugh with him, or even smile. Steiner's manner became more serious. 'Permit me to ask you, my dear Sarah – I may call you Sarah, may I not? – but you are here toute seule?'

'Toute seule,' she replied, as the waiter placed a glass of innocuous-looking pale orange juice in front of her.

'Your health, my dear!'

They touched glasses and drank. Sarah sipped hers, swallowed, sipped again, then took a deep drink. 'It's good. It's very good indeed, Mr Steiner. Just what I needed.'

'You can always trust me, Sarah. I am a man of my word. And please – call me Shiva. It is not a beautiful name, but it is my own and I cherish it. It is Armenian in origin – a memory of my mother. I am, I fear, what you pure-blooded English would call' – he gave a supplicating gesture, palms upwards – 'well, you probably have several very rude words for it, but the politest I can think of is "mongrel".' He smiled. 'My pedigree is really the most awful mess. However, I can honestly claim to have a dash of royal blood. I am distantly related, on my father's side, to His Imperial Highness.'

She was clasping her glass in both mittens, only half listening as he made some joke about blood not being as thick as oil. 'Who is Harvey Wallbanger, anyway?' she asked suddenly. D'Arcy-James, who had come up to their table just as she spoke, answered, 'Probably some dirty old Yank who likes tossing himself off against walls!' and laughed uproariously. Sarah did not even look at him. Shiva Steiner smiled with oriental blandness.

D'Arcy-James pulled up a chair. 'Is old Shiva giving you the low-down on the oil business, darling? Well, I warn you, don't believe a quarter of what he says. If even that much was true, we'd have the whole Western world declaring a state of emergency. I've told Shiva' – he winked knowingly across the table – 'that the best thing the West can do is team up with the Russians and take over every oil-field in the Middle East.'

'You would find nothing to take over but sand,' Shiva Steiner replied. 'There are contingency plans to destroy every well and pipe-line within twenty-four hours of such an event.'

'Twenty-four hours, my foot! The wogs take longer to tie their shoe-laces – those that wear shoes, that is!'

There was an awkward silence. The waiter returned with

Sarah's fresh drink. Steiner, with a veneer of discreet insult, neglected to ask D'Arcy-James what he was drinking. They were joined by Jocelyn Knox-Partington. 'Hello, Sarah! Shiva! Wonderful air for blowing away the night before!' He turned to D'Arcy-James. 'Feel like being a hero, DJ? Simon and I are doing the Alpspitz after lunch. You on?'

D'Arcy-James' tough baby face looked up at him. 'You know Roddy Sampson broke both legs on that run last week?'

'Yes, but think of all the girls he can get to sign his plasters!' He raised his hand. 'Farewell, gang! I must get that damned wife of mine out of the hairdresser's.'

D'Arcy-James took his leave and followed. When he had gone, Steiner said, 'Has that man been a friend of yours for long?'

'Oh, I've known him on and off for years,' Sarah said. 'He's a bit of a fool, I'm afraid.'

'Not a fool. He is merely typical of the society which invades St Moritz for the season. Unfortunately, they do not realize that this is one of the most vulgar places in the world.'

Sarah smiled. 'That's not very flattering to us, is it?' She glanced round the terrace, where most of the tables were now empty except for a few elderly couples swaddled in blankets, and a solitary man in a raincoat and dark glasses who looked as though he had damaged his face skiing.

Shiva Steiner was saying, 'Last night I saw at once, my dear Sarah, that you have rather more grace than the rest of your friends. I find your company most refreshing.'

'Thank you, Shiva. But you know D'Arcy-James too?'

'Yes. Occasionally my work has involved me with him. As you probably know, he is a public relations consultant, and in the oil industry – as in most industries – one is obliged to use such people.'

Sarah sipped her second Harvey Wallbanger, then tilted her head to one side. 'You don't mind me being direct, do you, Shiva?'

'I should be delighted! – providing you do not expect me necessarily to give you a direct answer.'

'I'm not going to sleep with you, Shiva.'

His bland expression did not change; she would have been less disconcerted if it had. 'My dear young Sarah, I do not wish to sound conceited, but I must inform you that if I want a pretty woman I have only to crook my little finger. It is perhaps a sad reflection on humanity – at least, on the female of the species – but the two greatest aphrodisiacs are wealth and power. When I say wealth, I do not mean the common millionaire with a yacht and a fast car – I mean wealth that can make and break the economies of nations. And I talk of power that is absolute. Power such as that held by Robespierre, of whom it was once said, "He woke in the morning with a whim, and by afternoon it was law". In the case of a certain individual, that law would have been passed by lunch-time.'

'Are you referring to yourself, Shiva?' Sarah asked, with uneasy sarcasm.

'My dear, I am not a modest man, but you claim too much for me.'

Sarah finished her drink. At the table across the way the man in dark glasses was paying for his coffee. She noticed again his bruised cheek and cut lips; then looked back at Shiva Steiner. 'You are talking about the Ruler, aren't you? Why?'

'Why?' Shiva Steiner's thick brown fingers with their winking jewels built tents on the table-cloth. 'I must make a confession to you, Sarah. I am a man of very humble origins, but everything I have tried my hand at has been a success. And not only in affairs of business. I also have a talent for weighing the value of people – particularly those of the female sex. I have weighed you, Sarah, and I have calculated that you are at least twenty-four carats' worth.'

The man with the damaged face passed their table, but Steiner did not appear to have noticed him. He was now leaning forward with the air of a player who already has the winning move in sight. 'You must not misunderstand me, Sarah. If you did, it would be a sad loss – not only for both of us, but for each other. Do I make myself clear, or am I talking in riddles?'

'Perfectly clear,' Sarah said calmly. 'You're pimping for the Ruler.'

Shiva Steiner gave his light rippling laugh. 'My dear! I trust that your language has not been infected by that of your social playmates? But I will be generous and interpret your remark as meaning that I intend to introduce you to His Imperial Highness. This is indeed true. For just as I am a fine judge of women,

perhaps been tactless, even provocative; though the Ruler had shown no sign of being offended. He showed no sign of anything.

The fact that just over twenty-four hours ago Sarah had been part of a well-concerted plan to kill this man sitting less than two feet from her, was too outrageous for her properly to appreciate. What did disturb her was the fact that the Ruler seemed not even to notice her.

She had never met anyone as rich or famous or powerful as the man on her left; but she was also not used to being ignored. Her initial nervousness was now giving way to petulance. She felt no ill-will towards the Ruler, for there was no contact between them – his very proximity made him seem all the more distant – but she was beginning to feel very angry indeed with Shiva Steiner. He had given her no briefing, no hint during the helicopter ride of how she was to treat her host, or react to him; and now Steiner was giving her no help at all. As for the Ruler, she had decided that a man who is revered by thirty million subjects must be allowed a degree of social licence; but for Shiva Steiner, the procureur royal, to abdicate all responsibility for her even before the second course, seemed unforgivable.

She was eating breast of wild duck in a bigérade sauce, sitting stiffly forward and pretending to listen to the garbled conversation about antiquities from the end of the table, when she became aware of a slender finger pointing at the centre of her breast. As she looked down, the finger scooped up the emerald on the end of the necklace which Pol had given her; paused as though weighing the gold, then let it fall gently back on to the velvet of her caftan.

'It is very beautiful. You are fond of emeralds?'

She nodded, with a vivid smile; but before she could think of a reply, the Ruler spoke again. 'The emerald is my favourite jewel. Although the blue of the peacock is the national colour of my country, I consider the emerald to be our symbol.'

He was looking at her again with his empty gaze, and her mind filled with a confusion of judgements.

Like all famous men whose faces are public property, in the flesh he was smaller than she had expected, with a yellowish skin stretched tight over his cheek-bones and a web of acne scars round his lips. It was a face which required to be framed, above

231

a breast-plate of medals, wearing a peaked cap encrusted with gold. His clothes this evening were quiet, faultless, peculiarly arrogant in their lack of lustre.

His most celebrated features – his hair and his nose, which endowed his portraits and photographs with imperious nobility – were disappointing. The hair, with its deep widow's peak, looked stiff and artificial, like a wig; and the nose was coarse and fleshy, with a slight shine that she had observed increasing during the evening. She also noticed, with distaste, that he suffered from blackheads.

Although she had drunk abundantly, she was still sober. The presence of the Ruler had cast a chill over her; for someone so drilled in the protocol of dinner parties, she now felt like an athlete who has gone lame.

The soft voice, with its faintly Teutonic inflection, sounded close to her left ear. 'You are from England.' It was not a question but a statement. 'Mr Steiner here informs me that your family possesses a famous and very fine country house.'

She nodded. 'Well, yes. But the Government has brought in this awful tax and my father thinks he may have to sell.'

'I understand. You in Britain pay very high taxes.' He paused. 'I like Britain. It has simplicity and charm. London is my favourite Western city. London – and perhaps Amsterdam. Do you know Amsterdam?'

She felt the saliva dry up in her mouth. 'Yes, I've been there once,' she murmured.

'I like the British people, too,' he went on, 'except that they are lazy. They ask for more money to do less work. That is ridiculous.' He paused again, and laid his hand on her sleeve. 'You must forgive me. I criticize the British only because I admire you, and am troubled by your problems.'

'Oh, I quite agree with what you say!' She had begun to feel more at ease.

'I have said nothing that is original,' he added. 'Criticism is too easy – it is the trade of a parasite. Action is what is important – action translated into work and discipline.'

She wanted to say something – anything – but was again stilled by that blank timeless gaze.

Across the table the Princess was now very drunk. She was waving her hands and shouting incoherently at the American archaeologist and his wife. Sarah distinguished the words, 'sar-cophagus!', 'tombeaux!' several times, then: 'How do you say it in English – these old bodies – in sarcophagus – ?'

'Mummies?' the American suggested.

'Yes, mummies! Dead people – always death! That's all you do – dig for death!' Her voice reached a pitch of insane fury, as she lurched round in her seat and faced the Ruler, her ragged face distorted by a macabre smile. 'You, Your Majesty – you do not fear death! Your people believe you are immortal!'

'I am not immortal, Princess. Like everyone, I too prepare myself for death. And when I die I take with me to the earth perhaps not even these clothes I wear. Perhaps just a piece of white cloth. But I also take with me a part of history.' He turned and looked at Sarah. 'Mr Steiner also tells me that he has ex-tended an invitation to you to visit my country?'

'Yes, he has.' She glanced uneasily at Steiner, seeking some flicker of confirmation, but found none.

'It is possible,' the Ruler went on, 'that I shall have the pleasure of meeting you again. I should be interested to hear you talk about your family's house in England. I very much like English architecture, particularly the eighteenth-century period.'

'Yes, ours is eighteenth century – or rather, some of it. The older part is Jacobean.'

'I am sure it is very beautiful.' As he spoke, the Ruler rose to his feet, gave a single nod to the table, turned and left the room, followed by three white-clad retainers.

Sarah reached with relief for her wine glass.

13

Owen Packer had chosen Béziers because it was a quiet town, a few miles from the sea so that it did not attract the rush of tourists, and far enough along the coast not to have been infected by the leprous opulence of the Riviera. He had once visited it on a bicycling trip, and now found it unchanged.

His hotel was half empty, overlooking a square lined with pigeon-grey shutters and trees that were just beginning to shoot green. The morning after his arrival he woke early, shaved, leaving his upper lip untouched; then inspected himself in the mirror to see what other changes he could make, and decided to rely simply on sunglasses, and a hat.

It was a pale grey morning, with the promise of a hot day. The square was still deserted, but in the street down to the railway station a couple of bars were open where workmen in blue overalls were bracing themselves with the first drink of the day. The newspaper kiosk was opposite the station. The local papers were folded out on top and one of them had a photograph on the front page of the panel-truck, with an arrow marking the bullet-hole in the window.

Packer selected both local papers and strolled across to the station, where he bought *Le Monde* and *Le Figaro*, not wishing to attract attention by buying all four papers at once. Then he went into the station brasserie, ordered coffee, pain et beurre, and started reading.

None of the papers contained one mention of him or Ryderbeit; nor of the discovery of the Fiat hired by Monsieur Cassis of Liechtenstein; and there was nothing at all about the Ruler. As for the abandoned truck in Näfels, with two dead men and their guns in the back, the reports – as released by the Swiss Police – struck Packer as wilfully evasive, even misleading. The identity of the victims was given only as 'foreign'; the ownership of the truck was undisclosed; there was no suggestion of motive; and no evidence from the young traffic policeman in Näfels.

The aftermath of the avalanche commanded only the inside

pages. Rumours of a shooting on the mountain had been dropped; and Packer's original conviction – that the Ruler's influence, together with the Swiss determination to avoid scandal, would abort the story before it was even still-born – seemed proved. It all depended on how the Ruler would now react, following the escape of his three would-be assassins.

Packer waited until the shops opened, bought a beach hat, espadrilles and bathing trunks; then located the central Post Office, two streets away. It was too early to expect a reply from Pol, but he wanted to get his bearings and make sure of what time the office closed.

Next he found the bus terminal and looked up the schedules to Valras-Plage and Montpellier. From now on he was going to avoid taxis. And with nothing else to do, he intended to get in plenty of swimming, so that he would at least be physically fit, if still morally wounded, by the time Pol's answer came.

He took the first bus to Valras-Plage. It was a clean white town with restaurants and cafés built out on to the sand. There was already a holiday atmosphere, without being crowded. Along the beach were stalls selling mussels and crêpes. The sea was still cold and sharp breezes stiffened the flags along the front.

When he returned to Béziers that evening, he called at the Poste Restante, at 7.55. Nothing from Pol.

There was nothing from Pol for the next five days. The newspapers had also dropped the story of the two murdered men in the panel-truck in Näfels. On the fourth day, however, *Le Monde* reported that the Ruler was cutting short his vacation in Klosters and returning to Mamounia, where there were rumours of political unrest.

On the sixth day Packer began to wonder if he wasn't wasting his time. In spite of Pol's insistent misgivings in the Silvretta Hotel on that last night, Packer considered whether the Ruler would not have to be a fanatic and a paranoid to want to hunt them down now.

What made him delay in Béziers, apart from exhaustion and inertia, was the knowledge that Pol would eventually contact him so that they could each collect their share of the half-million pounds. When he called at the Post Office that morning there was still nothing. But Packer was not discouraged; however much Pol had already been paid, he would be just as eager as Packer to draw on their joint account.

That day it clouded over, with a strong wind, and he had lunch inside his usual restaurant, behind the glass-fronted terrace on the beach. He had finished reading *Le Monde* and was drinking his coffee, when he was aware of someone watching him.

'Monsieur, je vous demande pardon.' The man had pulled his chair sideways from the next table, and was pointing at the folded newspaper beside Packer's bottle of Vichy. 'May I trouble you to borrow your paper?'

'Not at all.' As Packer handed it to him he realized that apart from the couple who ran the hotel and the clerk at the Poste Restante, this was the first person who had spoken to him in nearly a week. Instinctively he pulled down his sunhat, adjusted his dark glasses, which he had worn religiously since that first morning, and brushed a forefinger over his young moustache.

He was afraid, for a moment, that he was going to be engaged in conversation. He drank his coffee, called for the bill; but when he glanced across, he saw the man intent on the paper, studying the financial page. He was a thin bony man, middle-aged, in a white shirt, shorts, plimsolls, and one of those caps with a flap over the neck which racing cyclists wear. He looked up only when Packer had settled his bill.

'Monsieur, your newspaper.'

Packer gave him a nod. 'That's all right, you can have it. I've read it.' He felt vaguely puzzled as he walked out of the restaurant, and as he waited for the bus he felt a distinct unease. Something about the man – that absurd costume, perhaps?

He found a seat at the back of the bus and slept almost into Béziers, waking with a stiff neck and a headache. The afternoon had grown prematurely dark, with the sullen smell of an approaching storm. Gusts of wind swept along the pavements. Across the street was a big hoarding advertising bonds in some industrial development.

It was as though an electric current had passed through him. Christ, what a fool I've been! he thought. The financial pages, of course! It was so obvious that it might have been a sign. A sign of what? For him to make the first move, perhaps?

The first drops of rain were splashing on the pavement and

he began to run. He reached the Post Office just as the storm broke. At the Poste Restante counter, he heard the rain drumming against the windows.

Both the morning and afternoon clerks knew him well enough by now not to ask for his passport, although he always carried it. The clerk was a waspish little man who gave a now familiar shrug. 'Rien?' asked Packer.

'Rien.'

Packer nodded and turned away. The marble hall was now full of the boom and sizzle of rain, and a crowd had come in for shelter. Packer stopped halfway across the floor and stood looking at a row of telephone kiosks marked 'Internationaux'; then suddenly walked up to the woman at the desk and asked how long it would take to call London.

'Not long,' she replied.

Packer wrote out the number of the Bond Street gallery where Sarah worked. The woman told him to go into the second cabin. It had a glass door and a mirror in which he watched the wet waiting crowd.

The phone buzzed and he hesitated before lifting the receiver. A chirpy English voice said, 'Rohmar and Mayhew.'

'Miss Laval-Smith, please. Tell her it's urgent, I'm calling from France.'

'I'm sorry, sir. Miss Laval-Smith is no longer with us.'

He didn't even thank her; hung up and stumbled out of the cabin, bumped into somebody, growled an apology, and felt a hand on his arm.

'It is I who should excuse myself – Monsieur Packer.'

The man was very wet. His T-shirt and shorts were sodden grey and the flaps of his cyclist's cap dripped down his neck. 'I think it better that I introduce myself somewhere quieter. There is a café at the corner – if you don't mind the rain?' He was already guiding Packer towards the entrance.

'You've been following me,' Packer said, stopping just inside the door.

'I have been following you for a week – although I prefer the expression "chaperoning".' As he spoke, Packer caught the gleam of gold teeth.

'But why wait until now?'

'I was waiting to see if you had unexpected company in Béziers. I also came to collect my telegram.'

'What telegram?'

'Come, we can talk better in the café.' And he led Packer at a dog-trot out into the rain.

Packer spread out the pale blue slip on the table and read the teleprinted message: BRT XL 9500/4/6 FRIENDS HAVE NOT YET ARRIVED BUT THE PARTY READY TO BEGIN – STOP – COLLEAGUE TO PROCEED AS ARRANGED – STOP – INFORM HIM PLEASANT SURPRISE AWAITING – GUIGNOL.

Packer turned the telegram over and reread the name on the front. 'He should have signed himself "Grand Guignol". Or am I guessing, Monsieur Sully?'

'You have guessed correctly. He is certainly fat enough!' The man smiled over his coffee, which he had ordered for both of them – having no doubt observed Packer's drinking habits. He had removed his white cap when he came in, and his toupée was less conspicuous now that his hair was lying flat.

Packer turned the telegram over again and tapped the first letters of the message. 'BRT – Beirut. Yes?'

'Yes.'

'And "friends" means certain foreign gentlemen who might be less than friendly?'

'Precisely. A stupid euphemism but – like many stupid tricks in our trade – it is often effective.'

'And what are the arrangements, Monsieur Sully?'

'You will take this evening's train to Marseilles, and the overnight express to Paris, where you will leave tomorrow morning by Air France from Charles de Gaulle Airport for Beirut. I will deliver the tickets to your hotel before five o'clock.'

'I'll need a visa for the Lebanon.'

'You will receive a twenty-four-hour transit visa on your arrival at Beirut Airport. After that, matters have been taken care of.'

Packer looked again at the telegram. 'And what's the pleasant surprise awaiting me?'

'That, Monsieur Guignol did not tell me.'

Packer sipped his coffee in silence. He felt the dawning of a fearful excitement. 'Who are you, Monsieur Sully?'

'It is not necessary that you know.'

'It is necessary.'

The man shrugged. 'As you may have guessed, I am an old friend and colleague of our mutual acquaintance with the beard. We met during the war. Since then our paths have somewhat diverged. But whenever possible I render our friend what services I can.'

Packer nodded. 'Meaning one of the French Government Services? And you put in a bit of overtime for an international crook? Must get risky sometimes. Either Charles Pol has got a pretty big hook into you – or else he's keeping you sweet with something tasty, like a nice Swiss bank account?'

Monsieur Sully gave his gilt-edged smile. 'It is more simple than that. He saved my life during the war – twice. Now, finish your coffee and I suggest you return to your hotel.' He stood up. 'Someone else will deliver the tickets to the desk. I shall not see you again. Adieu.'

They shook hands across the table. Packer turned and walked out into the street, which had turned into a canal blistered by the slashing rain. He put up his collar and began to run.

14

The car seemed to set a new tone and style, even after the private sleeper to Paris and the first-class flight to Beirut, where Packer's clearance through Customs and Immigration had seemed less a formality than a privilege.

It was a midnight-blue Mercedes 600 SL, with a glass partition between him and the driver. The windows were closed and he tasted the chill tang of air-conditioning. The driver – who appeared to be symmetrically oblong from his shoulders to his ankles, with a neck as thick as his head – had greeted him at the gate without a word and carried his case to the car.

After leaving the airport they had turned off the main highway into the city and followed an unmade road which skirted an automobile cemetery – a vast wasteland littered with the carcasses of taxis, trucks, cars, buses and military vehicles, all in various stages of decomposition. Their speed increased as they reached the edges of the shanty town – a sprawl of huts that looked like bits of broken biscuits, propped up with oil-drums and strips of corrugated iron. Through the shimmering midday heat, the only colour came from the slogan and political posters, which were uniformly red. The driver was using his horn continuously, executing a skilful slalom between donkeys, push-carts, stray children, static beggars, and the occasional armoured car with its hatch shut. Through the window Packer caught fleeting faces turned to watch them, their eyes button-black with hatred.

The landscape changed. The cracked dusty road was now metalled, between red earth and orange groves fringed with eucalyptus trees. They began to climb. Mountains grew ahead, a dark wall against the steel-blue glare of the sky. They drove for three-quarters of an hour, with the road winding out like an elongated intestine, twisting up the ribs of mountain into the shade of cedar trees that opened out over wide green valleys patterned with vineyards, moulting into black gullies which spouted thin waterfalls or were scarred with dry streams like shards of scraped bone.

Snow had appeared, like a distant wreath of cloud, as the Mercedes plunged into an alley of cypress trees that ended between high white walls. A man of the same size and shape as the driver squeezed between the wall and the car, slipping his carbine down beside his leg. He stared in at Packer as though he were a piece of luggage; nodded to the driver and withdrew.

The car slid under an archway in which a steel door had automatically opened. It closed behind them and the inside of the car was flooded with neon. Packer made to open the door and found that he was locked in. The driver released him, and he stepped out into a garage where he counted half a dozen long black cars and three jeeps painted with desert camouflage.

The driver motioned him towards the door of a lift. Inside, the man pushed the bottom of five buttons and they began to move downwards. He stood, legs slightly apart, hands at his sides, facing the door; his only movement came from the shoulders, in slow heaves like a man doing breathing exercises. He smelled of camphor.

They stopped, and Packer walked out into the cool sunlight. Shallow steps of white marble curved down to a patio, walled in on one side with green glass, and open on the other with a parapet overlooking the ridges of mountain rising to the snow. In the middle of the patio was a kidney-shaped swimming pool in which a girl in a polka-dotted bikini and a flowered bathing-hat was basking face-down on a lilo. At a corner of the pool, three men sat in wicker chairs round a table on which stood an opened bottle of champagne.

As Packer stood shading his eyes against the light, one of the men below raised his arm, and a familiar voice reached him like a clear bell. 'Ah, mon cher! Welcome to your new home! You had a good journey? They looked after you at the airport? Meet my two friends.'

Packer reached the foot of the steps and walked round the pool, where the girl had drifted away so that he could not see her face. Her body was small, well-rounded, lightly tanned; she reminded him, with a stab of bitterness, of Sarah. He reached the table where there was a fourth, empty chair.

'Messieurs, I would like to present le Capitaine Packer' – Pol's fat little fingers closed tightly round Packer's wrist – 'Mon Capitaine, I present to you my good friends and associates, Monsieur Shiva Steiner, and le Docteur Zak.'

Shiva Steiner nodded; otherwise the two men did not move. They were a strikingly incongruous pair: Steiner, in a grey mohair suit matching the colour and texture of his hair, exuded an aggressive opulence, while Dr Zak's old thin body was exaggerated by a loose striped pyjama-like costume, with no collar or tie. He had large sad eyes and hair like wire wool.

Pol drew Packer down on to the vacant chair and beamed at him, his silk suit shining under the filtered green sunlight like fish scales. 'So? You have no complaints?'

'No. But I've got some questions to ask.'

Pol chuckled and his fingers played a trill along Packer's arm. 'Of course you have, mon cher! I too have questions to ask.'

'Right, down to business. I made a deal with you, and we signed a contract in Aalau, and then things started to go wrong. You disappeared, for a start. Let's begin there.'

Pol shifted his buttocks with a crackle of cane. He reminded Packer of a porpoise, benign and playful, ready at any moment to splash into the pool. 'I left for an excellent reason, mon cher – to save my life.'

'Why didn't you tell me?'

'Because I had no wish to advertise my fear.' Pol removed his hand from Packer's arm and poured himself some champagne. He was the only one who was drinking. He looked at Packer and smiled. 'I can offer you coffee or mint tea.'

'Neither. Charles, you left Sammy and me in a very awkward situation back in Switzerland.'

'It was an agreed situation. We had discussed it fully in Klosters before I left. You were to proceed with the plan, as arranged. Unfortunately, the Ruler played a trick for which you cannot be blamed.'

'Sammy was right, of course,' said Packer. 'The Ruler knew our whole drill from the start. And the only way he could have known was from you. He had a stand-in propped up on that T-bar like a red, white and blue target – but what for? To see if you and I carried out his orders, and I'd shoot Sammy? A pretty devious way of proving a point. And risky, too.'

'The Ruler is a very devious man,' replied Pol. 'He is also

prepared to take risks – provided they are calculated risks. This one was, and it paid off. No publicity – no scandal.'

'The Ruler may be devious,' said Packer, 'but so are you. You hired Sammy for this operation because he was being a nuisance to you and you wanted him on a leash. So you paid him enough to keep him happy – and it doesn't take much to keep Sammy Ryderbeit happy, as long as he's given a gun and can play with it. As for you, I still don't know what passed between you and the Ruler – and I don't honestly care, as far as you're concerned. What I do care about is the fact that the Ruler not only wanted Sammy out of the way, but was out to get me too. In fact, he was taking no chances. Apart from trying to get me to shoot Sammy on the mountain, he'd also laid on another scheme for both of us.' And Packer went on to describe the two sets of booby-trapped ski-sticks.

Pol nodded gravely, while Shiva Steiner and Dr Zak sat watching the pool, as though they were no part of the conversation.

'Surely you understood,' Pol said at last, 'that the Ruler was simply hedging his bets? If you had killed Sammy, that would have been convenient. You might even have been picked up by the Swiss Police and gaoled for life. That too would have been fine. Whatever you confessed about the plot – even if it was believed – could not have hurt the Ruler. On the contrary, the Ruler wanted a plot. The perfect, bungled assassination attempt.'

'So that's why he sent a man who looked like him up the mountain to get his head blown off?'

'My dear Capitaine Packer, you do not suppose the deaths of two servants would trouble the Ruler – even in Switzerland?'

Packer leaned forward in his chair. 'Charles, how the hell do you know there were two men killed? How the hell do you know anyone was killed on that mountain? I mentioned a red, white and blue target just now, and you didn't take me up on it. Nor did you read about it in any newspaper or hear it on the radio. The Ruler gagged the Swiss Police all down the line – including his attempt to kill Sammy and me on the road to Zürich.' He stared hard at Pol, whose expression remained unchanged.

'Mon cher,' Pol said at last, 'you must know that I am not an amateur – that I have much experience in these matters – many

243

friends, many sources of information.' He made a faint, ambiguous gesture in the direction of Shiva Steiner and Dr Zak. 'How I found out need not concern you. The Ruler intended an attempt to be made on his life, but that does not mean he wished it to be publicized.'

'Why go to the risk unless he could cash in on the publicity? It doesn't make sense, Charles.'

'Ah!' Pol tilted his head back and stared at the sky, as if waiting for something to drop down. 'It is all a matter of politics, mon cher. Delicate, internal politics' – Packer heard a splash and the mutter of wet feet on marble, but his eyes were fixed on Pol – 'politics of an intricate Byzantine nature which you and I would find hard to explain.'

Packer was aware of a dripping behind him. He looked round and saw the girl from the pool, just as she snapped off her bathing-cap. 'Oh God,' she said in English, 'it's terrible!'

Packer gaped up at her. She laughed and shook out her black hair, every casual strand dry and falling into place. 'Your moustache,' she added, 'is just about the most horrible thing I've ever seen. It makes you look like a seedy commercial traveller.'

Pol giggled. 'Sarah, ma petite, sit down and make friends with Capitaine Packer. As for his moustache, it is like civilization –it takes a long time to grow, but can be destroyed within minutes.'

Sarah perched her neat little haunch on the arm of Packer's chair, her thigh touching the back of his hand. Pol poured her a glass of champagne. 'Santé,' she said, with a short nod to Shiva Steiner.

Packer just sat. His emotional responses had been short-circuited by amazement. He had forgotten his fury and grief at losing her; and was too stunned to think of all the questions he needed to ask her.

Pol was meanwhile shaking with quiet laughter, trying to look at them both, but hindered by the silk handkerchief which he was having to dab to his eyes.

'Gentlemen, let us waste no more time.' Shiva Steiner spoke with the measured command of the boardroom. 'As Monsieur Pol has explained to you, the plan remains unchanged except for the location. Instead of Switzerland, we must now turn all our attention and resources to eliminating our subject on his own ground.'

'In Mamounia?' Packer glanced at Pol for reassurance. Sarah had left them, and he was alone with Pol, Zak, and Shiva Steiner. Zak had not spoken a word, while Shiva Steiner reminded Packer of a mamba dressed by Cerutti: he would give no warning before he struck, and he would strike without being provoked or frightened.

'In your absence, Capitaine Packer,' Steiner went on, without answering the question, 'we have devised a provisional plan. It is unorthodox, and quite different from the one you attempted to execute in Switzerland.' He turned to Pol. 'I think, Charles, in view of certain delicate aspects of this affair, Capitaine Packer might prefer to hear the details from you.'

Pol took a sip of coffee, leaving a muddy smear along his lips. 'You have been anxious to learn, mon cher Packer, what Mademoiselle Sarah has been doing in our company? You have even made the absurd suggestion that I have been entertaining amorous intentions towards her.' He wagged his head from side to side: 'Such a compliment, mon cher! But fear not – the Germans released me from all such appetites in Lyon in 1944.'

'Don't worry, I've got no illusions about your sexual proclivities,' Packer said brutally; 'I'd even prefer it if your interest in Sarah was that simple. But you like to play games – and sometimes pretty expensive games, when it comes to throwing in a gold and emerald necklace. You still haven't explained what that was for. Some kind of down payment?'

'I really think,' said Shiva Steiner, in a voice like falling leaves, 'that such matters are irrelevant.'

'Not to me,' said Packer. 'Charles gave her that necklace as what we call a "sweetener". And that was just for openers. By this time he's no doubt got a full contract drawn up – joint bank account, with small print to his advantage, if she hasn't read it carefully and beaten him to the draw. She's a banker's daughter, of course,' he added, with a bleak smile at Pol, who did not return it. 'All right, Charles, what's it all about?'

'She has said nothing to you so far?'

'I've hardly had the opportunity to speak to her – especially since you've assigned us separate rooms. Was that your idea, or hers?'

'Ah, mon cher, it is indeed unfortunate,' Pol said, stroking his goatee, 'that you and Mademoiselle Sarah have had this little contretemps. It would be in all our interests if you became friends again.'

'I'm not prepared to discuss my affairs in front of two strangers,' said Packer. 'My personal relations with Sarah are even less relevant than your little cadeau to her.'

'That could be a matter for argument,' Pol said. 'In the kind of operation we are planning, I must emphasize that personal disharmony could be as damaging as mutiny or betrayal.'

'All right, Charles. So what you call "Operation *Shah-Mak*" is still on, and this time it's to be played on the Ruler's home ground? And where does Sarah fit in?'

'Mademoiselle Sarah,' Pol said, leaning back with his hands folded across his immense stomach, 'will be the instrument of death.'

'"Instrument?" Packer paused, his thoughts disorientated. 'What instrument?'

For some time no one spoke. The silence was broken by the faint scratching of Pol's finger-nail on his goatee; while Packer was aware of the pale hunched figure of Dr Zak watching him with his large sad eyes.

It was Shiva Steiner who finally spoke. 'I should explain, Capitaine Packer, that under my auspices, Mademoiselle Sarah made the personal acquaintance of the Ruler in Switzerland before she left. I have also extended to her an invitation to visit Mamounia, where I shall arrange that she should again meet His Imperial Highness – this time under more intimate circumstances.'

Packer turned and stared at Pol, with confusion and dismay. 'Oh, for God's sake!' he yelled, suddenly in English, with a look of hopeless rage. 'You don't really intend to get *her* to kill him?' He paused. Again, none of them spoke. 'She's never killed anything except a few pheasants,' he added in French, 'and she's not even good at that!' He turned to Shiva Steiner. 'You talked about a provisional plan. What is it?'

'Let us take this step by step, Capitaine Packer,' Steiner said blandly. 'It is sufficient for the moment that she should be successfully introduced into the Ruler's intimate presence, under circumstances in which he will be both highly vulnerable and unsuspecting.'

'And how's she going to kill him?'

Pol began to speak, but Packer cut him short. 'No, I want Monsieur Steiner to answer. He seems to be the one who's taken over this operation.'

Shiva Steiner inclined his head. 'Certainly, mon Capitaine. We have devised a plan with care – and, I may add, with considerable ingenuity. I do not claim that it is a perfect plan, but it is a very good one. The Ruler is fond of entertaining female company, particularly of select origin, and when he does he always uses his private apartments in the Palace, which are separate from those he occupies with his family. On these occasions he is guarded by a small group of specially chosen men who are familiar with his habits. When Mademoiselle Sarah leaves His Highness' apartments, it will be worth literally more than the lives of any one of these men to stop her, even to ask her name. But what is more important – under no circumstances do these guards enter the royal apartments until they are summoned by His Highness himself.

'The Ruler entertains many women in this way,' Steiner went on, 'and it is not uncommon for him to tire of them before the night is out. Therefore, if Mademoiselle Sarah is seen to leave his apartments early, not only will she arouse no suspicions, but she will have ample time to make her escape. That is where you will come into action, Capitaine. You will be waiting in a car close to the Palace Square and will drive her to a spot outside the city where you will rendezvous with a private aircraft. We will discuss the precise details later. But that is the broad provisional outline of the plan.' He paused. 'I am interested to hear your opinion, Capitaine.'

'And why have you chosen me to drive this car, Steiner?'

It was Pol who answered. 'Because you will inspire confidence in Mademoiselle Sarah. I know that you are angry with her, and that she behaved in a foolish and selfish way –'

'I said, I will not discuss my personal relationships here!'

Pol smiled indulgently. 'But *I* have also said, mon cher, that your personal relationship with Mademoiselle Sarah happens to be of critical importance to this operation.'

'Why?'

Pol sighed and patted his belly. 'In the last few days I have had the opportunity of getting to know the young lady quite well. She is most discreet about her private life, but I have been able to detect that her emotions are somewhat confused, at least as far as you are concerned. She will not admit it, but in a situation where she finds herself exposed to danger, she has come to rely upon you.'

'Did she tell you this?' said Packer.

'Not in so many words. But I can assure you that when I informed her you were arriving here, she was not displeased.'

'You still haven't told me how she's going to kill him.'

There was another heavy silence. Pol's eyes had rolled up again towards the ceiling, his lips parted in a half-smile. Shiva Steiner spoke.

'We have naturally considered this aspect of the affair most carefully. The use of a gun – even a small one – equipped with a silencer, is not practicable. For although the Ruler's guards have orders never to detain or question any of his private guests when they leave his apartments, they are empowered, on occasion, to search visitors on their arrival.'

'There are guns and guns,' Packer murmured. 'What about that little gadget that looks like a cigarette lighter – what they call a Mexican gun-knife?'

Shiva Steiner's eyes slid sideways towards Pol, who lowered his head, and for the first time Packer saw the Frenchman blush. 'For reasons which I need not explain,' Steiner continued, 'I happen to know that the Ruler is especially suspicious of such gadgets.'

'Well?'

Steiner pressed his broad flat finger-tips together and stared into the middle distance. 'The obvious weapon would seem to be a knife, or perhaps a needle or hatpin, disguised in a nail-file case.'

'You'd never get her to do it. She practically faints at the mention of blood.'

'Quite. Besides, the use of such weapons would require considerable skill and knowledge of anatomy, which I happen to know the young lady does not possess.'

'Well, come on – what have you decided?'

Shiva Steiner explained, in brief, precise, medical detail; and while Packer had difficulty controlling his bewilderment and fury, he had to concede that whether the plan was Pol's or Steiner's, it had a certain revolting simplicity.

The decision to carry it out successfully must now rest with Sarah; but he also knew, from weary experience, that to try and dissuade her would be self-defeating. The fact that he was to connive not only at her committing murder, but at her fornicating with an almost total stranger, was a moral peccadillo which would not concern the three men round the table. In any case, Packer realized that he had no rights over Sarah. He had never had any. Since their last meeting, in the Vereina Hotel in Klosters, his relationship with her had ceased to be even precarious, and from now on would be simply professional. It was not a situation that he liked, but one which he would have to accept. For he was only too well aware that while Sarah might be indispensable to the operation, he was not.

He looked at Pol. 'I want to talk to you, Charles – alone with Sarah. I think it right that we should hear what she has to say.'

'D'accord.' Pol glanced across the table. Steiner nodded, but Dr Zak sat in his baggy pyjamas, silent and motionless. Pol heaved himself to his feet and Packer followed.

'By the way, Capitaine Packer,' Steiner called after them, 'what make of lipstick did you say Mademoiselle Sarah uses?'

'I didn't. But if you choose one of the expensive ones you won't go wrong.'

'It's mad and it's obscene! What's more, it's probably a trick anyway.'

Packer had been pacing the floor, picking his way through the litter of Pol's personal effects; while Sarah sat on a couch under the open window in Pol's bedroom.

'If your friend Steiner is that intimate with the Ruler's habits, he might well tip him the wink. Steiner could be sitting it out to see which way the cat jumps. My guess is, the Ruler still holds a pretty strong hand – a lot stronger than that wizened old creep, Dr Zak who, from what I hear, is some sort of a leftist guru for the Ruler's dissidents. Anyway, that's the way I see it. And Steiner probably does too – he's not stupid.'

Pol himself lay on the double bed, jacket and shoes off, his tie loosened and shirt undone, his egg-shaped head resting like an invalid's in a nest of cushions. He let his hand flop down on to the crumpled sheet beside him; the bed looked as though it had not been made for a week. 'It is our only chance, mon cher. Unless we kill him, he will kill us – it is as certain as if it were a law of Nature.'

'You and I aren't going to kill him,' said Packer; 'Sarah is.' He turned, looked at her, and spoke in English. 'How much is he paying you?'

'Why do you want to know?' she said, also in English. Her profile was silhouetted in black against the window and he could not see her expression.

'Because I want to make sure you're not cheated,' Packer said, reverting to French. He looked at Pol, who had judiciously closed his eyes. 'How much has Steiner paid you, Charles?'

Pol opened his eyes with a start, as though aroused from sleep. 'Don't play the innocent,' said Packer, moving to the foot of the bed. 'Between you and Steiner, you may have fooled Sarah – but not me. His Imperial Highness had you badly scared back in Klosters – scared enough to make you run, but not enough to have you scurrying back for a second try. Not unless somebody made it worth your while. Shiva Steiner, for instance, acting as a front man for Dr Zak's cronies, who probably get their backing from those Arab states who'd like to get rid of the Ruler. What I don't understand is why the Ruler has let Zak run around loose for so long – unless he thinks a dummy opposition is good for his democratic image.'

Pol nestled back on the pillows and closed his eyes again. 'Why must you always concern yourself with the politics of the situation, mon cher? You are a soldier – you obey orders.'

'You're wrong,' said Packer. 'I'm an old-fashioned mercenary — which means I'm *paid* to obey orders. And I don't do the same job twice for one fee. I want your cheque book out, Charles – not the one on our joint account, but the one you kept for yourself when the Ruler made you the initial payment. Don't worry, I'll still leave you a nice margin of profit.' He leaned out and squeezed Pol's big toe. 'You're going to write out one cheque, made out to our join account at the Volkskantonale Bank, for £500,000.'

'You are ridiculous.'

'Shut up.' Packer jerked the toe backwards and Pol squealed. 'You will airmail it yourself, this evening, from Beirut Central Post Office, with instructions for the bank to cable me here immediately it is received and cleared.' He ran his thumb along the soft cushion of Pol's toes, reached the little one and slowly pinched. 'And I'm not making a move until I get that confirmation.' He pinched harder. 'It's something you taught me yourself, Charles – life insurance. Because if anything unfortunate should happen, and I should get killed, that half million is buried in the frozen vaults of Aalau. Think about it, Charles. That's nearly three-quarters of a million you're going to have tied up in me.'

Pol gasped with pain. 'You are a fool. What makes you think you are so important?'

'You do – or you wouldn't have gone to all the trouble of getting your old hush-hush friend with the wig to wet-nurse me in France, then air-freight me out here, with full board and lodging.' He had relaxed his grip on Pol's toe, and the Frenchman's face was beginning to sweat.

'Why do you think I need you?' Pol asked feebly.

'To protect your original investment. And, as you said downstairs, to convince Sarah that she's going to get out of Mamounia alive. That's what I was hired for originally, remember – longterm planning and instant improvisation.'

Slowly Pol rolled his head from side to side, leaving damp patches on the pillows. 'It is not worth half a million pounds sterling,' he murmured.

'A quarter of a million,' said Packer.

Pol blinked. 'Hein?'

'It'll be in my name, but half of it goes to Sarah.' Packer sensed, rather than heard her begin to speak, but held up his free hand, still holding Pol's little toe in the other. 'She's going to be the one taking all the risks, Charles. You don't even have to shift your arse out of this fortress, let alone put yourself inside the Ruler's jurisdiction.'

Sarah now spoke from the window. 'Don't be stupid, Owen. Charles and I have made our own arrangements, thank you. And if you want the truth I trust him rather more than I do you, after what happened with the necklace he gave me.' She gave an icy laugh. 'A quarter of a million pounds tied up in you? I just wonder what I'd have to do to get it!'

He turned stiffly, letting go of Pol's toe. The light behind the window was fading, but Sarah's expression was still unclear.

'These arrangements you've made with Charles,' Packer said slowly. 'Have you agreed to them all, unconditionally?' He waited, but she said nothing. 'When will you do it?' he went on. 'While he's on the job? Or just afterwards, while he's still exhausted, but hasn't had time to get bored and summon his bodyguards to throw you out?' He took a step towards her. 'Or maybe you'll choose the moment of climax – that glorious historic moment, never to be forgotten, when the Imperial penis anoints the vaginal font of Miss Sarah Laval-Smith before she –'

She crossed the floor and slapped him hard across the cheek, her finger-tips leaving a burning ache in front of his ear. He stepped backwards into the tangled heap of Pol's sheepskin coat, lost his balance and sat down. From the bed came a shrill laugh.

'Ah, quel joli spectacle! The great Capitaine Packer floored by a young girl. You see, my friend, she is a young lady of spirit! You should be proud of her.' Pol had sat up on the bed and was groping for his shoes. 'I am going to call for some champagne for Sarah and myself. As for you, mon cher, I suggest some fig-juice. It may help to purge some of your bad humours.'

15

'I am dissatisfied, Minister.' The Ruler sat on the chesterfield, a varnished bamboo cane with a leather-bound handle balanced across his knee. 'If I did not honour you with my most profound and absolute trust, I would be tempted to believe that you were deceiving me.'

'I assure Your Serene Highness' – Marmut bem Letif stood with his sleek narrow head tilted to one side, his shoes pressed together like a pair of shiny slugs – 'assure you with all my faith – swear to Your Highness on the dust of my father – that I do not deceive you.'

The Ruler watched him in silence. 'Perhaps you do not deceive me. But you do not satisfy me. And how, Minister Letif, can I be convinced of the former when the latter is wanting? I do not judge by intentions, but by results. The results, Letif, are inadequate.'

Letif's limp white features sloped downwards, his eyes following the ridges of bamboo as the Ruler now drew the cane in a sawing motion across the knife edge of his trouser leg. 'With deep and humble respect to Your Highness – without the services of NAZAK, my resources are severely limited.'

'NAZAK' – the word reached Letif like a bolt of cold anger – 'you speak as though NAZAK was the driving force, the soul of the nation. Do you think I appointed you Minister of the Interior – my direct second-in-command, in charge of the nation's Security – in order that you might go cowering to Colonel Tamat and his menagerie of licensed torturers and psychopaths?'

Letif's chin drooped on to his chest. 'No, Your Serene Highness.' There was a long silence.

'You tell me that Dr Zak left the country five days ago and has not returned. And Colonel Tamat also tells me that the Doctor has flown to Damascus. But then, as we know, Colonel Tamat can no longer be trusted. So what do *you* tell me, Letif? You tell me only that you do not have enough resources, not enough men. And perhaps I should not be surprised, after what happened to your two apes in Switzerland. You must do better. Colonel Tamat and his organization do not have exclusive rights to the ablest men in the country. Why, Letif, are your men so inferior?'

'Your Most Serene Highness –' Letif hesitated. The Ruler fondled the leather handle of his cane and waited. 'Your Highness, permit me to ask a question which, I pray, Your Highness will understand –'

'Speak. My time is valuable.'

Marmut bem Letif raised his head and licked his bloodless lips. 'I humbly ask of Your Serene Highness why he does not arrest Colonel Tamat?'

'Because he does not wish to. Do not ask for reasons, Letif. Even for a man in your office there must be secrets. Be content that your Supreme Ruler, the Holder of Almighty Power in our nation, enjoys the luxury of good enemies. Sham Tamat is very efficient, he is very proud, above all he is very self-confident. He is also stupid, base, and morally odious. He thus makes a very, very good enemy.' He gave a quick white-fanged smile. 'You see, like all good hunters, I bide my time. You too, Letif. Only you do not have much time. You have perhaps only a few days.'

He leaned forward and the cane slipped through his fingers, its wooden tip bouncing with a hollow click off the mosaic floor. 'In the next few days, Letif, there will be men entering this country – foreigners with evil intent against our nation, and in particular, against my person. Remember, these men are not fanatics – they are impelled neither by ideology nor hatred of my Imperial Being, but by greed, by money, by great sums of money. We already know something of these men from the agent, Chamaz. But Chamaz has done the work of ten men, while the other nine have lain idle.'

He swung the bamboo cane lazily against Letif's knee. 'Stand up straight. For a Minister of my Court, your posture is a disgrace.' He paused, his eyes half closed. 'It is a pity that you are not younger, not better looking, Letif.'

His eyes opened again, aroused by some inner thought. 'It is strange that the great and noble Hamid the Martyr, to whose memory even I bow my head in reverence, should have begat such a feeble, paltry creature as you, Marmut bem Letif. I even hear word – from tongues forked with envy and ambition, no doubt – that your paternity is in question, Letif. That such a wretched body could ever have sprung from a seed of the Great Hamid. But I am not troubled. I know that your body enjoys a good brain – and intelligence is always a virtue, even among my most obedient servants. Let us trust you use that virtue.' His eyelids were drooping again, too far perhaps to see that Letif's face had gone white. 'Go now.'

The little man bowed three times and began to back down the long room.

'Remember, he is very fat,' the Ruler called. 'He is as fat as the very fattest merchant that you ever saw when you ran as a child barefoot through the bazaars. Find him for me, Letif. Find him for me quickly.'

16

'I'm not going to discuss anything with you until you get rid of that ghastly moustache.' Sarah turned away from Packer and gave Pol a tantalizing smile as she lifted the champagne glass to her lips.

Packer watched her sullenly from a chair by the door. 'Charles prefers it. Tell her, Charles – she listens to you.'

Pol sipped his champagne and giggled. 'You do not find him handsome like that, ma petite?'

'Il est horrible.'

'Ah, but it is also one of the simplest and most effective of disguises. A small precaution, perhaps – but a more important consideration than vanity, I think?' He looked at Packer. 'You still have some questions to ask?'

'Several.' Packer turned to Sarah, who had closed the window and pulled a cashmere shawl round her shoulders. 'Do you know what will happen, Sarah, if you get caught?'

'I've no idea.'

'And you're not interested?'

'Why – are you? Or are you just trying to put me off?'

'I'm just trying to make certain that you know the score. Because this time the rules are going to be different, and it won't be a few years in a Swiss gaol, with the chance of parole if you're a good little girl. The Ruler's people do things rather less generously.'

She pulled the shawl more closely around her shoulders. 'Well, what would they do?' she asked, in a flat voice.

'Sammy only told me what happens to a man, but no doubt they have an equally exciting recipe for women.'

Pol broke in with a wince of distaste. 'Sammy has a vivid imagination.'

'So, no doubt, have the Ruler's boys. It runs in the blood.'

'You know something, Owen,' she said slowly, 'I honestly believe that you rather enjoy thinking about what they'd do to me. Well, go on – tell me what'll happen to us both, if it goes wrong and we get caught.'

'Ah, please, mes enfants!' Pol looked distressed. 'Such a morbid subject! It will spoil our evening.'

Packer spoke without looking at either of them. 'The Ruler has the pick of every luxury whore outside the Iron Curtain – and he could probably get his leg over there too, if he bothered. So what guarantee have we got that he's going to choose our little Sarah here?'

'It is precisely because Sarah is not a luxury whore that she qualifies so well,' Pol replied, and Sarah laughed:

'Thank you, Charles!'

'The Ruler has a very select taste,' Pol went on. 'And as I told you, he has already met Sarah and was impressed.'

'What you mean is, he'd like to sleep with her?' Packer scowled.

'That is what was indicated.'

'To whom?'

Pol took a sip of champagne. 'His Imperial Highness confided in his close associate, Monsieur Shiva Steiner.'

'How very touching.'

There was a pause. 'Do you have any further questions, Capitaine Packer?' Pol said at last. 'Of a less personal nature?'

'Yes. How did you get involved with Steiner and Zak?'

Pol slid off the bed and waddled over to the window, where he poured more champagne for Sarah. 'Ah, mon cher!' he cooed over his shoulder, 'that is an indiscreet question, and it would require an indiscreet answer.'

Packer nodded. 'So the final show was always planned to be played over in Mamounia – with Sarah in the star role, and me just walking on in the last act carrying a spear? It was just a matter of talking Sarah into it – convincing her that you'd got a back-up plan to rescue her. It doesn't matter if it's a good plan or a bad plan or a hopeless plan – just as long as she's convinced.'

He gave her a tired smile. '*Are* you convinced, Sarah?'

She was looking at Pol, like a novice seeking spiritual guidance, but Pol did not respond; he just stood, grinning impishly, and said nothing.

'That was why you chose me in the first place – even before Amsterdam?' Packer went on. 'I was to be your trained gun-hand and strategist. But it was Sarah you were really after, wasn't it?'

'Is this true, Charles?' she asked, in a low tight voice.

Pol simpered over his champagne. 'Our friend simplifies everything, ma petite. He is so very suspicious. And it is too late now to start distrusting each other.'

Packer said, 'All right, Charles. Get out your cheque book and your gold pen. And make the first cheque out to Mademoiselle Laval-Smith.'

'Owen, I feel cold. Is it cold in here?'

'No. They've got the central heating on.'

'That sounds funny – central heating in the Lebanon! And it's nearly May.'

'It gets cold up in the mountains at night. Like the desert.'

'Yes.' She gave a quick shudder and her teeth chattered. 'Owen' – she reached out with both hands, in a stiff theatrical gesture – 'come here.' Her eyes were large and bright with fear. He walked over to the bed where she was sitting, and stopped just beyond her reach.

They had gone back to her bedroom, at her request. Pol had disappeared – hopefully, Packer thought, on his mission to Beirut's Central Post Office – and they were waiting for dinner which Pol had explained would be served in their rooms. It was now dark beyond the drawn curtains.

'Owen, I'm frightened.' She seized his wrist. Her fingers were very cold, and he allowed her to pull him up against the bed, but did not sit down beside her.

'I need you, Owen. I'm all alone.' Her other hand reached out and began to pull him down towards her.

'You need me, Sarah. But it's not because you're alone. It's because you think I'm the only one you can trust. The trouble is, you're too bloody right!'

She began to cry. He touched her shoulders, and she grabbed at him with both hands, her whole body shaking against him. 'I'm frightened, I'm frightened!' she moaned, between quick heaving sobs, and he could feel her tears trickling over the back of his hand.

'It's all right,' he whispered, and they sat on the bed, rocking gently against each other; then suddenly she stiffened, pulled the shawl off her shoulders, and fell back on to the pillows, kicking off her shoes and wriggling her toes between his thighs.

He undressed her quickly, more from habit than from skill, turning her over to unhook her skirt, breathing calmly now, with her face turned away from him, as he pulled her bra from under her and peeled off her pants. He paused, looking down at her, and a giddiness swept over him.

He felt sick and the floor seemed to be moving, rising up to meet him, while the whole room had turned red, the walls expanding and contracting like a pair of lungs. He closed his eyes, and the darkness was full of ugly swirling patterns, with Sarah still on the bed, lying on her belly with her legs parted and her whole body bathed obscenely in red. He blinked and looked away, but her body was still there, still red, but horribly distorted. Things were happening to it – strange, vile, unspeakable things that were the product of disordered imaginations, fed on centuries of cruel desert lore.

He switched off the bedside light and lay down beside her, and her hands closed round him, her fingers sliding across his body like scales in the dark. He started to say something, but she choked the words off with her tongue, letting out a long hiss of breath as he went into her, and he felt her tremble and contract with a steady rhythmic frenzy which he had never known before. It was over very quickly and simultaneously. For several seconds he lay sprawled across her, drained and dizzy. In the quiet of the room he could still hear the sharp cry she had given when she came; and he felt another rush of sickness as he squeezed his eyes shut and tried to banish that horrible red image on the bed.

He pulled away from her, and she gave a little gasp. 'Owen, what's the matter?'

'Nothing. Nothing at all – except that either you, or I, or both of us, is going to be killed in the next few days. All I hope is that it's quick.'

They lay together, listening to the black silence. 'Oh God, don't say that!' she cried at last. 'It was so good just now, and you want to spoil everything.'

'It was spoilt before we started. And what wasn't spoilt, you killed off for good back at the Vereina Hotel.'

'Oh no!' Her hands groped for him blindly. 'Please. Owen, that's all past and forgotten.'

'I haven't forgotten,' he said, and felt her stiffen beside him, but she did not speak. He traced her features in the dark and kissed her mouth, without opening his lips. 'Sarah, tell me how you feel about being screwed by the Ruler.'

This time he felt her flinch away from him. 'I don't want to talk about it.'

'I don't want to talk about it much, either. But it's not just personal interest – it's business. Big business.'

He paused; she lay tense and quiet beside him, as though holding her breath. 'How are you going to do it, Sarah?'

Again she said nothing. He reached out and felt for her chin, which was turned away from him, and yanked it round towards him, although her features were only a dim blur. 'How are you going to do it?' he repeated savagely.

'I don't know. Honestly. They haven't told me yet.' She suddenly scrambled up in the bed and slid off the other side. 'I'm going to wash,' she said. A moment later the light came on in the bathroom.

He lay back and tried to think.

17

She had all day with nothing to do but sun-bathe and water-ski and go to parties where they ate caviar and drank champagne and danced until the dawn came up, pale pink and grey across the wide sweep of the Gulf which was flecked with fishing boats, their nets suspended behind them in the clear air like insect's wings.

At least, that was how Mr Shiva Steiner had described it to her in Beirut, and in a manner of things he had been right. What he had not told her was that the sky was a dome of burning glass, extinguished only at night, and occasionally by the howling, biting brown fog of a sand-storm; and tolerable only in that brief half hour after dawn and just before sunset. This was when the young and privileged of Mamounia went water-skiing; but Sarah was no better at this than at snow-skiing, and had to explain to Steiner and his elegant cosmopolitan friends that she was forbidden this sport owing to a serious riding accident.

As for the parties, she had never greatly cared for caviar, and the champagne seemed to have a gritty brackish taste, as though it had been filtered through sand.

Steiner had also failed to inform her that the company at these parties, while affecting a suave Western chic, mostly looked like what her father was fond of describing, rather ambivalently, as 'coming from the wrong side of Lombard Street'; nearly all of whom spoke languages which she had never heard before. And long before Shiva Steiner's promised pink-grey dawn, half the men had usually offered, in broken but explicit English or French, to take her to bed – or rather, down to one of the huge American cars in the garage, where they suggested doing elaborate things to her – some of a weirdly mechanical, asexual nature which was quite unfamiliar to her; others more basic and foul, which she knew you could read about in special magazines, but had never been in the least tempted to try herself.

These men bored and disgusted her. One evening she told Steiner so, and he dismissed her remark with a shrug.

The women hated her – the older ones even more than the young. On her fourth night in the Ruler's capital, three of them had lain in wait for her in the downstairs toilet reserved for the women, where two of them had spat scientifically in both her eyes, while the third had stabbed her in the forearm with a pin. She had staunched the blood, and slipped back to her room unseen, where she had had violent hysterics.

On the fifth day a high, hot wind had blown up, and by noon the city had grown dark with sand. That morning she had also woken afflicted by an acute stomach disorder, and stayed in her room until evening, eating nothing, speaking to nobody.

It was then that she began to feel like a prisoner. The windows were double glazed against the sand, and the air-conditioning was kept permanently on, its steady hum pitched at a note that always seemed just about to break off, but never did – blowing cold all day, hot at night.

Her mouth and lips and skin had that same parched feeling that she'd had almost from the moment of stepping out of Shiva Steiner's twin-engined Executive jet, to walk the few yards across the bubbling shimmering tarmac to the black air-conditioned Fleetwood sedan. This had driven her to Steiner's marble palace outside the city. The place reminded her of an old film she had once seen in which an ageing Hollywood movie queen acted out the last days of her career in a macabre setting which Steiner seemed to have copied with a demented sense of kitsch.

Sarah now lay naked on the bed, and listened to the wind booming against the glass, and shivered – perhaps with the dry chill of the air-conditioning, but more likely at the thought of this house.

She assumed it must have been built quite recently, with the coming of oil; but despite its polished floors, glossy buhl furniture and luscious indoor plants, the place already exuded a sickly sense of decay. In most houses she would have diagnosed mildew, dry rot and wood-worm; but here the disease eluded her for the first couple of days, until she realized that she herself was contaminated.

It was the sand. Not the healthy pebble sand of a salt-washed beach, but a creeping silver-grey grit – a cloying fibrous substance which was not quite wet, not quite dry, not quite sticky – somewhere between mercury and powdered glass. It rubbed and itched and ate its way into everything, piling up under the windows like a fine layer of ash; collected round the tops of her bottles and jars in the bathroom, clung to the bottom of the bath and the seat of the lavatory, clogged the spray of the shower, and worked its way into the fabric of the towels, the folds of her clothes, the roots of her hair, under her arms and between her legs and toes, into her eyes and mouth and ears.

On the sixth day she was appalled to find a rash beginning round her groin, where the edge of her pants chafed against the top of her thighs. She rubbed on cream, but by the eighth day the rash had spread and become inflamed, until it was uncomfortable to walk. That evening she gave up wearing pants at all, but the rash persisted, and she was now thinking of asking Shiva Steiner if there was an English doctor in town.

Her inbred sense of what was right and proper excluded all possibility of venereal complaints; and the thought that she should get stricken with some horrid little affliction so far from home, so utterly far from friends – and at the one time in her life when she must appear at her most glamorous and unsullied – filled her with humiliation and panic. She pressed her breasts against the stiff gritty sheet and wept.

Her discomfort, as well as her growing fear of humiliation, was increased by the state of her stomach, a condition which deteriorated during the day in equal proportion to that of the plumbing in the Steiner mansion. By mid-afternoon – either because of the storm or through some decrepit malfunction of the city's water supply – the gold-plated taps ran to a dribble, coughed and dried up. The green onyx lavatory refused to flush.

She made the best of things by damping down both the bathroom and the bedroom with Guerlain's 'Chamade', using the best part of a bottle before Steiner called her on the house phone to ask if she would like to go to a party at the British Embassy. He was not going himself, but his chauffeur would drive her there and wait for her.

She accepted only in the hope of meeting an English doctor. She dressed casually, not taking her customary care over her make-up, swallowed ten milligrams of Valium, and went downstairs feeling drained and feeble.

It was a twenty-minute drive to the city, through the scrambling rush-hour traffic of American limousines and donkeys and bicycles, and occasionally the lurching shape of a camel.

Apart from the sea-front, which she had seen on a trip into town on her second day, it was an undistinguished city, remarkable only for the ugliness and speed with which it was being developed. She noticed a great many supermarkets, some only half built; shops packed with colour televisions, hi-fi equipment and cassette players; and numerous modern dress shops, several of them full of obscene life-size plastic models, naked and bald.

And everywhere the Ruler's eyes followed her from large coloured posters.

The Embassy was in a quiet residential quarter on the other side of the city : a modest stone building behind a large garden. There were about two dozen guests in a brightly lit room with a chandelier and Annigoni's portrait of the Queen. She knew at once that she was in for a heavy evening.

An English footman, looking like an actor, offered her the choice of a sherry or gin and tonic. She asked if he had any vodka, and he said he would look.

She was introduced to the Ambassador, a worried-looking man who seemed to be frowning even when he was smiling. He, in turn, introduced his wife, who was as tall as himself, and larger, with a lot of pale yellow hair and an unhealthy bluish complexion that might have been caused by drink, or just the climate.

The footman had found Sarah a vodka, and the three of them talked about England, the English theatre, and the prospect of the National Theatre coming to Mamounia. It was all very smooth and leisurely and trite, and struck Sarah as being just the kind of conversation the British Ambassador and his wife were supposed to have with visiting compatriots. Only later did it occur to her that not once had either of them asked her a direct question about herself – about what she was doing in Mamounia, how long she was staying, or what she thought of the place.

The Ambassador circulated, leaving Sarah to chat with his wife from whom she learned that their last post had been Buenos Aires – 'which was heaven compared to this – the climate, anyway' – this being the only opinion that Sarah heard the woman express. She managed to secure a second vodka and then broached the subject of the British doctor, but was dismayed to learn that there was none; the resident Embassy staff had the choice of a Swiss or an American – 'both of them good', said the Ambassador's wife, 'but horribly expensive. It isn't anything serious, I hope?'

'Upset tummy, that's all, Mrs Braintree.' At this stage, she was not going to confide her other complaint to a stranger.

'Oh, I've got *just* the thing!' the woman cried, and hurried Sarah upstairs and led her through the connubial bedroom into a bathroom, where she closed the door and began sorting through bottles in a medicine chest. 'All runny, are you? Or can't keep anything down?' She turned and was smiling down at Sarah with a square-toothed grin.

Sarah, who had always been embarrassed about discussing such matters in front of anyone except her mother, her ex-nanny, or a recommended doctor, suddenly distrusted this big, bluff, toothy woman.

'All right, I can see – you're shy! Runny, are you?' She patted Sarah on the arm and laughed. 'Goodness, what a thing to be ashamed of! We all get it when we first come out here. Now, this'll put you right.' She handed Sarah two bottles – a small one with pills in it, and a larger one full of brown liquid. 'Two pills now – two before you go to bed – two when you wake up – and two every four hours until it clears up. And take a big slug of the other now.' She picked up the tooth glass from beside the basin, together with a decanter of mineral water. 'This ought to seal you up for the next forty-eight hours. I know what these abominable loos are like. I'd be surprised if Shiva Steiner's were any different.'

Sarah gave a start at the mention of her host's name, then remembered that the Ambassador's wife must have known where she was staying to have sent the invitation. She swallowed two of the tablets, and drank an inch of the brown liquid which tasted of chocolate. Both bottles, she noticed suspiciously, had labels printed in Arabic script. She considered mentioning her rash, but before she had time to decide –

'Sarah Laval-Smith!'

The woman was staring down at her, with no smile now, her face like a slab of pumice stone. 'Listen, you bloody little fool.'

Sarah felt herself stiffen with a rush of anger. 'What on earth do you mean by speaking to me like that?'

'If you were my daughter, young lady' – the woman's breath smelled of gin – 'if you were my daughter, I'd give you a darn good hiding and send you to bed without your dinner. But unfortunately you're not –'

'No, I'm not,' Sarah said furiously, and was turning on her heel, dropping the bottles into her handbag, when the woman grabbed her arm.

'No, but you *are* a British subject. And that makes you our responsibility.'

'I'm perfectly capable of looking after myself, thank you, Mrs Braintree.' She moved towards the door, but the woman stepped round her and leaned her bulk against it.

'I've got something else to give you, my girl. Good sound advice. And you're going to stay here for as long as it takes me to give it. Get away from Mr Shiva Steiner. Get away as quickly as you bloody well can. Have you got an air ticket? Or did he fly you here in his jet, like he does most of his girls?'

'In his jet.'

Mrs Braintree shook her head melodramatically. 'What on earth is a girl like you doing getting yourself mixed up with a man like that? Your father's Henry Laval-Smith, of Laval-Smith's Bank, isn't he?'

Sarah gaped at her; the sound of her father's name coming from this grotesque woman, in this unlikely outpost of British territory, shocked her rigid. 'How do you know?' she asked, in a weak whisper.

'Well, it's hardly a common name, is it, dear? And we do keep a copy of *Who's Who* in the Embassy.'

'What are you warning me against, Mrs Braintree?'

'Mr Steiner. Are you sleeping with him?' she added casually.

'Certainly not.'

Mrs Braintree frowned. 'That's rather what I was afraid of. I'd be happier if you were.'

'What's that supposed to mean?'

'Listen, you silly, spoilt, arrogant little bitch!' She grabbed Sarah by both shoulders; her face was flushed dark, her eyes bloodshot. 'You may think I'm just another toothy old hag who spends all her time organizing bridge and cocktail parties, and swapping catty stories with the other Embassy wives.

'But I also keep my eyes and ears open. The Argentine was

good training, with all the kidnappings and terrorism. But let me tell you – even the Argentine had nothing on this place.' She fixed Sarah with a fierce, sober stare. 'I suppose, before Shiva Steiner got you out here – for whatever purpose that is – he told you about NAZAK?'

Sarah gave a faint nod.

'Well, they're bloody terrifying. And they don't need any proof against you – just a whiff of suspicion, and you're likely to be picked up and taken to their headquarters where they go in for things like sticking broken bottles up middle-class girls. With a pretty upper-class girl like you they'd have even more fun.'

'I don't understand,' Sarah replied, with blank innocence.

'Well, that's too bad,' said Mrs Braintree, 'because *I* certainly don't understand. All I know is, a lot of strange rumours have been going around lately, and they all suggest that this country's on the point of bloody turmoil. And a lot of these rumours concern your friendly host, Mr Shiva Steiner. And if you're not sharing his bed out here, I'd just like to know what you *are* doing with him. I expect the two gentlemen in the car across the street would as well.'

'What do you mean?'

'When you leave, you'll see what I mean. They'll follow you. I'm surprised you didn't notice them on your way here – or perhaps you weren't given the right training? It'd be like Steiner to pick some pretty little innocent to do his dirty work. Less chance of your being able to talk afterwards.'

'Mrs Braintree, I don't understand what you're trying to say.' Sarah spoke with a frightened dignity, 'And I don't wish to be rude to you in your own house, but I'm beginning to think you've had too much to drink.'

The woman gave a hoarse laugh and took Sarah firmly by the arm. 'All right, I can't beat it out of you. And I can't keep you locked up here, or have you deported. But don't say I didn't try to warn you.'

She opened the door, led her back across the bedroom and out on to the stair-case. Halfway down she stopped.

'Sarah, for the last time, I don't know what you're doing out here with Steiner, but – *get out while you've still got your skin*!' She took a deep breath. 'And remember one thing. You can be sure that everything I've told you tonight – about you and Steiner

– has already been noted by the authorities here. If you don't believe me, take a look at the car when you go outside. It's a grey Ford Falcon, with no numberplates' – she cackled – 'which is supposed to make it inconspicuous, like wearing no trousers.' And she marched on down the stairs.

Several more guests had arrived, including a number of sleek-haired locals whose fishy eyes darted at once in Sarah's direction. She evaded them skilfully, and left unnoticed.

Outside, the wind had dropped and the air was full of the scream of cicadas. Steiner's car – one of the big Fleetwood sedans – was parked where she had left it at the gates, with the chauffeur asleep at the wheel.

About fifty yards down the street, on the opposite side, a low dark coupé stood facing them, without lights or numberplates. Sarah could just make out the shape of two men inside. She shivered as she climbed into the air-conditioned chill of the Fleetwood. The chauffeur had woken as though by instinct; seen her in, closed the door, and started the engine. As they slid away, the coupé's side lights came on and began to follow them.

The traffic had cleared and the chauffeur kept up a steady speed which the coupé had no difficulty in matching. A couple of miles from Steiner's house, the lights behind suddenly swerved round and vanished. Sarah and the chauffeur were alone on the straight desolate coast road.

18

Owen Packer was shaving, after a late Continental breakfast, when there was a loud knock on his door. He went through and opened it, with the foam still clinging to his neck and cheek.

Three men stood outside. Two were household goons who might have been twins – oblong bodies, blue jaws, and black square crewcuts. Packer throught for a moment that he recognized the driver who had brought him up from the airport, but he could not be sure. He was not interested, anyway; he was looking at the man in the middle.

Like the other two, he was very tall, but much thinner, and hung between them, his head lolling forward under a wide bush hat, his legs dragging behind, like a broken scarecrow.

One of the goons growled, and the three of them entered, the middle one scraping his boots across the cedarwood floor. Packer backed away in front of them, and stood aside as they hauled the man on to the bed and rolled him over on to his back. The bush hat rolled free, and a yellow eye stared dully at the ceiling. Its companion opened slowly, squinted round, fixed on Packer, blinked, and lit up with a dry glitter. 'Oh shit. Sh-sheeeeit!' The goons withdrew.

Packer stood by the bed and scratched his cheek where the shaving foam had already dried into sticky flakes. 'What did they do to you, Sammy?'

Ryderbeit twisted his head round and made a vague effort to lift himself, then sank back with a groan. His face showed no visible injuries, but had lost all its tan, and again had that sunken greenish pallor which was as smooth as old ivory.

'Pissed,' he said at last. 'Pissed as a snake. Footless! Been footless now for nine days. Three days in a wop can – that makes twelve. Right? Twelve fucking days since I saw you, soldier, and I can't remember a fucking thing about any of them!' This time he managed to get himself up on to his elbow, but it didn't seem to make him feel any better.

'I'm going to finish shaving,' said Packer. 'You stay here.' He paused. 'What *are* you doing here, by the way?' he added.

'I drive planes, remember?' Ryderbeit replied weakly.

Packer nodded, went back into the bathroom, shaved, put on a clean shirt, and poured the last of the tepid black coffee into a cup; but when he brought it to the bed, Ryderbeit was asleep.

There was another knock and Pol came in, jauntily dressed in a floral beach shirt, white flannel trousers and embroidered slip-on shoes. 'Ah, so the great warrior sleeps like a child!'

'He's been on a bender for a week. Where the hell did you find him?'

'The Italian Police found him for me. He was enjoying himself in Genoa, when he was seduced from the charms of the fallen ladies of the port district by his old friend, the grappa bottle. If he hadn't made a nuisance of himself, which necessitated the intervention of the carabinieri, it would indeed have been very difficult to find him. Fortunately, Sammy has remarkable powers of recovery.'

'I hope so, if he's going to fly,' said Packer. 'He's only got one eye, even when he's sober.'

Pol nodded. 'We will leave him to sleep a little, then after lunch, perhaps, he will be ready to join us in conversation.'

'Are you leaving him in here? What's wrong with Sarah's old room?'

'Ah yes.' Pol paused, sucking the heel of his thumb. 'Tonight we are rather crowded, mon cher.'

'You mean, I'm going to have to share a bed with Ryderbeit?' Packer cried, genuinely appalled.

'No' – Pol giggled – 'no, mon cher. Tonight Sammy will be flying you to Mamounia.'

'How the hell did you get in?' said Packer. 'This is the one part of the world where that virgin Israeli passport of yours is about as popular as the proverbial pork chop in a synagogue.'

'Yeah' – Ryderbeit drew on a twisted black cigar whose smoke hung heavy and foul, even in the clear mountain air. 'Well, I'm no longer officially one of the Chosen Race. Danny Spice-Handler's been left in the cat houses of Genoa, and Samuel D. Ryderbeit is back in business, complete with his Rhodesian rebel passport.'

'What about your visa?'

'Twenty-four-hour transit. We're not going to need longer – and if we do, we're going to have more to worry about than a few wog Immigration officers.'

Packer nodded thoughtfully. His own visa had been extended for a month, after Pol had taken his passport away for a few hours on the second day of his visit. Next evening he and Pol had each received telegrams from the Volkskantonale Bank, Aalau, confirming the further payment of £500,000 sterling into their joint numbered account; and four days ago – the day after Sarah had left with Steiner – Pol had handed him an express airmail letter, also from Aalau.

It contained photostated documents relating to the payment, together with a letter reminding him, as a new client, that the money could be drawn only against both account-holders' signatures, and that in the event of the decease of one or the other, the entire funds reverted to the bank. Packer had accepted – with contradictory emotions – the fact that he was now finally and irrevocably committed: the departure of Sarah had already decided him emotionally, and the money was merely a further practical inducement.

They were sitting on the open terrace beyond the swimming-pool. Pol, who had said little so far, was sweating, although the heat was not oppressive. He poured some arak into Ryderbeit's cup of black coffee and opened a folder on the table in front of them. 'Let us attend to details. First, the aircraft.' He turned to Ryderbeit. 'Fortunately, here in the Lebanon there are gentlemen who, for a consideration, will supply almost every modern instrument of war, short of nuclear weapons – and those, perhaps, are only a matter of time. Antiques, however, are more difficult. But there again, the Lebanon is a country rich in both the old and the new. An advertisement in one of the local papers put us in touch with the owner of a private museum for veteran equipment from the last two World Wars. The price he asked was abominably high, but I was forced to agree.'

'Come on – details,' Ryderbeit said impatiently.

Pol bent over the sheet of paper in front of him. 'Fieseler Storch, Luftwaffe, North African Campaign,' he read slowly, moving his finger under each word, as though unfamiliar with his own handwriting.

'A Storch, eh?' Ryderbeit shrugged. 'Not bad, though I'd have preferred a Lysander, mostly because they were on the winning side and didn't get mauled around so badly. Date?' he added.

'1941.'

'Holy Moses!' He gulped his coffee and arak. 'That's a real old-age pensioner! If she survived that long, either they dug her up out of a graveyard and stuck her together again, or she was bloody lucky.'

'Do you mind telling me what you're talking about?' said Packer.

'Getaway plane,' said Ryderbeit. 'We're going to need something with a long range, that flies low, handles like a kite, and can put down and take off in sand. And the Storch fits the bill beautifully. These modern tricycle jobs are useless. You touch the nose-wheel down and hit just one bump or patch of soft sand, and go arse over tip and usually land upside down with a broken back. But those old World War Two babies were tough. They didn't look it, but they were. Tied together with string – sometimes literally – and no fancy problems like stress. The Fieseler Storch was a reconnaisance plane, used for tank spotting in the desert, and could cruise at around 150 knots for up to six hours – which, with modifications, gave it well over a 500-mile range. And that's just about what we need.

'They have other advantages too. You can shoot them full of holes, and unless you hit the tank or the prop-shaft, they stay flying. They're also tree-hopping jobs, and with no trees we can come in and get out well under any radar system.'

'What about sand-storms?' said Packer.

'Even better. They really bugger up any radar. And while you wouldn't get most modern planes through one, a Storch just bounces about like a ping-pong ball and doesn't get hurt.' Ryderbeit leaned out and gave Pol a huge slap on the shoulder. 'Well done, Fat Man! Now tell me where she is.'

'At Beirut International Airport. In the section reserved for private aircraft. You and Capitaine Packer are cleared for take-off this evening at 18.30 hours for Nicosia.'

Ryderbeit was suddenly suspicious. 'Has she been tested?'

'The vendor has assured us that the plane is in perfect flying order,' Pol replied.

'Yeah, these wogs never lie!' Ryderbeit poured some more arak into the dregs of his coffee. 'But don't mind if I make a detour up to Tripoli, and if I don't like the way she handles, I reserve my right to come back.' His eye peered at Packer. 'I take a hell of a lot of risks, soldier, but where flying's concerned I take careful risks.'

'One thing you don't seem to have thought about,' Packer said, 'is that our 500-mile range may get us to Mamounia, but it's going to be a one-way trip.'

'Yeah, but there's another thing I didn't tell you about these Storch babies. They're put together like one of those toy aircraft – and they come apart the same way. Wings, engine, tailpiece – all detachable, and the rest folds up and can be put in a truck. We can refuel her in Steiner's back-yard.'

'And a truck's been laid on?'

Pol answered, 'Do not concern yourself – all arrangements have been made.'

'Which presumably means,' Packer said coldly, 'that the Ruler makes his personal dates well in advance? Or perhaps Steiner makes them for him?'

'You must surely understand,' said Pol, 'that a man in the Ruler's position does not have time to attend to such details.'

Such as a royal bunk-up with Sarah, thought Packer, but he made no comment.

19

For the driver and his passenger the journey was a familiar one, though the route of the first stage, out of the city, varied slightly each time.

Today, Marmut bem Letif had left the Ministry at his usual time, just after noon, and had ridden in his official car, flanked by two outriders with sirens to clear the traffic, to a restaurant in the commercial centre. The car had waited outside until the last diners had left; but when it finally drove away the two men sitting in the unnumbered Ford Falcon a few doors back down the street saw that it did so without picking up its passenger.

Letif had slipped out of the back after the first course, crossed a garden and let himself into a small ground-floor flat from which he emerged a few minutes later wearing sandals and a burnous with its hood up. He went out through a gate in the garden wall, and down an alley into a small street where a taxi was waiting.

Outside the Armenian quarter, on the edge of the city, they had been stopped at a roadblock where the troops had been sleepy with the heat, hardly glancing at his card in its celluloid frame. Two hours later, they had climbed the foothills and were driving over a bleak plateau with the wall of white spiked mountains on one side, the empty glare of the desert on the other.

As soon as he saw they were coming close to the gorge – even after all these visits – Letif felt a faint ache in his bowels; but today he was more confident, sustained by his anger and outraged pride, following his last audience with the Ruler. He was even looking forward to this meeting.

The sight of the gorge was so sudden that it still amazed, even alarmed him. After driving across nearly 100 kilometres of monotonous stony wasteland, the ground stopped, like the edge of the world. Beyond was a great void, ending in a distant wall of dark sunless rock, veined and blotched like raw marble.

The Doctor's guards appeared, as always, from some mysterious covert: ragged men dressed in bits of uniforms from many armies, strapped about with an arsenal of light weapons, all of which looked modern and in working order. They examined Letif's pass with the usual meticulous curiosity, passing it from one to the other before handing it back to him and signalling that he could get out.

It was only when he reached the edge of the precipice that he could see the bottom – a ribbon of black water several thousand feet below. The air was already cool up here, but the emptiness below seemed to give off a chill of its own. To his right rose a pillar of sandstone supporting a bridge across the chasm : a narrow cat-walk sustained by steel cables that drooped away into the distance, and reinforced by two more cables attached to the top of the sandstone. These also steadied a pair of rope hand-rails.

Letif knew that distance and height were deceptive, and that the true span of the bridge was less than 400 metres; but whenever he stepped on to those short wind-worn planks he felt the bile rising in his throat, and turned his eyes upwards, narrowing them until he could only just make out the blurred rim of the cliff ahead. A few steps from the edge, the bridge began to sway, then to rock with a slow lurching rhythm that made him feel as though his small body were being magnified to monstrous proportions.

He was greeted on the other side with ritual courtesy. Here the men wore no uniforms, carried no guns – at least, not visibly. Letif was never introduced to them by name, but their hands were soft and they had the refined, thoughtful faces of students from good families who had rejected fashionable Western clothes and had reverted, instead, with almost religious zeal, to the plain tribal costume of their ancestors.

Beyond the summit of the cliff was a short drop into a silver-green oasis of olive trees; in the middle stood a small house with a flat white roof. A couple of goats were tethered under the trees. It was a scene of Arcadian simplicity which always struck Letif as being irritatingly mannered, as did the costumes of the young men who had greeted him. They, in turn, reminded him of those students he had met in Paris and America who wore Lenin-type caps and workmen's boots, and had charge accounts at all the best shops and restaurants.

But he consoled himself with the image of that long room in

the Palace, its walls and ceilings gilded with gold leaf, its red carpet climbing the steps to a throne of solid gold studded with 780 emeralds. The thought revived his anger and hatred, and he entered the house in a spirit of resolve.

It was a simple peasant house, with one main room, its white-washed walls covered with ornamental hangings, except for one which was lined with books, many of them in European languages. The floor was stone, the furniture in traditional Arab style – low couches draped in woollen rugs, leather stools, small round tables of beaten brass.

Letif's escort withdrew through the bead curtain. The windows were small and the light poor, and it took Letif several seconds to appreciate the scene.

There were only two men in the room. One was Dr Zak, sitting quietly in the corner sipping a glass of mint tea. The other was Colonel Sham Tamat.

Letif was surprised; for although Dr Zak had long enjoyed the status of being head of a licensed opposition, the old man had never before held court to both the Minister of the Interior and the Chief of the Committee of Counter-Terrorism and Public Safety. Letif's instinct, as well as his trade, led him to suspect a trap. In any case, he decided that matters had clearly reached a climax.

He bowed, gave the ceremonial greeting, and sat down, against the wall opposite the two men. The Colonel's appearance was certainly not that of a conspirator: he was wearing cavalry twill jodhpurs and calfskin boots, and an English chequered hacking jacket with a yellow handkerchief flowering from his breast pocket; and was drinking from a bottle of good Scotch whisky on the table beside him. Letif guessed that he had brought it with him. For Dr Zak – like the Ruler – discouraged alcohol.

Tamat gave his big fleshy grin. 'So, Minister Letif, we meet in the wolf's den!' His smile shifted to Dr Zak, who sat without expression. Tamat raised his glass to Letif: 'Well – what is new at the all-powerful Ministry of the Interior?'

Letif licked his lips. 'I have spoken again to His Imperial Highness. He is angry that I cannot tell him more than we have already discussed. He does not believe the report that our honourable host' – he nodded at Zak – 'was in Damascus. In fact, I had

276

the impression that he no longer believes even what *I* tell him. I believe that he knows more than we suspect.' He sat with his fingers locked together, his face grown taut and pale. 'He also insulted me. It was not even a subtle insult. It was a vicious wound to the memory of my father.'

Tamat drank some whisky. His expression was relaxed, benign. 'Poor Letif. But we who work so close to the Devil must expect the occasional jab from his horns. Did he tell you anything new?'

'He told me I had little time – that I must hurry. He expects foreign assassins to enter the country at any moment. It is my impression that he is no longer impatient, but is becoming nervous.'

Tamat shrugged. 'Impressions are not sufficient, Letif. I, like His Imperial Highness, require facts.'

Letif stared at the floor. He wondered why he was not accorded the accustomed formality of mint tea. He also wondered if he should tell Tamat that the Ruler knew about the fat man; whether Zak had confided to the Colonel the existence of this Frenchman who was known under the names of Cassis and Pol, and perhaps other names too.

He wished that Zak had spoken to him first, had forewarned him of this meeting; for Letif loathed and feared his encounters with Tamat – doubly so now that the circumstances were so sudden and unexplained. He looked at Dr Zak, but the old man seemed to be dozing. 'Tell me what is happening,' he said, in a clear defiant voice.

Dr Zak opened his eyes and gave a slow sad smile. 'Come, Minister, I have something to show you.' He unfolded his thin legs and stood up, beckoning to Letif with his clawlike hand. Together the two men moved up to the wall of books. Zak paused, then ran his finger along a row of yellow paper-bound volumes in French. He smiled again at Letif. 'One day, Minister, when I have more time, I must try and arrange my humble little library. I can find nothing when I want it.'

Letif smiled back. 'What are you looking for?' He heard the rattle of the bead curtain and wondered if this was his mint tea arriving. He was about to turn when the Doctor's bony fingers closed round his wrist.

'I think I have found it.' Zak's free hand was reaching up for a book on one of the higher shelves. Letif heard the pad of footsteps on the stone floor behind him. Zak had pulled out the book and Letif was trying to see the title, when something was thrown round his shoulders. He thought at first it was a rug, though it was too light, and had a shiny surface like a waterproof cape or oilskin. He felt hands round his neck and across his face, and began to scream.

It was a loud, choking animal scream, accompanied by a frenzied struggling . . . the noises of the farmyard and the abattoir. The man used the ceremonial dagger, with its long scythe-like blade worn thin on a whetstone, like a well-used carving knife.

He cut Letif's throat with one swift movement, opening it from ear to ear, slicing the oesophagus, windpipe and tendons as far back as the spinal cord, until the narrow head was lolling back from the shoulders, while the face, stretched in its frozen scream, hung upside down until the man carefully lifted it, let the body down, and wrapped the head and shoulders in the plastic sheet whose folds were already brimming over with blood.

A second man had appeared and together they carried the body outside. 'Bury him at once,' Zak said, and put the book back on the shelf. 'Then signal to the guards.' He turned to Tamat. 'I have given instructions that they are to dispose of the driver and the car in the gorge.'

Colonel Tamat nodded and finished his whisky. 'This has been most satisfactory, Doctor.' He glanced towards the bookshelves. 'I congratulate you – hardly a spot of blood! Is that an omen, I wonder?' He chuckled and refreshed his glass.

20

Sarah woke late and breakfasted alone in the air-conditioned
salon, where there was coffee and mint tea, yoghourt and honey,
and bread loaves the shape of stones. Beyond the French windows she could see a few of the other guests, all of them men,
basking on long chairs under the arcades round the pool. The
women rarely appeared before dusk.

She had a headache and was still tired, although she had slept
heavily. She was also hungry. She had slipped in unnoticed last
night after the Embassy party, and had gone straight to her
room. Mrs Braintree's warnings had been muted, if not neutra-
lized, by her agreement with Charles Pol, who had promised her
that if she did what she was told, she would be as rich as she
required.

The thought filled her with febrile excitement; and the best
she could say for Mrs Braintree was that her medicine seemed to
have worked. Not only had her stomach recovered, but her rash
seemed to be clearing up too.

Steiner found her in a mood of tentative elation. 'Good morning, my dear Sarah.' He looked fresh and at ease. 'I apologize
most sincerely for the disgraceful lack of water. But I am afraid
we are not in the West any more. However, I trust you have not
been too greatly inconvenienced?'

Sarah said something noncommittal and waited. For a long
moment Steiner gazed out at the pool, which was still covered
with a film of grey sand, like the skin of a toad.

'We are taking a trip into the city,' he said at last. 'There are
some things I want to show you. And things I want to discuss.
Are you ready?'

'I'll just get my bag.'

She felt a guilty excitement as she climbed into the upholstered
gloom of the Fleetwood, sitting well back in the seat away from
him. She remembered Mrs Braintree's warnings against the man,
and although Sarah had never found Shiva Steiner anything but
courteous and charming, she could not help feeling that it would

take quite a lot to shock an old bag like the Ambassador's wife.

Steiner said little during the drive. When they left the house the road was empty, but a few miles on, when Sarah looked back through the smoked rear window, the unnumbered grey car was there again with two men inside. She pointed it out to Steiner, but he seemed uninterested; then she told him about the car last night.

'You are very observant,' he murmured. He sounded pre-occupied or bored; and she was reminded of his behaviour during their dinner with the Ruler in Klosters, when he had dropped his easy social manner, suddenly, like an actor abandoning his role once he has stepped off stage.

'But who are they?' she asked.

He turned slowly and looked at her. 'Why are you so interested, my dear?'

'I talked to the British Ambassador's wife last night. She said some very odd things – not only about being followed, but about you.'

'I do not suppose they were very complimentary. In my experience, the wives of Western diplomats live on rumours and gossip, as some people live on vitamins.'

There was a long pause. They were coming into the city now, leaving the private villas with their gardens and swimming-pools, and were driving between squalid modern buildings divided by dark alleys and crowded bazaars. The traffic had not yet built up, but there seemed to Sarah to be a great many troops and armoured vehicles about. Near the city centre, they were to be seen in every door-way, at every street corner: most of them carried short-muzzled machine pistols, and several of them had radios.

She asked Steiner about them, and he gave a small, patronizing smile. 'You must know, my dear Sarah, that this country has one of the largest armies in the world.'

'But why so many today?'

'They are probably on manoeuvres. An army has to be given something to do. You cannot keep it locked up in barracks all the time.'

His reply struck her as a trifle too glib, but she did not feel qualified to argue. She looked back through the rear window; and after a moment she saw it again, a few cars back. She turned again to Steiner and said fiercely, 'You still haven't told me who they are.'

'Who?'

'The men in the car behind – the ones who followed me last night. *Who are they?*' Steiner's lack of interest was not only irritating her, it was making her nervous.

'Security police,' he replied.

'But why do they follow *us*? Why did they follow me last night?'

Steiner sighed. 'My dear, they follow anyone they think is important. Particularly foreigners. It is partly a form of protection for, regrettably, there are still many beggars in the city – wild men who have come in from the desert and the mountains where they used to be brigands. And this is a very security-minded country.'

Again Sarah found that the explanation seemed a little too elaborate, and not quite convincing.

They had reached the end of a street which opened on to a large deserted square: at the far end was an ornate white building which reminded her of a French casino. On one side of it stood a mosque, with a glittering dome and a pencil-shaped minaret; on the other, a long building faced with colonnades.

The street was blocked by a couple of jeeps and a row of troops in leopard-spotted uniforms. The driver turned the car so that it was facing across the street, then stopped. Steiner nodded in the direction of the square.

'That is the Royal Palace you see directly ahead – the Ruler's official residence. On the right is the Great Mosque, and on the left the Senate Building.' He spoke with the indifferent precision of a tour guide.

She looked at him, puzzled. 'Shiva, I saw all this the other day when we all came into town together. But then we were able to go right round the square. Now it's all blocked off.'

'Quite.' There was an uncharacteristic note of irritation in Steiner's voice. He gestured with his squat flat fingers. 'It is precisely this roadblock that I wished you to see. You will be passing through it tonight.'

She caught her breath and stared at him.

'They will not be the same troops on duty,' he continued, 'but they will have received instructions to let you through. The car will drop you here.'

'Tonight?' she said, in a dry whisper.

'His Highness has expressed his wish to entertain you tonight.'

'Me? But he won't even remember me!'

Shiva Steiner smiled, dead eyed. 'My dear Sarah, you do not suppose that we have gone to all this trouble and expense without first being sure of at least the basic details? Your last remark suggests, I hope, merely a degree of modesty on your part? Not, I trust, a sudden lack of self-confidence?'

He leaned forward to touch her knee, but she flinched away. 'You have nothing to fear. His Highness has also expressed to me, personally, that he found you a most agreeable and attractive person.'

'Nothing to fear!' she repeated, and glanced again through the rear window: the car was there, waiting, 100 yards behind. 'And what about those Security people? You're really telling me that they're following us just in case we're attacked by a few beggars?' She was sitting forward, her finger-nails digging into the deep leather seat.

'Calm yourself, my dear.' Steiner had not even bothered to follow her glance back through the window. 'We have come so far – you really must trust me.'

Again she remembered Mrs Braintree's words on the Embassy stairs – 'Get out while you've still got your skin!'

She opened her mouth to speak, then shut it again. She looked out at the troops. A few of them were looking back at the car. 'Shouldn't we be going?'

'You in a hurry?'

'But won't they recognize us – recognize me?'

Steiner's voice was as caressing as ever. 'They cannot see in through the windows. Even if they could, they are only soldiers. Why should they be interested in you, except to dream about you at night?' He gave a guttural order to the driver, who started the engine.

She watched as they passed the stationary grey car on the other side of the street. It pulled out and did a swift U-turn a moment later. The Fleetwood was driving deliberately slowly. Two hundred yards from the entrance to the square Steiner murmured something and the driver almost stopped.

Without looking at her, Shiva Steiner pointed towards a narrow side street leading between two tall concrete buildings.

'That is Passam Street,' he said. She peered over his shoulder and saw the name on a plaque in Arabic and Roman script. 'Your friend, Captain Packer, will be waiting for you at the corner from midnight tonight.' He added something to the driver and the car speeded up.

Sarah sank back into her corner, and for several minutes they drove again in silence.

'Sarah, it is time I explained to you the final, and perhaps the most important, detail of this whole operation. It concerns the method by which His Highness will die.' He paused. 'When you first agreed to this plan, did Charles Pol ever discuss this aspect of the affair with you?'

'Not exactly.' She was trying to control her breathing and found it hard to speak. 'He promised me that there wouldn't be any blood. That's all he said.' She was very frightened.

Steiner nodded. 'Monsieur Pol was quite correct. We have all agreed that you should be spared any unnecessary unpleasantness. Fortunately, there are new techniques which are both simple and highly effective.'

Her voice was a whisper. 'Poison?'

'In a manner of speaking, yes. However, we cannot risk having you offer His Highness something to eat or drink. He follows the ancient tradition here of employing a taster at all times of the day and night. So we have decided on an anal suppository.'

She swallowed hard, saying nothing.

'It is an almost universal practice among the French,' Steiner went on, 'for taking most common medicines, including aspirins and sedatives. But for some reason the Anglo-Saxons – including the Americans – find it disgusting, despite the fact that, as a method, it works much faster.'

'You want me to stick it up his arse, you mean?'

'Precisely.' Shiva Steiner sounded relieved. 'You must merely think of yourself as a nurse, or even a woman doctor. They have to perform far more disagreeable tasks every day of their working lives.'

'I'm not a nurse or a doctor!'

'No. But not even the most famous doctor in the world could command a fee a fraction as great as that which you are being paid for tonight's work.'

Sarah closed her eyes, as Steiner's soothing voice continued. 'The only real skill you will have to employ will be in the matter of timing. Like most experienced men of his age, the Ruler often enjoys diversions from the usual sexual play. But I have no doubt that you will handle this aspect of the situation correctly. Whatever His Highness suggests, it is essential that you neither resist nor show the least reluctance. If you do, he will merely throw you out. And that would be a pity. A pity for us all.'

Sarah still said nothing. After a few minutes, Steiner's voice reached her again, full of cajoling reassurance. 'There is one thing I should add, my dear. You will be given two of these suppositories. The poison belongs to the same group as cyanide and acts very quickly. He will be dead within thirty seconds. Before that there may be violent spasms, but even if he is lying on top of you he will not be able to hurt you, nor will he be able to make any sound. He will be unconscious almost at once.'

'What is the second one for?' she asked.

'It is merely a reserve – in case you drop or mislay the first one. Of course,' he went on gently, 'if something were to go seriously wrong, and you were to be apprehended, you could always use it on yourself.'

She shrank back into her corner again and watched the palm-shaded villas sliding past them as they drove through the suburbs, with the Ford Falcon still behind them.

'It is no business of mine,' Steiner added, 'to advise you to kill yourself. I am merely giving you the option.'

'That's very kind of you. And at what time is my presence required at the Palace?'

'His Highness is dining early with a delegation of Japanese industrialists. He does not expect to be late. I have received instructions to have you driven to the roadblock at 11.30. From there you will be escorted to his private apartments. Just one other thing . . .'

He paused, as though unexpectedly embarrassed. 'Of course – I rely entirely on your judgement in this matter. But it is possible – in this heat, perhaps – that your period might be premature?'

'No.' She gave a sharp humourless laugh. 'And what if it had been?'

'It might have been awkward. For you, I mean.'

They did not speak again until they reached the house.

21

They took off from Beirut International Airport at 6.42 p.m. local time. Customs and Immigration formalities had once again been leisurely and affable; the official who had inspected the Fieseler Storch was obviously more interested in the plane than in anything it might be carrying.

Their only visible luggage was a paper carrier bag containing two bottles, of Scotch and arak, which Ryderbeit had bought at the duty-free shop. For the moment, these worried Packer rather more than the two M16 carbines, with six clips of ammunition each, screwed down under the main tail-strut.

Packer guessed that somewhere along the chain of command at the airport, and probably fairly high up, the right words had been said, the right money exchanged; for the Lebanon was still in a state of civil war, and the Fieseler Storch did not look like just another playboy's toy.

Among the shoals of brightly coloured small aircraft in the area reserved for private planes, it stood out like an old cutlass on a dinner table. As a museum piece, it was still camouflaged – sky-blue on the underneath, desert-brown on its sides and roof and the top of its high wings – though someone had tactfully painted out the black indented crosses on the wing-tips and the swastikas on the tail.

Ryderbeit had spent a quarter of an hour inspecting her, unscrewing the cowlings and groping around in the engine until his hands and arms were smeared with fresh oil. His silence seemed to indicate a morose, professional satisfaction.

There was a fifteen-minute delay before they reached final clearance for take-off, while they waited for a jumbo and a DC 10 to come in. The cockpit, which was the size of the front seat of a sports car, was fitted with a large modern radio that took up most of Packer's leg room, in the rear observation seat. The screws looked brand-new. And Packer guessed that it had been installed in the last forty-eight hours.

Just before take-off, Ryderbeit reached back for the carrier bag and took a long drink of whisky from the bottle. His eye looked back at Packer and crinkled. 'Take it easy, soldier. Most times you fly commercial airways you don't see the pilot – nor do you see him the night before or the morning after. But that doesn't mean to say you haven't got a piss artist up front.' He cackled. 'I've known pilots – real respectable ones – who'd no more fly without a bottle than without radar. Most of them are never drunk, never sober. Me, if I don't have a drink I fly lame.'

The engine was not anxious to start, and Ryderbeit talked to it in a mixture of English and Afrikaans as though it were some new pet. To Packer the controls appeared remarkably few and simple. An American voice finally came over the radio: 'German bird-dog, you are cleared for take-off. But shake it up – we've got a Pan-Am 747 coming in on your tail.'

Ryderbeit grinned, and the little plane began to move. They took off in less than forty yards. Packer watched the floating compass settle on to north-north-east; the altimeter needle quivering up to 2000 metres.

It was already very cold, and very noisy. Packer pulled a thick sweater and anorak from behind his seat. It had been too hot on the ground to put them on, but up here it was like dressing inside a deep-freeze. Ryderbeit, on the other hand, seemed immune to the cold: he was still wearing his bush shirt under a light canvas jacket, khaki trousers and black suede boots, with his snow goggles pushed up on to his forehead. His hands on the controls were supple and perfectly steady; the only trace of his Italian rampage was his greenish pallor. He had shown no symptoms of tension or anxiety since waking at noon; and his one emotional outburst had been annoyance at not being able to get any Havana cigars at Beirut Airport.

He had stuffed the weather reports into the canvas pocket of his door; they were cleared to fly only as far as Tripoli, then west to Cyprus. The long leg east across Syria and Iraq would have to be flown blind, without radar or storm alerts.

The weather report indicated no cloud, with light south-easterly winds. Perfect conditions, Ryderbeit had said: perfect conditions, that was, for anyone wanting to go water-skiing or give an outdoor barbecue in Beirut or Limassol. It did not take into account sand-storms or mountain turbulence 500 miles to the east.

Ryderbeit had the maps – given him by Pol – spread out on his lap. Communication was difficult except by shouting; and once they were airborne Ryderbeit's expression had become one of serene but intense concentration. He was in a world of his own, and he loved it.

They followed the coast for twenty minutes, until they saw the grey smudge of a city ahead. Tripoli. Ryderbeit had kept the radio switched on, in case someone in Beirut changed his mind and told them to come back, in which event he was going to do a sharp right turn into Syria. He intended to do that anyway, but he wanted to keep the Lebanese happy for as long as possible.

He dropped to 800 metres, made a wide inland sweep as though he were about to hook round and come in over the dust-grey outskirts to the north of the city; then yelled at Packer: 'Sit back! – we're rolling over!' The floor seemed to slide away, the patchy brown below tilted up until the margin of veined green-blue sea was hanging above them; then with a swooping roar the Storch levelled out, with its detachable wings swaying giddily, and the city and the sea gone behind them.

The compass wobbled and settled down to due-east. The radio came on with a loud jabber of Arabic. Ryderbeit switched it off. From now on, whatever came over was not going to be polite, even if they could understand it.

The altimeter had dropped to just above 300 metres. Below stretched scrubland and semi-desert, spotted with olive trees and the occasional smallholding, racing towards them at over 140 knots. Ryderbeit had said he was not worried about the Lebanese; the real danger was that the Syrians would pick up Tripoli radio, and if someone got jittery enough, they might send up a fighter. There was an air-base at Homs, he'd said, just inside the border; and the Syrians had MIG 23s – not to mention SAMs.

But the light was already going. The sky was black and the desert ahead was turning the colour of a blood orange. Fifteen minutes after leaving their northerly course to Tripoli, the Storch sank to within 100 metres of the ground, its high-tailed shadow, with the long fixed undercarriage, rippling over the rocky sand like a great bird gliding in for the kill.

Packer could see no signs of the frontier; nor were there any tell-tale streaks from MIG afterburners or missiles. The landscape was now flat and featureless, bare of even the few scraps of cultivation they had crossed in the Lebanon.

Suddenly it was night: a wide deep blue-black nothing, except for the tiny green glow from the instrument panel. For the next three hours, and the next 500 miles, they were going to be flying what Ryderbeit called 'dead blind' – no lights, no radar, no radio, just a gyro-compass and an altimeter – in an aircraft that had been built when Ryderbeit and Packer were both in short trousers.

Packer settled back and tried to sleep.

22

At the moment that the Fieseler Storch was illegally crossing the Lebanese–Syrian frontier, a sand-coloured jeep with four men stopped close to the great Gorge of Darak, some eighty miles east of Mamounia.

In the quiet dusk the jeep showed no lights. The four men descended swiftly, their rubber-soled boots making no sound on the rocky slope up to the edge of the precipice. They wore grey denim battle-dress and walked in pairs, two carrying what looked like pieces of drain-pipe attached to a tripod, the other two lugging a heavy metal box.

When they reached the edge, one of them signalled with his hand and the tripods were set down on the ground. No spoken orders were given. From the black abyss in front of them came a cold dead hush, broken by the whine of distant wind. The pale rim of the sky still showed the jagged treeless horizon.

The man who had given the signal now raised a pair of night-glasses and scanned the far side of the gorge, turned and swept them over the rugged ground ahead. Against the fading light he could just distinguish a blurred pillar of sandstone, with two black threads curving down into the darkness of the gorge. There was no trace of life.

He looked at his watch. They were not to act until it was completely dark, he had been told: which would be in five or ten minutes – no more.

The other three were adjusting the tripods and rangefinders. One of them had opened the steel box and carefully, silently, arranged the pear-shaped bombs in rows between the two mortars; then they lay flat and waited.

They waited eight minutes. The sky was now black and full of stars: a good night, the men thought, because the moon was low and thin. They were all watching the same spot, on the sheer, faintly discernible ridge of cliff ahead, when a light blinked twice. The leader swung the glasses round to the foot of the sandstone pillar. There was no answering light, but a quick moth-like movement.

Half a minute later a second, feebler light flickered over the ridge ahead and meandered down to the edge of the invisible footbridge. Here it paused while four more lights joined it from above; then the five of them began wobbling out over the chasm.

The leader with the night-glasses nodded. Two of the soldiers reached out and each picked up a mortar bomb. They rested on their elbows and held the bombs over the mouths of both barrels. The man with the glasses followed the luminous second hand of his watch; after fifty seconds, the cluster of lights had progressed a third of the way across, swaying visibly. He waited another thirty seconds. The lights had passed the lowest dip of the bridge and began to climb, more slowly now. He raised his right hand.

The group on the bridge was within fifty feet of the rock base when he brought his hand down with a quick slicing movement. The two commandos dropped the bombs into the barrels of the mortars. In the silence there was a rattle of metal, then two almost simultaneous clonks and a whistle of air. A couple of seconds later a pair of flashes appeared on the sandstone pillar ahead, followed by a loud double crack that bounced off the opposite cliff with a long rolling echo.

The leader had his glasses up and gave a rapid order. One of the men fed his mortar again, while the other made a slight adjustment to his rangefinder. The explosions now came in fast succession, amplified by the walls of the gorge, until they sounded like an artillery barrage. The lights on the bridge had paused for a moment, then began hurrying forwards and upwards.

All four men were feeding the mortars now, watching the bursts of light on the top of the sandstone pillar. The leader had dropped in the ninth bomb and ducked down, when the four torches on the bridge appeared to glide sideways, then drift down into darkness where they spread out like fireflies and vanished. Above the booming echoes, a thin scream rose from the depths, with an answering bark from the walls of the gorge. Then silence.

The four men had already grabbed up the mortars and ammunition case, and were trotting back towards the jeep. A bullet cracked into the rock a few feet from them, and a second ripped through the jeep's canvas hood, as they clambered aboard and bounced away, without lights, into the darkness of the desert.

In the back the leader switched on a powerful short-wave radio.

Eighty miles away, in his office in the turret of his marble mansion, Shiva Steiner received the transmission. Dr Zak had departed to his Maker.

23

For the last two hours they had been flying at treetop level, although there were no trees. There was also no moonlight, but the stars had a brilliance that was reflected in a weird glow off the broken naked landscape.

Ryderbeit had consumed a quarter of the whisky by the time they had crossed Iraq, flying terrifyingly low until they reached the mountains that formed the natural barrier with the Ruler's kingdom. Here they had climbed steeply, with the little plane bouncing and lurching in the treacherous upcurrents, while Ryderbeit's fingers slid swiftly, surely over the controls, his lips moving in the dim light from the instrument panel, soothing, coaxing the little antique machine up through the winding corridor of a pass which marked the highest and most remote point of the frontier.

Packer had not been able to see the sides of the pass, but could make out their shape by the absence of stars. Ryderbeit, however, seemed endowed with some especially sensitive night-sight. He had a pencil torch with which he occasionally consulted the charts on his lap; but most of the time he seemed to be flying by instinct.

Packer was no aviation expert, but he guessed that Charles Pol would have had to spread a very wide net indeed in order to find another pilot like this one-eyed Rhodesian pariah. He wondered, too, what extra inducements Pol had offered, beyond the £100,000 that Ryderbeit had already received, and whether it was in a joint account, subject to the same dual signature conditions as Packer's.

He had fastened on this thought – on any thought – for as long as possible. Anything to keep his mind off the immediate fears of the flight, and the more ominous speculations of what lay ahead that night.

For more than an hour, after crossing from Iraq and leaving the mountains, Ryderbeit took them back up to 1000 feet, and they flew to the steady rattling roar of the engine, without seeing a single light below – not a town, not a village, not one pair of headlamps to mark a road. Packer felt like someone who has swum too far out over a deep lake and wonders if he can make it back to the shore.

At 10.35 local time – an hour ahead of Beirut – they reached another ridge of mountains; and again they came in so low that Packer felt that at any second the long rigid wheelstruts would be snapped off by a rock. But Ryderbeit's natural antennae seemed to detect every contour, every hump and peak and crevice, until they were drifting down the long empty slopes towards the Gulf. Lights were now sprinkled across the blackness below – and ahead Packer could see the glow of a city.

Ryderbeit signalled with his thumb and passed him the torch. Packer unstrapped himself and crawled back over his seat into the cramped tapering fuselage whose vibrating sides made his teeth rattle.

His fingers found the screws, and with the torch in one hand he got out Ryderbeit's pocket-knife, opened the screwdriver blade and went to work. He slipped three of the spare ammunition clips, each containing thirty rounds, into the deep pockets of his anorak; climbed back over his seat and laid the two M16s on the floor under his legs, before passing the other three clips to Ryderbeit, who tucked them into his belt.

They were again flying so low that Packer had the sensation of riding in a very fast car, skimming over the shadowy mounds of sand-dunes, expecting at any moment to see a house speeding towards them.

Ryderbeit had switched on the radio, and moved the dial slowly round, picking up the occasional static crackle; then a blare of music – a woman wailing to the twang of some primeval instrument. Mamounia Radio. Ryderbeit adjusted the dial to a precise wavelength, with the volume turned up full. A couple of minutes passed; there was a loud swooping howl, and a voice with a thick accent shouted through the cockpit: 'Please over to forty-three degrees . . .' It went on repeating numbers, while Ryderbeit altered direction, again with the speed and ease of a racing driver.

A pair of lights appeared over the next hump of sand – two burning oilcans, with the flames flapping sideways in the cross-wind. Ryderbeit flew between them, touched the wheels down with a gentle jolt, reversed the prop with a screaming, howling shudder, and pulled up within fifty feet.

He had his straps off and one of the M16s in his hand before the engine died; opened the flimsy door and jumped down, crouching under cover of the wing, with the gun snapped on to fully automatic – capable of firing all thirty rounds in 1.5 seconds – sweeping the muzzle round in a swift arc. Packer followed, with the same movements.

Two men were already beating out the flaming beacons, and two more were approaching with hurricane lamps. There was a high container truck parked on the dunes about thirty yards away, above the salt-pan on which they had landed. One of the men came forward and shook them both by the hand. He did not smile. 'We have little time. The aircraft will go to the truck.' It sounded like the voice which had talked them down on the radio.

Packer and Ryderbeit slung the M16s over their shoulders and joined the four men behind the wings of the Storch, and they began pushing it towards the truck.

The time was 10.54 p.m.

24

Sarah had been able to eat little for dinner. At nine o'clock she went up to her room and tried to sleep. At ten o'clock she had a shower and began to prepare herself. Shiva Steiner sent her up a vodka martini which she found disappointingly weak. All evening Steiner had appeared unusually fussy and anxious, and had twice given her the same warning. 'Sarah, it is most important that you do not have too much to drink. The Ruler detests people who are drunk.'

Sarah would have liked very much to get drunk. Instead, she took twenty milligrams of Valium and tried to avoid thinking of what lay ahead. But tonight her imagination was unusually busy, playing – against her will – on the persistent and repulsive theme of what it was going to feel like to slip a poisoned suppository up the anus of a man she did not even know. Her upbringing had left her with a lingering revulsion against the mechanics of the human body.

She wondered, with a slight shiver, as she squeezed the tube of glue along the edge of her false eyelashes, whether he was hairy. She had once seen a man on the beach, in Turkey, who had tufts of hair on his shoulders and down his spine, and thick black hair sprouting out of the edges of his bathing trunks, and the sight had sickened her. The Ruler came from a tribe very close to the Turks.

She wondered, too, what he would want to do to her.

Her mind, with malicious curiosity, wondered how she would react if he insisted on subjecting her to some outlandish Oriental perversion; she realized with dismay how relatively inexperienced she was. The Ruler, Steiner had told her, was a worldly man who would want diversions – he would certainly not be satisfied, as poor Owen Packer was, with conventional coitus.

Again she tried not to think about it, but the thought was imperative : how was she going to manoeuvre him into a position where she could insert one of those odious little waxy grey, bullet-shaped objects which Steiner had given her earlier in the evening, disguised in two Estée Lauder lipsticks. She could already imagine several mishaps, any of which would cause immediate disaster.

She would have to secrete at least one of the lipsticks under the pillow, and bring it out while he was already mounting her, her hands all the time caressing him against her will, her fingertips having to explore and locate the exact point of entry, and then carry out the act of murder with a deft precision which must allow for no margin of error. The least hesitation, the smallest degree of clumsiness, would alert him at once – he would grab the lipstick out of her fingers and summon the guards.

What would happen then was something she wanted to think about even less than the idea of probing with her index finger to find the rubbery ring of the Serene Imperial sphincter.

It was essential, Steiner had emphasized, that the poison be inserted as deep as she could reach, so that it was drawn up into the rectum. From that moment the convulsions would start and he would be totally incapacitated. It was the few seconds beforehand that would be critical.

She felt slightly sick as she removed the varnish from her finger-nails, and cut each of them almost to the quick; then checked herself again in the mirror, and put a spare pair of pants in her bag, along with her wallet and passport and cosmetic purse, her silver pill box from Asprey's containing her Valium, and the two lipsticks.

At 10.30 precisely Steiner appeared, alone, and escorted her down a side stair-case, on to the sandy forecourt in front of the garage. He hardly spoke, except to ask her if she had everything she needed – her passport, in particular. She knew she would not be returning here, and Steiner had assured her that her luggage would reach Beirut safely. It was not a detail that greatly concerned her now.

As she stepped out into the muggy darkness, her mind seized on small irrelevant details. She noticed that Steiner was oddly dressed: instead of one of his impeccable suits, he looked as though he were going out on some hunting party – olive-green smock shirt and baggy matching trousers tucked into green rubber-soled boots.

The Fleetwood sedan was waiting on the forecourt. Steiner showed her in and said nothing as he closed the door on her. The engine was already running and the driver pulled away a second later, between the marble gate-posts, on to the empty coast road into the capital. After a couple of miles she noticed that the familiar Ford Falcon had not joined them.

They reached the suburbs and there was still no car behind. The streets were almost empty of traffic, except for light military vehicles – jeeps, trucks, occasionally an armoured car or weapon carrier.

Beyond the sealed smoked windows she was aware of a ghostly stillness. The city seemed far darker than last night when she had ridden back from the Embassy; yet it was not deserted. There were men in every door-way – shadowy figures with invisible faces; static groups of men round the squares, on the steps of official buildings, near the entrances of the big international hotels.

Here, at the very centre of the city, it became so dark that she lost her bearings. Theirs was still the only car in sight, driving now on dipped headlamps, very slowly. Several times soldiers in leopard-spotted battle-dress and steel helmets stepped out and peered at them closely, the muzzles of their machine pistols trained on the front window.

They came to a street lined with camouflaged buses, and she could just make out rows of more helmets behind the windows. There were also buses up all the side streets; and the roadblock at the entrance to the square leading to the Royal Palace was now manned by at least fifty troops and two armoured cars.

The Fleetwood slid to a halt. An officer strolled up to the driver's side. He had a thin savage face with a black moustache and sunken black eyes under the shadow of his helmet. He stepped forward and opened the door for her. As he did so, their eyes met and he looked at her with an expression of contemptuous indifference.

She got out and steadied herself against the car door. Her knees were trembling. The officer gestured towards a jeep with two men in it. She walked over. One of the men jumped down and pulled the front passenger seat forward to let her into the back. The officer said something behind her and the man grinned, but did not reply. She sat down and clutched her shawl round her, although it was a warm night.

The jeep drove off, slowly, with a single spotlight cutting through the blackness of the square. Two points of light marked the entrance to the Royal Palace ahead. The rest of the square was in total darkness.

They passed the statue of Hamid the Martyr, his head and shoulders splashed with bird droppings, his cape and boots mouldering with verdigris. The gates to the Palace were open and unguarded. They drove up to the steps leading to the pair of massive bronze doors.

The jeep stopped and the man in the passenger seat leapt down. Sarah followed, moving carefully as though she might trip and fall. She felt giddy with a sensation of being suddenly very drunk; and feared that if she did fall she would not be able to get up again.

The next few minutes passed in a silent trance in which her mind and body did not seem to be properly related. It was as though she were being wheeled through a hospital, only half conscious, aware of people round her without really seeing or hearing them.

The corridors were long and brightly lit, and there were men stationed at intervals at the high ormolu doors. Two men walked with her, but did not support her: her main concern was the highly polished floor, which seemed at every step to be sliding away beneath her feet.

They came to the end of another corridor and stopped at a smaller brass-studded mahogany door, with no handle. One of the soldiers rapped on it twice: it was instantly opened, just enough to allow Sarah to pass through. It slammed shut behind her.

She stood blinking into the room. Her imagination had anticipated a chamber of sumptuous elegance, discreetly lit, with perhaps a whiff of incense. The Ruler would be there, alone, casually attired, and would offer her champagne and golden caviar. He would take up their conversation about English country houses, and she would describe her family's ancestral home in detail, particularly the famous garden with its lake and grottos and Palladian bridges. She had not even needed to rehearse this part, for she knew the speech off by heart. She would continue until the Ruler stopped her; he would expect her to be nervous, and with his experience she knew that he would take up the conversation without effort.

She was shocked to find that it was not going to be like this.

All the lights were on, so bright that the room seemed to be floodlit. It was not a large room, but some kind of antechamber, lined with high-backed wing chairs and Louis XV sofas. It was crowded with men, all of them standing, many of them armed with pistols or sub-machine guns.

They were silent as she came in, and watched her this time with a lewd curiosity. A man in plain clothes came forward and seized her bag. Two uniformed men stood on either side of her, very close, without touching her. The plain-clothes man riffled expertly through the contents, glanced at her passport, then passed the bag to a second plain-clothes man who nodded and disappeared with it through a pair of folding doors at the end of the room.

The first plain-clothes man turned and looked at her; then, with a dispassionate expression, slapped her across the mouth. Her head spun round and the room went red, then black, full of dancing lights, as she felt hands close round her arms and her feet seemed to leave the ground. Doors opened, then shut. She heard a man laughing and peered across a much larger room containing a four-poster bed with peacock-blue hangings.

The man was large, with a broad fleshy face. Her handbag was slung over his left arm, while in his right hand he was holding something between his thumb and forefinger. She dimly recognized one of her lipsticks. He carried no gun, and he was smiling. Beside him, spread out on the bed, was the smooth naked body of a man. His hands had been folded gracefully across his groin, and his face was turned away, hidden by the shadow of the hangings. At first all she recognized were his wings of dark silver hair; and with a dreadful clarity which contrasted with the numbness of her brain, she remembered thinking that the rest of his body seemed quite hairless – an ageless, alabastine figure which even in this moment her distracted senses found almost beautiful.

She drew closer to the bed, aware of the man still watching her, still smiling. Then she swung round: 'What is this? What are you doing here? Are you staying to watch?'

The man smirked, without sound. She turned again, her fear becoming confused by anger. 'I did not agree to a ménage à trois!'

'You did not agree to anything,' the man beside her replied, pleasantly.

She took a closer look at the bed. The eyes were tiny slits and a small pool of yellow liquid had oozed out on the peacock-blue pillow under his ear. She felt the floor sway, and the outlines of the room became dim and fuzzy. She wanted to be sick, but her throat contracted. The man said, 'You are too late, Mademoiselle Laval-Smith' – and bowed – 'but fortunately you come in excellent time for me !' He spoke English in a deep sensual voice with a musical accent.

'Who are you?' she gasped.

'My name is Colonel Tamat. You may have heard of me – I have a very bad reputation' – he chuckled – 'I am Chief of the Security Police, NAZAK. And what you see over there is the last vestige of the Tyrant of the Emerald Throne.'

His words faded with a singing in her ears; she grabbed the back of a chair and tried not to look at what lay on the bed. 'What has happened? Oh God ! Oh God, what's happened?'

'You are under arrest,' Colonel Tamat replied in his friendly voice, and held up the lipstick. She saw now that it was one of the grey suppositories. 'You are a very wicked girl, Mademoiselle Laval-Smith.'

She looked at him, her mouth hanging open, her face feeling swollen and lopsided. 'What have I done?' she moaned.

Colonel Tamat laughed heartily. 'Young lady, you have just killed His Serene Imperial Highness. And what I have in my hand is the evidence.'

'But I didn't.' Her mouth was dry and she forced her knuckles between her lips.

Colonel Tamat shook his head, his face suddenly grave. 'It is foolish to protest, Mademoiselle.' He lifted the lipstick to his nostrils. 'This unpleasant little device contains cyanide, as you are no doubt aware. And you do not suppose that one of His Highness' most loyal subjects would dare to commit such an outrage?'

She gave a choking gasp. 'But that – *that* !' – she gestured towards the bed without looking at it – 'I didn't do that !'

'What has been done to the body is immaterial. The fact is that you, and your Imperialist foreign masters, have murdered the Supreme Ruler of our country. As such, you will be subjected to the full rigours of the law.'

The room became blurred, then went black.

25

The Fieseler Storch had been folded up and put in the back of the truck, which had then driven off with Ryderbeit and the rest of their reception party, leaving Packer alone with the man who had first come forward and spoken English. The rest of them had seemed in a hurry, and Packer and Ryderbeit scarcely had time to cross-check their plans and schedules for the rest of the night.

The plane was to be refuelled, brought back to the salt-pan and reassembled within one and a half hours: midnight plus thirty minutes. Ryderbeit had snarled something about waiting no more than ten minutes; and if Packer and his rich little dolly bird didn't show up in that time, he'd take off. That was his contract, and he was sticking to it.

Packer thanked him, adding an ungracious epithet, and Ryderbeit cackled and waved good-bye. Packer watched the truck grind off into the night; he missed Ryderbeit, as much for his company as for his expertise with a gun.

He and his English-speaking guide now began to walk back along the metalled road. The man seemed to be unarmed and carried only a hurricane lamp. Neither of them spoke. The silence and darkness were broken only by the soft scuffing of their boots and the distant flare of burning gas from the oil wells of Barzak, twenty miles north-east of the capital.

After a few hundred yards the hurricane lamp picked out the dim silhouette of a Range Rover. As they reached it, Packer's hands tightened instinctively round the M16, which was still slung from his neck. His companion, who had a young clean-shaven face under a Castro-style forage cap, opened the door on the driver's side, nodded to Packer to get in, then joined him in the passenger seat. The keys were in the ignition.

'Start the engine, please,' the young man said; 'we do not have much time.' He leaned over and switched on the lights. 'You are familiar with the geography, yes?'

Packer nodded and slipped into gear. During his stay outside Beirut, Pol had given him a map of Mamounia, extending to the outer suburbs, with one-way streets marked by arrows in red crayon. Pol had also provided photographs and postcards of certain buildings, squares, and monuments.

Packer's route was shown by a dotted green line which stopped at the corner of Passam Street, an intersection leading off the main avenue – a total distance of some 700 metres from the entrance to the Royal Palace. It was going to be a long, lonely walk for Sarah, Packer thought.

The young man had told him to keep the headlamps dipped. The edges of the road were ill-defined, heaped with wind-blown sand that sometimes covered the whole road until the wheels of the car sank almost to the axles.

Neither of them seemed disposed to talk. For the first few minutes the silence between them was tense; then the young man switched on the car radio and tuned in to the local station.

Packer now noticed two curious things : instead of the mournful wail of traditional music, the radio was playing strident martial tunes; he also saw, beyond the white arc of the headlamps, that the glow of the city, which had been clearly visible from the air, had disappeared. He supposed that the citizens of Mamounia, deprived of alcohol and the diversions of Western life, retired early, and that the street lighting was extinguished before midnight. But even as he thought of it, he was not entirely happy with this explanation.

According to the map, it was twelve kilometres to the outskirts of the city. He had checked the kilometre gauge before leaving, and saw that they had covered just over half this distance, when they ran into a roadblock.

Two jeeps and an armoured car were positioned along the road so that he would have to do a slalom to get past. Half a dozen soldiers in battle-dress and helmets stood on either side. They all looked efficient and alert. He slowed down and stopped, even before they had ordered him to. Several carbines and rifles were pointing at his head, and there was a finger on every trigger. The man beside him switched off the radio. 'We must get out of here,' he whispered. He sounded nervous.

As Packer opened his door a sound reached him that he had not heard for a long time : a sound both fearful and exhilarating, sending at once a needle of excitement up his spine and making his heart race.

It was the distant sound of battle : not just sporadic firing, but a steady grumble and roar, punctuated by the rattle of machine guns, the crack of mortars, and the slow thump of artillery.

He looked at his guide, who stood white-faced in the light of more hurricane lamps beside the road. He was talking earnestly to one of the soldiers, who appeared to be an officer. Packer waited, without speaking. The young man finally turned and was about to speak, when the sky was split open by a streak of white-hot flame, followed by the tearing shriek of a jet. The troops ducked instinctively as the fighter swooped away towards the city.

The guide turned to him again. 'I do not understand. There is big fighting in the city.'

'Can we go on?' said Packer.

'They say it is difficult. That the road is blocked and that it is very dangerous.'

Christ, thought Packer. Those bastards, Pol and Steiner, had to choose this night of all nights! In normal circumstances he would have driven back and waited for Ryderbeit at the salt-pan. But he remembered that somewhere ahead, in the chaos of battle, was Sarah. He didn't suppose that the Ruler would have much time for her tonight: the Royal Palace would be the central target of the fighting. He just hoped to hell that it had all started before she had been despatched on her mission.

At least he had the consolation of knowing that Ryderbeit, going with the Fieseler Storch to refuel, would be taking a different road away from the city, and might even have an uneventful ride.

He said, 'Let's get going.' He moved back towards the Range Rover and no one stopped him. The guide got in beside him and Packer restarted the engine. 'They didn't even ask to see our papers,' he added, nodding at the troops as he swung the Rover round between the jeeps.

'They have instructions,' the guide said uneasily. He switched on the radio again: the same monotonous martial music.

'Have you any idea what's happening?' Packer asked.

'No. But I think there are bad things. Maybe a revolution.'

'Who makes the revolution?' said Packer.

'I do not know. Maybe NAZAK. There are many bad men in NAZAK. But maybe it is the Army – and that is not so bad.' He shook his head. 'It is very complicated.'

After another two miles the headlamps picked out the rear of a Chieftain tank, straddling the whole road. When Packer stopped and got out, he saw that it was the last of a column of six. One of the crew came round, wearing the padded leather helmet and ear-flaps of tank troops ready for combat. The guide had again begun talking in a rapid undertone, while Packer listened to the cacophony of gunfire ahead, which had grown perceptibly louder.

The young man turned to him at last, with worried eyes. 'It is not good. The Army has surrounded the city and is fighting with NAZAK. It is impossible to go further.'

Packer stared at him hopelessly. 'I've got to be in the city in twenty minutes!'

The guide shook his head. 'It is not possible.'

'We can bloody well try.' Packer glared at the helmeted soldier. 'Will he let us pass?'

The guide shrugged, with a miserable defeated movement. 'The road is blocked. Maybe when the tanks have gone –' He shook his head and got back into the Range Rover. Packer followed reluctantly, with a sense of furious frustration.

In less than twenty minutes now, Sarah might come running to the corner of Passam Street to find no one there. In the long year of knowing her, and loving her, this was his one chance to play a role of high drama and gallantry; and at the final moment he was going to fail her.

26

Sarah found herself lying on a couch in the brightly lit anteroom. Her face still felt swollen and sore. Shifting her legs under the long evening dress, she realized, to her horror, that she had wet herself.

She tried to sit up and found that her hands and feet were tied together with sash-cord. She was also aware that her nose was running, and that one of her eyelashes had come unstuck.

All the men in the room were standing very still, listening. From somewhere outside came a loud, distinct sound which she had heard many times on films and television; but the reality of it was so alien to her that she thought at first she must be mistaken. It was heavy gunfire.

The next moment, she knew there was no mistake. The floor rocked with a shuddering explosion, followed by the crash of glass; the lights dimmed, went out for a couple of seconds, then came on again. Half the men in the room had rushed through the outer door. Under the chandelier, clouds of dust were rising like smoke.

The gunfire outside seemed to be coming closer; quick chattering bursts, broken at steady intervals by a pulsating boom. Then another ear-cracking explosion, and the lights went out for good.

The room was full of dust and shouts. Several torches flashed on, catching the confused shapes of faces, wild-eyed, open-mouthed, frantic with fear. A bulky figure paused beside her. 'Little girl' – Tamat's hand fastened round her elbow – 'don't think your friends outside are going to help you.' He was bending over her, and she caught the harsh smell of saffron on his breath.

His fingers began to squeeze and pinch the flesh of her upper arm, while in his other hand he was holding something. In the uncertain light of the torches, it took her a few seconds to recognize the lipstick. Colonel Tamat followed her horrified gaze, and began to laugh.

His voice was shut out by an explosion which seemed this time to come from within the room; the chandelier lurched and tinkled like sleigh bells, and Sarah felt fragments of plaster spraying over her face and hair. She began to cough from the dust. Colonel Tamat had released her arm, but went on speaking in the same silky voice.

'I would like to have had more time to spend on you, but one is forced to bow to the winds of history. You came here to kill a man, so it is fitting that you should be despatched by the same method that you intended for your victim.' As he spoke he rolled her quickly, expertly on to her stomach.

She began to scream, as much with shame as terror. She tried, by pressing her knees into the couch, to prevent him from pulling up her dress; then she remembered that she had soiled herself, and became hysterical with humiliation. Her screams were carrying even above the sound of firing, when she felt a violent blow across her buttocks which stopped her breath in a gasp of pain.

Tamat was talking to her all the while, but in his own guttural language now, as he ripped her dress up to her waist. She felt his big brown fingers at the base of her spine, gripping the elastic of her pants; there was a long volley of bullets, so close that she could hear the swish of air and the crump as they sank into the wall above her.

Tamat had suddenly moved away, with two loping steps, and now stood swaying as though he were drunk. There was another bursting roar and she saw the front of his jacket flatten against his body. He stumbled, jerked his head up, did a quick two-step shuffle, fell over backwards, and lay still.

Sarah was not sure whether she had fainted or not. At first the darkness and noise and confusion were so concentrated as to be totally unreal : she was overcome by that detached, timeless sensation which she had experienced once after she had fallen while hunting.

The cords round her hands and feet had been cut, her dress had been pulled down, and someone had sat her up like a doll on the couch, and put a handkerchief into her hand. Her immediate concern, besides the pain in her buttocks and the embarrassment over her loose eyelash, was whether she had stained her dress.

There were more lights in the room, and more men, but they were different from the ones before. They wore combat uniforms and their rubber-soled boots made no sound on the polished floor. Several of the plain-clothes men were lying in odd lifeless positions along the wall, their bodies ash-white with dust and plaster.

A group of men came through the folding doors from the bedroom. The gunfire outside had slackened to spasmodic bursts. Sarah became aware of a hush in the room.

A man had come through the small outer door. He was wearing an olive-green smock shirt and carried a pistol. He looked slowly round the room, then at Sarah, and nodded. She stared blankly at him, as he came strolling towards her.

He stopped next to the couch, his pistol pointing at the floor. 'You have been exceptionally lucky, my dear Sarah. For my part, I must apologize for these rather dramatic events, but they were unforeseen.'

'What has happened?' she pleaded, in an exhausted voice.

'There has been a change of government,' Shiva Steiner replied. 'What is called a coup d'état. To be exact, it has been a coup within a coup. Certain mischievous elements within the Secret Police managed to subvert units of the Army, and with the backing of the Pan-Islamic Socialists, tried to take over the country. Fortunately, the rest of the Armed Forces acted in time to forestall disaster.'

'But the Ruler?' she cried.

'The Ruler?' Steiner sighed, with a glance at the closed bedroom doors. 'It is a matter of little importance who really killed him – you, or the head of the Secret Police. The fact is, he is dead, and over his corpse a new government will be formed. However' – his eyes were now fixed on a point just above Sarah's shoulder – 'when I say it does not matter who killed him, I do not mean that it is not important for the people of this country – and the outside world – to be told who killed him.

'You must understand that many millions of his subjects – simple, illiterate people who know no better – believe their Ruler to be a divine power. They fear him, but they love him. And it would be very bad for the morale of the nation if it were learned that the Chief of NAZAK, which was the Ruler's right arm, had turned and slaughtered his master. Therefore it is necessary to find – what is called in English, I think – a scapegoat.'

She felt a cold creeping terror from the bowels up to the nape of her neck. 'Me?'

Shiva Steiner's mouth creased into a saurian grin. 'Considering the amount of money you have been paid for tonight, for doing absolutely nothing, I think it both apt and convenient that you should take both the credit and the blame.'

'Blame?'

'Why not? You agreed to commit murder. In most countries, including your own, that is a crime in itself.'

'You can't kill me!'

'Of course not, my dear. When the fighting has stopped, you will escape. Your arrest and trial would only lead to embarrassing complications with your country's government at a time when our new régime will need to be on the best terms with all the Western nations.'

He turned to go. She leaned out, with a puzzled, frightened gesture, as though to grab his sleeve. 'Shiva, please!' Her voice became a weak shout. '*How* do I escape?'

'My dear, do not be foolish. We have discussed the plan in detail. If he has done as instructed, your friend Capitaine Packer will be waiting for you at the corner of Passam Street. It will take you no more than ten minutes to walk.'

'But I was supposed to be there at midnight!' – she glanced frantically at her watch: it was 1.10 – 'and if I wait until the fighting's over, I'm going to be hours late.'

'My dear, you are not the only one whose plans have been disturbed by the events of tonight. Your friend has no doubt been held up himself by the fighting. However, if he fails to reach his rendezvous, then that is simply a misfortune with which I cannot help you. In the meantime, one of my officers will take you to a private apartment where you can make yourself comfortable until it is safe for you to leave.'

27

Packer had tried rolling down the Range Rover windows, but it did nothing to relieve the heat, and only brought with it the smell: a burnt bitter-sweet smell of cordite and shell-smoke, scorched stone and dust, and the clammy foetid stench of roasted flesh.

It was not until past nine in the morning that he had been let through the roadblocks outside the city, and then only after protracted conversations on field telephones. He had reached the commercial centre of the city shortly after ten. The streets were lifeless, deserted. Trucks, jeeps, and armoured cars stood crashed, abandoned, burnt out, amid the litter of human debris on which the flies were already settling in glistening swarms. It looked like some obscene playground.

Near the corner of Passam Street, a couple of personnel carriers stood locked together in a tangle of crushed, blackened steel, their wheels burned to the rim, their crews scattered along the sidewalk – a row of tiny charred figures lying on their backs with their arms and legs drawn up in the air, their bones sprouting like bamboo shoots from the cobweb ashes of their uniforms, teeth grinning at the sky. One of them had escaped the flames and lay further up the street, a coil of silvery intestine wound out beside him, still steaming in the heat, while two bald dogs were already setting to with their fangs.

Packer backed up the street, far enough to be out of sniper range from any of the buildings leading to the Palace Square. He took a tepid drink from the plastic canteen, rinsed out his mouth, opened the door and spat into the street, where the water bubbled and shrank into a dusty gob and disappeared.

The heat was so intense that he was having to breathe slowly, between panting gasps, like an asthmatic. Through the aching glare the city had a bleached naked look, with every window smashed, as dark as empty eye-sockets, walls blistered and blasted, balconies hanging down like broken jaws. Behind, the minarets rose in shimmering clusters – gold and pink tulips thrusting their way up from the scrap-heap.

He leaned against the wheel, the plastic cover slimy under his fingers, the sweat stinging his eyes, itching down the backs of his legs. For twenty minutes nothing happened. Nothing at all, except the ghastly canine meal behind him. He wanted to get out and put an end to the creatures with the M16 which still lay under the seat; but he feared that the least sound of gunfire would at once arouse the city to further fury. For the moment it was as though Mamounia had been stunned.

Packer now felt a new, strange sense of unease – something that was oddly at variance with the untimely chaos of the night. He was still uncertain of exactly what had happened, except that his final passage had been remarkably, uncannily smooth. Even at the four roadblocks in the centre of the city, which had been manned by hard, battle-weary troops, there had always been an officer ready to check his credentials on a telephone or radio, and to let him through.

His brain felt clogged and swollen with the heat; but one thought persisted: a trap, if it is to be effective, has to be well-oiled. He thought of Pol and Steiner and Dr Zak; he trusted none of them – probably no more than they trusted him – and remembered that his only insurance was his joint account for three-quarters of a million pounds with Pol.

In any normal circumstances, such a sum must have constituted a copper-bottomed, gilt-edged insurance. But Pol was a long way away; and whoever had mounted this coup was playing for stakes worth not thousands, but hundreds of billions of pounds.

He had wondered at one time how easy it would be to get to the Embassy. But what would he tell them? What would that crimped diplomatic mentality make of his presence with no luggage, no visa, no entry stamp? If he told them everything, he was likely to meet little sympathy; for Packer was part of a conspiracy to commit murder and high treason, and if Sarah had succeeded in her mission the two of them could expect little mercy.

It was the thought of Sarah, alone in that beleaguered, silent palace 700 yards away, that decided him.

The presence of Ryderbeit, back on the salt-pan with the refuelled Fieseler Storch, he took oddly for granted. Ryderbeit had said that he would not wait more than ten minutes: but

Ryderbeit was a soldier – if only a soldier of fortune – and the idea of his deserting his post at the final hour struck Packer as not so much improbable, as totally out of character. Ryderbeit might be capable, as well as guilty, of many infamies; but he would never run the risk of being called a coward.

It happened so quickly, and with such planned precision, that his suspicions were only strengthened. Across the blinding, dusty street ahead a tiny figure had appeared, walking awkwardly, heavily, as though wading through water. She was bare-headed and wore a long dress.

He leaped out and waved, frightened to shout. She saw him and began to run; tripped and nearly fell, then caught sight of the row of miniature black corpses. Her hand flew up to her mouth and she stumbled forward and reached him, gagging, her make-up streaked with sweat. For several seconds she clung to him, and he felt her whole body quivering as he dragged her up into the Range Rover.

He started the engine and reversed back up the street. As they passed the two dogs, who had been joined by several others, he put his arm round her and told her to close her eyes. It was some minutes before she could speak.

He was driving through a network of small streets, shadowy and deserted, following a route which he had already prepared from the map. He drove fast, without using his horn, and hardly checking the intersections before racing across, burrowing into another tunnel of alleys and crooked backstreets between shuttered shops and bazaars.

She sat pressed against him, still shaking, and began, in hushed breathless sentences, to tell him what had happened. His attention was distracted before she had finished. In the mirror he had caught sight of a long black car. It was the only vehicle he had seen moving anywhere in the city. He doubled back down a one-way street, the wrong way, and turned up a steep alley so narrow that the sides of the Range Rover scraped against the shutters of the shops. He came out on to a bare yellow square with a hump-backed mosque. The car behind had gone.

But now something else was beginning to worry him. The needle on the temperature gauge had crept up to maximum and was almost touching the red warning zone. The radiator would have been filled with a chemical cooling fluid which could not boil; but he knew, from his experiences in Aden, that under intense heat it could evaporate.

He slowed down, avoiding low gears wherever possible, and cut through a couple of side streets to join the main avenue to the north-west, out towards the desert and the salt-pan. Somewhere to his left a great fire was burning, and the air was full of coils of oily black smoke that left flakes of soot clinging to the dust-caked windshield.

There was a roadblock ahead, and as he prepared to stop he saw the officer in charge wave him on. Again, it happened too smoothly, too easily.

He was now driving through the Armenian quarter, where there were tanks and troop-carriers drawn up in the side streets; but everywhere was the same macabre stillness; again no one stopped him. The atmosphere in the Range Rover was suffocating, as though drained of all oxygen; when he again tried opening the windows he was blinded by dust, and the air blew in with a baking heat that was not like air at all, but hot gritty fumes.

He had been going for half a mile along the avenue when he saw the black shape shimmering again in the mirror. It looked like a Cadillac or a Lincoln, but it was still too far behind for him to make out how many people it carried. He guessed that it could easily outpace the Rover, and so made no effort to lose it; instead, over the next couple of miles, he waited to see what it would do. Sarah did not seem to have noticed it, and for the moment he did not draw her attention to it.

But he did reach down for the M16, which he kept balanced across his knee.

The car was now about 300 yards behind, and was still making no effort to catch them. Packer was puzzled, as well as worried. Sarah had told him how Shiva Steiner had said he wanted a scapegoat. Yet he had let her go. He had also greased the wheels for their escape, through the roadblocks in the dead city. An explanation dawned on him, with a nasty sinking in his stomach : they were being set up for the kill at the salt-pan. He wiped the sweat out of his eyes and put his foot down flat on the floor.

The temperature gauge was now within the red danger mark; but he had already planned what to do. If they were waiting at the salt-pan he was going to put up a fight; but first he was going to try a diversion, in the hope of losing the Cadillac.

It was a desperate decision, but not totally irrational; nor was it dictated by fear, but by anger – a cold relentless fury at the treachery of Pol and his scheming Levantine master, Shiva Steiner. Or was he just panicking? And was the Cadillac behind just a friendly escort? He didn't think so – but there was only one way to find out.

He had now reached the road out across the desert, and was driving flat out. He had unfolded the map over the M16, and was calculating, from the kilometre gauge, his approximate distance from the salt-pan. At the same time, he noticed wisps of smoke beginning to drift up from under the bonnet. His view behind was obscured by a dense veil of dust.

After another four kilometres they were in open desert, and he could feel the engine starting to grumble; his foot was still right down on the accelerator, but their speed was slackening and the floor had begun to shudder.

His anger had given way to a sense of futile recklessness. He was now certain that they were driving into a trap; yet they had come so far that he was determined to get to the bitter end, and to take as many of Steiner's henchmen with him as he could. He also had one immediate advantage. The Range Rover is probably the best equipped wheeled vehicle for negotiating the roughest terrain, in extremes of climate; while a Cadillac is built for highways and graceful forecourts. In the open desert it would be as helpless as an elephant in a dance hall.

Packer guessed that they would be expecting him to reach the salt-pan from the road, down the same route that he had followed last night. If he could approach it from another angle, he might have a small chance. At least he would try, or go down fighting.

He calculated that he was about three kilometres from the salt-pan, when he swung the Rover off the road and felt the wheels spinning furiously as they plunged into the soft sand. Like a fox reaching a wood, he looked back and saw, through the trail of dust along the road above, the Cadillac slow to a halt.

The Range Rover's four-wheel drive howled and skidded and slithered through two deep trenches in the sand. Ahead, the dunes rolled away like shorn sheep's rumps into the blinding blur of the horizon. Packer steered in a direction parallel to the salt-pan, allowing the Rover to follow a course of least resistance between the white-hot dazzle of the dunes.

But even so he could feel the wheels sinking deeper, their speed down to walking pace, while the black smoke from the cooling fluid was now belching out of the bonnet. But as long as he kept moving, he thought – even if it was at no more than a mile an hour. For he knew that once they had stopped in this heat they would be dead before siesta time – even if the Cadillac didn't get to them first.

Again he peered behind and saw, across a hump of sand, the dusty black snout of the Cadillac crawling into view. Sarah now saw it for the first time, but made no comment. It was as though her capacity for fear was exhausted. She was breathing in short gasps. 'What are you doing?'

'I'm trying to outflank the bastards. That big American job back there will burn up in no time – another five minutes and those fancy tyres will start melting like treacle.'

It was now almost impossible to see ahead, through the smoke and glare and clouds of sand churning round them. The temperature needle had passed right through the red zone and was off the dial; and the speedometer was registering zero. They both drank some water from the plastic canteen, but it seemed scarcely to moisten their mouths.

The heat had clamped round Packer's head like a steel brace that was being slowly tightened. He leaned over the wheel, trying to steer the Rover's deep sluggish course away from the banks of sand, where it would become landlocked for ever.

In the mirror he could just make out the black shape of the Cadillac sliding clumsily down the side of a dune, like a huge wounded beetle. When it had righted itself, he guessed that it could be doing no more than two or three miles an hour. The broad black bonnet was also wrapped in smoke, and with any luck the air-conditioner would blow, or the carburettors explode.

He gave a sudden, savage laugh. 'Well, if we've done nothing else, we must have established a record for the world's slowest car chase!'

At that moment the Range Rover bumped into a bank of sand, gave a clanking roar, and stalled. For a few seconds Packer rested on the wheel. He felt calm and very, very tired. Sarah drank some water, and Packer wasted some more by splashing it on his face and neck. It dried almost at once. Then he reached over and kissed her on the mouth. Her lips and tongue were parched and did not respond.

He looked back again at the Cadillac. It was moving so slowly that he thought at first it had stopped. His fingers tightened round the M16, his thumb slipped it on to semi-automatic – five rounds a burst – and he got out. His hands and face burned under the sky as though they were being held under a red-hot grill. The air was full of the acrid fumes of the cooling fluid and the smell of scorched rubber.

He peered back across the dunes and this time saw the Cadillac lurch to a standstill, its nose buried in sand, under a pall of black smoke. Its windows and doors were still closed.

He tried to position himself against the rear wing of the Rover, but burned his hand and elbow on the metal. He would have to fire from a standing position, using the sling as his only support. He had brought the muzzle up, when two things happened.

A voice began yelling from somewhere behind him, and two bullets clanged into the back of the Range Rover. A second later a double crack reached him from the direction of the Cadillac. The voice yelled again, 'Packer, you crazy bastard – !'

Sarah had climbed out on her side and was scrambling up the steep dune. On the ridge, against the glaring grey sky, stood the tall thin figure of Ryderbeit. Packer, half blinded by sweat, blinked at him, just as a spurt of sand appeared a couple of feet away from him and another sharp crack came from the Cadillac.

He began to run, stumbled, and fell on his hands and knees. There was another shot and he heard the second, smaller crack of the bullet's sonic boom as it passed by his ear.

He was crawling up the dune on all fours, hardly feeling the pain in his burned fingers. He heard more shots, but they seemed to come from a great distance, like echoes; and the dune was becoming steeper, until he felt as though he were clawing his way up a sheer wall of sand. His fingers and face were burned raw, and he could feel the searing heat through his shirt and trousers, and a deep dull pain in his back and belly.

A pair of boots came slithering down beside him, kicking hot sand into his face. Hands grabbed him under the armpits and he heard Sarah crying, sobbing, 'Oh my God, no! Is he all right?'

Then Ryderbeit: 'Shut up, and give me a hand!'

They dragged him between them, down the spoon-shaped

bowl of the salt-pan, across the fifty yards to where the Fieseler Storch stood ready for take-off.

Sarah, in her preposterous evening dress, was almost too weak to climb aboard; and it was Ryderbeit alone who hauled Packer's inert weight up into the oven-hot perspex capsule of the cockpit, where he dumped him down in the observation seat. Packer found that he had lost all sensation from the waist down; and when he opened his eyes he noticed that there was blood on Ryderbeit's hands and shirt – only Ryderbeit wasn't bleeding.

Packer sat propped against the flimsy door, feeling nothing. A long sleep came over him. It was only when Sarah squeezed herself awkwardly in beside him, having to sit half in his lap, that she realized that Packer's dreamy expression was one of death.

She did not move, did not shift her hand from the pool of blood that was seeping on to the seat beneath them. Her hands closed round Packer's head, and she began rocking it, weeping with no sound above the roar of the engine.

They took off at a steep angle, and far below could see the two cars, tiny and remote, like a pair of dead insects caught in the vast grey wilderness of the desert. Ryderbeit began to laugh. Sarah did not seem to hear him. 'There's a certain lovely poetry in it!' he yelled.

She stared at him, uncomprehending.

Ryderbeit shook his head, still laughing, and jabbed his thumb at Packer's upright body. 'That bullet is going to work out pretty bloody expensive. In fact, it's going to cost Fat Man three-quarters of a million fucking quid!'

He was laughing again when they landed in Beirut; and Sarah began to cry again.

All-action Fiction from Panther